Tamara Goranson holds  Neuropsychology as we University of Victoria in British Columbia.

She published several academic pieces before she turned to writing short stories, creative non-fiction, and historical fiction, winning 3rd prize in the 2019 Vancouver Island Writers' Association annual general contest for her non-fiction piece, 'A Voice in Time'.

Tamara lives in Victoria with her husband and two daughters. When she is not writing, she enjoys spending time outdoors hiking in the Canadian wilderness.

www.tamaragoranson.com

instagram.com/tgvikinggirl

Also by Tamara Goranson

The Flight of Anja
The Oath of Bjorn

THE VOYAGE OF FREYDIS

TAMARA GORANSON

One More Chapter

a division of HarperCollins*Publishers* Ltd

1 London Bridge Street

London SE1 9GF

www.harpercollins.co.uk

HarperCollins*Publishers*

1st Floor, Watermarque Building, Ringsend Road

Dublin 4, Ireland

This paperback edition 2021

First published in Great Britain in ebook format

by HarperCollins*Publishers* 2021

Copyright © Tamara Goranson 2021

Tamara Goranson asserts the moral right to

be identified as the author of this work

A catalogue record of this book is available from the British Library

PB ISBN: 978-0-00-845571-2

TPB ISBN: 978-0-00-849533-6

Printed and bound in Great Britain by

CPI Group (UK) Ltd, Croydon CR0 4YY

Content notices: domestic abuse, physical violence, and use of the historical descriptors "Red Men" and "Skraelings" for the Indigenous peoples of Greenland and Vinland.

For my parents,
Elaine and Alan Goranson

She was a domineering woman, but Thorvard was a man of no consequence.

Saga of the Greenlanders, c. 13th century, translated by Keneva Kunz

Prologue

THE GREAT AUK TRAVELS FREE

Harpa, 996 AD

The icy wind whistles past my ears, whipping my unruly red hair into my face as I clamber out of my hiding spot, panting heavily. It has taken months to plot a course to freedom. It could take only moments to lose it if my husband finds me here.

He won't now that they have come for me.

Savoring the moment, I scan the seashore, and my heart skips a beat and then slowly settles when all I see is a group of Icelanders wandering down the beach. No one is hiding amongst the rocks. No horse is galloping down the vast stretch of sedge meadows full of tundra browns and saxifrage purples and lichen-covered mossy greens. Truly, I have managed to escape. Even the screeching wind cheers for me.

Like a fool, I release a carefree whoop as another blast of chilly air hits me squarely in the face. My husband can't touch me anymore. He no longer has any power over me. There is a sudden urge to wrap my arms around the dragon's head that adorns the prow in giddy celebration.

From the longboat's helm, I watch the waves come crashing in to shore, rolling across the rocks, dragging through the rattling pebbles. Lifting my hands into the air, I close my eyes and feel the tickle of sweet success, knowing that I have duped the great Thorvard of Gardar. Soon I'll be free of this so-called husband, this three-headed monster whom I've been forced to honor and obey, this hawk whose eyesight is so keen.

I stare down at the Icelanders beetling across a beach strewn with bulbous strings of seaweed hosting swarms of sandflies.

"*Góðan morgin*, Freydis. Did you sleep well?" Finnbogi shouts in the voice of a conqueror. The helmsman's smile is like the brilliant sun.

I wave to him, not trusting my voice to speak.

"My ship is a good one. You'll soon see how it steps through the waves." He shields his eyes against the morning sun hemorrhaging onto the horizon and spilling sunbeams across the white-capped seas. A moment later his wife comes into view.

"As soon as we pack the remaining goods, we'll be ready to set sail," Logatha calls up, shooing Finnbogi off. "Praise Óðinn, you are almost free of your husband."

Just then, I catch a blend of voices rattling through the deck planks from down below as the Icelanders begin hoisting the livestock crates, the freshwater barrels, and the smoked meat and fish on board. Only Logatha knows how bloody anxious I am to leave Greenland shores and take back my worth and build a new life where I won't have to endure my husband's wrath or his brutal fists.

By the gods, this is a new beginning, a chance to make my broken self whole again, a way out of the nothingness. I am dead already so what is there to lose?

Behind me, there is a sudden crash as a barrel is dropped with a heavy thud into the belly of the ship. The longboat creaks and shudders as it is hit by another wave. Someone curses loudly, which makes me jump. For a moment, I hear him yelling, and I get pulled into the darkness, into the memories of Thorvard's fists landing on my body. He is bruising me on the outside, crushing something deep on the inside.

In the distance, a great auk calls and I surface out of the fog, listening to its low, deep, gurgled cry echoing through the chilly air as if it is screaming a farewell blessing. Tilting my head back, I follow its flight path as it catches air currents, travels free.

For a moment, all is still, and I find my peace knowing that I have tackled Fenrir, the Hel-wolf.

Thorvard has stolen much from me, but I am not broken. I am standing on the brink, pounded down like sand but willing to go in search of peace. I have found a way to trick him and now I am about to soar.

Part One

HE STOLE HER FUTURE

Chapter One

THE WEIGHT OF THE KNIFE

Feast of Lithasblót, 993 AD

Summer Solstice

My husband's mood is foul. I sit up straight, hoping he won't notice the perspiration marks underneath my arms because he hates it when I look unkempt. The longer I sit, the more difficult it is for me to share the news. Selfishly, I want to savor my victory and keep the joyful secret to myself. My silence provokes a scornful look.

"Show me the bruises on your wrists," he says as he stabs a chunk of walrus meat and stuffs it whole inside his mouth.

Gingerly, I extend my arm. He flicks a glance at the purple welts.

"You brought it on yourself. You must learn your place,"

he says as he opens a flask and pours more wine into his drinking horn.

I hang my head and slowly bring my frozen fingers to my cheek feeling like a groveling fool, a whining mammet.

I never used to be like this. Before I wed Thorvard of Gardar, I was the envy of every maiden in the western settlement. The bride-price he offered Faðir for my hand in marriage was greater than any other *mundr* anyone in Greenland had ever seen: sealskin hides, arctic fox pelts, and sheepskin fleece, narwhal ivory pieces, an expensive iron pot and tempered scythes, twelve ounces of silver, one horse and oxen, and four milking cows. Now he tells me that I am always wrong, that nothing I do is ever good enough, that I am as worthless as a grain of sand. Perhaps I am. He has a way of making me feel small.

"As my wife, you must do your duty and obey my rules," Thorvard yells. His eyes are bloodshot, his lips slick with grease.

"I have been dutiful," I mumble, keeping my face stone-cold. I have no more tears to shed, no more of anything left to give.

"Ach, Freydis! You disgrace your *faðir's* house. No Eiriksson are you. Your comportment needs to change," he says as he takes another bite of walrus stew. The flickering firelight highlights the tattooed knotwork on his muscled forearm. I used to think that he was handsome, that his body was lithe and toned. Now his looks don't matter. Nothing does.

"You slug," he spits.

By Óðinn's beard, I'll not give him the satisfaction of

bringing me lower than I already feel. It is his habit to treat me as though I am a child. He tells me what to wear and whom I can see. He even controls the foods I eat. Tonight, I am not allowed to have any of his favorite dish. The feast of seabird eggs dipped in salt lies untouched on his pewter plate.

"I have tried my best to conceive a son," I say. Thorvard's eyes narrow into slits. He leans in closely, and I lick my lips and stare at my folded hands as my muscles begin to shake.

"Believe you me, no other husband would tolerate your barren womb."

I begin picking at the pilling wool on my shawl. I can feel his eyes burning into me.

In one smooth motion, Thorvard heaves himself off his chair. Startled, my hands fly up, and my head snaps back as he shoves his face into mine.

"You wench," he hisses. "You think I don't know that you leave my farm? You think I haven't had you followed when you sneak out of my longhouse and make your way into my meadowlands? I know where you go. I know whom you see. Your trainer keeps me well-informed."

He *tsks* his tongue and shakes his head, and I keep my fingers splayed across my face. I have been an utter fool to put my hopes in Ivor, Thorvard's trusted bondsman.

"Have pity, Thorvard," I blubber pathetically. He begins belaboring my shortcomings in a long monologue, his spittle spraying across my hands. My ears are tingling. My throat is dry. I would kill him if I had the chance.

Thorvard's voice ratchets upwards, and my heart picks

up a beat and I begin to shake as a chill creeps into the room. Very carefully I go to reach for the hidden knife stashed inside my boot, but in one quick move, Thorvard grabs my wrist and squeezes hard. Wincing, I try to swallow a building sob, knowing that he is breaking skin. If I kill him, his clansmen would accuse me of being a murderess.

Thorvard yells again, and my thoughts snap back. On instinct, I leap out of my chair and push him hard so that he stumbles backwards and lets out a vicious growl. A moment later, he recovers and runs at me with a menacing grimace on his face. There is no time to think. Falling backwards on my chair, I draw my knees in closely to my chest and kick him viciously in the groin. Thorvard roars in pain as he trips and falls and narrowly escapes falling into the firepit that runs the length of the room. In a flash, I am up again and scampering backwards, shielding myself with my knife in hand, acutely aware of the building pressure in my chest that feels like a calving iceberg of fear shearing off as a surge of boiling hatred pushes up.

"Come and get me," I whisper in a daze.

"You weasel! I'll make you pay for your defiance," he growls, cursing loudly as he rights himself. "You'll beg for mercy when I am done!"

I reach inside and find my strength hidden in a half-dead place. The weight of the knife is heavy in my hand. The blade is sharp. Shuddering, I imagine seeing blood dripping from the tip as the hazy light from the midnight sun trickles in through the smoke hole directly above Thorvard's head. For a moment, I am frozen as I watch his mouth moving but hear no words. A moment later, there is a sudden surge of hatred, a burst of anger, a red-hot rage. Without thinking, I run at him with the dagger aimed directly at his heart.

Thorvard ducks just in time. I go to strike again, but Thorvard blocks me, yelling fiercely as he grabs for me and twists my arm. Wincing, I feel the knife tang slipping from my grip and hear the metal hit the slate. From somewhere distant, Thorvard laughs.

"Freydis, you are too strong-willed," he gurgles. I cock my head and catch a glimpse of his angry face, his crooked smile. My eyes shoot wide when he shifts his weight and draws his muscled forearm back to drive his fist into my face.

Please help us, mighty Thor…

From a woozy place, I feel my knees buckling as a scream escapes. Oh gods, please don't let him hurt the child growing in my womb.

I beseech thee, Óðinn!

Help me.

Please.

Chapter Two

ONE MUST HOWL

I lurch forwards with a sudden gasp. My head throbs, my lip is fat, and I can barely see. Clawing for air, I struggle to sit, but I sense a presence – a shadow – towering over me. The room begins to spin. I freeze until my right ear pops. Then I suddenly realize that my mind is playing tricks. The speckled shadows are climbing up and down the longhouse walls. Thorvard isn't here. For a moment, I sit and stare up into the rafters and taste the iron tang of blood. Ivor will be expecting me in the yard to practice my grappling drills. Fie on him! By Óðinn's beard, I expected more from Thorvard's overseer, that two-faced snake!

The thoughts come in swarms, pinging off one another so that I can hardly breathe. Ivor must have tracked me into the hills where Einar and Éowyn tend their sheep. The shepherd and the shepherdess have become one of my few and only friends. I visited Éowyn just the other day. We ate together and her youngest fell asleep in my lap. By the gods, what if Thorvard hurts them to punish me? Ivor, that piece of dung, betrayed us all.

I sift through memories as carefully as I sift through a sack of barley looking for weevils before making porridge. How did it come to this? All I did was slip out for target practice with Einar who was eager to teach me how to use a slingshot. I didn't think. I should have asked Thorvard for permission. Now my face feels bruised and puffy, and my eye is swollen shut.

This is Ivor's fault! He is a righteous troublemaker who panders to my husband and treats him like a white-plumed swan. When I think on it, I scarce know whether to scream or cry. Ivor was the one who told me that I should learn how to defend myself against the musk oxen wandering through Thorvard's meadowlands. I never should have gone behind his back and asked a lowly shepherd to help me learn the shieldmaiden ways. I should have asked Ivor instead. Gods' bread, it makes me mad! Do they not realize that I am desperate to learn from *any* man?

My mind begins to float into a sea of mist. There are memories of Thorvard standing in the shadows of the byre, cooing as if he were a dove, whispering sweet nothings in Ivor's ear. I am in hiding in one of the empty stalls, watching my husband through the slats of the ill-placed planks where slivers of wood are sticking out like bristled hairs.

Slowly, Ivor steps forth and plants a long, wet kiss on Thorvard's mouth. The memories hiss, or is it me? Even now, there is a cold and nauseous feeling that makes my heart twist so I can hardly breath.

Staring into the memory well, I hate myself for becoming a trophy wife, a woman who was married off to a lawless cheat. Thorvard tied the knot to protect his life, to escape from the scrutiny of his clan. He would be banished to the hinterlands if others found out that he liked men.

I cast my eyes upwards, replaying everything. Thorvard tricked my family. He stole my dowry. He duped Faðir and dishonored me.

What horse dung!

Someone shouts outside, and I fall back into the room with a heavy *thunk* and the sudden awareness that I am lying on my back staring at a beam of dust-speckled light streaming inside from the only shuttered window above my head. The rushes thrown across the slate grope my bruises and itch my welts.

Ivor must have followed me. He must have suspected that I would tell Einar about his great love affair with my husband, Thorvard of Gardar. Who does he mistake me for? A gaggling goose? How would I benefit if others knew?

My head is spinning. My bruises hurt. Poor Einar. He is a valiant shepherd – a *drengr* who is brave and honorable, someone with a sense of fairness who possesses the strength to do what is right. As my protector, he has warned me about the dangers of walking alone in the meadowlands where there is always the possibility of encountering vicious beasts. He would be shocked to learn that inside the dim, dark extravagance of Thorvard's longhouse, I face this fear every day. Truly, I should show him the small hammer-shaped pendant that I wear to honor Thor and ask him to teach me how to defend myself against wicked men. I close my eyes, imagining what he would say.

Éowyn's soothing voice tinkles in my ear. In a singsong tone, she reminds me that she, too, has met Fenrir, the wolf, and Jormungand, the world serpent, in Thorvard's longhouse when she was his thrall. Perhaps this is why we share a bond. In that wretched place, I, too, have experienced my own living Hel.

Trying to breathe, I attempt to steer my thoughts away from Thorvard of Gardar. By Óðinn's eye, Ivor betrayed my trust and hooked me as though I was a fish, baiting me with the promise of teaching me a few grappling moves. I see it now. I bet he thought Einar would train me up to kill my husband. Perhaps he worried that Einar himself would try to avenge my honor and kill Thorvard without penalty.

Gingerly, I feel my cheek. The blood is crusted over. Wincing, I finger the gash, and it suddenly begins to bleed again. Curse my husband! Curse all Norsemen who abuse their women because they think it is their right. I won't stand for this cow shit anymore, but what can I do? I have no rights. I was married off two months ago and now I am stuck on this godless farm forevermore.

My mind drifts back to my wedding day, and I see my *gyoja*, an old woman without any teeth, crouching at the water's edge where I am bathing in the mineral pools. She wants to prepare me for the marriage bed. She is stirring the bridal herbs and the oil, the elixirs that will encourage my fertility. I am floating in the hot spring, weighed down by the heaviness of my red hair fanning out around my face with my arms spread wide.

Faðir's only care was to have me well-matched, but Thorvard played a jest on all of us. What lies he told! That two-faced bastard never loved me, and he never will. Mother told me that the *inn matki munr*, the mighty passion, was less important than great wealth. I disagree. Thorvard is a wealthy man, but I lost my life when I married him. Now I must do my duty and produce an heir. It is what is expected. Faðir needs a grandson to guarantee his ancestral line.

There is a knock at the longhouse door. In a panic, I shimmy backwards and almost bang my head against a post until I recognize the familiar voice. Slowly, I get up and stumble forwards and lift the latch to let in the stocky Norseman who did me wrong. Ivor is a thick-necked warrior with a muscled gut. Short in stature, his gait is stiff and purposeful.

"My lady! How come you are so late?" Ivor asks as he steps inside. Behind him, the sunshine streams in through the open door and irritates my swollen eye. "When you didn't show, I worried that you were ill." He closes the door and turns around. Then he stops. "Your eye is black and your cheek is bleeding!"

"It is nothing but a scratch," I say. I am afraid to be alone with the overseer, this owl with his swiveling neck and keen, bright eyes. I now know why Thorvard elevated him above all other Norsemen on this wretched farm.

"Did Thorvard do this to you?" Ivor asks as he takes my elbow to steer me to the nearest bench. I shrug him off and shy away. Ivor eyes me hard. "Last night I sensed that your husband was in a mood."

"There is no need to worry," I lie. "The hour was late, and I was clumsy. I tripped and fell." I dig my fingernails into my palms, and feel a burst of pain shooting through my temples.

"May the gods take pity on your poor, poor face. It looks so painful," Ivor murmurs with sympathy. Another surge of anger ignites faster than the driest piece of flint.

"I am well enough. I took a fall, and that is all."

"Freydis, I am a friend," Ivor whispers carefully.

"You have proven yourself to be most loyal. Now leave me be."

I wince in pain as I limp towards the back of the longhouse where I have a ready supply of arnica and yarrow mixed with seawater, salt, and a drop of wine to apply to my oft-broken skin and throbbing welts.

"My lady, where is Thorvard now?"

I am as disoriented as a longboat without a rudder. I can hardly stand on my own two feet. The pain is too sharp.

"Get out!" I spit as I bend over the wash basin and splash some water on my face. The cold is good for my black eye. There is a sudden cramping in my gut and I panic, fearing for the baby growing in my womb. Ivor reaches out and steadies me. I freeze.

"Please leave, Ivor. I can't afford to have Thorvard come barging in only to discover that we are alone. You know his jealousy."

"Freydis, you need my help!" Ivor begins again.

I cut him off. "You have helped me well enough," I mumble, spitting out a gob of blood.

Out of the corner of my eye, I see Ivor's brow constrict,

and I almost break. I remember what I've endured since my wedding day – the day when I first set eyes on Thorvard's handsome face and my heart thrummed like a well-played harp.

To think that I cared about Thorvard's dress! His blue kaftan jacket with borders of decorative silk and golden embroidery stitched up and down his sleeve; his belt of fine, polished embossed silver; his black hair swept back and oiled. By the gods, I tremble to the core of my being when I think of how I longed to sip the honeyed mead imported by Faðir – the "honeymoon gift" as he called it. My husband shared the entire keg with my brother, Leif.

The memories fade, and I leave Ivor standing awkwardly by the door and feel my way to the nearest bed platform where I collapse. Stealing a glance in his direction, I see the concern creeping into his weathered face. I have learned that looks can be deceptive, that some men give kindness like they throw bones to dogs.

"Your services won't be required anymore," I manage.

For a moment, Ivor doesn't move, but when I turn my back on him and curl up tightly in a ball, he quietly takes his leave. The door bangs shut behind him as another surge of hot, searing pain builds and bursts.

Then, I sleep.

It is almost nearing suppertime when I wake again in a state of agony. My face is throbbing and my ribs are sore. The savory scent from the roasting meats cooking on the outdoor spits entices me to try to sit, but it is hard. I am too sore. Glancing around, I see that there is no more drinking water in the pail. My throat is parched and a headache pounds. With a grimace, I struggle up, praying I won't be noticed when I step out into the yard.

I am never lucky. On the way back to the longhouse, I meet Finna who meekly tells me that Thorvard has ordered her to help me dress.

"Help me dress?" I ask, confused. The thrall looks at me with her big doe-eyes.

"He wants you in your very best for the feast that has been prepared." She lowers her eyes, refusing to acknowledge that my eye is black.

I look down at the coarse smock I am wearing and realize that I arm myself with toughness before allure in an effort to unsex myself. After tasting blood instead of tender lips, I have no desire to look my best, but I also worry that Finna will pay a price at Thorvard's hands if I refuse to let her dress me for his godless feast.

One must howl in the presence of a wolf.

In silence, I follow Finna into her hut where she fits me into finely pleated linen garb with sleeves that fasten at the neck. My pregnant bump isn't showing yet. I thank the gods. I don't want others to know before Thorvard does. He would not be pleased. Besides, these are early days.

Over the linen shift Finna places a tightly fitted woolen gown with shoulder straps held on by oval brooches with decorative chains that loop across my chest. Around my neck she hangs another heavy chain with beads of colored glass. I hardly care. The novelty and expense of the glass mean nothing anymore.

After tying a belt around my waist, Finna beckons me to take a seat so that she can fix my hair. The thrall works fast. Her nimble fingers form fancy plaits that she deftly positions into place. When she offers to fit me with the tall headdress that marks my high position as Thorvard's wife, I push her hand away.

"I won't wear that," I say. For a moment she simply stares, but then she places the headdress aside.

"Your husband is waiting," is all she says.

I tremble like a leaf in autumn before enduring another wave of sickness and a jolt of pain.

"My lady, you must go to him," Finna urges. "Here, take this shawl. You're shivering."

Chapter Three

HER CLOAK OF FALCON FEATHERS

I hem courage into my skirts and do my duty even though I feel like a tiny mouse about to face a fearsome cat. As I retrace my steps to the longhouse that I have come to hate, I can't help but notice Thorvard's men beetling across the yard to the dinner hall. I keep my head down, knowing I shouldn't care what others think when they see my blackened eye. I shouldn't care, but I do. The rumors are that I am a clumsy bat.

I am perspiring heavily when I cautiously re-enter the longhouse where it is warm and I can smell the roasting meat. Thorvard is sitting on his dais dressed in all his finery. He invites me to come and sit with him.

"I will come by and by," I say stepping back to smooth out my crinkled skirts. Thorvard quickly stands and comes to me. He smells like mint.

"Please excuse the thralls. They couldn't catch your favorite fish," he says in an even tone as he stretches out his hand to me. I force myself to endure his touch without flinching.

"Let me first find some beer for you to drink," I manage awkwardly.

"I have some here. Come dine with me," Thorvard counters as he takes my elbow and draws me forth. Underneath his touch, there are goosebumps rising on my arm.

I brace myself for another fight, but instead I find a feast. Two goblets have been set out beside a flask of wine, and Thorvard has ordered a savory stew of roasted duck for us to eat. The iron pot hangs over a low-burning fire. Glancing sideways, I feel a chill. The blazing firelight highlights Thorvard's chiselled jaw, but his smile is stiff. I shift my gaze and focus on his well-manicured nails, his long fingers, his glistening clean hands.

"What did you do today, Freydis?" Thorvard asks as he pats the seat of the elaborately carved chair with the fancy runic inscription on the cresting rail. He knows full well.

"Today I wasn't feeling well," I say stiffly. "I stayed in bed."

"Ivor told me that you don't want to learn from him anymore. I thought you were *shieldmaiden born*?" Thorvard's voice is silky smooth.

"I couldn't see much, husband. My eye was sore."

It is a stupid thing to say, but I feel smug when I see him squirm. He is ashamed and this is why he hosts a feast. He always does something honorable the day after he beats me hard.

"May the gods have mercy, Freydis," Thorvard purrs. I

feel my brows arching as Thorvard continues serving food. "Next time, do not blame me for your clumsiness. The rumor is that your eye is black because you tripped and fell getting into bed." He pauses and reaches across my arm for the carving knife. "They say that you were too eager to bed me." He grins, and I gawk at him and feel another jolt. What is there to say to this?

"This very day is almost done, and I have thought about you way too much."

I stare at him, feeling miserable as he begins to eat. He chews his food slowly and carefully before sitting back to study me.

"Freydis, I worry about you all the time. You never get to see your kin. I am surprised that you refuse to visit your mother and your favorite brother, Leif."

I have never refused to travel back to Brattahlíð. Thorvard always says he is too busy to accompany me on the long ride back to Faðir's farm. Time and again he has told me that he cannot afford to spare his men to accompany me. There is a giant in the room, and I am too small and weak – indeed, too scared – to stand up to him. In truth, I wish I could scurry away and hide like the little mouse I have become.

"Freydis, I'll not have my bondsmen thinking ill of me. In truth, there is a code of honor this farm keeps." He stops speaking to take another sip from his gilded wine goblet before inviting me to do the same. I shake my head. I hate these dinners. I dread sitting alone with him. I feel as tightly strung as a minstrel's lyre as I watch him begin to suck the

23

grizzled fat off a chunk of bone. An instant later I hear a crack before he spits out the broken bits.

"I have thought long and hard about how to please you," he drones as he flails his knife blade in his fisted hand. I poke at the stew with my pewter spoon and listen to him prattling. I have heard this remorseful, repentant speech before, this heap of cow dung, this desperate attempt to make things right. He stands and moves to the darkened corner at the back where he pours himself another drink. I can hear him fumbling. Panicking, I eye the latch.

"Freydis, I wish to start again, but you must do your part. You have married a wealthy man who has no need of a peasant wife to light his hearth fire and tend his sheep. *Neinn!* I am not that man. My thralls can do all that for me." He returns to the table and takes a swig from his drinking horn. "By Óðinn's beard, my clansmen must see that I treat you well. Your only job is to provide me with a dozen bairns to bear my name. I promise you with my heart's blood that if you do your duty and give me heirs, I'll be content. There will be no cause for grief, and I'll not ask Ivor to follow you anymore."

Outside the wind begins to howl. A headache throbs. My bones feel weak.

"I am grateful," is all I say, trying to hide my trembling hands. They are cold and clammy. I rub them on my apron dress and feel a hangnail catch before I sit up tall and draw in air.

"Husband, there are times when I am afraid to walk alone in the meadowlands. Can you spare a shepherd boy to walk with me?"

"Fie!" he says dismissively. "Ivor has taken great pains to teach you how to defend yourself. You are not in need of protection anymore. Just make certain to take a knife. The one in the calf-leather sheath should serve you well." He does not mention that this is the knife I almost stabbed him with, that this is the weapon he gave me the last time he bruised my cheek. I shift a little in my seat, but I somehow manage to hold his gaze.

"By the gods, Freydis, you may walk freely in my meadowlands, but just be careful and don't blame me when you trip on the hidden boulders that line the fjords. It will not be said that I abandoned you when you go out walking on your own and return with your face all bruised because you slipped and fell against a rock."

He reaches for a slab of bread that he uses to sop the juices from the stew. I can't recall a time where I have ever slipped and fallen during one of my jaunts to the meadowlands.

Just then the door to the longhouse blows open. I wonder if the ancestral ghosts are wandering in to see how we fare. I hope they see that my eye is black and my cheek has cuts and purple welts. I hope they see the darkness inside my husband's soul.

Thorvard stands. In a few quick strides, he travels across the room where he struggles to bolt the latch against another sudden gust of wind. When his back is turned, I dare to give a little smile. I am shocked that Thorvard isn't forcing me to do women's work, that he is still going to allow me to take outdoor walks alone. I should tell him that I am with child, but there is an awkwardness that comes with telling a man this kind of news.

"Husband," I say quietly. I feel a surge of heat in my cheeks as the wick of the whale-oil lamp sputters and drowns and flickers out. I can barely think. "I am pregnant with your firstborn son."

Thorvard slowly turns. "What say you, wife?"

"I am with child."

For a moment, there is silence in the room. Then he rushes forth and pulls me into his massive arms, and I feel nothing.

"Dear Freydis! This is great news, indeed!"

Trembling, I can't help but think that I am giving him a chance to be a *faðir*, that I am giving him protection, that I am allowing him to maintain his other life. I have come to love my hate and hate my fear, but today there is something else. Today there is pure disgust. I know that I have been wronged and that Thorvard is the guilty one. Someday I hope that my bones will dance when I find a way to shame his name.

"I will restore all the privileges that you have lost," Thorvard sputters with a gentleness I can hardly stomach. I swallow bile and turn my head away from him so he can't see the daggers in my eyes. I can hear the shepherds herding sheep into the yard, calling to the stragglers, yodelling.

"Thank you, husband," I say with effort before I take a shallow breath. "I'll make a sacrificial offering to the gods for your continued good health."

"What good is that?" Thorvard sniffs. "I have no need

for rituals or useless hexes that are meant to convince a man that the only way he will be protected is if he kills a goat and makes a sacrificial offering with sprinkled blood. Come now, wife. Look at me! Your news proves that there is great virility in my lower parts. Curse Freyja and her cloak of falcon feathers."

Shivering, I feel the burning in my cheeks, knowing it is bad luck when men curse gods.

"To celebrate the joyous news that you are with child," Thorvard continues, "we will throw a feast and you will look your very best."

I inhale slowly. I will dress in my finest garb, and Thorvard will drink too much. It is what he always does. I draw my hands together. They feel ice cold. "Can I assume that you will invite all your thralls and freedman to this feast?"

"*Já*, of course," Thorvard says as he moves back to the table and pops a cloudberry into his mouth. "All of my clansmen will be invited. They will rejoice for us when they hear the news."

"Einar and Éowyn will be invited too?" I ask a little too quickly. Thorvard stops chewing and looks at me.

"If you want them there," is all he says as he drops his eyes, "although I find Einar to be a dim-witted bore. Tell me, wife, do you have eyes for him?"

"Eyes for him?" I ask, feeling dumb.

"O noble Freydis! I think your red hair seduced him."

"I beseech thee, husband, I don't catch your drift."

"I sometimes wonder if my bride-price was overpaid."

"I feel queasy. I should go to bed," I mutter as I grip a

longhouse post. There is a sharp pain in my womb, but I am careful in the way I stand. My instincts tell me that Thorvard is studying me for a reaction, expecting me to blush. Panicking, I try not to wince. The hearth fire flares.

"You must rest your body for the baby's sake," Thorvard finally says, throwing me a little pity. He pours himself another drink. Behind his head, the shadows dance across an imported tapestry displaying an elaborate hunting scene.

"Freydis, rest assured that I will do well by you," Thorvard sighs. His face is half-silhouetted black; his dark eyelashes are glistening in the flickering firelight. "Einar and Éowyn are as valuable to me as they are to you. I promise not to harm them in any way or to hold them accountable for your misdeeds."

My throat constricts; I am so relieved. Perhaps my pregnancy will make Thorvard into a better man. Perhaps he will be a devoted *faðir* who will come to love me in his own way.

In the days following the announcement that I am with child, the tundra turns all brown and golden and silver-rose, and Thorvard accompanies me for many long and peaceful walks into the hills. Despite his lavish treatment, I have difficulty trusting him. I have learned that his promises are as fickle as the sands rolling in with the foaming surf before they suddenly drift out again. Guarded and on edge, I startle easily at every unexpected sound, but Thorvard continues to dote on me. I begin to look forward to receiving his special gifts: wool to spin; flax for linen; a speckled sealskin pelt he brings home after he goes out hunting with his men; a beautiful rock he promises to have made into a brooch; a treasured piece of soapstone that will make a perfect spoon. He becomes a different man, and I hold out hope that he has changed as I begin to imagine a life for both of us and our little bairn.

When my bruises finally fade to yellowish-green, I tell Thorvard of my intention to hike into the meadowlands to visit Einar and Éowyn on my own. He waves me off.

"Watch where you place your feet. The ground could be slick with frost at this time of year and I'd hate for you to trip," he says without looking up from his counting table. I smile when I hear the tenderness in his voice. How I've longed to hear him speak to me in such a gentle way that makes me feel my worthiness.

"I'll take special care," I mumble as the emotion bubbles up.

The wind is blustery in the meadowland as I trudge through ribbons of grass bordering the pristine fjord, searching for the shepherd and the shepherdess. It is not long before I hear the call of their eldest boy. Arvid, a lanky youth with barely ten summers to his name, holds a shepherd's staff in his hand. The bleating sheep are following him. Some playfully skip around his legs.

"Mistress, 'tis a fine day fer a walk, is it not?"

A sudden gust of wind lifts his mantle and tousles his white-blonde hair. I am so relieved to see that he is safe that I rush forwards, skipping as though I am an unmarried maiden. Three large, ragtag sheep are grazing in the distance where the loam-green grass is lush and plentiful. Arvid calls to them in a warbling voice before tossing me a lopsided grin.

"We haven't seen you much around these parts," he says with a spirited energy I have missed. His gaze sweeps over my fading bruises.

"The elk are rutting at this time of year. Mistress, I spotted them over yonder where the cliffs drop down. They are half-crazed and highly irritable. I'd hate for you to be attacked. Best you avoid them large beasties grazing near the cliffs."

"I'll heed your words," I say as I glance out to sea.

"Mistress, the chieftain says you need protectin'. He says you don't always pay attention to the things you should."

I prickle when I hear these words coming from this freckled-faced boy with barely any peach fuzz on his chin.

"Perhaps I should turn back," I mumble as I draw my mantle tightly closed. "I only came here to ensure that you and your parents were faring well."

"You can't leave so soon," Arvid says. "My parents will want to see you. There is some news to share." Arvid smiles an impish grin. He reminds me of how carefree I used to be before I was wed.

"Come, my lady, follow me. My parents moved the location of their tent away from the gully because of the wind. When the cold weather comes, we'll need to return to the farm."

We walk together in comfortable companionship with the flock of sheep following us. It is not long before I spot a tall, thin shepherd dressed in a woolen overtunic with baggy trousers and woven leg wrappings, standing underneath a lone willow tree surrounded by three little ones. Behind him, Éowyn is bustling around the cooking fire. I am so overjoyed to see them that it takes me a moment to compose myself. Éowyn waves just as a ray of sun comes pealing out from behind a wisp of passing clouds.

"Your husband told us your happy news. We were so pleased to hear that you are with child," she says as soon as I reach their snapping fire. In three quick steps, I am in her arms.

"Freydis Eiriksdöttir, we have missed your presence around our fire," Einar says with a toothless grin. I catch his eye. He sees my face. If only I were a little sheep, the thickness of my woolly coat would hide the bruises around my eye. Éowyn bites her lip as she studies me. An awkwardness hangs between us, thick as smoke.

"Was Thorvard here?" I murmur, speaking low.

"He came ten days ago."

The wind picks up and pushes the campfire smoke in one direction and then the next.

"The chieftain brought all kinds of news," Arvid says. I glance over to where Einar is standing and staring at his feet.

"What did he say?" There is a taste of ash in my mouth, a rippling cramp jabbing fiercely in my gut.

"As you know, the blacksmith's only son died one year ago," Arvid continues as he tries to suppress a growing smile. "By Óðinn's eye, the blacksmith is looking for an apprentice. He wants someone about my age. May the gods be praised! The chieftain, your husband, asked me if I want to learn the trade."

"What did you say?" I ask, feeling ill.

"I agreed. If all goes well, I will start working for the blacksmith in two weeks' time after we have finished shearing all the pregnant ewes that are due to lamb. Faðir said that Thorvard of Gardar has granted our family the highest honor in choosing me to learn the blacksmith trade. He says that our family's social standing on this farm will improve. I am so grateful for this opportunity – the opportunity to be honored above the other boys. My lady, your husband is a generous man."

I cannot focus. I cannot think. Einar steps forwards and busies himself attending to the fire. I sense his shame. Curse my trust of mortal men! In one fell swoop, Thorvard has bought Einar's loyalty by elevating the shepherd's son to one of the highest positions on his farm. As soon as his son is apprenticed, Einar will never speak out against Thorvard of Gardar. He wouldn't dare.

"It's time to eat," Éowyn says softly as she offers me creamy goat cheese and hot steaming flax-bread cooked over an outdoor fire. I look at her and furl my brows. No food will mend the friendship we once shared.

Éowyn finishes serving up the food, eyeing me as she flits around. When she comes to take me by the arm, I let her drag me out of earshot as her youngest *döttir* begins to whine.

"Dear Freydis, it may not be my place, but I know your husband abuses you. I am sorry that we are not in a position to bear witness to the brutalities you face." There is a fierceness I have never heard before in her voice. "We couldn't possibly speak out. Not now. Please forgive us. We had no choice. The chieftain's offer was something we could not refuse."

Behind us, Einar is consoling their little one.

"I understand," I lie. I take a step backwards and try to still my shaking hands. "It is not fair to ask you and Einar to get involved in my affairs."

"Mistress, aren't you happy for me?" Arvid asks in a breathless voice as he approaches from behind.

"*Já*," I say, turning. I hold his eyes. "My husband has honored you for good reason. You are capable and responsible."

The boy lifts his chin and puffs out his boy-man chest. He is an innocent whose youthful, self-important look spears me.

"The chieftain knows that I am quick to learn. Someone told him that I am good with my hands." His eyes throw sparkles. He can barely contain a growing smile. "I am grateful, mistress. He told me you spoke highly of me."

I touch my belly where my own bairn sleeps, wondering if I am fit to be a mother, if I am wise enough to Thorvard's ways. Éowyn sighs.

"I hope you'll continue to come and visit us," she says. "The outdoor air is good for a woman in your condition."

"It is," I say.

Chapter Four

IF I HAD WINGS

Towards the middle of *tvímánuður*, after the harvest, I find myself in the longhouse with Thorvard and my husband's inner circle of trade advisors who are discussing whether to hunt for caribou or jig fish before the winter sets in and the sea ice comes. I have just finished carding a basketful of wool when I hear someone's loud whistle announcing the approach of a visitor.

Ivor quickly stands. I drop the wool carder and follow him out into the sun-drenched yard where a cool autumn wind is stirring up the sedge grasses. Faðir's messenger looks spent. Alf's leggings and his wolfskin cloak are mud-spattered, and it looks as though his horse has been run hard all the way from Brattahlíð.

"*Góðan dag*, my lady," Alf pants as he rides up. "I am here to tell you that your *faðir* suffered a broken leg after falling off his handsome horse."

"By the gods, is it bad?" I ask, feeling my stomach drop. Alf's brows furrow into knots. He dismounts quickly.

"Your *faðir's* leg is festering," he says.

Unable to speak, I try to remember how to breathe.

"Is there news of Leif?" Thorvard barks. His breath is hot against my neck. Alf glances at Thorvard before he turns back to me.

"My lady, I also bring news from your brother, Leif."

"What is it, man?" Thorvard yips.

A lopsided grin breaks out on Alf's dirt-speckled face. "Leif's fortune is on the rise."

I stare at him, uncomprehending, as my husband devours the messenger with his carrion eyes.

"Before I explain, I need a drink to quench my thirst," the messenger continues, spitting out a wad of phlegm. A dread comes over me when I catch a glimpse of Thorvard frowning.

"Come," I say as I hastily usher Alf towards the well. The messenger doesn't realize that he is a moth fluttering around a fire.

"If it is news you bring, then tell us quickly. I've work to do and a farm to run," Thorvard barks as he trots behind us.

Alf takes a drink from the drinking pail and then rights himself. In the process, his back cracks. "The tale is long," he grunts as he runs his forearm across his dripping beard. Thorvard turns on me.

"Do you know what this is all about?" His words slice through me, sharper than any sword. The messenger eyes the two of us.

"Leif Eiriksson sends you peace," Alf pipes up uncomfortably. "The chieftain's son is gone—"

"Gone?" I ask. I feel my mouth go dry. "Not dead, I hope?"

"*Neinn*. He sailed away. He went to explore the northern seas."

"The northern seas?" I repeat. My stomach drops.

"*Já*. There came a man who had a ship. Bjarni was his name."

Bjarni Herjolfsson. He was a mammoth of a man with a missing tooth and giant's feet and a nervous tic that made him blink. He wore a fox pelt around his neck. His ship had been anchored in the fjord when I first came to Gardar as Thorvard's bride. Bjarni had just returned to Greenland after spending a winter with the Thules. We have always done well trading with those northerners. The helmsman talked too much, but he brought me trinkets, including a fancy spindle made of antler bone and a pure white bear hide that was as soft as fleece. It was the perfect pelt. Bjarni had wanted Thorvard to purchase it so that I could put it on our bed. Thorvard had beaten me for it, stating that my want of it shamed him.

"Bjarni was a stupid fool for venturing north before Rogation Day," my husband huffs. He motions to a thrall and flicks his wrist and orders drinking horns. "Surely Eirik the Red did not take him in?"

"There was no other place for him to stay in the western settlement. Bjarni has been with us now for months on end." Alf wipes the droplets of water off his beard.

"Freydis, your *faðir* is too generous," Thorvard sighs. "That Bjarni was a bore. He told us that he had no desire to explore the lands he found. I have no respect for men like him. How could he travel all that way across the northern sea and show no curiosity?"

"Apparently, the *skraelings* with their red faces scared him off," Alf says, addressing me. "That is why he returned to Greenland."

"We heard the tale repeatedly," Thorvard scoffs.

Poor Faðir. I can't imagine having to listen to Bjarni's saga repeatedly. The story was very dull. The only intriguing part was when he met the Red Men. Even then, he didn't have much to say about the encounter.

Alf clears his throat. "Eirik Eiriksson treats Bjarni as though he is a king. 'Tis true, I say! Eirik the Red knows how to throw a feast in honor of men who give him news."

Thorvard eyes me hard, as if to blame me for Alf's sense of entitlement. A sudden misgiving trickles into a lake of fear.

"Messenger, I don't have time to roast a pig just because you arrive here unannounced from Brattahlíð. Rest assured, we will give you food and shelter for the night, but you shouldn't expect too much hospitality given that it is the harvest month."

Alf's smile reveals a mess of blackened, crooked teeth. He clears his throat. "Freydis, you might not be surprised by this, but your brother, Leif, was eager to know all about Bjarni's travels. On the first night the helmsman was with us, the two of 'em debated the merits of making another *vyking* expedition across the northern sea. In the end, Bjarni said that he had no desire to go back, but Leif was eager. You'll never believe this, but your brother purchased the helmsman's ship."

"What?" Thorvard snaps. His voice sounds wild.

"He did it with his *faðir's* help."

"Faðir would have enjoyed the bartering," I say quickly, thinking of my brother back in Brattahlíð. At my wedding feast, Leif asked Thorvard if he knew of a good shipbuilder with wood to spare. Thorvard laughed. I remember that. Then the two of them bent their heads together and talked all night about sailing across the northern seas. I had to sit there listening. Afterwards, Thorvard blamed me for finally asking my brother to leave us so that we could be together on our wedding night. It shames me to think on it, but I wonder if Thorvard demanded a kiss from Leif when I wasn't looking and that is why my brother left so fast.

Someone shouts. There is a rumble of voices. A crowd is gathering in the yard. The messenger squares his weary shoulders and stands up tall. "Eirik the Red sends good cheer to all of you, but the real reason I am here is to tell you that Leif Eiriksson has left Greenland's shores in his own *vyking* ship to sail across the northern seas. He will be gone for at least a year."

I draw in air. How could Leif abandon me? How could he leave me in this fox's den when he used to defend me when we were young? Why didn't he come to tell me he was leaving? Do I mean nothing to him anymore?

"Did Eirik the Red go with him?" the blacksmith asks as he eyes my husband hard.

"Eirik Eiriksson is getting on in years," the messenger tells the growing crowd. "He won't be leading any more *vyking* expeditions across the sea. The chieftain jokes that at his age, he wouldn't be able to bear the cold, but truth be told, he couldn't have gone. He is recovering from a broken leg."

I turn my back on all of them and begin to pace, walking back and forth in front of the chicken coop.

"Eirik the Red is feverish," Alf announces uncomfortably. "The good chieftain's wife sends greetings. She is worried about the chieftain. She is in need of Freydis. She has no one to help her now that Leif is gone."

"What about my other brothers?" I mutter. "Where are Thorvald and Thorstein?"

"They are too young to manage a chieftain's farm, Freydis. Besides, your mother always relied on you and Leif."

"When did my brother leave?"

"Leif put to sea two days ago," the messenger announces as he takes another swig from the proffered drinking horn. His body odor wafts towards me so that I need to turn my face away.

"Your brother took a giant risk leaving at this time of year," Thorvard says as he glares at me. I go to speak but he cuts me off, silencing me as if I am a bug to squish. "He is a foolish man."

"Leif Eiriksson is wise enough to set down anchor and go into shore before the ice sets in and clogs the channels," Alf says carefully.

"Summer is too far gone to make it across the northern sea," I sputter. "He will not return to us this year."

"'Tis true, good Freydis," Alf affirms. "He'll have to find someplace to winter before the snows set in."

"Wintering in the north can be dangerous," my husband

mutters before he reaches out and grabs my arm to make me stop walking back and forth. When my heart finally settles, I extract myself from Thorvard's grip.

"Why didn't Leif come to me?" Thorvard rants. "Why didn't he ask me to help him build a ship?"

Alf releases a heavy sigh. "Leif has always been his own man."

I feel a sudden cramp. "I must offer sacrifice to the gods for Leif's safe return."

"The gods are useless," Thorvard sniffs. "As mortals, we must trust our instincts and rely on ourselves."

"Hush, now, Thorvard," I whisper anxiously.

"Don't 'hush' me, woman. Did you know your brother was planning this great escape from Greenland's shores?"

"Stop," I fret as I wring my hands. I feel embarrassed to hear him berating Leif. "I trust that my brother will be praised for his bravery. He has always wanted to explore new lands. May his name be spoken by the bards. May there be numerous sagas told about his northern quest."

Thorvard glares at me. I feel another sharp stomach cramp.

"Truly, I am afraid for Leif," Alf says as he rakes his fingers through his hair, "but Leif has always been lucky. He will return to us, and he will enjoy sharing the saga of his adventures overseas."

Thorvard folds his arms across his chest and looks out across the churning sea.

"We need to prepare the evening meal," I say to Alf as I smooth out my apron skirt with my sweaty palms. "Take a drink with the freedmen and then return to us. I'll have our thralls attend to your horse."

Alf steps towards me. He dips his head, positioning himself so that only I can hear. "Freydis, your *faðir* wanted you to know that he misses you. He sends you blessings from the gods."

That night the men are loud, and the mutton is tough and smells like feet. Sitting at the banquet table feeling ill, I am barely able to touch my food, but Thorvard is a glutton. He calls for more wine, carmine-colored, before he begins to belch and brag about his plentiful harvest and his flocks of sheep. Alf listens avidly. He reminds me of a busy squirrel gathering nuts and stockpiling them for later use. When he is short on news, the story of this feast will be the acorn he retrieves.

"Freydis is with child," Thorvard says. "You must tell her *faðir*. Eirik the Red will be pleased to hear that I am doing well. His *döttir* has done her duty to my house."

I hang on Thorvard's words, feeling cheated. Not once has Thorvard glanced my way.

"My lady, this is great news indeed!" Alf exclaims. Then, gently, "Should I tell your mother first?"

I nod, but my cramps worsen. In front of me, my untouched food grows cold. Thorvard leans towards me, trying to be discreet.

"You must eat a little for the bairn's sake," he whispers fiercely in my ear.

"I have no appetite."

"Prithee, Freydis, have I said something to injure you?"

I shake my head, grimacing when another cramp attacks me.

"Perhaps you should go to our bed chamber and rest," he says impatiently.

"I'll stay until Alf retires," I say quickly. Secretly, I can hardly wait for the fire to die and the charred criss-cross embers to crumble into ash so that the men are forced to go to bed.

As I lower my head like a chastised thrall, a shadow moves across Thorvard's face. The fire spits. I sneak a peek beyond the dirty chargers strewn across the table and feel the presence of ghosts floating through the room as they stop to search for morsels and pick through bones. Time runs as fast as a river current and my back stiffens as I endure another cramp. Without turning to look at me, Thorvard waves his hand dismissively.

"Go," he says. "Run off to bed like you always do."

In pain, I quickly stand only to feel blood trickling out of me.

"Don't be rude," Thorvard whispers fiercely as he suddenly reaches out and tugs my arm to hold me back. He sounds perturbed. "You must first say *góða nótt* to our guests."

I blink and brace myself so I don't double over.

"Wife, you'll heed my order or make me mad. You do not look well. Now take your leave of us and go to bed."

I feel a building pressure in my gut, a stab of pain, and another vicious cramp.

"Freydis Eiriksdóttir, did your mother not teach you the importance of obeying your husband and listening carefully to his commands?"

I flinch. Thorvard's face looks deadly calm. As he draws back his dais chair, he glares at my stomach with his dragon eyes.

"Good men," he announces in a booming voice as he turns to address the crowd. "My wife is pregnant with our firstborn son and she is feeling tired after a long day of work. Please excuse her from this feast."

Alf smiles and I smile back. I am on display for Thorvard of Gardar. Gripping the table and feeling faint, I don another brilliant smile for the sake of showing Thorvard's clansmen that all is well. I understand the importance of these banal platitudes, and I have learned how to wear a mask. Then, retrieving my grace, I lift my chin and walk in a stately fashion across the banquet hall.

I have barely made it out the door when I keel over from another vicious cramp. In the yard, there is a raven croaking out a gurgled cry. It is a sign – a sign that Óðinn is visiting Thorvard's farm.

I try to right myself, but I can barely stand. Below my skirts, I see a trail of blood. Cringing, I stumble, certain that some monster is passing out of me. When I endure another rush of crushing pain followed by a burning wave of agony, a cry slips out.

Finna is suddenly at my side. The thrall bends down and tries to support me, but her thin frame wobbles underneath my weight.

"Mistress Freydis, should I call the midwife?"

"*Neinn*," I blubber as I grit my teeth. "I'll go to her myself. I don't want the men to know that I am ill. Alf especially. He will return to Brattahlíð and worry Mother."

Finna nods. Her eyes are large. When I let out a little cry, she darts forwards and helps me begin to hobble in the direction of the midwife's hut. As we walk, I try to clamp my legs together so that I can keep the bairn inside my womb, but the pain comes in vicious waves. Beside me, Finna is muttering fervent prayers.

"Please," I grunt. "Please be quiet until we reach Mairi."

Mairi, the midwife, is a thin, austere-looking woman who whisks me inside a stuffy room where the hearth fire is far too warm. When she instructs me to squat, her face looks calm in the firelight. Then she reaches underneath my skirts.

"Your womb is slightly small, but it is certainly big enough to birth another healthy bairn," she whispers as soon as she withdraws her hand. She reaches for some foul-smelling herb.

"What about this little one?" I moan as I arch my back. Without looking, I know that my bairn's lifeblood is draining out of me.

Another contraction comes, and a scream slips out. In anguish, I place my hands in a triangle on my womb, knowing that something precious and irreplaceable is being stolen from me, knowing that it is too late.

"Push, mistress!" Mairi mutters fiercely.

By the gods, I have failed as a woman. I have failed as Thorvard's wife. Everything looks blurry in the hazy light. The whale-oil lamp flickers in the wall sconce where the cobwebs sit.

"Boil some water, Finna. Thorvard's wife needs hot cloths." Mairi scowls before removing what remains inside of me.

I cry out again, relinquishing any dignity I have left. I am sweaty and bloodied. My smell is bad. Outside, I hear men's voices. Someone shouts.

Another cramp twists me up in pain and fear before tossing me into a great abyss where my mind struggles to make sense of things and my body aches as dark thoughts come. By the gods, if my knife could only dig out this pain, I could stop thinking about all that has happened and all that won't.

There is another sharp, stabbing jolt that makes me arch my back.

Sweet Óðinn! Send me your ravens to raise me up and bear me off into the sky. Oh gods, please hurry, I beg of you.

I'll do anything to be free of what's inside of me.

In the morning when I wake, they tell me that Alf has left. Mairi brings me goat milk and tells me to drink deeply to restore my health. I squint up at her and see the coldness in her eyes.

"Did you take your *gojya's* fertility herbs?" she asks bluntly as she leans over me. I purse my lips. My body aches so much I can barely move. Someone has covered me with a bearskin hide. I push it down and try to struggle up.

"Lie down," Mairi snaps. "You can expect some bleeding yet." She turns from me and busies herself sorting jars of tincture and a mess of herbs. "Truly, mistress, I am sorry that you lost your bairn."

"Does Thorvard know?" There are welling tears. I brush them off.

"You should not have told him that you were with child until you were sure," Mairi scolds. I stare at her. "It is only the middle of *Tvímánuður*. There is nary a mistress who would have announced her pregnancy quite so soon. It is too disappointing to the men."

"How did my husband take the news?"

"Your husband is grieving still. Didn't you hear him sobbing in the yard last night?"

"I heard nothing," I whisper, feeling only the rhythm of the throbbing pain. Underneath my garments, my belly is distended and my nipples ache.

"Your husband needs to be consoled."

"Have him come to me."

"He wants to have nothing to do with you, mistress," Mairi says. Her voice sounds strange. "He told me to attend to you."

Two days later, when I am still feeling heartsick from the loss, Thorvard unexpectedly enters our bed chamber. I keep my eyes closed, feigning sleep, until I feel his breath on top of my head.

"Freydis, it is time to wake," Thorvard whispers quietly as he gently runs a soft finger down my face. I am startled when I open my eyes and he is suddenly in my face.

"You are more like an annoying gnat than a wife," he sighs in his softest voice. He slowly stands. "You can't even bear me a healthy bairn who stays alive long enough to see the sun."

I glance up.

With a sudden thwack, Thorvard hits the bed platform's post so hard that it vibrates and the dust filters down from the rafters.

"Thor restrain me, you fail at everything," my husband shouts.

Instantly I pull back in fear as the hides get caught around my waist. "I'm sorry, husband,"

"You good-for-nothing ugly old woman! I'm sick of you!"

I try to draw back from him, but he slaps me hard across the face. In shock, my neck snaps back, and I knock my head into the wall. When he hits me in the mouth again. I feel the blood slipping down my teeth.

Mairi slinks into the shadows just as Ivor bursts through the door and claws at Thorvard, trying to hold him back and calm him down with soothing words. My ears are ringing, but through the buzz I hear Thorvard shout.

Then Ivor swears, and I scuttle backwards, cowering against the wall. Someone throws a pewter mug that clashes and clangs as it hits the slate.

"Watch out!" I scream as Thorvard punches Ivor's jaw.

"Hold up, man, I've lost my tooth," Ivor groans. Blood is slipping through his fingers and splattering in big, fat droplets on the floor.

Thorvard stares at Ivor and then he folds, blubbering pathetically like a little child.

In stunned silence, Ivor blinks. Cradling his jaw, he stares at his lover who drops to the floor and curls up in a little ball, moaning and crying unconsolably.

"We shouldn't have to put up with this," Ivor mumbles as soon as our eyes connect.

"*Neinn*," I say. "We shouldn't have to live in fear."

After that, Thorvard ignores both of us for two full weeks. Then, on the night of the Feast of Haustblót, he dismisses Mairi and orders me to spread my legs to try again to make a child. Reluctantly I obey, but my insides hurt and my heart is a broken vessel of nothingness.

As I struggle to lift my skirts, Thorvard turns away to unbuckle the belt that holds his sword. The weapon was a wedding gift, a replacement for his *faðir's* burial sword, a leg biter that I now own. As tradition demands, I gave it to Ivor for safekeeping until our firstborn son comes of age. Tonight, I wonder about the whereabouts of the weapon. Will I ever be able to pass it on? Will I even be able to bear Thorvard sons?

"Lie back," Thorvard barks. His eyes are bloodshot and he is drunk.

He spreads my legs apart with his bony knees, and I let him maneuver me into place. To still my angst, I focus on his ice-fog breath pluming from his big, fat lips and will my heart to settle. Fumbling awkwardly, he yanks my skirt up only to discover that I still bleed.

"Shit!" he swears. His spittle splatters across my chest. Turning my face away, I let him fondle my breasts with his cold hands. When he stops to take another gulp of wine, I try to wiggle out from underneath him until he slaps me hard across the face.

"When you finally find the wherewithal to bear me a healthy son," he mutters angrily as I lie there mewling, "what is mine shall never do you any good."

Grunting, he falls on top of me like a slab of rock. In the process, he snags a lock of hair. Stifling a yelp, I tug it free and feel the beginning of a rumbling – a black and thunderous rage that feeds the hate. The wolf inside me snarls and I call to it, ready to act on that rebellious part that feels the coils wrapping around my heart, smothering reason, stifling fear.

With narrowed eyes, I begin to punch and roll and kick and grapple hard like Ivor taught me in the yard. Consumed by resentment, I am filled with vengeance, fuelled by rage.

An instant later, my world goes silent.

Completely still.

"No man will ever hurt me again," I hiss as I reach underneath the furs for my knife. I focus on Thorvard's crazy eyes and gnash my teeth, but before I can dig the knife out, he lunges. In the nick of time, I dodge his blow.

But he is fast. A moment later, he grabs my hair, not knowing that I've become a wolverine with vicious, sharp, and nasty teeth capable of biting down on his tattooed arm.

"You bitch!" he screams, wincing as he pulls back his shoulders, favoring his bleeding arm. Without pausing, I grab hold of his balls and squeeze them hard. He yelps again, and I feel a tiny smile moving into my lips.

With my other hand, I raise my knife and aim it at his stubbled beard. A moment later, I jab his cheek and allow the blade to dig in deep and rip the flesh open to expose the bone. Then I drag the blade down and blood spurts out from the mess of flesh. Thorvard reels backwards, thrashing and struggling to get free of me, swearing that I am a witch-ridden. In one quick move, I scramble up.

There is a sudden sickness in my gut. Standing there, frozen, I gawk at him.

"How now? Are you badly hurt?" I finally mutter in a shaky voice. My hand is bloody. My shift is ripped. In front of me, Thorvard writhes in pain. When he finally rolls over, the open wound – a flap of bleeding skin – reveals cheekbone fat. Gasping, I lean forwards, but just as I am reaching out to help stanch the blood, Thorvard grabs me with his bloodied, sticky hand.

"Thor's hammer, you amaze me, Freydis Eiriksdóttir." On his tunic there is an ugly smear of blood. Slowly, I lift my head. His cheek looks like some vicious animal has chewed him up. Horrified, I pull back. His grip tightens around my wrist.

"Blood has made you cowardly," he says through gritted teeth as he squeezes hard. "You should have finished off the deed and stabbed me in the chest."

"Blood does not make me cowardly. It makes me bold," I

say in a stone-cold voice. "It reminds me of who I am and what I've become living here on this godless farm."

Thorvard reaches up to touch his bleeding cheek. "Who are you, my blood-thirsty wife?"

"I am Freydis Eiriksdöttir! I am the *goði's döttir*. I am a warrior. By the gods, the next time I have a chance, I'll kill you with this fearsome blade."

Thorvard laughs sardonically as he struggles up. In silence, I watch him pick up his drinking horn and wander out of the longhouse. As the door slams shut, I am left standing there knowing I have left my mark on Thorvard's cheek, and in exchange, I've become a monster, just like him.

Far away in the distance, I hear the seabirds shrieking. If I had wings, I would leave this wretched longhouse and fly back to Faðir's farm. Brattahlíð calls to me. It is the place where I left myself.

Chapter Five

DUST DEVILS

By the time the first big snowstorm comes, I am black and blue with broken bones inflicted by a wolfish husband whom I despise. Thorvard blames me openly for the knife scar that marks his cheek. Then he blackens my good name by telling others that I am a thankless wife, that I am headstrong and feisty and shamelessly bold. When his clansmen shun me, I ask Óðinn, the god of divination and of war, to keep me safe and restore my position on Thorvard's farm.

One cold, grey, frosty day I ask permission to go out with a group of huntsmen to harpoon seals. To my surprise, I score a kill. Ivor tells me that my hunting eye is keen. My husband tells me that my tracker's instinct needs some work. I ignore them both and celebrate my success by drinking too much wine. While most of the huntsmen ignore me, Ivor is agitated.

"Freydis. I worry that you are not yourself," he says, taking me aside.

"I'm not," I say.

"Just watch yourself," he whispers softly in my ear.

"I always do," I reply.

"You don't," he says, throwing me a look of pity as if I am a starving dog, a flapping fish out of water.

"Peace," I stammer.

"I advise you to do your duty and show your husband the respect he deserves so that it will be better for both of us."

I smile at him.

"This is not a game," he says.

"I didn't think it was," I say, faltering.

In the coming weeks, I hunt so much that the smell of fat and blood and smoke and fresh outdoor air hangs heavily in my clothes and hair. I learn to check hunting traps and follow tracks. Even Einar congratulates me for using my slingshot to target a rabbit from halfway across the yard. I should be proud but I feel nothing. I should be proud but I feel nothing. Worst of all, I no longer laugh, I can't relax, and sleep evades me. I am too afraid.

When the weather worsens, Thorvard gathers the good people of Gardar together. "You must come to live in my longhouse instead of suffering in your drafty huts."

He makes the announcement in the yard and his clansmen are so pleased that they praise him openly. From a distance, I study Ivor's face. He is standing with his arms crossed, leaning against a post, looking cross. I swear on Loki's statue that my 'generous' husband is never generous to those he loves although he treats Ivor much better than he treats me.

As I listen to Thorvard's speech, I watch the sheep with their scraggly wool coats, grazing on top of the longhouse, nibbling the brown grasses short. Some of Thorvard's clansmen are studying me and I know they think my face is surly and I am slow. How is it that Thorvard convinces others to think ill of me? How is it that he makes me second-guess myself? Why does he question me about everything? Why does he blame me when things go wrong?

Ivor sidles up to me. "It will get better. Thorvard is always at his best when there are others around."

"The fox inside his lair remains a fox."

"Lower your voice, Freydis."

"I can protect myself. I have a knife."

"Careful," Ivor whispers without looking at me. "Your husband is the chieftain. He has the power to banish you to the north."

"Others would condemn him for it."

"Just watch yourself," Ivor says.

By the Feast of Dísablót – the festival honoring the female spirits of protection and fertility at the beginning of winter – the longhouse is crowded with farmers and thralls who huddle together near the hearth fire. In their company Thorvard drinks too much, but he leaves me be. The relief I feel is notable, but I still feel like I am walking on eggshells, constantly needing to protect myself.

When Thorvard takes a thrall to his bed after getting extremely drunk one night, a sour taste fills my mouth, and I have to sit on my hands to stop them from shaking. During their outlandish coupling, the bed-slave shames me openly. Everyone can see her breasts dangling over

Thorvard's chest, her long hair trailing down her back. When I hear her wanton moans, a shiver racks my body as I fiddle with my hands and stare at the longhouse walls, wishing that I was dead.

Éowyn tries to console me by handing me her hand spindle. I take it, but my eyes mist up and I can't see straight. The only grace is that my kin back in Brattahlíð do not know of this great dishonor. In the hot, smoky room, I stare into the fire, not caring whether I live or die, not caring about anything.

The next day, Éowyn finds me in the coldest corner of the longhouse wrapped inside my sealskin coat, shivering with my eyes half-shut.

"Please take this little creature off our hands," she says as she comes to sit beside me in the dark. She holds a caramel-colored baby goat in her arms. I scratch its head as she continues, whispering low: "This kid was rejected by its mother after a difficult birth. The poor creature needs to be fed by hand. By the gods, I know this goat will be a welcome distraction. He'll feed your heart. It's what you need."

Éowyn's words are meant to comfort, but I despair. How is it that a worthless thrall replaced me – a bed-slave who might even be the one to conceive Thorvard's firstborn son? Thorvard seems to have forgotten that I am his wife, that I should hold a place of honor around his fire. Curse him for not visiting my bed anymore. Curse him for loving Ivor instead of me. Curse this longhouse. Curse this life.

The next day, Éowyn comes to sit beside me as soon as she has done her chores. Once again, she brings the baby goat with her. "Thorvard's thrall is far too bold," she mutters carefully. "May the gods frown on her. You must find a way to take your power back."

I am silent – perhaps even a little rude as I reach out and take the baby goat into my lap. The creature is an energetic little thing. He looks at me with his long-lashed eyes waiting for me to scratch the top of his bony head. An instant later he releases a high-pitched bleat, and just like that the little goat becomes my own – my entry into motherhood.

In the coming weeks, I spoil the kid. To my delight, the little thing follows me all around the longhouse as I do my chores. In the eyes of the good people of Gardar, he is a jumper and a climber who falls off things as often as he is successful. To me, he has a playful attitude and an energetic, funny bounce which lifts my spirits and helps me forget about Thorvard's bed-slave and her seductress ways.

I give my goat a name: Brúsi. At night I like the way he nuzzles his little body in close to me. I tell myself that I can endure Thorvard's disrespect as long as I have Brúsi with his soft pussy-willow ears and his bristled coat that I like to brush. When the women try to shoo him out of the weaving room, I remind them with a few well-placed words that I am the chieftain's wife and that I have influence whereas they have none.

My vindictiveness flares one day when I announce to a group of Norsewomen that Thorvard's thrall, a thin, plain-looking maiden, is not of woman born. The thrall is cooking stew. To my delight, I see her head snap up and I continue berating her, feeling gleeful that I can shame her with some well-placed words.

"I hear tell that she was sired by a giant and that she sucked the blood out of cold corpses before she came to Thorvard's farm." My words slip out as easily as a musician's prickly bone-flute trills.

The women gawk. The chatter stops. Thorvard's bed-slave hangs her head. Her hands are shaking as she stirs the pot.

That day I lose another piece of myself when I take pleasure in belittling her. As the weather worsens and the snowdrifts bank so high that the top of the byre is hardly visible from the longhouse door, I work hard to make the thrall's life miserable. I task her with dumping the urine bucket and dealing with a hunk of spoiled foul-smelling meat. I know that I am hard on her, but by publicly rebuking her, I restore my seat around Thorvard's fire, which forces Thorvard back to me.

One morning I wake to the howl of a brutal wind and blowing snow. The sky is bleak, but my husband convinces his men to go out hunting with him anyway. The party returns empty-handed, which brings great disappointment. What is worse is Thorvard's red frostbitten foot. Mairi worries that he'll lose some toes. After mixing herbs, she tends to him while muttering prayers to Hlin, asking Frigga's handmaiden to lay her hand on Thorvard of Gardar and heal him.

Someone has carved Hlin's figure into a piece of bone that sits upon a longhouse beam. I stare at it and take note of the sword and shield in her hand, and she inspires me.

There is a wood-axe hanging on the wall. I could use it to strike Thorvard on the foot. I could thrust it through him. I could deal him a death wound. I am capable.

I imagine striking him on the spine and splitting him in two. The thought brings a tiny smile that quickly fades.

Afterwards, they would banish me.

When the storms persist, I can't stop worrying. There is Leif's absence and Faðir's leg. I even fret about starvation setting in on Faðir's farm. If Thorvard's food supplies are low, Faðir's must be low as well.

One night when I have trouble sleeping, I turn to Thorvard, who is lying beside me in the dark and breathing heavily, half-awake. "I can't stop thinking about my kin. What if they are faring poorly in this spell of cold weather?"

"Freydis, I can hardly walk, but if I could, you know that I would do my best to ensure that all was well on your *faðir's* farm. I am sure that they are well-provisioned. Even if my toes weren't black, there is no way that we could travel to your *faðir's* farm. There is simply too much snow." He grimaces as he repositions himself on our bed of furs, shifting so that his back is facing me.

I feel my heart thudding heavily. Suddenly I see myself as a little girl sitting around Faðir's fire, listening to him sing a song about a far-off land, about a princess who leads a *vyking* expedition to the north. It is sad to think that that life held sweetness then and that Faðir thought of me as his most precious pearl. He said I was worth more than a storage shed full of his finest pelts.

I dream that night of being at home in Brattahlíð with my kin, listening to the skald telling stories about my pathetic life. When I wake, a shiver runs through me, but I get up and go about my chores. As I stoke the fire, I watch my little goat working hard to break the thin sheet of ice on the water bucket. Afterwards he comes and nuzzles my hand for food. Sadly, I have nothing to feed him. There is only my skin for salt. That afternoon when Thorvard brings up the need to ration food, Brúsi lets out a long, noisy bleat that startles me.

We pass a rule that until the weakened sun passes noon and the shadows begin to lengthen on the walls, we cannot eat. Feeling desperate, I petition the gods, but they fail to help. A few days later as I am carrying a bucket full of snow inside to melt, I overhear two Norsemen speaking quietly amongst themselves in the dark back corner of the longhouse.

"The animals are growing lean and weak. Have you seen the cattle's bones?"

"Gudrun tells me the chickens are no longer laying eggs."

"The chieftain ain't gonna be pleased when you tell him that. Soon we'll be forced to eat his horses if we can't get us meat."

My thoughts swirl into dust devils of despair. When they finally spot me standing half-hidden behind a barrel, they offer an apology for speaking about my husband behind his back. I wave them off, but I understand beyond all doubt that the situation is very dire. I can only pray that we won't be forced to boil hides for soup to fend off starvation. Fie! Eating hide-soup would be ludicrous. Surely it won't come to that.

As soon as the snow stops, Thorvard organizes another hunting party to go out in search of meat. The huntsmen leave at dawn. By early afternoon when the shadows begin to snake up the wattled walls, I fear that the men are lost – or worse, that they lie frozen and buried in a bank of snow.

Outside it is deathly quiet, deathly cold. I am so vexed that I make a sacrificial offering to Thor, hoping that he will protect the men from the winter hunting god, Skaði. I place the offering – a piece of my hair cut from the forelock – on the *hørg* and lie prostrate in front of it. The altar of heaped stones has not been used in many days because there has been nothing to sacrifice – no remaining sheaves of wheat, no she-goats for the offering.

"Hail to thee, defender of us all. We humbly ask that you protect us from the frost giant's *döttir*, she who hunts on skis. Mighty Thor, hasten to help us. Give our hunters strength to bring home meat. With blithe eyes look on us and prevent the god of winter from robbing our hunters of victory. Help them so they don't freeze to death in the snow. Make them victorious in the hunt and help them return to us by nightfall."

After that we wait in silence, stoking the peat fire when it burns low. The room grows cold as darkness falls. When we finally hear a barrage of muffled voices at the door, I quickly stand. The sound comes again. Soon after, the huntsmen stumble inside, bringing with them a rush of cold air that slithers up my skirt. Their beards and moustaches are covered in thick white frost. Their leggings are frozen hard and dusted over with matted snow that clings to their hides in clumps.

"We didn't find any caribou," wheezes Thorsen, a large barrel-chested man. He drags himself closer to the fire as the melting snow slips off his furs.

"No meat again?" Thorvard grouches as he struggles up from his trading desk. In silence, he limps across the flagstone floor.

"The daylight was too meagre. We could barely see," Thorsen replies as a puff of steam billows from his tunic.

"Are any of you fisherfolk? When you couldn't find game, could you not have tried your hand at fishing?" Thorvard bellows irritably. Wincing, I pull back into the shadows.

"It was impossible to crack the ice," Ymir, a tall, lanky huntsman, mumbles as he pulls off his coat. "I broke the tip of my harpoon trying." His voice sounds tired and almost hoarse. He glances at Thorvard. I hold my breath.

Hild, a Norsewoman whom I hardly know, is standing beside me and she leans in closely with her baby screaming at her breast. "We'll starve to death if they keep returning empty-handed," she whispers as she rocks her child back and forth. Ignoring her, I study the men standing around the fire.

"It was hard to break a path through all that snow, but we labored hard until Gulbrand's snow blindness made us all turn back. He is lucky we didn't leave him stranded in a snowbank," Thorsen says. He thrusts his hands towards the fire for warmth. When I see his red fingers, I glance at my husband.

"The next man who brings back meat will be greatly rewarded," Thorvard announces as he wipes his nose across his hides. His eyes narrow into slits. "There again, the next man who returns here empty-handed will be punished. We can't afford to fail at this. I expected someone to bring back meat."

Hearing the bite in his voice, I take another step backwards and unexpectedly bump into Einar's chest. Éowyn and her children are huddled on a bed platform looking hungry. One of her girls throws me a toothless smile.

"The gods have truly abandoned us," Einar mutters in my ear. "The flax is gone, only a handful of dried fish is left, and there is no more seal blubber in the pot."

"The gods are fickle," I respond.

"They don't like something in this longhouse, I'm sure of it. Why else would we be cursed?"

"Einar, I beg of you," Éowyn whispers to his back. "The gods will certainly hear your words and double-cross us just for spite. It is better to hold out hope than to blame the gods."

I crank my neck. "He didn't blame the gods."

She drops her eyes. "He always does," she simply says.

One week later, Einar finds Thorsen lying frozen in the far corner of the yard. We figure that he came out of the byre when the visibility was poor and lost his way in the blowing snow. Poor Thorsen. Reflecting on the futility of life and on the stupid ways in which men die, I can't help but thank the gods for one less mouth to feed.

Burying my face in Brúsi's coat, I take comfort in the way the bristles tickle me. Then I scratch his little head. He responds by licking me.

"We'll wrap his body and store it behind the shed," Thorvard tells his kin. "When the spring thaw comes, we can send Thorsen off to the next life by pushing his body out to sea on a burial barge."

Just then, his voice cracks, and a sob escapes, and Brúsi crawls into my lap and tries to nibble at my hair.

Nothing is better than having a little goat. Nothing.

A few weeks later when we run out of food, Thorvard makes the decision to slaughter some of the livestock in the byre. The meat is stringy and tasteless because the animals have gone hungry for far too long, but at least we eat. As I am sucking the last of the gristle off the bones, I can't stop worrying about everything.

When the next hunting party returns empty-handed, Thorvard is livid. He throws an axe and narrowly misses hitting Einar's child. Ivor tries to calm him down while I stand in the doorway to the women's room, feeling sick. Eying Thorvard, I take a breath.

"I've walked the hills in summer. I know where to find bull caribou. I could go out hunting. I could bring back food." The men shoot me a waspish look before they start muttering.

"She is capable," Ivor announces. I catch a whiff of smoke radiating off his grimy furs. "Thorvard's woman has a damn good eye. She can shoot an arrow twice as far as the rest of you."

Thorvard spits a wad of phlegm between his boots. "Truly, Ivor, do you believe that my wife is trustworthy enough to go out hunting with all these men? Is she good enough to score a kill?"

"Your wife possesses good hunting skills. If it were me, I'd let her go."

"Your tongue drips too much flattery," Thorvard chastises. He turns to me, and my back goes stiff. "Wife, I'll give permission just this once, but only because your trainer speaks so highly of you."

I bow my head and bite my tongue and hate myself for being so weak in Thorvard's presence.

"You can take my crossbow when you go," Ivor says as he reaches out to stop me with his arm.

"I will find us meat, I promise you." My husband is staring at the two of us. Lifting my chin, I square my shoulders and stand up tall and glare at him. Then slowly, I take a breath. "Ivor, you should come with us," I boldly say.

"Freydis, be off with you," Thorvard orders in his harshest voice.

"Husband, if I could be so bold—"

"Freydis, I thought we had an understanding. Did my commission bid you to forget yourself? Now, be off with you and leave us be. Ivor will stay right here with me. I need him in my counting room. I need him to help me because of my poor feet."

That night I barely sleep. I can't stop thinking about how my husband makes me feel so troublesome. I am so wound up when I rise in the morning that I almost forget to say *far vel* to my little goat, who likes it when I scratch behind his soft little ears just before I go outside. As I am tying up my boots, Brúsi comes to me, trying to get underneath my arm to nibble at the leather drawstrings in my hands. Gently I push him back.

"These leather tassels aren't for you," I whisper. When he looks up with his round, sober eyes, he releases another playful bleat. Laughing, I lean into him, knowing that my little goat has melted the ice around my heart and broken into that part of me that is not quite dead. I have survived this place because of him.

Just before I slip outside, Brúsi scampers away with a spark of energy I do not possess. I watch him go before I pick myself up off the ground and retrieve my hunting spear. Soon after, all thoughts of Brúsi fade as I slip outside where I am met with a blast of cold that sucks the breath right out of me. Immediately, the snow starts eddying around my feet, and I hear the cry of the winter wind hissing in my ears as I stare into a sea of white. For as far as the eye can see, there is only frozen earth and ice-blue sky.

We leave the yard on snowshoes, tracking through the ice-hardened snow that crunches underfoot, making our way to a stretch of open land. Along the way the frigid air burns my nose and sears my lungs, but I am grateful to be outside in the open air where I am free of Thorvard of Gardar.

Swishing forwards, we see no signs of life, no tracks, no

hidden entries to animal burrows buried underneath the drifts, no frozen animal droppings anywhere. Then, in late morning, we hit a trail that meanders up a hill. At the top, we find fresh caribou prints that peter out when we lose the trail in a patch of ice. In sheer frustration, someone releases a string of curses while the most seasoned tracker among us, a man with a frost beard and a red, bulbous nose, scans the area for more markings.

"Why don't we continue in the direction of the headlands where the caribou used to be plentiful?" I suggest.

"I don't like that idea," Gunnar sniffs.

"Let's draw for it. If Freydis pulls the longest stick, we'll follow her," Ospak says.

In the end, I win. In the growing darkness we crest a hill and find a barren wasteland of frozen rock stretching out towards the sea. My eyes sweep the snow-covered plains, but there are no herds, no deer, no anything, not even birds.

"Let's go further beyond that point," someone shouts overtop of the wailing wind.

"*Neinn,*" I shout. "I have come this way before with Einar when it was summertime and the sheep were grazing in the fields. The cliff edges are unstable. There are slippery rocks underneath the snow and a sheer drop-off straight ahead."

Leaning down, I remove my snowshoes. Then I stand up tall and turn around, shielding my eyes to look beyond the land towards the sea. Just then, I spot a seal whose head is partially sticking out of the still grey waters where there are sheets of floating ice. I lick my lips. Then I grab my spear. A moment later, I start to run, even as I hear the men cry out.

"Stop. You'll scare it off!"

"You'll fall through the ice!"

Heeding their warnings, I slow my pace and take stock of where to place my feet as I continue to track the seal. In one quick move, it dives down deep and disappears. When it fails to resurface, I grow impatient. My breathing is ragged, my thoughts are sharp. Fingering my spear, I take aim below the water line. An instant later, the seal returns and without hesitating I release the shot.

"You hit it!" someone shouts amid joyous cheers.

Shading my eyes against the frosty brilliance, I try to spot my kill. Far off in the distance, I see its body pop up again with my spear sticking out of it. An instant later, the seal dives down deep, taking my spear with it. Behind me the shouts echo through the blustery white against the cries of the moaning wind.

My throat begins to close.

"Your aim was good," Thorgrim says as he runs up, followed by the rest of them.

I ignore them all as I continue to scan the open sea. Nothing moves. In the winter haze, the grey sky turns dark and the northern lights begin to dance in a display of purplish-blues. The patterns gyrate wildly, morphing into bands of greens and orange-red, swirling hypnotically in the dark.

Thorgrim looks up. "It's clear that you've been well-trained, Freydis Eiriksdóttir. I will be sure to tell the chieftain that I'm impressed."

That night I shuffle into the longhouse in a dejected state. As soon as I step across the threshold, I catch a whiff of roasting meat and my stomach growls. Warily I look around.

"Freydis. Come and receive your share," Thorvard calls. I remove my sealskin boots and my heavy frozen hides. He is rotating a roasting stick full of sizzling meat that sits across an open fire.

"Come eat," Thorvard says again. "By Óðinn's beard, I can't have you starve to death."

The room grows silent. The fire spits out sparks. My mouth starts to water as I step forwards into the light. As I pass Éowyn, she glances down.

"Where's my goat?" I suddenly ask as I scan the faces in the room.

"Here," Thorvard mumbles. He is chewing meat. Grease layers the hairs that line his whiskered lips.

"Where?" I ask.

"We are eating mutton for dinner at my hearth tonight."

"Where is Brúsi?" I ask carefully.

Thorvard turns to Ivor. "Didn't I tell you she would be difficult?"

Ivor sighs. His hands fall open. His shoulders slump.

"The good people of Gardar would like to thank you for fattening up your goat in these harsh times," my husband continues as he leans forwards to pluck the chunks of meat off his roasting stick. He almost burns himself when he goes to bite the remaining piece of chevon that has been cooked to perfection.

Staring stupidly, I have difficulty discerning what is real and what is false. Nothing seems as it should.

"Where is my goat, you bastard!"

Impulsively, I lunge, and Thorvard is caught off guard. With a little cry, he falls backwards as my fists fly up and I begin to slap him repeatedly. As if in a fog, I hear the high-pitched wail of my own cry. Then, with a fiendish look, I take a giant breath and give a tremendous shove that propels Thorvard backwards into the fire.

Swearing, he regains his footing and struggles up, but I am ready. My hands lock around his throat, and I kick his balls and hear him choke. The wad of meat clogs his airway so he can't breathe. Gleefully, I watch his eyes go wide before his face begins to turn a shade of purplish-grey. In a panic, he struggles to pull my hands off his throat, but he gurgles wetly and I see the terror in his eyes.

When it looks as though he might pass out, I run my fingernails down his cheek with such force that rivulets of beet-red blood spurt from the gash. Gleefully, I spit on him, drawing on my villainous she-devil's blood, my dragon's fire, my shieldmaiden self.

"May your stomach writhe with cramps and your arse bleed in pain from the waste you shit out after ingesting my little goat," I scream hysterically. I am aware of horrific heart pain, of a grief so raw that I am sliced in half. My head reels and I see stars as my toe delivers such a vicious kick to Thorvard's balls that he doubles up in pain.

They pull me off him. It takes three men. In the fray, my nails connect with Thorvard's flesh, and I delight when I hear his desperate sounds – the sweet blood-gurgling breathless gasps. By the gods, I hope to leave him scarred for life, he is such a dog.

In the end, the settlers of Gardar do not understand my grief. I listen uncaringly as they grumble about my hot-headedness and my lack of respect for starving men. Hild's husband – a sour-faced Norseman whom I do not like – labels me "a difficult wife" which makes me frown. Einar and Éowyn say that I am overreacting to Brúsi's loss. Even when the children look at me with their hungry eyes, I say nothing in my own defense. No one seems to understand. Even the Asgard gods have failed me.

I have no one.

Chapter Six

I HAVE NEVER WORN A JORVIK CAP

In the weeks that follow I am morose and moody, a husk of a woman with no more to lose, no more disappointments to endure. To distance myself from Thorvard, I volunteer to go out hunting almost every day. I get good at harpooning and gaffing seals, but when I make the kill I feel nothing – no pride, no joy, not even the relief that comes in knowing that we will have food to eat for a few more days.

When winter turns to spring, the settlers, still reeling from the hardships faced over the long winter months, return to their huts. After they leave, Thorvard has no reason to restrain himself, and I grow more and more afraid of him. In working hard to pluck out the worry that thistles deep, I suffer sleepless nights and abhorrent thoughts. Thorvard has made me into someone cruel, someone who is consumed by so much fear and sorrow that I cloak myself in anger and push them all away.

I am standing with Ivor in the yard one day when we

hear the galloping hooves of a fast-approaching horse. Glancing up, I am surprised to see Faðir's messenger.

"We haven't seen him all winter. If he came all this way in the melting snow, the message must be dire," Ivor mutters underneath his breath.

"Hear ye! There is news for Freydis Eiriksdöttir," Alf calls as he reins his horse in and dismounts. His face is mud-splattered and his cheeks are flaming red. He throws the growing crowd a hasty glance and then he bows to me. "Mistress, the message concerns your *faðir*."

"Speak," I command.

"Our great *goði* of Greenland, the fearsome Eirik the Red, has..." He glances sideways, and my body stiffens. The messenger leans in closely. "Freydis, your *faðir* has died."

I gawk at him. Far off in the distance, I spot an eagle flying in circles and instantly I know that it is Faðir's *fylgja*. They say that when a person dies, the guardian of his spirit appears in a different form. How fitting. The powerful eagle is the bravest of all birds, symbolic of freedom and victory, of inspiration and the courage to look ahead. As I stare at it, the eagle leaves me, swooping low across the land.

"I swear by Óðinn's eye that it was for the best," Alf continues in a rush. "Your *faðir* was suffering. After he fell off his horse, the wound festered, and his skin turned green. The good women of Brattahlíð tried herbs and salves and blood-letting to no avail. The *gyoja* even advised that the leg be removed, but your *faðir* pushed her off."

I feel the urge to cry, but no tears come. The wind cuts

into the furs that line my back and I flip up my hood as the seagulls begin to shriek.

"Your goodly mother wants you home," the messenger whispers softly. I resist the urge to throw myself into his arms. "She asks that you return before the body starts to smell. We kept him frozen in the snow, but the ground is thawing."

I turn away and stare across the ice-capped sea.

"Come, mistress. Sit thee down," the messenger whispers softly as he takes me gently by the arm. "I'll go find your goodly husband and share the news. Gods willing, he will see the need to return at once to Brattahlíð only because my lady, your poor mother, is not doing well."

"Is the path clear of ice and snow?" I whisper, my voice breaking.

"Yes, but the mud is bad and some areas were flooded so we needed to take a different route."

Faðir's image flares, and for just a moment I see his laughing eyes. Then the vision fades and all I hear is the whistling wind, a rise of voices, thin moans, and gasps.

"Your mother needs you, Freydis," Alf says, squinting as he looks at me.

Faðir is dead. He is lost to me. He is dead and gone. I would have gone to him, but I had been waiting for the snows to melt. Now there is no one to defend me from Thorvard's fists.

"I will go to her," I say just as Thorvard comes to sit beside me on the bench.

Taking charge, he orders a thrall to fetch my best apron dress – the one with tailored panels and an embroidered *kyrtle* to mark my rank as mistress of his house. The thrall scurries off and quickly returns with the dress in hand. She also brings a wool caftan with a single silver-rimmed chest-brooch.

"I'll have nothing to do with these garments!" I say hotly. I have never worn a Jorvik cap, and I am no longer accustomed to the embroidery, the couched cords, the colored strips of fabric, the woven bands, and the fancy stitch work that a woman of my station should be displaying in an attempt to demonstrate her husband's wealth. *Neinn!* These garments are not for me. My shieldmaiden breeches should suffice.

"Come now, Freydis," Thorvard admonishes. My husband keeps his voice low and his tone even. I smirk when I see him working hard to hide his shame. "You'll dishonor your *faðir's* memory if you don't dress finely."

"Faðir wouldn't care about my clothes," I say, glancing up when he sniffs. I do not tell him that I have no fear of Mother. She will understand when she discovers what I've been through living on this godsforsaken farm.

I call for my horse, feeling my husband's eyes burn my back. Behind me I hear shuffling feet. When I turn around, Alf is fiddling with his cap. I wouldn't put it past him to gossip about my defiance and disrespect. By Óðinn's beard, I'll be glad if my manly garb becomes the talk to beat in the coming days.

"Let's be off," I announce. No longer will I wait for men. No longer will I pander to my husband, the mighty Thorvard of Gardar.

We ride into valleys still half-covered in dirty clumps of ice and snow. It is hard going, and my horse whinnies as it struggles to plough through the mud.

When we reach the mouth of the fjord, Alf advises Thorvard to take a different route – a longer one where the snow is not waist-deep. Thorvard follows Alf's advice, and we pass through areas with slippery rocks covered with a matting of frost crystals that sparkle brightly in the sun. When thoughts of Faðir pop up unexpectedly, I try to close off thought and focus on the speech I'll make when I tell Mother about Thorvard and what I've lived through. Even now, he disgusts me, dressed in all his finery.

As soon as we arrive in Brattahlíð, Mother, Thorvald, and Thorstein come out to greet us. Mother's hair has greyed since I've been away, and there are crow's feet and dark half-moon circles that line her eyes. Dismounting quickly, I fall into her outstretched arms and drink in her homey scent before registering just how bony she has become.

"Welcome home, *döttir*," she whispers with a tired smile that quickly fades when she pulls back to study me. "Your appearance is much changed."

"How so?" I ask. I do not break. Her eyebrows arch into a frown.

"Your nose," she says. I shrug. Thorvard is hovering behind my back.

"We've missed you," my brother, Thorstein, interrupts as he steps forth. He is a handsome boy who has grown taller since I've been away. Respectfully he bows his head and fumbles with the brooch that holds his fox furs together at his throat. I throw him a sad little smile, and he blinks at me and smiles as he steps into my embrace.

"Faðir called your name before he died," he mumbles so softly I can barely hear. His voice snags. The room falls silent. Mother draws a hand up to her mouth and I release myself from Thorstein and go to her and clasp her hand. She draws me in.

"I am home now," is all I say. For many months I have longed for this moment, imagining how it would be. Strangely, I feel nothing.

Mother rubs my back before she lets me go. Then she invites us to follow her to the gathering hall where Faðir and his advisors used to meet. The place is eerie and dark and far too quiet. As I glance around, I see a spider web hanging from a blackened beam.

"It doesn't seem the same now that Faðir isn't here." The words come out in whispered breaths.

"I'm glad you came," Mother says.

Thorvard coughs to clear his throat. When he steps forwards, he places his hand on the small of my back. "Freydis couldn't stay away," he says, glancing down at me.

"Come. I'll show you to your bedchamber," Mother says. "I've put you in a private annex at the back beside my two remaining sons."

Thorvard sighs. "As a family, it is important that we grieve together."

"There are also other matters that we must discuss," Mother manages. Her face goes pale.

"Good lady, you mustn't worry now that I am here," Thorvard says. I glare at him.

"I knew I could rely on you," Mother smiles. Her eyes well up.

"Thorstein, bring us all a flask of wine," I say quickly. There is smoldering rage that I must stomp out before the anger flares, morphing into a wildfire I can't contain.

"We'll drink to Faðir's memory," Thorvald says. He looks uncomfortable.

"He would like that," I say simply.

That night we hold a feast in Faðir's honor. Thorvard insists I wear my Jorvik cap, and he sits beside me in his finest garb holding himself like the rooster he has become. I am certain he anticipates great things now that Faðir is dead and Leif is gone.

As for my grieving mother, she orders the thralls to serve dish after dish of Faðir's favorite foods. While we are eating, she becomes a woman of decorum who floats around the great hall, asking our clansmen about their farms, about their families, about their health. When our kinsmen offer their condolences, Mother assures them that even in Faðir's absence, the land will flourish and more settlers will come to Greenland's shores. Hearing her speak, I am convinced that she is blind. Even I know that Faðir's advisers are fighting men who plot to steal Faðir's land. She fools herself if she thinks these so-called trustworthy pirates will allow her to keep her farm and all her wealth – unless, of course, she weds again.

The feast drags on and the *skål* is refilled with beer and shared among Faðir's friends many times. Then the *skald* takes up his lyre and begins to tell the saga of Faðir's life, strumming softly as the hearth fire flares. As he speaks, the crowd goes silent and Mother stills. Afterwards, she comes to sit beside me on the bench. We are surrounded by Faðir's most loyal men, who blink like owls and drink like fish.

Mother takes a breath. "Freydis, you have disappointed me," she says, leaning into me so that no one hears.

There is a cacophony of rumbling voices whirling around us. It is all I can do to contain myself. Shocked, I shoot up tall.

"Thorvard told me that you are difficult to live with and that your womb is barren," she continues soberly. "Your *faðir* worked hard to make the match. How come you have not conceived a child?"

I feel the insult so deeply, it is like someone stabbed me with a knife. I draw my shaking hand across my mouth. "Mother, life with Thorvard is not what you think," I manage.

"Tomorrow at the break of dawn you'll go to see the *gyoja*," Mother sighs in a brittle voice. "I asked her to prepare a bundle of fertility herbs. She will bless your marriage once again."

A volcano of hot anger bubbles up and I vow to avoid the *gyoja* and her vexing spells. Mother silences me when I go to speak.

"You should do your duty to your *faðir's* house and speak with his advisers. They are pleased to see you wearing such a fine Jorvik cap."

She turns her face away from me, and as she gazes out into the crowd, I study her in the firelight.

"I need to speak with you alone," I finally sputter as I feel my hands balling into fists.

"Not tonight. I am too tired," she whispers without moving.

"Tomorrow then."

"Tomorrow is a long way off."

"I see," I say.

"You don't," she says.

When it is time for bed, I tell Thorvard that I am craving the quiet of an evening stroll. He asks where I plan to go. I lie and tell him that it is my intention to wander over to my *gyoja's* hut. Even as he waves me off, I see him eying one of Faðir's young advisers – a tall Norseman who hails from a powerful family east of here. Disgusted, I turn my back and wander outside where the midnight sun is easing into a bed of clouds tinged the color of bruises.

Soon I find myself following a well-trodden path leading to my favorite hot spring. The meadows are loamy green and eerily quiet at this time of night. With the bugs nipping at my ankles, I scamper through the grass, breathing in the crisp, fresh air and tasting the freedom that I have greatly missed. After cresting the last hill, I see a shroud of mist rising from the hot pools that give off a sacred scent.

In the sky, the moon is rising, its white pearly face half-distorted in the steam rising from the blue water that burps bubbles and lures me in to its steamy extravagance. As soon as I shed my clothes and ease my body into the warmth, I try to dismiss the childhood memories that threaten to overwhelm as thoughts of Faðir unravel like balls of wool.

When he was alive, Faðir always said that if he could

not reach Ragnarok by dying an honorable death in battle, living in Helgafjell – the holy mountain – would have to do. I am sad that he will never have the chance to admire the golden shields mounted on Valhalla's walls, that he will never be able to marvel at the magical stags roaming freely across the golden grounds.

"Find peace, Faðir," I whisper into the evening sky as midnight sun flares behind a ridge of hills.

By the gods, I wonder what it would be like to allow myself to fall asleep and drown, to succumb to death. I'd be free from the wicked husband I had been forced to marry. I'd escape from all this misery, from having to worry about Thorvard's threats, his violent fists.

Turning my face into the water, I feel the pain of everything as the steam begins to lick my face. The mineral bath cradles me and I let the water drag me down, filling my ears with its liquid peace.

There is a sudden gust of wind just before I go down, and my eyes pop open as a patch of mist in front of me clears. Faðir's spirit presence hisses in the wind, telling me not to end my life, warning me not to die a coward's death. Suddenly, the wind picks up and the rippling water is pushed towards me, and I am enveloped in a cloud as islands of memory surface and Faðir's breathy voice creeps towards me through the steam.

Let nothing threaten you, döttir. *Do not be intimidated or hindered by difficult men. You must leave them to be punished by the gods.*

I swallow hard, knowing that the gods are gone. They, too, have abandoned me. As Faðir's image fades into nothingness, I am left with only wind whispers scattering the steam.

"I will miss you, Faðir," I murmur underneath my breath. "I will miss you terribly."

~

The return journey back to Brattahlíð is uneventful in the dark. When I arrive in the quiet yard, I do not join Thorvard in his bed. Instead, I find a dark, dry corner in the byre where I can be alone in my struggle to fall asleep.

In the morning, I snap awake at the sound of the startled boy who comes to milk the cows. He gapes at me as I scramble up and begin dusting the pieces of hay off my lap.

"Lo! It is Freydis Eiriksdóttir," I quickly say. In response, the boy jumps back and spills the contents of his slop pail. He gawks at me as if I am masquerading as a *Valkyrie* intent on taking him against his will to the afterlife.

"I am in need of the *gyoja*," I sputter. "Do you know where she sleeps these days?"

"Up there." He points his finger towards the hills.

"Could you take me to her?"

In a flash, the boy turns and runs, and I follow him. Frenzied, he stumbles past the stores shed before following the frost-covered footpath where he stops and throws a look over his shoulder as if he is expecting to see a giantess or something worse. Panting, I wave him forwards. He takes off again at a run, quickly mounting a sloping hill.

Halfway up, I am so winded that I stop. The boy beckons me to hurry before he disappears around a bend.

When I finally reach him, he is standing outside a hut that has been newly hewn into the side of a grassy hill. On the bank, a cow sits lazily, backlit by the rising sun, its tail swishing back and forth as it swats away a swarm of flies.

"*Góðan morgin!*" the boy calls out as he pokes his head inside the hut. He darts back when I approach and shuffle past, panting. It is dark inside and I am suddenly hit with the pungent smell of herbs. For a moment I stop and listen to the sounds of the busy farm I left behind: the bleating sheep, the lowing cows, the sounds of Norsemen waking up, a crying child. Then, from somewhere in the inky black shadows, I suddenly hear the dry rattle of my *gyoja's* cough.

"Freydis, you have returned," she croaks. She clears her throat. As soon as my eyes adjust, her wizened face comes at me as if she were an apparition in the dark.

My *gyoja* is as stooped as I remember. Her long greyish-white hair hangs down in strings. Her leathery face, mapped with wrinkles, looks stern.

"Freydis, the gods have not been kind to you," she wheezes as she squints up at me. "You look too thin and your nose is twisted out of shape. Offer sacrifice to our lady, Frigga, who has abandoned you, my child."

She drags me outdoors where a raven pokes around the cooking pit before hopping to a flat altar rock. Then it begins to croak, its calls echoing down the slope.

Hobbling forwards, my *gyoja* picks up an elaborately carved walking stick. I notice that her hunchback has grown more noticeable and her eyes are filmy, almost blind.

"I see the blackness of your soul," my *gyoja* moans, her voice rasping like rustling leaves, dead and brown in fall.

"Freydis, my girl, you must come closer so that I can feel your bones."

Reluctantly, I do what she asks, bracing myself when I smell the stink of onions on her breath.

"Even though my eyes are dim, I sense your grief and feel your pain. Poor child. I want to see you. Come hither. The light is poor."

Leaning down, she feels around the dirt until her hand comes to rest on a smooth, speckled rock. With effort, she holds the pebble up to the sky.

"Oh great mother, your *döttir*, Freydis, is a good child. I bear witness to it. Bless her with noble gifts and make her barren womb conceive. Hail, Queen of Asgard, holder of heart and home. Lay your hand upon this child's womb and work your threads. You are the weaver of the web in which we live, the friend of mothers, the giver of new life. I ask that you please bless this child, this friend, this gentle woman who reveres the gods."

When her incantations are almost done, she reaches out to feel my face. Then her forehead kneads into a frown. "I hear tell that you have not done your duty to your husband, Freydis Eiriksdöttir?" She pauses and my anger erupts like a spray of water shooting up from a mussel bed.

"Too often have I heard of duty," I round on her. "Forsooth, my duty is done. I have lain with Thorvard and worked hard to conceive a son, but no seed takes root. Now I have found a different path."

"You are bound to your husband, Freydis Eiriksdöttir. He will want you to bear him sons."

"He hinders me." I will not tell her the all of it. I will not tell anyone anything anymore.

"Hinders you? Fie! You are a fool to reject the likes of him. He will make trouble for you. He will punish you. I know it."

"You are an old woman who knows nothing."

She squints. Her forehead crinkles into an even heavier frown.

Down the hill, the child begins to wail again as the wind picks up. The cry startles my *gyoja* whose long white hair whips forwards into her face. Fumbling, she struggles to reach underneath the folds of her woolen caftan and brings out a small ivory box. Then she lifts the lid so that I can peer inside at the bundle of herbs that give off an aromatic scent.

"Take these. They will help you to conceive a bairn."

We hear another piercing scream. My shoulders tense.

All my life I have been taught to revere the gods, to offer them daily sacrifice. What good has come of it? Today my *gyoja* instructs me to burn some herbs. She gives me lady's mantle, thyme, flax, and shepherd's purse, and tells me to offer these up to Freyja, the fertility god.

"The Queen of Asgard has the power to help," my *gyoja* says as she holds her heart. "You must light the herbs and put yourself into a trance. Allow the scents to linger in your hair, to infuse your clothes."

I wait for her to finish instructing me on the ritual that will bless my womb. Just as her eyes fall shut, her lips release an unearthly chant. "Think of your belly growing round and watch the smoke carry your heavy burdens up, up, up into the sky. See wishes rise in wispy curls to settle around the Queen of Asgard's feet. The god, Freyja, will see your needs in the heart of all that smoke and bless you, Freydis of Gardar."

My *gyoja's* filmy eyes go round, and I find myself breathing hard.

"Take inspiration from our lady. Her story is much like yours," my *gyoja* manages in the middle of a coughing fit. "Frigga gets her way by using careful planning to dupe her foes. She never opposes Óðinn, her powerful husband, the chief of the Aesir tribe. Truly, I tell you, Frigga is very wise. She tolerates Óðinn's retinue of beautiful Valkyries and giantesses without complaint. Because she recognizes Óðinn's improprieties without allowing his indiscretions to weigh her down, she remains married to a great, great god. Follow her lead, Freydis, and heed my warning. It would be dangerous and ill-advised to divorce Thorvard of Gardar."

Bending low, she stoops to pick a fallen sprig off the ground and I study her, thanking her for planting a tiny seed. I will speak with Mother about divorce after Faðir's burial ceremony is over and my inheritance makes me mistress of my own farm. Only then will I demand to be released from my marriage bed.

In fact, I will insist on it.

I do not have the opportunity to pull Mother aside until well after Faðir's *sjaund* when we drink the funeral ale and toast Faðir one last time.

We come together in Brattahlíð's great hall for the death

feast, a sober ritual during which all of Faðir's belongings are laid around him: his swords and shields, his favorite furs, his drinking horn, a stringed instrument he used to love playing. Someone has dressed him in his very best, and his hair has been combed and groomed with scented herbal oil. Even in death he looks strikingly handsome and strikingly fearsome. Everyone remarks on it.

When I learn that Faðir's treasured horse has been run hard in a nearby field in preparation for its butchering, I still can't shed a single tear. The horse is frothing at the mouth, and after the hunters spear it to death, my *gyoja* cuts out its heart. Then she orders my father's men to place the carcass alongside Faðir's body in all his finery.

"We should sacrifice your *faðir's* favorite thrall as well," Thorvard announces as soon as the funeral pyre is ready. "She can serve him in the afterlife."

"Faðir was not a man who liked to waste," I reply as I eye the frightened girl.

"'Tis the proper thing to do, but I am tired of all this death," Mother sighs weakly. Her opinion settles things, and Faðir's thrall is spared. I watch the poor woman crumple in a heap.

After she has been carried off the beach, the barge is lit on fire. The wind propels Faðir's remains towards the afterlife in a pillar of smoke, and I feel nothing. Nothing.

Behind me, Faðir's loyal clansmen push in closely as they honor the greatest *goði* who ever lived. Mother is so weepy that my younger brothers squirm uncomfortably. Their youth leaves them ill-prepared to fill Faðir's shoes. Thorvald and Thorstein are boys not men.

On the seventh day following the burial, I follow the clan custom and order Faðir's thralls to serve the funeral ale. Mother calls for me to join her in Faðir's counting chamber as soon as the toasts are finished and the guests have left. Thorvard is standing by her side surrounded by Faðir's most loyal men. My two younger brothers, Thorvald and Thorstein, are there as well.

"I wish that Leif, my eldest, was home to manage this," Mother begins uneasily as she turns towards Thorvard. She takes up his arm and pats it before drawing her head in close to his. "As my *döttir's* husband, I ask that you oversee the transfer of the lands."

Thorvard throws me a curious look. Then he smiles. "Of course, my lady," he replies.

The meeting starts. I have trouble following all of it. Faðir's advisers talk amongst themselves. When they pose questions that Mother can't address, Thorvard answers for her before comforting her with soothing words. Her tears well up. In silence, I study all of them.

When it finally comes time to bequeath my inheritance, Mother stands. "Thorvard," she sighs heavily. Her cheeks have a rosy glow. "Am I to understand that my *döttir* is the rightful heir of one fourth of all of my deceased husband's lands?"

"'Tis the arrangement Faðir made for me," I say dully.

The room falls silent as Thorvard taps his index finger against his chin. I stare at the beard ring that holds his whiskered braid. "Who will manage all of this land for her?"

"You are her husband. 'Tis your right," Mother sighs.

"I see," Thorvard says. I look up. My hands grow cold. Thorvard draws in air, ignoring my outrage, pretending that he doesn't see. "And who will manage Leif's lands while he is gone?"

"My husband did not say," Mother sputters. Her face crumples. She begins to weep.

"What if Leif does not return to Brattahlíð?" Thorvard presses. "What then?"

Mother dabs her eyes. Faðir's closest adviser holds her up as she turns to address us all. "In Leif's absence, I deem Thorvard of Gardar to be in charge. He will oversee our family farm."

Behind me, my brothers whisper amongst themselves. My heart thuds so loudly that I worry that it will burst apart. Gods' bread, Mother lacks discernment! How can she be so blind? Can she not see the dragon who stands before us breathing out a stream of fire that scourges all?

"Thorvard of Gardar will be the chieftain of our clan," Mother blubbers. We wait as she struggles to collect herself. "He can be in charge and take my husband's place until the next *goði* of Greenland is chosen at the next Althing."

In shock, I stare at her, feeling woozy, as if in a nightmare.

"Now give me peace, my loyal friends," Mother continues with a heavy sigh. "I need to be alone and mourn my husband. I grieve for my missing son as well. Even now I worry that Leif has drowned. Njörd's undersea gardens will be his grave."

"Dear lady, you mustn't fear the worst," Thorvard

soothes. "Your oldest boy is surely safe. We'd feel it in our bones if it were otherwise."

I glare at him. Thorvard is a two-faced snake.

"'Tis true," Mother says as she sucks in air and turns to me. "Freydis, this must be hard for you." Her voice cracks. I pinch my wrist to stop myself from spitting on her. She has no idea what she has done. Studying me, she reaches for me with her fine-boned hands. "Thorvard will help to ease the pain of your *faðir's* loss. He will oversee your lands."

"Oversee my lands?" I repeat dumbfounded. "My lady Mother, I had hoped to manage my own affairs."

"Lay hand on heart," Mother says in a tired voice. "You inherited a large parcel of land on this very day. Let your good husband do his duty to our house. From here on in, you must allow Thorvard to be in charge."

"'Tis not needed."

"Please, Freydis. I don't want it said that you have become a domineering woman."

"I beg pardon, lady Mother, but I am confused. Why should I give my husband full control?"

"Why should you give him full control?" Mother stammers. Her forehead knots into a frown. "It is his right. It is his duty to protect your *faðir's* wealth!"

"You tax your mother, Freydis," Thorvard whispers in my ear. I shrug him off.

"Good mother," I say in a pleading voice, "I had high hopes. After the ritual drinking of the funeral ale, I had hoped to ask a favor. I want to raise some sheep on my own lands."

The room goes silent. I catch a glimpse of Mother's stricken face.

"Freydis, your *faðir* is dead, and your brother gone. If it was not for your husband, our family would be in ruins. By the gods, your *faðir* worked hard to build this farm and earn the respect of this clan. Thorvard and these good men will help to keep our family strong."

I gawk at her. "Lady Mother, please hear me out—"

"What a ready tongue you have to speak on matters such as these," Mother admonishes. "Forsooth, your spirit has become too wild. I see a strangeness in your face, *döttir*. Have you changed so much since your wedding day?"

There are tears of frustration brimming in her injured eyes. Thorvard slithers forwards to comfort her and she clings to him, and just like that, she is lost to me.

There is a sick smugness in Thorvard's face. "Perhaps you should leave," he mutters underneath his breath.

My stomach sours. "I'm sorry. I didn't think Mother would—"

"If Leif is living, he will return to us," Thorvard interrupts as he suddenly turns to address Faðir's men. "Until then, I will happily manage Freydis's lands. I am sure my wife will come to understand that it is for the best."

Nothing Thorvard does is for the best. All he wants is to steal from me, to amass his fortune and claim the *goði* title as his own! If Leif is lost at sea, my husband will rule as a tyrant does.

"Mother," I plead softly in a pathetic voice. "Thorvard of Gardar is mean and false. He beats me hard. He is a wolf." I take a breath. "Please help me seek divorce."

Mother's eyes grow wide.

Thorvard's eyes grow sharp.

Then Mother faints. In the chaos, someone yells for help. I feel my legs buckling and my mouth go dry. An instant later, Thorvard grips my arm and squeezes hard before pushing me towards the door.

"You'll pay for this," he threatens in a seething voice.

I call out to Faðir's *fylgja*, but there are no eagles to be seen.

His spirit presence is truly gone.

Chapter Seven

CHIPS OF SILVER ICE

T horvard slaps me across the face and insists I wear an apron dress to leave Mother's farm. Not only that, but he takes away the knife he gave me.

"You will not need this weapon anymore."

"It offers protection when I walk alone."

"Hold your tongue! I'll no longer allow you to wander freely in my meadowlands."

Fear burrows deeply in my bones as Thorvard escorts me to the waiting horses that are laden with goods for the ride back to Gardar. I say nothing to Mother, who waits, pale-faced, to say goodbye. Even though I see her weepy eyes, she fails to see the wounds that I've endured at Thorvard's hands. She has reduced me to nothing while raising Thorvard higher than the sun.

Thorvard bids farewell to Faðir's most loyal men, and we make our way down the bumpy path leading to the rolling hills. With effort I cling tightly to my gelding's mane and guide him over the hills and plains with flocks of birds skirling overhead.

After crossing a riverbed, I see a patch of crocuses with purple petals unfurling in the sun, and then I break. Spring was Faðir's favorite season. I let my horse fall behind, remembering all that I have lost. Remembering my sweet *faðir's* face.

My husband's party goes on ahead. Their backs are barely visible as their horses plod along a snow-covered stretch where the bog blueberries sit frozen on twigs ready for the mice and ptarmigan to find and eat.

At the summit, I contemplate returning to Mother's farm, but Thorvard is the kind of man who would come for me and drag me back and beat me hard for inconveniencing him. Weighing this, a shiver runs through me and I draw my arms around myself and feel the heaviness of everything.

It takes two days to reach the cliff overlooking Thorvard's farm. Gazing down at the longhouse, I go numb until my horse whinnies long and low. I can see the ruins of my life down there amongst all that wealth. What of pelts? What of herds of sheep and balls of wool? It means nothing to me anymore.

Shivering, I brace myself to re-enter a life that I don't want to live – a life controlled by a duplicitous man, a man with fangs and a fierce appetite for blood.

As soon as I guide my horse down the bank, I sense that something is wrong. The corral is empty. There is no one scurrying about the yard. In the silence, I lift the latch and shove the longhouse door open. Immediately, I am met with the smell of burning herbs. The pungent smoke is so overpowering that I need to cup my hand over my nose and mouth to breathe.

"Thorvard?" I call out uncertainly. Wincing, I bat the smoke away with one hand.

"Here," he says from the back. My mind is full of screeching seagulls and cawing crows. Slowly, Thorvard materializes in the smoke.

"Divorce," he says hotly, "is just not right." He takes a step towards me; my vision blurs and my knees go weak. "Help me understand why you are being so difficult. I've made no mocking verses about you or your family, and your poor mother is not causing me hardship in any way."

With his every word, my heart beats faster in my chest. Wincing, I take a step back.

"Freydis, I should cleave your lying tongue from your pretty little mouth and feed your liver to my dogs. At your mother's house when you raised the subject of divorce, it wasn't fair. I've never inflicted any large, ghastly wounds on you nor have I penetrated your body with my spear. How is it, then, that you feel justified in asking for divorce?"

With a sudden growl, he slaps his hand against a post and the beams shudder. Startled, I flinch.

"Thorvard, I didn't mean—"

In a few quick strides he is beside me, taking up my shaking hand in his and placing it against his heart. "Come, now," he says in a gentle voice. "Let's discuss what happened on your *faðir's* farm."

I try to pull away, but he grips my hand and with a

sickly grin he lowers his lips to my arm and begins planting wet kisses on my flesh. When he pulls back, I give another tug and lose my balance, but he catches me. For a moment he just stares, and I feel a rush of heat moving into my cheeks. Without thinking, I close my eyes.

"May you choke on Óðinn's missing eye, you two-faced bitch!" he suddenly spits as he grabs a chunk of my red hair and yanks so fiercely that my neck snaps back and my eyes shoot wide. "I let you walk unchecked in my meadowlands for many moons and this is all the thanks I get? Did that whore of a shepherdess tell you to slay my cheek? Did Éowyn encourage you to seek divorce? Tell me, woman!"

I feel dizzy. My stomach hurts. The color must be draining from my face.

"Look at me, Freydis. Look what happens when I've had enough!" His spittle sprays across my face. I claw for air. "You stupid cunt. I know you are hungry for my land."

Grunting, he gives me a violent push and I stumble backwards, cracking my shoulder against the table and tumbling upside down. His sword belt is lying on the ground. I reach for it. He kicks me hard.

"Don't you dare try to use my sword against me," he howls like a bloodthirsty wolf. There is an explosion of pain in my bones and I draw back in fear. Inhaling deeply, I smell the stink that fills the air and curl up tightly in a ball. Thorvard circles me. I feel his spider-web presence at my back. Then something happens. Thorvard heaves a heavy sigh.

"Don't make a mockery of me!" he yells, and the sound echoes through the room. Unkinking my fists, I peek out from between my fingers and watch him make his way to the table where he stores his drinking horn. "Freydis, I forgive you for uttering those silly words about divorce but listen well. If I ever hear you complaining about your treatment on this farm again, I might not be able to restrain myself." I watch him take a swig of ale. "Now, do your duty to my house and spread your legs. Tonight, we will beget a child."

"Not now, surely?" I whimper, feeling a rush of panic in my chest, an ice-cold sensation in my lower parts.

"How can it be that other wives give their husbands heirs?" he spits.

"I don't know," I moan, cringing.

"You barren whore!" he cries as he suddenly rushes at me, and drags me up, and foists me onto a bed of furs. I gasp. He groans. With a heavy thud, he falls on top of me and grabs my wrists and pins me down.

"Remember this?" he smirks as he pulls out a knife and waves it wildly around my head. My vision blurs. I've learned that to resist him at this stage is dangerous.

"As I said, there will be no more walks." He struggles to lift my dress, and his cock hardens as he fumbles with my clothes. "Instead, you will make me meals and knit me socks and sit with the other women in the women's room."

I try to squirm away, but he is fast and strong. Holding me down, he tries to force his way into me and I feel myself turning limp in his clutches.

"Your day will start at dawn, and your work will end when I say you're done," he seethes with a forceful grunt.

He bears down roughly and thrusts up hard. I brace myself, vowing not to pleasure him by crying out.

Behind us the door squeaks open in the wind before banging shut again. Thorvard sniffs. "Turn around and hoist yourself up on all fours."

In a frozen state, I blindly do what I am told, bracing myself when Thorvard mounts me roughly from behind like an animal. As he dumps his seed into me, my spirit floats up and out the venting hole, and I am enveloped in a heavy fog that carries me out to sea. There I drift through clouds, looking down at the churning sea until I free-fall into the giant waves. For a while, I ride the ocean swells, plunging low then climbing high until I am pushed back into Thorvard's bed. In the longhouse, the smoke sits heavily in the air, choking me so I can barely breathe.

"Get up," he barks.

I am so stiff and sore that every muscle vibrates like overplayed strings on a minstrel's lyre. From the darkness of the bed platform, I study Thorvard as he shuffles around the longhouse to find new clothes. Then he pours himself a dram of wine, burgundy-colored, dark like blood.

"You deaf newborn rat. Get up, I say!" His eyes are chips of silver ice. From somewhere distant I hear a fly buzzing. Eventually I unstick my feet.

"I'll bring you water to quench your thirst," I mumble, grabbing the water bucket.

"Go quickly, wife. My throat is parched after all of that." He rubs his hand across his beard.

In the yard, the sun is setting in a ghoulish pool of red that flares, bathing me in blinding light as I follow the path leading to the byre. Once inside, I collapse. In the walls, I hear the mice. By the gods, I wish I were one of them – small enough to disappear into some tiny space and be alone, clever enough to hide myself from the hungry owl that is watching and waiting for its prey.

In the coming weeks a mundane routine sets in as I help the farmers' wives shear fleece from sheep, clean and dye the yarn with piss, weave and make strong thread for sewing shirts for the men. One of them – a thrall with a large bosom and nimble fingers – encourages me to use the loom. My hands work awkwardly and I am slow. Worst of all, I can't concentrate. Without meaning to, I lose my place as I think about walking down my favorite beach, breathing in the outdoor air and tasting freedom with the feel of the wind against my face.

By *miðsumar*, I miss my courses and suffer sickness and fatigue from dawn 'til dusk. The fact that I am pregnant brings no joy. In fact, I worry constantly, knowing that I can't afford to disappoint. In my weakest moments, I fear my body and doubt myself, fretting that I will not be able to care for a bairn like a mother should. Thorvard likes to tell me that I am inept. He says that all I care about is myself. He tells me that I am a stupid wife, that I have a turkey's brain and that I all I am is a useless slug. By Óðinn's beard, I am beginning to believe that nothing I do is ever right.

For weeks on end, I slink around, trying to avoid Thorvard, who is consumed by his duties as the newly appointed *goði* of Greenland. When Thorvard arranges to move the seat of the clan gathering from Brattahlíð to Gardar, he is worried about making a good impression, and he falls into a vicious mood. I am unsympathetic when I think about how he has torched my spirit and watched it char.

"Have you heard me, woman?" Thorvard yells at me one night while I am making him a pair of socks. "Unplug your ears. We will have the whole of Greenland entering our yard in only a few days' time for the annual Althing, and we are out of mead to serve."

With downcast eyes, I see a dirty charger in Thorvard's hand. I go to take it, but Thorvard blocks me with his hand.

"What is wrong with you? You should have asked Ivor about the mead. Did you do it? Your tongue is silent. Who cut it out?"

"You are usually in charge of things like this," I remind him without looking up.

"I told you about the mead a few days ago," he snaps. "I told you to ask Ivor to count the barrels in the shed. I was too busy overseeing other things."

I am almost certain that Thorvard would never trust me with such a task, but given how things are between us, it is typical for me to be forgetful. His eyes rake my face and I draw back.

"What should I say, husband?" It comes out in a pathetic squeak as I stare sightlessly at the wall behind his head.

"Are you so dim-witted that you continue working the wool when there are other jobs to do? Help is needed in this house in order to prepare the food. See to it that the onions are chopped and peeled before this day is through."

"I will follow your command," I say, struggling to keep my voice flat.

"My command?" he shouts. "Do not vex me, wife."

"It is not my intention," I murmur as I back away.

"Do not speak to me that way!"

"What way?" I ask as I blink, owl-like. His arm draws back. His face is mottled red. I take a breath. Drawing myself up, I look into his stone-cold eyes.

"I am with child," I manage, swallowing.

He stares at me, and the silence that floats between us stirs up fear.

"With child?" he repeats. "Prithee, Freydis, is it mine?"

It is a stupid thing to ask considering that he has imprisoned me inside his longhouse for months on end, but instead of being petulant, I bite my tongue and bow my head and brace myself to receive his fists. Instead, he reaches out and touches my face with tender hands.

"This time it will be different," he says. My body stiffens. When I attempt to pull away, he pulls me to him and I inhale his flowery-smelling sweat.

"Dear Freydis," he murmurs, "I am grateful for all you've done. As the mother of my firstborn child, I will bestow honors on you when you birth a son."

"I promise not to lose this child," I say, struggling to unhook myself from his clutches. Thorvard smiles and nods his head. "I know," he says.

"We should announce the pregnancy at the annual

Althing," I mumble almost incoherently. "Mother will be there."

"She will be pleased to hear that you are with child. I will tell her for the both of us."

When the good people of Greenland gather for the annual Althing, Thorvard is a generous host. There is much music and festivity with plenty of food and drink, and it seems as though everyone wants to give me a runic inscription to keep my baby safe.

In keeping with tradition, the Norsemen honor the gods by feeding the ritualistic fires with the harvest grains. Afterwards, the settlers celebrate by building a giant bonfire where the *skalds* sit and tell stories late into the night. The next day, the chieftains levy fines and adjudicate longstanding feuds that involve gripes about injury or insult that have been inflicted by one farmer upon another. I take no interest in what is said, preferring to stay out of sight until it comes time to announce the betrothals and to discuss the petitions for divorce.

There are some cases of men complaining about ornery wives, but it is the case of Thord and Aud that holds my interest most of all. Aud is a simple farmer's wife who requests divorce from Thord, whom she claims to be a licentious man.

"He wears tunics that are cut too low," she cries out indignantly. "I have brought witnesses to back my claims.

They will tell you that he walks around in damsels' clothes."

Thord's family is offended by Aud's accusations. Rebuking her, they try to blacken her good name. They tell the assembly that she is too active in the family trade, that she shears the sheep and cards the wool and takes the trading profits for herself. Then they make the case that she only married Thord to gain access to his lands.

Aud stands her ground. Her brothers are there to back her up. In the end, Aud narrowly wins her case, and she is set free from the marriage bed. I am elated. By the looks of things, three witnesses is all I need. Three. Just three. All must be men.

That night I toss and turn and cannot sleep. Who will speak up on my behalf? Who is brave enough to face my husband and endure his wrath? I think of Leif and weave my thoughts into a wish that I toss into the bonfire sparks.

Please send my brother home to defend me from Thorvard's fists.

I am bruised and broken and angry, too.

Come home, brother. I beg of you.

Chapter Eight

O BROTHER, WHERE ART THOU?

The birthing pains come in the middle of a snowstorm. The midwife says that the time of the bairn's arrival is fortunate. New calves born during this time of year are a sign of great prosperity, or so Mairi says. In pain, I arch my back and bite down hard on a piece of wood as the baby – a would-be giant inside my womb – cracks my hips in an attempt to enter this brutal world.

After a long night passes, my baby boy arrives with the birthing cord wrapped around his little neck. He is greyish-blue, the color of the sea. Contrary to Mairi's predictions, nothing about the birthing process leaves me feeling prosperous. I ask to see the bairn, to hold him just once and rock him in my arms. When they take him from me, my heart bursts apart, shattering into a thousand pieces that melt into tear puddles.

Thorvard comes to comfort me. He gathers me in close and holds me and rocks me back and forth, whispering softly in my ear. When Mairi leaves the room so we can be alone, I grow afraid, but nothing happens. Thorvard pinches his nose between his right thumb and index finger. Then he lowers his head and cries. I can't. By the gods, I am the walking wounded, a woman who has lost everything.

When the spring thaws finally come and the fields are planted and the sheep begin birthing little lambs, I am still heartsick. I hate my empty life. I am tired of being Thorvard's wife, tired of all the suffering.

In one final desperate act, I carve a stave on a piece of wood using my own blood. My hex on Thorvard bears no fruit until I learn that he has lost a herd of sheep after they were chased by charging muskox and driven over a cliff into the seas. Einar tells me that the shepherd boys were not around. Thorvard had ordered them to help shear sheep. In his misery, Thorvard fumes while I card wool and work my fingers to the bone. I feel elated each and every time my husband has to endure a loss.

In the coming months, I am kept busy in the women's room weaving blankets and spinning wool. The women gossip about their men and about the workings of the farm, and I worry that they pity me. Everyone knows that I am a disappointment to the *goði*. My womb is barren. I have failed in my duty as a wife.

All that summer, I can barely sleep. Thorvard comes to me each and every night, but he is usually drunk and miserable. After the coupling, I toss and turn, feeling too afraid to close my eyes in case I get stuck in an endless stream of black and ugly nightmares where I am chased by dragons breathing fire, helpless to defend myself. In the mornings, after barely any sleep, the misery usually starts up again, and I can barely concentrate. Thorvard is a man who punishes me for everything. His mood is often black and foul, and I get tired of living in a half-dead state.

Just before the dark, cold winter months arrive, we celebrate the Feast of Ullr where the weapons are blessed. The next day, Alf arrives from Brattahlíð.

"Hail to you, Thorvard of Gardar. I bring joyful news from the Eiriksson farm. Your good brother, Leif the Lucky, has just returned to Greenland."

In my excitement, I lose the rhythm of my spindle work. A ball of wool falls off my lap and unravels as it rolls pell-mell across the floor.

"By the gods, we must rejoice," Thorvard announces carefully as he stands. His lips are bloodless; his eyes are hounded by anger amidst a wash of confusion. For the first time in many moons, I feel alive when I see the panic trampling across my husband's face.

"Sweet Óðinn, Leif has come home to us!" I exclaim, glancing uneasily at Thorvard.

It is as though I can breathe again.

"I thought we had lost the boy!" Ivor exclaims as he emerges from the dappled grey shadows at the back. The room erupts.

"How long has Leif been back on Greenland's shores?" someone shouts overtop the noisy din.

The messenger is given a drinking horn. "Leif the Lucky came home two days ago."

"Leif the Lucky? What name is this? That boy never courted Lady Luck," Ivor says good-naturedly.

"Thor's hammer, I'd like to know his tale," someone yells.

"Leif will tell his tale himself," Alf announces loudly. He wipes the sweat off his ruddy face. "Forsooth, he is soon expected in your yard."

"In my yard? Does he bring his men?" Thorvard frets. His brows furrow into knots.

"Já. Not only that, but he brings his bride."

"His bride?" I gasp as my head swivels. I look towards the door and feel a sudden shift, almost like the ground is moving.

"Her name is Thorgunna," Alf informs the gathering crowd. The messenger takes a swig of ale and then swipes his forearm across his moustache hairs to remove the froth. "She is the *döttir* of a Scottish chief – a *vyking* raider from one of the Hebrides islands."

The redness in Thorvard's face works its way into his neck. "Does your tongue have thistles in it? Speak up so all of us can hear," he barks in a harsh tone that squelches the jocularity in the room.

"Leif chanced upon her ship on his way back," Alf replies as he eyes my husband uneasily. "It was Greenland-bound when it was driven off course in unfavorable winds. Leif says he found the skerry grounded on a rock." He clears his throat before nudging the blacksmith, Bjarke Akselsen, with a wink. "Leif tells me he had his work cut out to save her kin, but he somehow managed to anchor close to the reef and send his rowboat over to rescue all fifteen of them. Despite his efforts, Thorgunna's *faðir* failed to like him. Thorgunna's brothers liked him even less, but Leif has wolf blood, as we all know."

The men laugh boisterously. I steal a glance at Thorvard who is slouching against a post, listening with his arms folded stiffly across his chest. I can almost feel the heat steaming off him from where I stand.

My eyes dart back to Alf who hooks his knobby thumb into his belt. His hefty gut sticks out as he throws himself back on his heels. Thorvard's men lean forwards to catch his words.

"The wreck had been carrying house timber to the Greenland settlement. Leif tried to salvage as much as he could, but his own holds were full. He'll go back for it next spring, I'm sure."

"What about the maid?" someone yells from the back.

"By the time the winds died down and Leif was ready to set sail again, Thorgunna said she was in love with him." Alf stops and grins. Someone whistles loudly overtop of a flurry of catcalls. Alf quiets the crowd with an outstretched hand. "Given that Thorgunna is a woman of such high birth, her kinsmen were not of a mind to let Leif marry her, even though they knew that the young lovers had been together in a carnal way, but Leif is a lucky bastard, is he not?" The messenger crudely points down low. Thorvard's men explode in laughter and I feel a rush of heat in my cheeks.

"Did he tell her that Greenland was her destiny?" Hoskuld, a Norseman with a grizzly beard and a hawk-like nose, banters teasingly. The messenger ignores the man, but his eyes sport a playful gleam.

"Leif was reluctant to elope, but he was even less inclined to make a formal offer of marriage to the maid's noble *faðir*. In the end, he gave Thorgunna a gold ring, a wool cloak, and a belt of walrus ivory, and they stole away like two young doves while her *faðir* slept. Praise Loki for giving Leif such trickster's luck!"

There are more heckles from the back. Alf is jovial as he fiddles with his drinking horn. "Save your toasts," he says good-naturedly. "Leif and Thorgunna will soon be here."

Thorvard pushes his way through the rowdy crowd. It is evident that jealousy licks him like a dog.

I circle around the crowd like the ethereal ghost I have become and follow Vali, a tall broad-shouldered Norseman, into the yard. When Leif and Thorgunna and their retinue of thralls ride into Gardar on well-groomed stallions that have been loaded down with furs and goods, I bite my tongue and hold back tears.

Thorgunna is a striking woman with white-blonde hair and unblemished skin. The polar-bear skins that trim her long-sleeved ankle-length coat contrast nicely against the pallor of her face and her rosebud lips. I gawk at her. Ivor glances at me from underneath a darkened brow.

Just then, I catch a glimpse of my handsome brother, whose face shines with tempered pride. With a burst of joy, my heart swells and a profound relief sweeps over me, and my hand flies up to cup my mouth.

Leif greets Thorvard with a magnanimous smile. My brother has fattened up since I saw him last. I marvel at the sight of his short-whiskered beard, at the beauty of the fox's pelt draped across his massive chest. He throws Thorgunna a lovesick look. From the expression on his face, he is clearly proud of his trophy wife. In truth, he has never looked so fine.

When Leif spots me in the crowd, I run forwards like a silly maid and throw myself into his outstretched arms. "Brother, my brother, you are home at last," I whisper before my voice cracks. Leif crushes me against his chest. Afterwards he holds me back and stares at the fading bruises working their way down my jaw and neck, at the scar that cuts across my cheek, at my crooked nose and the black smudges underneath my eyes.

"Dear sister…" A shadow falls across his face. His eyes are pools of flickering light. "How now? Dost thou weep for sorrow or for joy?"

For many moons I have yearned to hear his gravelly voice, to see his handsome face. By the gods, there are no runic inscriptions long enough to encompass the prayers that I have invoked to see him safely home.

"I have some news to share," Leif says as he leans in and whispers in my ear. "I have brought my goodly wife to your farm. Her name is Thorgunna. She knows how much you mean to me."

I am suddenly shy and awkward, a little jealous, and somewhat vexed. Leif grins at me with his dimpled cheeks, the ones I used to like to pinch.

"I am glad that you are wed," I finally manage as Leif turns from me and scans the yard.

"Come, Thorgunna. Meet my sister, Freydis of Gardar."

Thorgunna greets me with the perfect mix of grace and charm. As she goes to embrace me with her outstretched arms, I unexpectedly feel something underneath her furs. A bump. A hard, round pregnant bulge. She has managed what I cannot. Leif eyes us closely with a beaming face, but there is something in his countenance. He has matured. Certainly, he has become a man during our time apart. In my periphery, I see my husband striding towards us.

"Welcome to my farm," Thorvard calls. He is agitated, a man uncertain of his place. "Why don't you shed your furs and set down your things. We will set a feast, and you can tell us all about your voyage across the northern sea. Of course, I will insist that you stay with us over the winter months."

"Your farm is not rich enough to host my men for all that time."

Thorvard takes the insult with a grin and I look away, embarrassed. Just then, Thorgunna tugs on my arm and I steer her into the longhouse that I have come to hate. A hearth fire has been stoked and the room is way too warm. Thorgunna rubs her hands as a joyful grin spreads across her face.

"The journey to your farm has been long and hard. I didn't realize you lived so far away from Brattahlíð."

Thorgunna is so stately and refined that I am suddenly conscious of my appearance.

"Thorvard's farm is remote," I say carefully, choking on the words. "I'll let you rest after bringing some food and drink. Then I'll show you to your own private bed closet. You can rest there for a while."

She lays her hand on my arm. "Thank you, sister," she says as she studies the bruises along my hairline with her ice-blue eyes the color of mountain water. "Leif was worried about you. He insisted that we come."

Pulling back, I snag a breath. "You'll be comfortable here on Thorvard's farm. He is a wealthy man, as you can see."

She stills her face. "I've heard Leif talk about Thorvard's wealth."

"I'm sure you have," is all I say.

By the time we sit down to a hearty feast, the longhouse is overcrowded with thralls and farmers who have come to welcome Leif back home. Thorvard is the perfect host and my brother is the perfect guest. I am seated between the two of them. The smell of men who have toiled all day wafts towards me, and I can barely concentrate for the stink of them.

"Leif the Lucky, we are eager to hear about this new land you discovered," Thorvard says officiously. I hate the false sweetness that drips from his serpent lips. Leif laughs openly before beckoning for a thrall to bring him wine.

"Let no man call me coward," Leif calls out as he begins his tale. "I was bold enough to travel to a northern land where I discovered heavily wooded shores."

The noisy din dies down and I study Leif carefully in the firelight. He is encircled by the men and women of Thorvard's farm who hang on his every word as the hearth fire smoke threads up and out through the smoke hole.

When he cracks a joke or addresses them by name, their eyes light up and they banter back and forth with him, treating him as if he were a god.

"After leaving Greenland, we sailed in calm, flat seas for days on end, surrounded by majestic chunks of ice. Then we hit a wall of fog and we had to wait for the winds to turn." Leif is confident as he addresses the avid crowd. Thorvard has had a wood fire lit, and the smell of cedar, pine, and juniper is luxurious.

"Eventually we passed a stone-slabbed land that was so flat we dubbed it 'Helluland'. There we cast anchor and went ashore. Finding nothing, we put out to sea again and found a second land that was forested with many white-sand beaches along its coast. I named that land 'Markland'. Even though my men begged me to explore some more, I took a chance and sailed for two more days. Then I found a third land where my longboat became stranded in a low tide just off the coast. Instead of waiting, we abandoned ship and went ashore with our sleeping-sacks and enough provisions for the night.

"Once on the beach, we discovered that the shoreline waters were teeming with all kinds of fish. The salmon and cod fed us well. And the land! It was plentiful with berries and fruits of every kind. So I said to the crew: 'This place will be our new home! Look yonder at those grassy fields. That land will feed our cows and provide the needed grasslands for our sheep.'"

"What did you do when winter came?" I ask as I stand to fill my husband's goblet with the berry wine my brother brought.

"Good sister, I see that you are eager to hear my tale. Have patience, Freydis. I'll answer as I go along."

"Take all the time you need," Thorvard says as he throws me a nasty look.

"I'll tell you this," Leif continues, ignoring us. "The land offered good hunting, but we all agreed that to venture inland and lay down traps before the winter snows began would be foolish. Instead, we dug a pit house into the ground with a turfed-over roof. When that was done, we immediately built a large byre with stalls for cows and sheep before turning our attention to finding the best turf for building a longhouse. We had no time to spare before the snows set in. Truly, I tell you, it was the harshest winter I've ever seen. Those storms! They almost froze us out, but we survived. When the spring thaws came, I called the place 'Leifsbidur'."

"I hear you brought back timber to trade." Thorvard's voice is lost in a sudden swell of noise as the food arrives. He clears his throat. "Were the forests plentiful?"

"Já! We felled so many trees that I lost count. Before I left, I loaded up my ship with enough timber to build another ship. If you want, I'd be willing to trade you logs for iron ore and a herd of milking cows. Thorgunna sure does like her cream."

"I'll think on it."

"I swear, wood is so much better to burn than peat."

Thorvard quickly reaches forwards to grab the arm of a passing thrall. Her eyes grow large when he orders her to bring out one of his few remaining kegs of wine that he imported at great cost.

"Thorvard, were you not saving the wine to mark the birth of our firstborn child?" I whisper quietly.

"Do not question me, woman! I have waited too long for you to conceive. I'll drink it now."

When the keg is tapped, Thorvard pours himself a generous horn and swigs it down in one giant gulp. Then he offers wine to all. Leif waves him off.

"I only thirst to tell my tale!"

My husband emits a harsh, raspy laugh. Outside, we hear a rush of wind pounding against the door of the feasting hall and rattling the hinges with a hissing sound. As the wind dies down, Leif leans forwards.

"Remember Tyrkir, from childhood?" he asks me with a wink. "He was the one with the protruding forehead and the darting eyes and deep wrinkles in his face."

"*Já*," I say. "I remember him fondly. He was a master of all types of tricks. You called him *foster-faðir*, if I recall."

"He sailed with me to Vinland's shores," Leif says as he fingers the tip of his drinking horn. "By the gods, he is a curious man – a true explorer with courageous blood."

"Why mention him?" I ask, glancing sideways. My husband is still fuming about the way my brother snubbed his wine.

"It came to pass that shortly after we arrived in Leifsbidur, Tyrkir disappeared for many days on end." Leif takes an earspoon and begins to dig out wax. "Only foolish, desperate men do that, considering that there are *skraelings* with red faces running wild in that wilderness on those distant shores."

"You saw *skraelings*?" Ivor asks. His eyebrows arch high as he stabs a chunk of meat with his hunting knife.

"*Já*, good man! We traded with those outlanders over many seasons. Those Red Men know their furs."

At this, Ivor sniffs and my brother laughs. Leif turns back to me. "After Tyrkir disappeared, we worried about his whereabouts. Some wondered if he had been captured by a group of natives who had been skulking around our settlement the day before. In truth, we wondered if Tyrkir had been eaten, beard and all."

"Do the *skraelings* eat men in those northwestern lands?" I ask, horrified. My brother shrugs. The hearth fire shimmies across his face as he reaches forth to snag a handful of grapes from a bowl.

"When Tyrkir finally returned to Leifsbidur, he came bearing clumps of grapes like these. The grapes were so sweet that we gorged ourselves until our bellies ached. The next day he showed us where to find these grapes on the vine. He also showed us fields of self-sown wheat and forests of trees that stretched beyond our line of sight. By Óðinn's beard, we will not have to rely on the Danes – those marauding pigs – to bring us anything anymore."

A shout rises from the men who feast. My brother grins and turns to Thorvard, who sits between us, nurturing another drink.

"Good brother, listen closely. Tyrkir sat me down the other day to calculate how much profit we made after sailing all the way to Vinland. He says I am a wealthy man. Trading for these wine grapes alone will make me rich. Next spring, I plan on making a voyage to Norway to sell my furs. Eventually I'll build another ship."

Thorvard's eyes linger on Leif's black hair as he slowly takes another sip of wine. From the back of the smoke-filled room, someone asks about Tyrkir.

"I'll tell you this, my friend," Leif announces as he stands up and motions to the crowd to simmer down. "Tyrkir is on board my ship guarding the trading goods we brought back." The noisy din crescendos until someone blows a cowhorn to hush the crowd.

"Good people of Gardar," Leif continues as his eyes scan the room. "I have dubbed the new territory that I found 'Vinland' because of these plentiful and delicious grapes that you see in my hands. These grapes make the most excellent wine. I have brought some for all of you."

At this, a noisy cheer erupts. Leif sweeps up Thorgunna's fine-boned hand and raises it to his lips. "The gods have blessed me many times," he announces as he grins at her. "I am Leif the Lucky, son of Eirik the Red of Brattahlíð. I am a *vyking* explorer of northern lands. Two *goði* titles I now possess. I am the *goði* of Greenland and the *goði* of Leifsbidur on Vinland's shores!"

A gleam of anger sizzles in Thorvard's hawk-like eyes. When one of his thralls offers him more wine to drink, he snaps at her. He has lost his title. He is no longer the favorite. Without power, he is a no one, and I am glad of it.

Thorvard waits for Leif to sit before he addresses him with stone-cold eyes. "Why are you so eager to reclaim the title of *goði* of Greenland?"

His baritone cuts through the chatter as sharply as the cracking ice on a frozen lake.

"You are newly home, and the council must meet to decide on who will rule," Thorvard continues, speaking fast. "In your absence I have been in charge."

"Good brother, be not so quick to take offense." The jocularity slowly drains from Leif's handsome face. "In the days to come we can divide the lands, debate the titles, and hold assemblies to determine who is best to rule this land. I'll even recommend that you are given compensation for what you managed while I was gone."

Thorvard's clansmen are not in the mood to hear him rant. As the hearth fire snaps, Vali calls for Leif to recount more of his adventures in the north. The request puts Thorvard in an awkward bind. For a moment I think he'll jump the table and start a fight. Instead, he leaves the gathering hall without a word.

The crowd folds around my brother as he shifts position on his bench. It creaks underneath his weight. "We traded with *skraelings* for furs and meat," he tells Thorvard's clansmen. "Those red-faced men with their chiselled, tattooed chests are a fearsome lot, but by the gods, their eyes are keen and they sure can hunt. I saw one of them arrange five or six arrows at a time between his fingers and shoot them off with great rapidity and an unerring aim."

I see a moth flit by. It tries to land on a darkened ledge above Leif's head, its wings shimmering in the glowing firelight.

"The *skraelings* carry their arrows in birchbark quivers on their backs. They like to hunt and fish, and they were willing to trade," he says to a group of men as they finish sucking on their feasting bones. "At first I had my doubts about them, but they brought me many luscious furs. They also paint their faces red. They revere the color. It is sacred to them. They offer three times more in trading goods for something red."

Eventually, the shadows lengthen and the fire burns low. Then Vali brings out his lyre and begins to sing about my brother's courage, but his warbles are drowned out by the talk of men. Out of the corner of my eye, I see Thorgunna stand and leave the room. When she returns, she is accompanied by my sheepish-looking husband.

"Tomorrow, I invite you all to attend a second feast," Thorvard announces to the crowd. "I insist on butchering my best cow to welcome Leif Eiriksson back to Greenland."

It is clear to me that he is drunk.

Standing quickly, I snag a breath. The room goes silent. All eyes fall on me. "Husband, we have already had a feast tonight."

"Silence, woman," Thorvard slurs.

"Come now, good brother," Leif manages with an awkward laugh. "Already my belly is far too full after eating your blood sausages and cabbage stew. Why not save your fattened cow for the winter feasts?"

Thorvard scowls, and Leif stands so quickly that the table shakes and my goblet wobbles and almost spills. With quick, efficient hands, Leif catches up my cup and rights it as his eyebrows crease into an anxious frown. Just then, Thorgunna's woven shawl puddles on the floor so that the roundness of her pregnant belly shows. Beside her, Thorvard's body stiffens.

"My wife is with child," Leif announces to the crowd. They gawk at her, and Leif's face breaks out into a boyish grin. One of Thorvard's advisers offers a hearty cheer and when he raises his drinking horn to toast my brother and his wife, Thorvard throws me a disgusted look. He is the fox and I am the rabbit about to be swallowed whole.

Just as the room erupts in cheer, Thorvard strides over to a side table to pour himself another goblet of red wine. On his return to the dais seat, he stops behind my chair and reaches past me to pick at a pewter platter full of grapes. In the process, he knocks my charger to the slate below. The noisy clang draws eyes.

As I am leaning down, I catch my brother's eye. Leif is speaking to his right-hand man but he reaches under the table and inconspicuously squeezes my shoulder with a kindness and a gentleness I am not used to receiving from anyone anymore. The small gesture is enough to make the tears well up.

When I return my charger to the tabletop where the candles are guttering in liquid pools of seal oil, Thorgunna's eyes lock onto mine. She looks deathly white and baby sick.

"We must offer sacrifice to the gods," I say in a sisterly voice. "We must ask them to keep you safe and protect the little one you carry in your womb."

"I pray to Freyr that I'll be able to deliver a healthy bairn," she frets. I feel the unfairness of the female plight, the burden that birthing babies brings. Self-pitying thoughts rise like fluttering bats when I remember my dead baby and the pain of childbirth that I endured, but I keep quiet. I always keep quiet. Talking has never done me any good.

When the last of the candles flickers out and the embers in the hearth fire start glowing red, Thorgunna announces her intention to go to bed. Before she leaves, she leans down to whisper sweet nothings in my brother's ear and her hair, glittering gold in the firelight, tumbles around her face.

Leif raises his eyes to her and his face lights up as they bid each other *góða nótt*. I study them, curious about what it would be like to hear words like that coming from a husband's mouth. Then Thorgunna drops a gentle kiss on my brother's lips and my shoulders slump. All around us, the din is loud and I suddenly feel as if I am being swarmed by biting flies. In that moment, I know what I have missed out on, what I have yearned for ever since Faðir announced my betrothal to Thorvard of Gardar.

After Thorgunna leaves, Leif's eyes meet mine. Thorvard's head is tilted against his chair. His eyes are closed. His mouth is pursed, his breathing soft. I jerk my chin to a corner at the back before quietly standing up. Leif points to the partition at the back and I nod my head and wipe my clammy hands against my dress.

Leif follows me, but as I pick my way over the remaining clansmen in the room, I look back nervously towards the dais chair where Thorvard sleeps. If he should wake...

"Sister, I've had reports that the lands you inherited from Faðir are doing well," Leif whispers as soon as we reach the shadowy back corner where the moths are flitting back and forth. We stand so closely that I feel the heat of his breath upon my face. "When you shear your sheep and sell the wool, your profits will be substantial."

"Brother, I do not know about these things," I mutter. "It is not my place. Thorvard is the man in charge."

"Freydis, those are Faðir's sheep – the ones he gave you," Leif says earnestly. The shadows scamper across his face.

"I am afraid," I manage.

"Afraid of what?"

"I am not myself," I say, stuttering.

Suddenly I hear footfalls. When I spin around, I catch my breath.

"The sheep have already been shorn. The profits from the wool were large indeed," Thorvard says in a vicious whisper forced through teeth.

"Calm yourself, Thorvard," Leif says awkwardly as he takes a step into the light.

"You speak of sheep but you are the fox!" Thorvard rants in a tone that makes me duck behind my brother's back.

"Our faðir left Freydis a large herd of sheep," Leif says indignantly.

"Freydis's herds are mine to oversee," Thorvard snarls. His breath comes out in ragged gasps. "My sheep are now mixed in with hers. They graze together in the same meadowlands. It would be impossible to ascertain which sheep are hers."

"Come now, Thorvard, you must be fair," my brother says as his tone drops low. "You gave Freydis a flock of sheep as part of the bride price. I witnessed the contract that was sealed in blood. Now I must see to it that she gets her land and her sheep as well."

Thorvard swears. "The bride price I paid to the Eiriksson clan was much too steep," he seethes. "Your useless sister cannot bear me sons."

"It was not my fault I lost the babe!"

In a flash, Thorvard pushes over the counting table with one quick shove that sends the coins and flasks and bags of flax and wheat rolling and tumbling to the ground. In the noise and confusion, Leif's men wake up and he orders them to grab their swords.

"Freydis is an infertile good-for-nothing ingrate!" Thorvard rants, his rage building like a tidal wave. Leif's men shimmy into the shadows and draw their swords, and as soon as Thorvard notices that he is surrounded, he changes like a rabbit changes coats in winter.

"Come now, brother, I meant no harm," he mutters as he lifts his hands in a gesture of surrender. A moment later, he extends his hand to me, but my fear of him makes me wary. Thorvard looks injured. He seems startled by all the fuss we are making, and his eyes pierce mine so that something dark floats between us, stinking like a wave of wildfire smoke ripping through mossy fens and heath shrublands.

"Come to bed, wife. Your brother is tired and I irk him with my words tonight. Let him retire with his pregnant wife who has done well by him to make an heir. Tomorrow we will discuss this business of your *faðir's* lands and your herds of sheep. Come. It is time to say *góða nótt* to all."

Leif eyes me and I quickly nod. "I'll be fine," I say, but I feel a chill.

That night, Thorvard takes me to a secluded annex usually reserved for sheep. As soon as the door is shut, he gives me a violent push and I whack my face into a wall. Struggling to stand, I brace myself when I see stars.

"Please..." I beg stupidly.

In the dark, Thorvard cracks his knuckles and sniffs, and I take a step backwards, listening to a thousand screaming voices in my head. Then another beating comes.

Chapter Nine

SOUL-SWORD WORK

I force myself to roll over in the hay in the early-morning hours. My head is throbbing and my ear has bled all over my sleeping hides, but I try to ignore the pain. Focusing on it just makes it worse. Instead, I return to the gathering hall and busy myself trying to light a fire. At first my fingers shake and I can't manage to hold the tinder steady, but after several tries I am successful.

As soon as the fire flares and I am able to see well enough to study all my bruises, I turn my arms this way and that and discover the hump of a purpling welt above my elbow. Behind me there is a sudden noise. When I spin around, I am startled to see Leif staring at me through the smoke.

"You look tired," is all he says. His whispers shatter the quiet stillness in the room.

"I didn't sleep."

"We need to talk," he mutters, speaking low. Glancing furtively around the room, I see Thorvard sleeping on a bed platform by the door with many other sleeping men sprawled out in different positions on the ground. Their bulky forms are buried underneath their cloaks and furs and their drunken snores are loud. Digging my knuckles into the pockets of my dress, I shiver uncontrollably.

"You'll return with us to Brattahlíð," Leif murmurs carefully as he studies my bruises. He speaks so softly I can hardly hear.

"How?" I ask as I lean forwards to poke the fire again. Another cloud of smoke rises and I work hard to suppress a cough.

"We will tell Thorvard that I need you to inspect your tenants' lands – the lands you inherited from Faðir when he died. We will say that you need to take an accounting from the farmers who rent from you to meet the requirements of your inheritance."

"He will want to come along," is all I say.

"I'll discourage him from traveling at this time of year."

"May the gods give you words," I whisper. I am beginning to feel like I will faint. My brother reaches out to steady me. I glance at Thorvard's sleeping form just as a wet gurgled snore escapes from his throat. "Gods' bread, if my husband learns that I conspire to cheat him out of any trading deal, there will be hell to pay," I mutter. "If you only knew what his fists can do."

"Freydis, I know what you've endured," he says.

I think to myself that he doesn't know, that he will never know, that he will never truly understand.

Leif eyes the fresh set of bruises on my face. His visit

here has weighed him down and made him see beyond his bride.

I inhale a series of jagged breaths that steeple high through my nose before turning back to resume my work, leaving Leif standing there, his forehead crinkled in a worried frown.

When the weakened sun finally climbs out of her horizon bed, Thorvard lifts his head. His bloodshot eyes blink wildly.

"Bring me a drink and bring it fast," he calls to a passing thrall. The thrall goes running as Thorvard struggles to swing his legs out of bed.

I stir the porridge and then find the jug of buttermilk. As I work, I glance at Thorvard, whose head is dangling weakly from his ropey tattooed neck. He looks so tired and beaten down that, for a moment, I feel confused and ashamed of myself.

When the thrall arrives with a drinking horn, Thorvard looks up with bleary eyes and grabs the drink. "This isn't what I asked for," he snarls after he downs the contents in one big gulp. There is water dripping down his chin. "You stupid slug. Now bring me ale!"

The thrall blinks. For a moment, she is a frozen block of ice, but when Thorvard's eyes, mere slits, come to rest on me, she scampers off.

"What's wrong with you?" he barks.

"Husband, let me bring you food," I sputter nervously.

"Bring me ale," he snarls, and I flinch before I, too, dash away.

That morning I tiptoe around the longhouse doing

chores, expecting to be chastised, shamed, or even hit, but Thorvard is silent as he recovers from his drunkenness the night before. Later, when my brother asks to see the farm, Thorvard insists on trailing behind the two of us as we walk the fields of Gardar, but he drags his feet and rubs his temples and shields his eyes, wincing in the bright sunlight. When I glance at Leif, he looks straight ahead, ignoring the wolf dressed in men's clothing who is following us.

As soon as we return to the longhouse, Leif suggests that the womenfolk be left alone to speak of female things. Thorvard disagrees. He says that leaving women alone has never come to any good. Leif laughs at this, but I know that my brother is looking for a way for us to talk alone. No opportunity presents itself.

I walk on eggshells all day long with Thorvard scrutinizing me from afar. He listens closely to what I say and tracks my movements with his eyes. I am sure he expects me to tell on him and shame his name, but I have learned to be silent in order to escape the darkness in this terrifying game of cat and mouse.

As the sun begins to set, Thorvard asks me to walk with him out into the meadowlands to find the sheep. I try to excuse myself, but Thorvard will have none of it.

"Don't you have a shepherd boy?" Leif asks. He slides a glance my way.

"My thralls are busy," Thorvard snaps. "Besides, I have business with my wife, and I must speak with her alone."

"My sister's business is also mine," Leif retorts, his eyes stone-cold.

"I am her husband, and what I have to say is not your concern."

I see my brother's face turn red. Throwing his shoulders back, he puffs out his chest and flicks his chin towards the path leading out of the settlement. "Tomorrow I will return to Brattahlíð at the break of dawn."

Thorvard glances up. "Have you seen the sky?" he asks. "It will surely snow."

"Freydis is needed to settle a difficult matter between some farmers who dispute a claim to land," Leif says as he stares into the western sky where the setting sun is piercing through a ridge of grey storm clouds. "The dispute is old, but recently the farmers have taken up the argument once again. The farmers' dispute relates to a land inheritance our *faðir* gave to Freydis before he died. They say that because she no longer lives on Faðir's land, she is no longer entitled to any of the profits from the crops. Her presence is required to sort this out before the winter comes. Afterwards, I will return her to your farm."

"If this business concerns my wife's inheritance, I will come along," my husband announces, glancing at me suspiciously.

"Suit yourself. We welcome you," my brother lies. He inhales the crisp autumn air. "Considering that it is the time for harvesting the crops, I hope your presence here will not be missed.

"It won't. I'll leave Ivor in charge. He is trustworthy and he knows what to do."

"Suit yourself," my brother says again, "but please

know this: Thorgunna is thick with child so we cannot be entertaining you and your men."

My husband glares at Leif before stepping forth to grab my arm and escort me out the door. As he leads me through the frozen yard, a flock of white-fronted geese flying in V-formation startles me with their honking cries. When I stop to gawk, Thorvard yells at me to hurry up. His voice is laced with irritation.

"I'm coming," I say, trembling at the look of him.

Thorvard drags me down the path. As soon as we are out of sight, he gives me a tremendous shove, and I fall down hard and cut my knee on a sharp, uneven rock. Wincing, I glance up. Thorvard's large frame is blocking out the wan grey sky, and in his hand he holds a rock. Instinctively my hands shoot up to protect my face. Thorvard laughs. I scramble backwards into the grass.

A moment later I am on my feet dodging rocks. With flailing limbs, I release a blood-curdling scream and begin to run, but Thorvard follows me in hot pursuit. Glancing back, I catch sight of the wildness in his eyes and pick up my pace, half-skipping around a boulder that lies in the centre of the path.

Panting and wheezing, I narrowly avoid a patch of thistles before making my way up a bank, but as I am nearing the top, Thorvard gains on me. With groping hands, he reaches out and grabs for me. With a squeal I try to wriggle free, but he grips my mantle and yanks me back. Then, pulling me, he throws me down and falls on top of my sprawled form, crushing me with his heavy weight.

Struggling, I begin to scream, but Thorvard muzzles me

with his hand. Underneath my flailing body, some itchy weed gets crushed into pulp, lodging itself deeply into my back.

"Stop!" I cry. I am not strong enough to throw him off.

Thorvard snarls and grabs my hair. When he yanks, my eyes grow round and my neck snaps back. Flailing, I try to fight him off using the grappling moves that Ivor taught me. With a sudden surge of force, I kick him hard and wiggle round to ram my thumb into his eye. His wolf-like howl cuts through the bloated silence of the meadowlands even as he comes at me again.

Panicking, I go to turn and run, but just up ahead the hill drops off so that I have no choice but to stop and curl into a little ball. An instant later Thorvard goes to deliver a brutal kick, but just before his foot connects with my chin, I propel myself over the steep, rocky bank. Careening wildly down the hill, I feel shards of rock tearing through my flesh as I pick up speed, vaguely aware that Thorvard is tumbling behind me in a cloud of dust, cursing vilely.

By the time I stop, parts of me are scraped and welting, bruised and raw. There are bits of pebbles in my knees, and my shoulder is a meaty mess of raw, oozing flesh. Sitting up, I brace myself when I see a gash on my shin oozing blood. A moment later, there are stars exploding in my periphery.

When my vision clears, I shake my head. Just ahead, Thorvard is lying flat and winded in a patch of arctic thyme. He looks so still that for a moment I wonder if he is dead, but then I hear a raspy rustling sound, a moan that sounds more like dying wind.

"Husband, are you alive?" I ask as I hobble over to where he lies. Leaning down, I run my thumb across his brow. His eyes are closed. His face is white. Bending lower, I take up his heavy wrist in my hands, but as I go to take his pulse he springs up suddenly and grabs my arms.

"By Óðinn's beard, I'll say this once," Thorvard threatens as he begins to shake me so violently that my teeth rattle and my eyes tear up. "If you ever turn against me and go to your brother to ask for help, I'll break your bones and throw all your bleeding parts to my dogs. Not only that, but Thorgunna will pay a price as well."

His eyes are like silverfish. His jaw is clenched. His breath is warm upon my face. I try to avert my eyes from the spittle dribbling down his chin, but he shoves his face in close to mine. When I catch a whiff of sour wine upon his breath, I try to wriggle free, but in one quick move, he twists my arm and flips me over and throws my face into the ground. My mouth tastes dirt. There are a thousand fluttering lights more brilliant than the summer sun, a whizzing swelling noise, like the nasty hum of circling flies.

The drone crescendos inside my head. With a burst of strength, I draw my knees up from underneath and feel his weight upon my back. An instant later, I drop my chin to my chest before lifting it with such a quick and mighty force that I bang my head into his chin. Yelping, he brings his hand up to his face. Instantaneously, I wriggle onto my side, and when I get my leg in place, I kick him hard. It does no good. He grabs my foot and, twisting me, he delivers a painful backhanded slap.

For a moment I am stunned. Then I lie back, playing dead. Eventually he turns away.

As soon as his back is turned, I shoot up tall and wildly scramble to get away, but Thorvard is too quick. His arm shoots out and he grabs me before I can escape.

"Oh, Freydis, whatever shall I do with you?"

I close my eyes and brace myself to endure another violent slap, but nothing comes. Instead, Thorvard begins moaning like a dying calf. Cracking one eye open, I watch him crumble. As he weeps, he stares at me with eyes that change, that soften up. He is a sea monster camouflaged amongst the rocks. I know this game.

Slowly and cautiously Thorvard leans forwards and begins to tenderly pluck the grass from my dishevelled hair, pulling gently at the ringlets and then letting them go so that my hair springs up around my face.

"Don't tell Leif about what happened here." He smiles and licks his thumb and smears his spittle across my cheek to wipe off the blood and dirt.

I nod, even as he turns away.

The walk back to the farm is slow and laboured in my injured state. My ankle swells so that I can hardly hobble into the yard, but when we finally make it safely to the well, my two-faced husband will not leave my side. To my dismay he orders a thrall to bring some salve that he gently applies to my welted, mangled flesh. I am too sore – indeed, too weary – to find the strength to play his mind games. I can't even muster the will to ask for Loki's help. The trickster god wouldn't help me anyway.

As Thorvard works hard to fix me up, a crowd begins to

gather. A thrall asks if I can stand on my throbbing foot, and when I shake my head, she studies me. All I want is to get away from all these curious do-gooders. If I could only go to sleep and not wake up...

"Bring me a goblet of wine," I say, tugging on the thrall's arm.

Thorgunna overhears. Pushing her way in closer, she takes up my hand in hers. "How bad is it?" she asks in her singsong voice as a million crinkles work their way into the folds around her eyes.

"She fell," Thorvard lies. Thorgunna blinks.

"It's true," I say in a shaky voice. "I tumbled down an embankment while I was out walking with Thorvard in his fields."

"She is lucky I was there," Thorvard mutters as he gathers up my boots.

At that moment Leif emerges from behind the well. I feel his probing eyes scrutinizing my scrapes and scratches and the growing welts on my flesh. A moment later, he spots my husband's bloodied scratches, and I silently breathe a prayer for protection. The god, Hlin, takes pity. Leif stays mum.

That night, Thorvard allows me to sleep alone but only because he stays up late in the drinking hall. In the morning, it is proposed that I travel with Leif and Thorgunna back to Brattahlíð. Thorvard insists on accompanying me in my injured state.

When the horses are bridled and waiting in the yard, Thorvard gallantly lifts me up onto my gelding, taking tremendous care to protect my foot. I am no fool. I have seen him nurse his guilt before by being overly thoughtful and attentive. He likes to prove to others that he is a valiant man, a Norseman like no other.

On the journey back to Brattahlíð, Thorgunna rides beside us. Her voice is cheerful as she talks about her kin and her life in the Hebrides. Keeping my back erect despite the throbbing pain, I stare off into the frost-covered fields and watch my breath puffing out clouds of mist as I listen to her babbling and worrying about everything. My soul-sword work needs to give me courage so I can try again to broach the subject of divorce as soon as I get the chance to speak with Leif alone.

Mother is there to greet us when we arrive in Brattahlíð. She scolds me for not visiting sooner, and I bow my head and close myself off from feeling responsible for her happiness. Then she tells me that she has had a guest for many months – a Christian priest who was sent by the King of Norway himself.

"I am thinking about converting," she whispers as she takes me by the arm. I go stiff. She clings to me.

"Thorvard and Thorgunna, you must come inside and receive a gift," she warbles as she throws a look over her shoulder. "It is something that should have been presented long ago when my husband was still alive."

Thorvard studies the two of us, his eyebrows arching high. "Freydis, come with me." He goes to say more, but Mother will have none of it. She drops my arm and waits for him to join her so they can walk together.

"Thorvard, I want to give the gifts in private without my

two children hanging over me. Go change, Freydis. Prepare yourself for the welcoming feast."

Thorvard's eyes cut into me. Leif says nothing. I can hear the turkeys gobbling loudly in the yard.

"I'll not keep your spouses long," Mother continues as she breaks away from Thorvard so that she can go and help Thorgunna adjust her elaborate headdress stitched in gold. "I'll present my gifts and then I'll bring them back to you."

A crimson flush rises in Thorvard's face. He is a prisoner in Mother's house, a man who is no longer able to use his power to get what he wants. For the first time in many months, I feel strangely smug.

As soon as Thorgunna and Thorvard are led away, Leif cautiously reaches out to touch the bruises along my hairline. Startled, I draw back. Behind him, the setting sun highlights the luscious furs draped around his neck with their bristles moving back and forth in the gentle wind.

"We should go inside," I say as he reaches out and gently turn my chin into the light.

"Did he do this to you?" he asks.

"Don't," I say in a pathetic whine.

"Freydis, we have little time," he pleads.

"I can't speak to you. He wouldn't like it." I want to tell my brother all about my husband's wrath, about the way he abuses me, about his fists and my broken bones, but I can't seem to use my tongue or find the words.

"It is just the two of us, and we are safe. You must tell me, sister. If your husband is abusing you, I'll demand blood money."

My lips are quivering. I pull away. In the distance, I hear a seagull cry.

"Come, then," Leif says calmly, his tone steady. "I'll walk you to your bed closet."

We walk in silence through the yard until we reach the smithy where Leif stops and turns. "Freydis, you are dear to me," he stammers. "When I left Greenland, I worried about you constantly." His eyes search mine as he presses on: "I will set things right beginning at the feast tonight. When you arrive, you must sit beside me and pretend that there is nothing wrong."

I stare at him, feeling numb. He wants me to pretend that there is nothing wrong when everything has been wrong right from the start.

"When tomorrow comes, you and I will ride out to inspect your lands." He slows his breathing and looks past me to scan the yard. When he is certain that we are alone, his eyes return to me. "The plan is simple so listen closely. We'll create a ruse using clever deception to trick Thorvard of Gardar. After we return from the fields, you will pretend that you are deathly ill and I will send you off to bed and ask the *gyoja* to attend to you. She will quarantine you inside your bedchamber and tell our kinsmen that you have the plague. If that trickster god, Loki, is on our side, our kinsmen will believe that you are too sick to travel back to Gardar."

"Thorvard will insist on seeing me," I moan. Leif cuts me off.

"*Neinn*. The *gyoja* will tell him that he would be a fool to visit you in your sickly state. She will tell him that it is best to leave and return to his farm. I'll reassure him that as soon as you are well, I will escort you back to Brattahlíð."

I glance up into the smoke-grey sky. "The threat of the coming winter storms will make Thorvard anxious to return to his farm," I say as I take a shaky breath. My mouth is dry.

"I am counting on it," Leif replies. "Let us hope that the god of winter is on our side. We should offer sacrifice. If Skaði is willing, the snow will trap you here over the winter months."

I bite my cheeks to hold back tears. When we were children, Leif used to fight injustices on my behalf. Now we find ourselves in a more dangerous game. I should tell him that by defending me, he risks his life – Thorgunna's, too.

"Freydis, do not despair," my brother sighs as he looks deeply into my eyes. "I will get you out of this."

"Óðinn has inspired you," I manage weakly.

"Praise Óðinn then," my brother says. He tries to give a reassuring smile before taking me by the shoulder and steering me down the hall. "Freydis, we must be careful. I won't tell anyone about our plan, not even Thorgunna. If Thorvard were to discover what we are all about, it could be our ruin."

I am ruined already, I think soberly.

Leif throws a glance.

"It was difficult while you were away," I whisper.

"Freydis, I am sorry that you were married off to him. You must have borne a terrible weight."

I have longed to hear these words, but now that he has spit them out, there is no relief. My sorrows have not been halved. There is only fear. I look down at my red hands, chafed from the work of dying wool.

"I'd best get back, brother."

In the end, our deceptive plan works well. With my *gyoja's* help, we manage to dupe the household thralls, my husband, and all his men. In a foul temper, Thorvard leaves the farm threatening to return for me before the snowstorms come. A few days later, the weather turns bone-chillingly cold, and the first snowstorm hits. In the blowing snow, ice pelts against the door of the hut and everything freezes solid overnight. I welcome the sound of the raging storm as I sit safely tucked underneath a sheepskin throw.

For days I remain hidden in the darkened hut where I light my herbs and return to giving sacrifices to the gods as I try to turn my wounds into scars. The thralls are too scared to bring me meals so Leif is the only one to visit me. He tells me that Thorgunna is worried about him catching illness. Poor woman. I wish that we could tell her that Loki has inspired us.

As time drags on, the guilt I feel for deceiving Thorgunna begins to itch. I am alone with my thoughts and plagued by a persistent building fear that Thorvard will return for me. While I am finally free of a vicious man, his hurtful words continue to tumble around inside my head, and I question every little thing I do. He has broken and changed me, made me doubt everything about myself.

One morning I tiptoe across the creaky planks and throw open the heavy door to catch some air. As the cold creeps in, I am met with the sight of my brother cutting a path as he snowshoes towards my hut. His shoulders are bent into the wind.

"Freydis, the *gyoja* says that you are cured."

For the first time in many months, I feel my lips curling into a smile.

"Here," he says as soon as he has unstrapped his snowshoes. "Take these berries and smash them against your lips and pinch your cheeks for color so that you look well. With that red hair of yours and your pale skin, you still look ill, and we can't have that."

"*Neinn*," I murmur. "We can't have that."

As the days grow shorter and the snow piles up, Leif helps me regain a place at his hearth. My clansmen embrace me, but I feel flat, like I have nothing to offer anyone anymore. I know that I am a tainted woman who is silently judged for abandoning her husband over the winter months. Leif has rescued me, but in many ways, I still feel trapped.

My brother, on the other hand, is full of stories. He likes to talk about his Vinland voyage to Leifsbidur. Our people love him for it. Especially Mother. In her eyes, he can do no wrong. With me, she blames and shames me. When I go to her, she tells me that she is relieved that I am well, but she accuses me of purposefully falling ill.

One day, I approach my brother who is stacking furs and counting tusks in Faðir's old counting room, an area at the back of the longhouse that has been partitioned off.

"I have grounds for divorcing Thorvard," I state simply as I use my teeth to rip off a piece of broken hangnail that is bothersome. Leif stops his work and glances up.

"Freydis, I know that you have not fared well at Thorvard's hands," he begins, "but you are safe here on this farm with us."

"*Já*," I say, "but what will happen when winter turns to spring?" I clench my fists and steel my nerves as a wave of anger overwhelms me. I could crush a giant, I am so worked up. "Good brother, please just hear me out. The way things are, I have fallen out of love with Thorvard of Gardar. Unless I divorce, I am not free to marry someone else and have children of my own."

"Falling out of love is not a reason for divorce," my brother says dismissively as he glances at a table where piles of shark and whale teeth lie in heaps.

"It is not just that," I continue, boldly locking eyes with him. "Thorvard has been cruel to me. He hits me hard. He has abused me openly in front of witnesses on his farm. If I am to understand the Althing laws, a husband cannot slap his wife more than thrice, and I suffered more than that when I lived with him. Good brother, don't you see? I know my rights. Divorce would be possible with your help."

"Where are your witnesses, Freydis?" my brother sighs. He is growing impatient.

"Back on Thorvard's farm," I reply, feeling a little less confident now that he makes me doubt.

"Would they be willing to testify against their chieftain?" he murmurs as he stands and begins sorting hides. I see a tiny bug scurrying across the counting table. In this cold, I am shocked to see that it is alive.

"I am unhappy with my union, brother."

"I can do nothing more than what I've done." He glances over his shoulder. "If there was mutual unhappiness with the union, a quick divorce would be within your reach. Your dowry goods would be returned in full. Even so, we would be forced to scrounge up funds to pay the bride-price and the morning-gift back in full. Forsooth, divorce is a very expensive proposition. I won't support it. Not right now. Quite simply put, a divorce from Thorvard is beyond my means."

He sees the bug on the table. In one quick sweep, he swats the insect to the ground and squashes it with his foot. When I stay silent, he looks at me.

"Freydis, don't be stupid. There is too much to lose."

"Too much to lose?" I hear my voice spiraling up. "If I divorce, my estate will grow. I am entitled to one-third of our common possessions including a portion of Thorvard's lands. You and I could both gain access to Thorvard's wealth."

"Come now, Freydis, calm yourself," my brother says in a soothing tone. "You assume that you will win your case. That is unlikely, sister, and I'll tell you why. Thorvard is a powerful man who can afford to pay off witnesses to tell his lies. Think on it. Lay hand on heart."

I lift my chin and study him. Squirming, he looks behind me towards the gathering room where our clansmen are sitting and talking while they work.

"Our family would easily lose a hefty chunk of land if you divorced. Is that what you want? Do you wish for me to lose the hard-won lands that Faðir settled when he first came to Greenland's shores?"

He stops to catch his breath. A moment later he stands up tall and scrutinizes me with his hard metal eyes.

"If Thorvard had full control of all your lands, he would have the largest farm on Greenland's shores. After that, he could usurp control. My position as the *goði* of Greenland would be jeopardized."

"I see," I mumble. In actuality, the only thing I see is that Leif has turned greedy since he became a married man. He likes the power that his title brings. He likes his wealth. His sister's fears are not his own.

"Freydis, you are happy here in Brattahlíð, are you not?" When I nod, he continues in an even tone. "I'll endeavor to either keep you here or settle you safely on your own lands. In any case, you must not fret."

He does not know me very well if he thinks that I will not fret and that I will settle for his selfish plan.

Leif continues to spew out words. His opinion clearly opposes mine. I sink down heavily on the bench. On the counting table, there is a silver coin, a single tooth.

"Give my regards to your pregnant wife whom you so adore," I finally say when he is done. For a moment, I stare at his handsome face, his handsome clothes. "Thorgunna is a fortunate woman to have your love."

"She is indeed," Leif replies. "It isn't every day that one finds love."

"*Neinn*," I say.

In the corner, the whale-oil lamp flutters.

In silence, I stand and take my leave.

In the days that follow, I practice using my slingshot, my knife, and my battle-axe to aim at targets that I place behind a partition at the back where it is cold. One night in my sleep I am visited by the love goddess who tasks me with killing a group of hardened foes. I ask her why I have to be the murderess. Freyja tells me that I must obey her wishes in order to win back love. When she wags her finger, I make a promise to serve her well. Then Freyja morphs into a falcon that flies towards an elaborate door. The shadows flicker before there is a burst of brilliant light. Freyja's face appears and she invites me to cross the threshold of love's golden gates. I tell her that I am too afraid. She reaches out her fine-boned blue-veined hand.

Come inside on tiptoes, my darling child. Come and see what you can find.

Come explore my world of love, but come quickly before the doorway closes and it grows dark again.

Chapter Ten

SORROWS SHARED ARE SORROWS HALVED

During the preparations for the Feast of Ostara, I meet Logatha and Finnbogi of Iceland, who arrive in Brattahlíð after snowshoeing in from a neighboring farm where they have been staying over the winter months, waiting for the ice to break up so that they can continue to go *a vyking*. Logatha takes up my hand in a friendly greeting. While she is all smiles, I feel my stomach knotting. If she has made it through the snow on foot, Thorvard could come for me at any time.

That night, I have trouble falling asleep. I worry that the nightmares will take me back to Thorvard's longhouse and trap me in an endless loop of suffering where I relive the beatings. I stare up into the rafters and feel the brush of my husband's ethereal spirit touching my clammy skin before I turn on my side, trying to get comfortable, trying to push the memories away as I feel my spirit haemorrhaging and my heart clamoring. Forcing myself to breathe in slowly, I listen to the rumble of laughter coming from the great room as Leif entertains his guests. The sound lulls me into a world of nothingness.

Sometime in the middle of the night, I startle awake to the sound of whispered voices on the other side of my bed curtain, and my breath snags until I discover that I am lying alone in sweat-soaked hides. When I peek out, I catch a glimpse of Finnbogi sitting with my brother. The two of them are all alone, and the fire is flickering low, spitting shadows across the walls.

"You are a lucky man to have found Thorgunna," Finnbogi sighs as Leif reaches forwards to stir the fire. Leif glances up. Finnbogi stamps out a flanker with his toe. "Like you, I want to be able to protect my wife. I am wondering if this journey that we wish to take across the northern seas will be too dangerous for Logatha."

I pull back, knowing that Thorvard of Gardar, my muskox of a husband, has never given a rat's ass about my safety.

"If Njǫrd, the god of the wind and sea, is on your side, you should have nothing to fear," my brother says. "But in Vinland, you must be vigilant. Don't let your woman out of your sight. I don't trust those *skraelings*. They might steal your wife and keep her as a trophy prize."

I hear a log snap in two. Finnbogi clears his throat. "If you were in my shoes, would you take your wife along?"

My brother laughs, and his chuckle is sedate and musical. "I would," he says. "I would be hard pressed to live without Thorgunna by my side."

My eyes well up. Finnbogi clears his throat.

"When we were still back home, I asked a fellow

Icelander, a helmsman by the name of Thorfinn Karlsefni, to swear an oath," Finnbogi says. His muffled baritone drifts into the shadows. "He wants to lead his own expedition to Vinland as soon as his shipbuilder finishes making him a ship."

"What kind of oath did you make him swear?" Leif asks. He sounds fatigued.

"We swore to protect each other's families if either one of us were to die. We found a stone with a round hole in it and clasped hands through it."

"It is rare to find such a stone."

"We also had oath rings made to cement our fealty." He holds up an elaborate silver arm ring that sparkles in the firelight."

"May Óðinn's Oath serve you well, my friend."

FinnbogI sighs. "I have no sons to call my own, but one day I will have a longhouse full of them, I'm sure of it. Karlsefni will be bound by his promise to look after them."

Behind the curtain, I stifle a silent yawn and wiggle back down into my bed, feeling a strange sort of jealousy.

"The problem is that Karlsefni might not sail his ship this way. He is a fickle man. What if he gets lost at sea? I might never see the man again."

My eyes feel heavy. The bed is warm. When the Icelander starts up again, I turn my face into the wall.

"Leif, you are somewhat of a legend because of what you've accomplished," Finnbogi whispers, speaking so low that I can hardly hear. "You've sailed across the northern sea and lived to tell the tale. I hope to follow in your footsteps, but if something were to happen to me, would you be so kind as to swear a blood oath to protect my family? If they were to make it back to Greenland's shores without me, I would want to make sure that they were protected. I know it is a lot to ask."

I spring awake. Who is this man? Never have I heard of an Icelander bestowing such a request on a Greenlander. It's just not done.

There is a burst of noise.

My brother has accidentally spilled his drinking horn.

"I see the way you treat your wife and your sister," Finnbogi says, speaking fast. "I sense that you would do well by Logatha and my heirs. A man can never be too careful in safeguarding what he treasures most."

My throat chokes up. Tugging on my hides, I draw the covers up to my chin. Logatha and Thorgunna have been favoured by the gods. I wonder if they even recognize what kind of lives they live because they are cherished by their men. I will never have this. I am not good enough.

My stomach turns. Thorvard of Gardar's shadow falls on top of me, and the memories take my breath away. I feel the weight of his hand against my mouth, cutting off my air supply. My head begins to spin. With a thud, I begin to fall, waiting for the nothingness.

~

In the nippy darkness of an early morning, I get up and join the others around Leif's hearth fire. Taking up my distaff attached to four bobbins, I numbly begin whipcording, feeling only bone-deep weariness. As my fingers manoeuvre the strands, Logatha studies me from across the fire. She is a tall, thin woman with blonde hair and piercing blue eyes.

"Last night someone told me that your husband is the wealthy landowner Thorvard of Gardar. Is this true?" she asks. My stomach sours. I give a little nod and force myself to concentrate on the hand rhythms, the monotony of the moves.

"I should have spoken with you more last night before I retired to bed, but I got to talking with your brother's wife. I can see why they call Thorgunna a priceless gem." She taps her head. "Not only is she beautiful, but she is intelligent. If she weren't pregnant, I'm sure she'd insist on traveling back with us to Leifsbidur."

The four-plait braid is almost done. Logatha leans in closely and I accidentally miss my pass.

"As you know, my husband and our crew sailed from Iceland last summer," she continues as she watches me. As she talks, she wildly flails her arms and I draw back. I have lived with a man whose flailing arms were dangerous.

"By Óðinn's eye, when we arrived here in Greenland, we were fortunate to find Gunthur and his wife, who took us in right before the blizzards came and our longboats got locked into the ice. Now my brother-in-law, Helgi, is anxious to leave Greenland's shores. As soon as the ice breaks up, we will travel across the northern sea on a *vyking* expedition bound for Vinland."

"My brother sailed to Vinland," is all I say as I tie off the string. "He founded a new colony there. Leifsbidur is what he calls it."

"Your brother is the reason why we came to Brattahlíð," she says with laughing eyes. "We wanted to learn more about his voyage and his experiences with the *skraelings*. We want to trade with them." I put down my work and Logatha takes my arm and draws me closer to the fire where I sink myself into her life.

"Finnbogi spent his life building ships. I spent mine studying the stars to learn how to navigate by them." Her smile is big and infectious.

"I envy you."

She emits a tiny laugh. "I want to go *a vyking* to learn even more about the constellations so I can map them out."

"I wonder if Leifsbidur is a peaceful place," I murmur as my heart begins to thud. She is sitting too close.

"I wonder," is all she says. When she turns, I notice the nest of crow's feet wrinkles etching the corners of her eyes.

There is a large celebration to mark the Feast of Ostara and the arrival of the new season. Leif dedicates the spring festival to Éostre, the goddess of growth and renewal. With the extra company, the longhouse is a busy place, but Leif is a gracious host. He keeps the hearth fire blazing brightly using Vinland wood instead of peat, but it is the sweetness of his Vinlandic wine with its rich, smooth taste that impresses most.

"I climbed those Vinlandic banks on my hands and knees to get to the place where I could pick the small red berries that had ripened after the first autumn frost. They make the best wine, don't you think?" His face is animated. His eyes are bright. "You must go to Leifsbidur and discover the riches for yourself. I tell you solemnly, the land yields abundant wealth. There was a river running adjacent to my longhouse where I stood knee-deep in water and plucked the salmon out by hand."

The Icelanders seem impressed. As Leif talks, I make my way around the room giving away dyed eggs to all the women who attend the feast. When I go to offer one to Logatha, she playfully tugs at my draping sleeves.

"I need the whole basket," she whispers dramatically before emitting a hearty laugh. The rumble of it reminds me of a white-fronted goose. "If just one of these eggs could help me bear a child, Finnbogi would be a happy man." She is suddenly serious when she crooks her finger and beckons me closer. The room is hot. A minstrel is strumming on a lyre.

"Freydis, do you think these eggs will bring me any luck? Finnbogi and I have been together for many moons and my womb is still barren," she says as soon as I sink down beside her on the bench.

"I'll give you some of my *gyoja's* herbs," I murmur in her ear. "They worked for me, and I birthed a boy." Logatha's eyes are glistening in the firelight. She cocks her head and glances down at my womb. Her face looks confused. I take a breath. "In the end, I lost the child."

"Dear Freydis, I am so sorry," she says after a moment, but her voice is so gentle that I almost break.

"It was a while ago," I manage. She takes up my hand, and in her company I find myself telling her all about the pain of giving birth. It is a story that I have never told – a story that I have longed to tell.

"You will conceive again," Logatha says encouragingly when I have finished telling her the sorry tale, but her voice snags. My eyes sweep the room.

"I will never bear a child again," I whisper. "My husband is…"

"Dying?" she asks.

"*Neinn*." My spirit plunges even lower. For a moment, I am sick with dread.

"He is abusive, then?" Logatha speculates.

"Abusive and evil," I reply, but I feel a chill when I envision Thorvard standing in front of me with his fist raised, threatening to break my jaw.

The image changes. Grows. I picture myself wrapping my arms around his bearded throat and squeezing hard, listening as his gurgles turn into a juice of blood.

Logatha's forehead creases into worry lines. When I see the expression, I tell myself to smarten up. If Thorvard were to discover that I had betrayed him to an Icelander, there would be Hel to pay.

"I'll fetch my man," Logatha says abruptly, looking grim. "Finnbogi can't stand men who mistreat their wives. He will challenge your wicked husband to a *hólmgang*. Such a duel will help you reclaim your honor."

"*Neinn*, I beg of you. Please don't tell Finnbogi. Please don't tell anyone." There are beads of sweat trickling down my back.

"Where is this husband of yours who abuses you?" Logatha spits.

"On his farm," I mutter, but as soon as I release the words, my head starts spinning and my heart begins to thrum. How is it that I have been silenced by every Greenlander I have ever met and now this Icelander is drawing this sliver out of me? I take a breath and struggle to suppress a surge of fear. A headache jabs. My legs feel weak.

"Please tell me the all of it. I want to know," Logatha murmurs as she takes my basket from me and places it on the floor. I blink and feel her warmth beside me. The hearth fire crackles and snaps as a log splits apart. All around us, Leif's kin are chattering. When a burst of laughter erupts, I glance up at the Norsemen who are sitting around the blazing fire.

I take a breath, and the trauma of my life slips out like dissonant chords slipping off a lyre. As I speak, it is as if I lift above myself. I find myself talking, but it is like I am listening to a run of ascending notes spilling from the panpipe, blasting from a cone-shaped lur held together by willow strings. I sing the song of my broken life, and Logatha listens with pity and compassion before admitting that she does not know what to say to comfort me. I tell her that her listening ear and honest words are good enough. Afterwards, there is some relief.

A few days later, I find myself seated between Logatha and Finnbogi at another festive dinner. Finnbogi is an animated talker with many interesting tales to tell. Tall in stature, he is a blond-haired, handsome man with broad shoulders and a ready laugh.

When the meat platters arrive, Logatha spots a pot of

rabbit stew and sticks her head into the wafting steam and drinks in the smell of the savory dish with a dramatic lifting of her hands and a brilliant smile. At the head of the table, Leif and Thorgunna begin to laugh. Even the thrall can't suppress a grin as she scoops out a serving of the stew into Finnbogi's bowl.

"Praise Óðinn! I am sure to have an heir in nine months' time," Finnbogi jokes good-naturedly.

"How can you be so certain?" a farmer heckles from the back. There is a burst of laughter as Logatha stands and bows to the crowd. Finnbogi takes another giant gulp of ale from his drinking horn.

"The rabbit is such a virulent offspring-producer that if my good wife licks her charger clean, I am certain she will ingest the fertility ingredient that she lacks. Forsooth, good man, reproduction in spring is not just for rabbits, is it, now?"

At this, Finnbogi throws his wife an audacious wink. I glance up nervously but Logatha takes it all in her stride. She clucks her tongue and wags her finger in Finnbogi's face.

"Rejoice and be fertile," Finnbogi says in a spirited voice as he lifts his charger into the air. His chuckles pop up in bursts as the crowd erupts and the revelry spreads like wildfire. Watching him, I have difficulty feeling anything. Thorvard of Gardar is a thief who stole the part of me that laughed easily, that took pleasure in life's simple moments, that was carefree and fun-loving. I don't know that woman anymore.

Finnbogi continues playing to the boisterous crowd.

When he jumps across the table and begins to hop around like a rabbit pretending to have big front teeth, Logatha laughs so hard she begins to cry. The crowd erupts with a thunderous roar, and Finnbogi laps it up. He returns to the table and sniffs at Logatha with his rabbit nose and nibbles playfully at her toes. When she swats at him, he hops zigzagged across the room. It is so absurd that I don't know what to make of him. I feel myself pulling back into a dark sort of ugliness, and I hate myself for it. Standing quickly, I call for water. When the thrall brings me a goblet, I am sorry that I didn't ask for more wine.

Eventually the crowd calms down, and Finnbogi and I find ourselves in each other's company, seated side by side. His mouth is full of rabbit meat when he asks about my land. At first, I am hesitant to disclose anything about my life, but he is so easy to talk to that eventually I open up. When the topic of his upcoming expedition is broached, he tells me all about where he intends to take his ship. Then he tells me that Logatha is an expert at reading stars, and I get so envious of their bond that I sit there stewing and chewing on my lip.

The hour grows late. When the *skald* begins his tale, I find myself surrounded by messy chargers and emptied goblets and couples with their heads bent together as they relax and listen to a saga that I have heard many times before. I feel strangely content knowing that I'll go to bed alone tonight. No bastard husband will use my bones.

I get lost in thought until I feel someone's eyes studying me. Slowly I turn my head only to see Finnbogi slowly raising his drinking horn in a toast to me. Nervously I look around. The shadows shift.

"Mistress Freydis," Finnbogi begins. He leans in closely. "My wife told me your sorry tale. I know about your husband, Thorvard of Gardar. That evil bastard must be held accountable for beating you. By Óðinn's beard, when the snows start to melt, I expect he will come for you."

Instantaneously I am on guard. "He has not come for me yet," I say, feeling a sudden chill.

Logatha comes to sit beside her husband. She frowns when she sees my stricken face.

"My dear Freydis, are you well?" she asks. I nod my head.

"I have no tolerance for men who intimidate or mistreat their wives," Finnbogi continues as he fingers his drinking horn and glances uneasily at his wife. "Mistress Freydis, I advise you to find an acceptable way to distance yourself from Thorvard of Gardar. He will not be pleased that you wintered here. By the gods, he will punish you. I have seen what other men do when their pride is stung. They do not like it when their woman gains the upper hand."

My fists ball up. Logatha sees me squirm and she fetches me a flask of water which I gulp down. Afterwards she helps remove my tattered shawl.

"I have spoken to my brother about divorce," I mumble uncomfortably, keeping my face downturned. The room is suddenly far too smoky and very warm.

"It is not the wisest course," Finnbogi cautions. He takes a sip from his drinking horn before continuing in a solemn voice. "You are a wealthy woman with much to lose. I am guessing that you do not wish to forfeit your inheritance. I understand that you own a lot of land?"

It is like this vibrant, carefree man has suddenly morphed into someone else – someone sober who clearly knows my status and knows the law. Still, I can't trust him.

"Divorce would be to your financial ruin," Logatha says as she works her hand into the crook of her husband's arm. "We have thought on it and there is something else that you could do."

In front of us the *skald* suddenly drops his pitch. He plays the audience to build suspense. Beside me Finnbogi clears his throat.

"You must come with us to Vinland's shores," he murmurs, and I glance up. The invitation hangs between us like a sticky cobweb.

"Vinland is far away," I finally mutter as I fold my hands in my lap.

"My brother, Helgi, would approve if he were here," Finnbogi says, speaking fast. "We need a sponsor to help us out, someone to outfit our longboats with rations and supplies. We own the ships, but we need a wealthy patron. We thought that Leif the Lucky would come with us, but he doesn't wish to travel." He flexes his arm, and the tattoo of a seagull pops out. I stare at it in the flickering shadows and it almost seems as if the bird begins to move.

"Helgi says that having an Eiriksson on board would be wise," Logatha whispers excitedly. "You could come with us."

"If you are wise," Finnbogi interjects, "you will heed our offer and leave this place."

Both of them suddenly stop talking and their offer sweeps me up like a fast-flowing current, spinning me into a whirling eddy of possibilities.

"Taking a *vyking* expedition is a perfect way to keep you safe from your husband's fists," Logatha breathes as she tosses a glance at Finnbogi.

"If I should entertain this proposition," I start to say, trying to squelch the panic leeching into my voice, "I would need to know the cost."

"The cost is nothing you can't afford," Logatha reassures.

The *skald* finishes, and my kinsmen stir. From across the room someone shouts for another round of drinks.

"It is curious that Leif refused the offer to go back to Leifsbidur," I say as I scan the room in search of him.

"He told us that he does not wish to miss the birth of his firstborn son," Logatha says as she studies the Greenlanders who roam the room.

"If I go, what type of trading profit could I expect?"

"On our successful return to Greenland,, we would give you half of any trading profits that we make. The deal works out well for us and well for you. If you provide supplies for the voyage there, we will supply the ships. Think on it. You will escape from Thorvard's abusive fists in a way that saves your reputation and protects your house."

Fingering my drinking horn, I contemplate the offer and keep my face shielded to hide my fear. *Oh gods, I need to move; I need to breathe the outdoor air*, I think as a rush of panic grips my bones.

"Prithee, give me some time to think this through," I

finally mumble as I finger the luscious furs that line the bench. "How will I convince Leif to let me go?"

"You must tell him that he will profit," Finnbogi grins. "Leif the Lucky is known for taking risks. He might let you go if he thinks that your presence in Leifsbidur will benefit him."

"Your brother is your closest ally, or so you mentioned when I asked," Logatha says in a careful voice. " Tell him that you wish to check to see if Leifsbidur still stands. Tell him that it would be best if a Greenlander was present – an Eiriksson. Offer to bring back timber and pelts for him to trade. As we said, we will split the trading profits. I think he might go for that."

"It is a far-fetched plan," I say quietly.

"But one that will save your life."

In the women's room, Mother is speaking with Bork, one of Faðir's closest advisers. Their heads are bent close together and Mother is laughing. She is widowed and laughing in the company of another man. Shame on her. She is no protector. I will never be able to rely on her.

How is it that these Icelanders have offered to rescue me from Thorvard's hands, and Mother has done nothing? How can I trust them to do well by me? By the gods, I have been known to give away trust too easily, and I can't afford to do that again. I wrap my arms around myself.

Finnbogi astutely reads my mind. "Fear not, Freydis. We only wish to do well by you. Come sail with us. We will protect you from your husband's fists."

Easing my back against the wall, I catch sight of a flittering bat that is trapped and agitated as it swoops up high into the longhouse beams where it is dark. Watching it struggle, I release a heavy sigh. Just as I am lowering my head, Logatha leans in closely. Her jaw is set.

"Please come with us," she pleads. "It is the only way to guarantee your safety. In Vinland, Thorvard won't be able to hurt you anymore."

Finnbogi coughs to clear his throat, and I study him through a misty fog that clouds my vision.

"Crying will only drench the problem further and we don't need that," the Icelander says practically as he throws me a gentle smile.

"May the gods bless our *vyking* voyage to the north," Logatha announces as she stands. She uses the bottom of her apron dress to dab her cheeks.

"As I said, I'll need more time to contemplate whether the benefits outweigh the costs," I say, glancing between the two of them.

Finnbogi shakes his head before he downs the remainder of his drink.

"Let's give her time to think," is all he says.

When I retire to bed, the memories of what Thorvard did to me come as fast as a waterfall tumbling over a hillside cliff. I try not to give in to the wall of grief, but I can't manage in my wretchedness. Soon I am moaning like an injured dog and rocking back and forth and stuffing my crumpled shift into my mouth, dreading what Thorvard will do to me, knowing that I can't go back. Then the shivers come as the darkness closes in and suffocates.

In the wee morning hours, my thoughts are a muddled pool of muck, my bones are sore, a headache throbs, and my eyes sting. Logatha and Finnbogi are Icelanders. I would be a fool to trust them. Icelander. Greenlander. It matters not. By Óðinn's beard, I am on borrowed time! Thorvard will come for me. I know the law. It is within his right to take me away from the safety of my brother's farm. Though I try to tell myself that I will be safe, everything feels dark and bleak.

When the sun begins to spill purple light across the eastern sky, I get up and wrap my sealskins around my shoulders, trying to still the shivers and stop the fear. My heart is cracked and bruised and bleeding still, and I feel bone-tired after suffering another restless night. Massaging my neck, I make my way into the dark passageway on the opposite end of the longhouse that leads to the bedchamber where Logatha and Finnbogi are sleeping. It is so dark that I can hardly see.

Thrice I tap at their door, but no one comes. As I wait, I shiver in the chilly air; my shoulders slump forwards and I rub my arms to generate a little warmth. Finally, someone cracks the door.

"Freydis, what do you want at such an early hour?" Finnbogi asks. His voice is still thick with sleep.

"I want you to get up and come outside," I state simply. "I have to talk with you alone."

To my surprise, Finnbogi does as I ask. As we make our way through the snow towards the well, he says nothing. In the frigid air, his breath emits a stream of icy fog-mist.

"I think I'll come with you to Leifsbidur," I finally say as soon as I feel that we are at a safe enough distance away from the longhouse. Finnbogi flicks a glance my way before he stomps his feet to get the blood moving back into his toes. I take another breath of the cold, crisp air. "Please, Finnbogi. Can you speak with my brother and tell him about the arrangement? He will have to give his approval. After all, he is the *goði* of Greenland and I'll need his permission to leave."

"Of course," Finnbogi says in such a gravelly voice that I almost fold.

"I'm scared," I say.

"What you are about to do is wise."

"If Thorvard of Gardar should find out that I am gone..."

"We will leave before he comes for you," he says grimly. He glances at the first rays of morning light piercing through the low-lying fog that hugs the ground. "Tell me, Freydis, why should I be the one to plead your case with Leif the Lucky? Your brother has been good to you, has he not? Surely he will allow you to go abroad if he knows that Thorvard has been abusing you."

A sliver of light splatters Finnbogi in shades of yellow and reddish orange. He shifts his weight and yawns, and I look away. The doubt comes again, and I shudder.

"If Thorvard learns that I have sailed away," I begin, "he will attempt to follow me all the way to Vinland's shores. My brute of a husband loves to live on carrion flesh. He will kill my brother and his goodly wife before sniffing me out with his bloodhound nose. Then, when he finds you, he will punish you for helping me."

"Don't worry so much," Finnbogi sighs.

"He will try to kill you."

Finnbogi's eyes search my face. "Ill-feelings we can all expect."

"I want to bring thirty-five fighting men on board your ship to offer us protection in case Thorvard finds a ship and follows us," I continue in a rush. "I think this might be best. If Thorvard attempts to harm me in a foreign land where there is no *goði* and no Althing to hear my case, my men can battle him with their swords and shields."

"It won't come to that, but I suppose I can agree to what you ask," Finnbogi replies in a measured tone, "if that will set your mind at ease."

"I am grateful, Finnbogi," I whisper. He rubs his eyes with his fist before releasing another tired yawn.

"We must remember Logatha in all of this," he sputters. "I don't want her to worry. She will be concerned if she thinks that we are sailing into an ambush, and she will want to avoid doing battle with a group of Greenlanders."

"Delay speaking to Logatha about me taking my own men," I say quickly.

"Be still, Freydis," Finnbogi reassures. There is kindness in his tired eyes. "Does Logatha not see what you've endured? Is she not wise to Thorvard's ways? Will she not protect you in any way she can? Fear not, good lady. You don't need to warn us about Thorvard and his abusive ways. With Óðinn's help, we can dupe him. You must

162

remember that Logatha and I have hatred of our own. If I know my woman, she would willingly take up her sword and cleave your bastard husband in half, but she would be reluctant to engage a group of his men in battle. She is a peaceful woman who prefers to avoid conflict." His dimple pops. "However, she can't tolerate ill-bred men who harm their wives."

"I worry that Thorvard will do her harm."

"Chopped logic," Finnbogi retorts. "Thorvard would turn on me instead. I know his type."

"How my fingers itch to have Thorvard's throat."

"He has harmed you and I am sorry for that," Finnbogi says as the rooster crows. "If Thorvard so much as touches you again, he will bear the wrath of my ancestral sword. By the gods, I will smite him down. I swear this to you."

"I am thankful for your hatred, Finnbogi," I whisper as I snuff my runny nose with my sleeve.

"Peace! My hatred of your husband has forged this friendship that we share." He gives a little shrug and cracks another dimpled grin as an awkwardness suddenly floats between us like a giant chunk of ocean ice. "With the gods on our side we will sail out with thirty-five of your men on board and thirty of my own as well. Think on it. When I build another ship on Vinland's shores, the extra hands can man the oars."

I push fearful thoughts to the back of my mind and let a wave of gratitude dismiss my doubt. Finnbogi comforts me with his reassurances and escorts me back to the door of the longhouse. As soon as I disappear inside, I tiptoe barefooted across the cold, drafty room to the shrine that I have erected to the gods. After lifting my arms in salutation, I bow my head and set fire to a bundle of herbs before offering words of praise, petitioning the gods to keep me safe. No one is up, and in the silence of the longhouse my mind strays to the Icelanders. I can't help but think that Logatha is lucky to be able to cuddle up next to a good man who protects and honors her, who knows her thoughts and fears, who always considers her wellbeing before his own.

A wave of sadness comes, and I feel my chest heaving as I try to squash a breaking sob. I can't seem to take my power back. I can't seem to regain control. As the envy leaks inside of me, pooling like dark octopus ink, I pinch myself, hating the woman I have become, hating everything about myself.

Chapter Eleven

RAVEN STARVER

As soon as the sun fully rises, Finnbogi comes to find me in the company of his wife and we begin to plan our *vyking* expedition across the northern sea. In addition to needing supplies to restock their ships, the Icelanders hope to use the longhouse that Leif abandoned on Vinland's shores. They want me to talk to Leif. They want to know how to contact the *skraelings* so that they can trade for furs.

I name my price for acting as their spokeswoman. In addition to paying me out in trading goods, I ask to be made the honorary helmsman of the ship and to be given a say in all decisions that are made. To my surprise, the Icelanders agree.

I find my brother in his counting chamber tallying coils of hemp rope. He barely looks up when I approach.

"I have come to ask for your blessing, brother," I begin. A dark shadow passes across my brother's face.

"I am busy, Freydis," he responds in a voice as dry as autumn twigs. "Speak quickly, sister. I have work to do."

He is so grumpy and irritable that for a moment I wonder if Thorgunna is being difficult. They say that his wife is accustomed to being spoiled. Apparently, the best isn't good enough for her here on Greenland's shores.

"Freydis, you vex me when you stare at me like that. Now speak your mind and leave me be."

"I wish to sail with Finnbogi and Logatha on a *vyking* expedition to Vinland. The Icelanders want me to supply the food and to take thirty-five fighting men. In exchange, they agreed to grant us half their trading profits. This arrangement seems fair to me. Faðir would be proud of my attempt to advance our family wealth by exploring a far-off land." I stop abruptly when I see my brother clench his jaw.

"By Óðinn's beard, what are you proposing now?" Leif snaps. "Another expedition to Vinland's shores? With the Icelanders, did I hear you say?" He pushes back his chair and stands up before flicking his hands at me dismissively. "Freydis, this is ill-advised. Just look around. I still haven't traded all the goods I brought back from my last trip there."

I feel my spirits fall. "Indeed, good brother. I see your goods, but please know this: I shall never be satisfied until I am free. Thorvard of Gardar is an abusive man. If I sail away, I can escape his fists."

My brother huffs. Emboldened, I begin to speak in earnest, to tell him how it really is for me, to tell him that Thorvard hits me hard, that he belittles me, that he shames me openly in front of all his thralls. I cannot stop the waterfall of words that tumble out, the gush of feeling, the spray of anger mixed in with fear.

"As long as my husband lives, he will try to usurp my

lands and squeeze us out of the most profitable deals," I snarl. I think of all the injustice that I have faced, and my anger sparks like a piece of flint. "By the gods, don't you see that Thorvard must be stopped? If he obtains more trading goods, he'll overpower you politically. You'll lose your place and your influence. Already Thorvard has duped our clansmen. Many see him as worthy of the highest Althing seat."

"Come again?" Leif interjects. His face turns purple. His eyes grow cold. "What nonsense do you speak of now?"

"As long as my husband, the villain, lives," I say, "he will try to make you pay a price for harboring me all winter long. You outsmarted him, brother. He will seek revenge. Only the gods know what his fists will do to your fine-bridged nose. As for me, I'm sure he'll break my jaw. I might even lose a tooth."

"Come now, Freydis," Leif says dismissively.

"Brother, please be reasonable. Thorvard is an evil man. He marks his territory like a dog and slithers into the best positions like a snake. Watch him carefully or he will rob you of the *goði* title you so well deserve. Think on it. This land is ours. Faðir was the first to settle it. He built a colony here in Greenland. Thorvard wants to rule these shores, but he doesn't deserve to take over. He has no blood ties."

"He'll never convince the clan that he is the best man to rule Greenland," Leif fumes. "No one will grant him the *goði* title."

"Paw! Thorvard played his *goði* games while you were away. He will do the same thing now. He will find a way. As for me, I must sail away on that *vyking* expedition bound for

Leifsbidur. If I don't, Thorvard will find me, and then I am dead."

"You have thought this through, I see."

"I have," I say.

"Watch yourself, sister. Making business deals with Icelanders is ill-advised. They will cheat us out of everything." Leif steeples his index fingers together and touches the tips to his lips.

"Finnbogi and Helgi are not like that," I say, my exasperation striking like a thunderbolt.

"Why has Finnbogi not come to me directly then?"

"Finnbogi and I agreed that I should come to see you on my own," I say defensively. Leif grunts in disbelief. "Good brother, I beseech you on bended knees, please, let me go. Faðir would want us to continue exploring the northern passages in his name."

As the sunrays creep towards us through the open door, Leif turns away. I know he will agree to let me go, but he bides his time to make me squirm. It is his way of reminding me that he is in charge.

"This is not a ploy to get you out of your marriage contract, is it, Freydis?"

"Dear brother, it is deception of a sort," I reply. "Long ago when I had the chance, I should have slaughtered Thorvard in his bed."

My brother lifts his brow. "Calm yourself," he says tiredly.

"I won't!" I yell, slapping my hand down on his counting desk with such force that the legs wobble from the jolt. "Thorvard has dishonored us. You should be challenging him to a duel. I never thought of you as a raven starver. What happened to you, brother?"

For a moment Leif just looks at me. "I see what he has done to you."

"You bastard," I seethe. "Just look at all my battle scars." I lift my hair, but as I go to roll up my sleeve, he stops me with an outstretched hand.

"I've seen enough."

"If you make me return to him, he will kill me, brother," I say, choking back my tears. Our eyes connect.

"What reason should I give for your disappearance?"

"Tell him that I orchestrated my own escape or that I died of sickness in my bed. Truly, it makes no difference what you say, just be sure to let him know that I'll never return to Greenland." I lift my chin and gather strength and let my armour fall into place. "I should never have been married off to him."

"Hold your tongue," Leif chastises.

"May the gods curse his bones."

"Freydis, you'll hex your voyage to the north and find yourself lying at the bottom of the sea in Rán's watery underworld with a piece of seaweed wrapped around your neck."

"Can I not speak freely in my *faðir's* house?" I ask, jabbing my finger at his chest. "Finnbogi is an Icelander who has provided me with an honorable way to end this abusive marriage that I've endured. He has been more helpful to me than you in my time of need. How pitiful. Truly, brother, I expected more from you."

"Then go," my brother spits.

"I need the keys to the longhouses you left behind on Vinland's shores if I intend to make Leifsbidur my new home."

"I left nothing behind of value in Leifsbidur," my brother snarls. "The door to the longhouse was left unlocked." He pauses to take a gulp of air. "I will lend the longhouses to you to winter in, but I will not give them to you outright."

"Why not?" I ask.

"I may go back," he says as he drums his fingers on his counting desk. Then he glances up. "Freydis, go in peace, but when you send the ships back, I'll expect to see the holds full of trading goods with my share of the profits."

I give a little nod, and in the silence, I hear someone shouting in the yard. Just as I am about to turn and take my leave, Leif clears his throat.

"Be mindful of the *skraelings* with their red faces," he says, blinking. "They love red so much that they'd slaughter you just to get your hair."

"I thought you said they were good to trade with and that they know their furs."

"I did," he says, "but I also said that we didn't seek them out. They came to us. In any case, I would advise you to be wary. The Red Men are stealthy on their feet, and they can easily intimidate. Truly, I tell you, don't take any risks and never let yourself be in their company alone. If you offer sacrifices to the gods for protection, I'll do the same."

"I'll heed your words."

Leif's face looks grim. "Tread lightly, sister. The ice is thin where you dare to walk."

"The ice is melting at this time of year, and I have a ship," I say.

Leif rakes his eyes across my face. "I anticipate that Thorvard will return before the next new moon comes. Until then you must hide yourself on Thorkel's farm. Be prepared to move if I send word."

"Don't tell Thorvard where I am," I beg. There is a churning in my gut.

"Rest assured, if Thorvard comes, I'll distract him by taking him to my seer. She came to me from the northern regions and Thorvard will be amused by her. She wears a string of glass beads on her head and a hood of black lambskin lined in white bear fur with fine gemstone charms that she uses to render predictions for her guests. I'll instruct her to survey Thorvard's flock and to inspect his horse. Then I'll ask her to perform a seeing so that he can learn about the future of his farm. Her attention should buy you time to get away on Finnbogi's ship."

"You are too good to me," I say, trying to sound grateful instead of harboring bitter feelings and resentful thoughts. I used to think that my brother cared. Now I am not so sure. His mercenary leanings have always guided the decisions he makes and I worry that I am just a pawn.

"Get thee gone, Freydis," my brother finally mutters as he absentmindedly blesses me without looking up: "May Thor's hammer keep you safe. May you find a way to return to Greenland's shores without being hunted by an abusive man. May you become a legendary woman of wealthy means whose name lives on throughout all time."

"Do you mean it, brother?"

Leif toys with a silver piece. "Just move yourself to Thorkel's farm," he says. "I'll send Alf to tell the farmer and his wife to expect you."

"I am obliged," I say, but when I take my leave of him, I do not fall into his arms like I was prone to do in a different life. Sentiment is no longer helpful in this place where nostalgia only serves to trip me up.

It takes one full day to travel to Thorkel's farm. When I arrive, I am introduced to Helgi, Finnbogi's brother, and another helmsman, a short, burly *vyking* by the name of Ulf. A few days later, the men collect their crew and return to their longboats in Eiriksfjord. There they begin to refit the ships. Logatha and I stay behind on Thorkel's farm, preparing for the *vyking* journey across the northern seas.

We are busy. I send Alf back and forth with messages for my brother, and Leif responds by sending me thirty-five men who are loyal to my family's house. I send them off to help Finnbogi prepare the ships after placing two men in charge. Gunnar is a Greenlander with a barrelled chest, and Snorri is a stocky sea dog with a tremendous build who is known for taking foolhardy risks. Leif also sends sheep and goats and chickens to add to the livestock the Icelanders already have. There also are barrels full of dried food and gear: weapons, tools, barley, flax, and iron pots. Logatha and I pack up all the supplies and trading goods, including baskets full of carded wool.

We all live peacefully for two whole weeks. One day,

Logatha and I are sitting in the yard milking goats when I feel a shiver running down my back. "When do you think we'll leave?" I ask, glancing at the melting snow in the meadowlands.

"Finnbogi says we shouldn't wait. He thinks the longboats can make it out of Eiriksfjord even though there is still ice floating in the fjord. He worries that Thorvard could come for you at any time."

A sudden gust of wind whips my hair into my face. "I am ready and packed," is all I say. I picture Thorvard riding hard from Brattahlíð, his anger fuelling a fanatical desire to hunt me down. In the distance, I hear the nesting birds and the water dripping from the longhouse roof. Each drop is the sound of doom, a tinkle of terror that freezes bones. Drawing in air, I reach for the knife stashed inside my boot as the fear coils around my chest.

"We must leave today," I whisper frantically. "I have this feeling in my gut."

Logatha fumbles with her furs. "I'll go and see where the ships are at," she tells me solemnly as a crow begins cawing noisily somewhere behind us in the yard. "For now, you must stay out of sight in case Thorvard and his riders come."

I shoot her a worried look. "What will I do if I see Thorkel's wife?"

"Tell her you are feeling ill."

"She will insist on staying with me."

"Be strong," she whispers with a worried smile.

As soon as Logatha leaves, I make my way to the farmer's hut, a small lodging hewn into a hill. As soon as I

173

push the heavy door open, I jump. The farmer's wife grins at me.

"Prithee, you'll catch cold in this chilly air," she says as she clucks her tongue and wags her finger in my clammy face. "Didn't I chastise you when you last went out without your furs?" I watch her bustling around the cramped earthen room as she fetches me a mug of tea.

"I'll rest in here," is all I say, feeling lucky that my voice sounds hoarse. Her wide girth bumps into me as I squeeze behind her to let her pass.

"I must go and grind some herbs to stir into the soup," she mutters underneath her breath.

To quell my rising panic, I sit down to spin some yarn, but I am so agitated that I can barely focus as I draft. A short while later, the farmer's wife leaves the hut and the silence settles, thick like dust. Very soon I get lost in the monotony of pinching and pulling the dull-colored strands in a slow and lazy rhythm as I listen to the world outside.

In the yard, the farmer's wife begins to sing as the wind picks up. Soon a cold draft is slithering underneath the door. Sitting there, I wish that a heavy rain would come and flood the land so that the boggy patches that line the mountain tarns between here and Gardar would flood. Perhaps I should offer Loki sacrifice. There again, if Thorvard has already made it through the barren, craggy peaks or to the trail lined with arctic willow and low-lying vegetation, I hope his horse falls and breaks its leg.

My impulse is to carve a stave. If I only had a dram of seal blood, I could make an inscription on some horse's skull and recite a verse to curse my husband and his men.

The wind rattles the door, howling. Every fibre of my being commands me to run, but I am anchored to my seat. With shaky hands, I pick up a small wooden figure of Óðinn that Thorkel's wife keeps on a shelf.

Please, Óðinn.

The ship needs to be ready. I need to leave for Vinland before my husband comes in search of me.

Chapter Twelve

THE SWIRL OF HOURGLASS SAND

Late in the afternoon, just as I am winding a final bit of yarn onto the shaft, I hear horses galloping into the yard. The thunderous, clattering noise shakes the mugs and chargers stacked in rows on the open shelves, and I brace myself, cocking my ear to better hear. When I catch the sound of his voice, my fingers freeze and my knees lock together.

Ivor.

He has come for me.

In a dizzy haze I drop the spindle. The whorl falls heavily to the ground as I scan the room to see where I can hide.

"Good woman, I am looking for Leif the Lucky's sister, Freydis of Brattahlíð? Have you seen her pass this way?"

I hold my breath. There are beads of perspiration dripping down my brow. My legs seem melded into the dirt-packed floor. The jingle of Ivor's heavy sword grows louder as he moves towards the door.

With mounting panic, I will myself not to faint. My muscles are as jittery as a flapping fish fighting to live on land.

"Freydis! Freydis?" Ivor calls. His gruff baritone brings back memories of the grappling drills he put me through.

My stomach clenches. My throat chokes up.

"She should be inside the hut," Thorkel's wife says loudly. I feel a jolt of fear jabbing its way into my heart and igniting my muscles, screaming at me to move. Someone lifts the squeaky latch, and my rib cages dives down low before rising like a rolling wave. An instant later I find myself squeezing into the dark recess behind the heavy wooden door, quickly manoeuvring myself into place.

Beside me I spot a woodcutter's axe hanging on an iron hook anchored into the earthen wall. I can't quite reach it. Instead, I lean down and retrieve my hidden hunting knife from my boot, brandishing it when I hear his voice again. With shaking hands, I wait for the door to open as I flatten myself further against the wall.

Thorkel's wife is the first to enter the musty room. As she steps inside, the smell of mutton roasting on a spit drifts inside.

"Freydis?" she calls as she looks around.

The panic swells. There is a moving tide of fear, a pounding surf inside my chest. Glancing up, I spot a tiny spider spinning an intricate web in the rafters. Its tiny body is illuminated by a shaft of light streaming through the open door.

"Freydis?" she calls again. Through the cracks, I catch a glimpse of the woman's chesty form, her distorted shadow spilling across the earthen floor. "Freydis was here a short time ago. She said she wasn't feeling well. Perhaps she left to get some air."

From my hiding spot I can clearly see Ivor's face. He has aged since I saw him last.

"Freydis?" Ivor barks in a biting tone. I hold my breath. The farmer's wife turns. There is a hair growing out of an unsightly mole on her chin.

"You could always ask the Icelanders who are working hard to prepare their longboats to go *a vyking* if they saw her. Freydis intends to sail with them across the northern seas as soon as the ice breaks up."

Ferreting into the shadows, I feel my hands begin to shake. White-knuckled, I squeeze my knife hilt hard.

"Did you say that Freydis Eiriksdöttir is soon to be leaving Greenland?" Ivor asks.

With my free hand, I wedge my fingernails into my palms. The only barrier that separates me from him is the heavy door.

"*Já*, good man! They say that Freydis is in charge of things."

"In charge of things?" Ivor's voice barrels low. "Does her brother know that she intends to lead a *vyking* expedition west of here?"

"The *goði* of Greenland? He has given his blessing. He told Freydis to go to Leifsbidur to check on the longhouse he had built. He also instructed her to bring back wood." The farmer's wife is panting heavily from the walk. Her large bosom heaves higher and higher as she draws in air.

"I'm certain you have got it wrong," Ivor says like an

annoying gnat. "It makes more sense that Leif the Lucky would strike a trading deal with the Icelanders who are Vinland bound. Surely he would not allow his sister to leave these shores without her husband's permission?"

Thorkel's wife is silent for a moment. "I am a simpleton," she eventually sighs in a worried voice. I close my eyes and will her not to say anymore, but she continues talking, blabbering like an idiot. When Ivor asks if she knows our plans, she tells him that we want to leave within the week.

I tilt my head back and see a beam of light skipping across one of the ceiling planks. Oh gods! I wish I had a powerful inscription to make me into something small. If I faint, the ruse is up.

An instant later, the shadows shift and Ivor fully steps inside. His silhouette claws its way up the wall and my heart becomes a booming drum where I feel the pounding in my ears. Then my body starts to sway, and I raise my knife and feel the weight of it shifting in my sweaty palm.

Just as Ivor is about to look behind the door, Thorkel's wife reaches out and grabs his arm. "She isn't here," she mutters impatiently.

Ivor swears.

I am so relieved that a fat, round tear spills down my cheek. Thorkel's wife pulls on Ivor to drag him out the door. As the two of them are shuffling past, I catch a whiff of Ivor's body odour, his musky scent.

They move into the yard, and as soon as Ivor leaps over a pool of mud, he turns and gazes back through the open door. With a sudden jolt, I pull my body back, breathing hard. My vision wavers, and I need to brace myself against the wall.

Squeezing my eyes tightly shut, I imagine Thorvard coming for me and pulling me towards his waiting horse and forcing me to ride with him. Then I hear his judgmental tone, his biting, threatening words, the irritation in his voice. Even my legs feel weak. Outside, Ivor's baritone fades then flares in with the wailing wind.

"The ships are anchored in the inlet behind that second ridge," Thorkel's wife announces before I can even catch my breath.

"If you see Freydis, tell her that her husband needs to speak with her," Ivor says. He mounts his horse and my knees buckle.

A moment later Ivor's horse gallops off. Immediately, another wave of strong emotion swells. Leif hasn't sent word that Thorvard is combing the area in search of me. He should have sent word, and he did not, and now I don't know what to do.

My thoughts begin to swirl like hourglass sand. Should I stay indoors or try to make it to another farm? Should I run? By Óðinn's beard, I yearn to have Logatha by my side. She would know, and she would help. Chewing my lip, I find myself absentmindedly picking at a scab until it begins to bleed. The red of it reminds me of all my scars, of all the pain, of my bastard husband, of my brokenness.

Outside, the cows are baying loudly. It is milking time. Thorkel's wife must be feeding the pecking chickens and turkeys in the yard with her clucks and incessant chatter. I'm sick of her.

When the shepherd boys return for dinner with the bleating sheep in tow, I have worn a rut in the earthen floor, dragging worry behind me like a ballast rock. Just then, Thorkel's wife rings the dinner bell. The repetitive jingle puts me in such a dizzy trance that I almost miss hearing the patter of feet scampering quickly down the path.

Without warning, the latch rattles and the heavy door swings slowly open, creaking as it scrapes across the warped boards of the lintel. I barely have time to tuck myself into my hiding place.

"Freydis?" Logatha calls. When she spots me hiding behind the door, she looks at me strangely. "Thank the gods that you are safe. We thought he came for you!"

I see the worry lines dotting her oily brow. Slowly, I crawl out of my hiding spot. "I'm safe for now, but Thorvard knows our plan. Thorkel's wife told him about our intention to sail the northern seas. Tomorrow he will come for me."

"Tomorrow is a long way off," Logatha blurts. "Finnbogi is dealing with Thorkel's wife even now as we speak." She swipes her face with the corner of her tattered sleeve. "My husband is making that stupid woman believe that you ran off without telling anyone. He said that you went to collect some trading goods from Gudrid's *faðir's* farm across the water from Brattahlíð."

I glance at her. "Thorvard will find me. I'm sure of it."

"Come with me," Logatha says, taking charge. "Throw on your heaviest cloak and take the personal items you have packed. We will sneak you out behind the byre and move you to our waiting ships. Hopefully the *goði* of

Greenland – your trusted brother – will know what to say to throw Thorvard off."

"What if Thorvard finds me before we can get away?"

She clucks her tongue. "Thorvard will not succeed in capturing you." She leans down to retrieve a heavy pack and groans under the weight of it as she lifts it over her shoulder.

"Make haste, my friend," she says as her voice eddies into a grunt. "Take your sword and shield and have at the ready your hunting knife in case we have to fight."

I follow Logatha into the empty yard, where it is uncannily quiet now that it is supper time. The two of us straddle the fence behind the byre, but once over, I linger briefly to re-tie the leather thongs on my boot. With a vicious hiss, Logatha urges me to hurry up.

Eventually we reach the beach where two lone *vyking* longboats are bobbing gently in the cresting waves. There is a large, wide-bodied *knörr* anchored further out.

"Freydis, it is best that you stay onboard our ship tonight," Logatha advises, breathing hard. Behind us, I see a string of footprints zigzagging through the sand. "I should only stay for a little while. I'll get you settled on the ship, but then I must leave to pack. Finnbogi and Helgi do not even know that I found you in Thorkel's hut. They are worried sick about you. When I tell them that you are safe, they will be relieved."

I stare into her sober face. She looks fatigued with her raccoon eyes. Even though I am afraid, I don't want her to worry about me anymore. I've been enough of a burden to her already.

"All of us will return at dawn," Logatha murmurs as she grabs my hand and pulls me forth. "If the weather holds, we will leave at the break of dawn."

I nod. Logatha clucks her tongue like a mother hen when she sees my face.

"Be still, my friend. Already you have beaten the odds. You duped your husband and got away. I am confident that you will fool him again when tomorrow comes."

"What if Thorvard comes for me and you aren't here?"

"I doubt he will come tonight."

"I'll be too exposed!"

Logatha reaches out and pulls me into a warm embrace. "Don't worry until a good reason presents itself."

I shiver and half-tune her out. She has not lived through what I've endured. She has not felt Thorvard's hands around her neck.

In my line of vision, I see the sandpipers on the beach using their long, straight beaks to go in search of food. They remind me that I am not alone. Tonight, I will have the seabirds to comfort me if I am afraid. I will have the fish that swim below me in the sea. I will have my talisman.

Oh gods! What if that vicious wolf attacks me in the dead of night?

I shudder like a shedding tree. Logatha stops talking. Her head snaps up. "Tomorrow morning when we sail for Vinland's shores, you will be free," she says.

I nod, listening to the creaking mast, the shrieking birds, the lapping of the gentle waves against the strakes.

That night when the twinkling stars emerge – those tiny pricks of light that gaze down like living eyes – I crawl beneath my hide coverings and draw the furs around my face. On the open decks, it is chilly. My breath hangs suspended above my head. Shivering, I try to find a comfortable position, but sleep eludes me, and I can't stop shaking. Eventually I get up, gather all my weapons, and place them next to me in case there is need. Even so, it takes some time for me to fall into a restless sleep.

In the dead of night, I bolt awake when I hear a thump. In the shadows, all is still. The longboat shivers, and I reluctantly extract myself from my bed of furs, moving silently across the deck, checking to see if I am alone. Just as I am making my final sweep, I look across the sea and see an eerie glow – a burst of light in iridescent rainbow hues. The swirling pools of greenish-blues and purples create dazzling patterns that dance underneath the glassy surface in twinkling sparkles that mesmerize.

It is as if the ocean is celebrating, exploding in whispered shimmers, proclaiming that I am soon to have a different life.

Shivering awake at the break of dawn, I yawn and push strands of frizzy red hair out of my face as I listen to the wind slamming waves against the prow. In my haste to leave Thorkel's farm, I forgot to bring Mother's comb, an ornately carved treasure made from antler bone. It used to mean so much to me and now all I want is to be rid of it, to find a different life – a life of peace.

In the distance, I hear voices. Men's voices. Springing up, I scan the shoreline before my eyes flit across the rocky ridges that surround the bay. Seeing nothing, I snag a breath and then let it out, but the voices grow louder. When I realize that there are men directly underneath the ship,, I glance around as my stomach drops and my heart begins to thunk. I can feel it pounding heavily in my neck.

I hear a shout, a gruff male voice. In an instant, I am scrambling to mould myself against a pile of furs.

The voices of heckling men and the jingle of a rattling cart make me paw the hides apart. Squinting, I can just make out a group of familiar-looking Norsemen carrying packs and shields and swords and spears with axes hanging from their leather belts.

The icy wind whistles past my ears, whipping my unruly red hair into my face as I clamber out of my hiding spot, panting heavily. It has taken months to plot a course to freedom. It could take only moments to lose it if my husband finds me here.

He won't now that they have come for me.

Savoring the moment, I scan the seashore, and my heart skips a beat and then slowly settles when all I see is a group of Icelanders wandering down the beach. No one is hiding amongst the rocks. No horse is galloping down the vast stretch of sedge meadows full of tundra browns and saxifrage purples and lichen-covered mossy greens. Truly, I have managed to escape.

Even the screeching wind cheers for me.

Chapter Thirteen

WATER MELDING INTO SKY

I t seems to take forever to load the ship. The animals are agitated and the men have difficulty hoisting the barrels full of salted meat, which causes Finnbogi to curse and yell. Even Logatha loses patience with a thrall. The poor woman hangs her head as she pulls on the tether of a stubborn cow. Asta, Groa, and Grelod, the three other women who will take the journey across the sea, call up to me, and I wave to them. The relief I feel is palpable.

By midday it is hot and sunny and impatience licks my weary bones as I watch the oarsmen crawl into place.

"We will follow Eiriksfjord out to the open sea," Finnbogi says. "Somewhere further up the coast, we will tuck the longboats into a more northern bay and wait it out while the ice clears up and summer comes. I pray to Loki that this plan will work. The trickster god is fickle and he revels in plotting against the honorable."

"There is no need to worry. I am in league with Óðinn,"

I say quickly. "I have pledged myself loyal and I trust that he will be the architect of my victory."

Finnbogi shoots me a tired smile.

"My husband has pledged to fight a duel against Thorvard if he should come for you," Logatha says, her voice chipped and slivered. "Finnbogi will make Thorvard cower in fear like a pale man forced to bite his shield rim. Finnbogi's spear will be dewed in blood. Now, still your heart. I know my husband to be a feeder of wolves."

Finnbogi throws another mischievous smile. "The duel would be fun enough, but I would much prefer to sail away so that you can find your peace," he says as he makes his way to the helm and gives the orders to set sail.

We have just nicely lifted the wadmal sail when we see a group of riders racing their steeds over the ridge of hills that line the bank. Thorvard's black stallion is in the lead. Without hesitating, I lodge myself between sacs and crates and animal pens where the stink is bad. A moment later, I hear Thorvard's men hollering at us, their voices echoing in the wind.

"Lower yourself further or he will see," Logatha hisses in my ear. My legs are cramped and squished, but I slither down so that my face is flush against that of a hairy-chinned goat and my hips are pressed tightly against a sack of grain. On my right, Groa leans forwards to cover me with another heavy fur. I am stifling hot, but I dare not move. Our *vyking* longboat creaks and groans before lunging forwards in the wind.

Suddenly, Thorvard's booming voice rips through the

air and mixes in with the sound of the screeching gulls. "Hail, Finnbogi of Iceland!"

"Stay still," Groa warns as Thorvard's voice comes to us in wind shouts.

"I hear that you are departing for Vinland's shores. Why leave before the ice is gone?"

The longboat surges forwards and the livestock pens half drag me across the deck. When all calms down, the only thing I hear is the water thumping against the strakes.

"Heave ho! Heave ho!" Finnbogi mutters desperately to the oarsmen.

From the shore Thorvard shouts again: "I am looking for my wife, Freydis Eiriksdöttir – Freydis of Brattahlíð."

"She is not with me," Finnbogi replies. His booming voice shudders the air as he leans over me.

"Is that Helgi's longboat I see? Perhaps your brother…?"

There is another surge of wind. Amidst the flapping sails, the shifting cargo, the crying gulls, and the baby goat bleating loudly in my ear, I lose some of the exchange. When I turn my face to better hear, a rough tongue tries to lick my face. Jiggling myself away from the ewe, I jump when I hear my name.

"Freydis isn't here, man! *Neinn*, she isn't on this ship," Finnbogi shouts in a baritone voice that slaps the air. A moment later, the longboat pitches forwards and I am thrown into the furthest corner where I narrowly avoid getting hit by sliding crates.

"*Far vel!* I wish you well. Travel safely, my good men." Thorvard's voice trails off. Beside me Logatha releases a heavy sigh, but Groa groans. Finnbogi cautions me not to move.

"Heave away!" he orders the oarsmen from somewhere high above my head. "The wind is picking up even more. You lot, there! Get ready to hoist the final sail!"

There is chaos and movement on the deck. Still I keep my head down low. My body is hidden amidst furs and barrels, crates and pens.

"Even now, Thorvard continues to run his horse up and down the beach. He is tracking the direction in which we sail," Groa announces as she makes her way over, trying to find her sea legs.

"Freydis, what do you want to do?" Finnbogi asks. He sounds annoyed as his words float down to where I am lying on the deck. Tentatively I lower the hide that covers my face to gulp in the cold, fresh air.

"Cover up! Don't be a fool," Groa orders. Glancing up, I see her panicked face.

"I can hardly breathe," I moan. Finnbogi shoots me a warning look.

"You're not safe yet," Logatha says, glancing down. From this angle, it looks as though she is a giantess. The seagulls swarm around her head.

"Considering that Thorvard is tracking us, we can't turn the longboats around and follow Ulf out to where we planned to meet," Finnbogi announces as he shields his eyes and looks out to sea.

"By Óðinn's missing eye, it is still too risky at this time of year. There is too much ice," Logatha frets. I catch a glimpse of Finnbogi scratching his neck as he scans the shore.

"If we hug the coast like Ulf's ship does, Thorvard will surely follow us," Gunnar, my most loyal Greenlander, says. He has the voice of a foghorn and a thick tree-trunk shadow.

"In truth, we have no choice but to follow Eiriksfjord directly out to sea instead of following Ulf," Finnbogi says as he chews his whiskered cheeks. "We can set down anchor before we hit open water, if need be. I'll send a runner ashore tonight to send word to Leif to track down Ulf. Someone needs to inform him of our change of plans."

"Finding Ulf will be very hard if we don't track his course," I say. My stomach is already sick from the rocking ship, and it seems as though I've pulled a muscle in my back.

"If the gods are on our side, we will be able to sail far up the coast and then head into shore where we can regroup. Hopefully Ulf will receive my message and find our ships."

I feel helpless as I stare up into the clear blue sky. Finnbogi is a practical man. It is his gift. I do not know him very well, but I sense that he will rely on no one but himself to safely navigate a route out to sea. Just then, the last wadmal sail flaps open in a sudden gust of wind, and I spot the great auk soaring high. Its presence is a good omen.

By suppertime my insides roll. I succumb to seasickness as the longboat rides the waves before dropping down into the rolling sea. Despite my queasiness, I revel in the fact that Thorvard of Gardar can't touch me anymore. There is no more panic, no more fear.

With a sudden surge of unbridled joy, I lift my face and drink in the air, listening to the poetry of the waves and allowing my spirit to sense the thumping of the war-god's heart, knowing that this is the beginning of a brand-new life. This oaken craft will take me to a distant shore. There has been no clashing of swords plinking off the edges of battle shields, no need to feed flesh to wolves. Thoughts of Faðir flint into flames.

He would be pleased to know that his only *döttir* is Vinland bound.

Part Two

SHE STOLE IT BACK

Part Two

SHE STOLE IT BACK

Chapter Fourteen

THE ENDLESS BLUE OF IT

In the days that follow, my stomach learns to tolerate the pitching waves, creaming as they stir up a frothy foam. The weather turns warmer and the ice breaks up into floating pans that allow for safe passage up the fjords. Each night the oarsmen take us into shore where we sit around a fire eating roasted fish or game depending on what the crew can catch. Despite the uncertainty that lies ahead, there is a feeling of carefree living that lifts my spirits and banishes the worries from my head.

The Greenlanders speak highly of Faðir. Pledging fealty to my house, they promise to protect me because I am an Eiriksson. I am profoundly thankful, but I refuse to tell them what truly motivates me to leave Greenland's shores. Memories of the abuse I endured at Thorvard's hands and his veiled threats are like shards of ice that pierce my heart and cut off air. Even now, I will not defame his name to the Icelanders. *Neinn.* I don't dare.

One night after we have set up camp on a patch of

tundra carpeted by wild flowers overlooking a stretch of sea where the migrating birds are nesting on the backs of a pod of humpback whales, I invite some of the men from Finnbogi's crew to spar with me. I use my shield in a quick succession of defensive moves and the rowdy men begin to cheer. Afterwards Logatha takes me aside.

"Energetic, feisty women who know how to fight can easily arouse the men. Sparring with them is ill-advised," she tells me with a heavy sigh. When I see her worried face, I heed her words and withdraw from everyone.

When we reach the western settlement of Lysufjord, we go ashore and visit the fishermen. We tell them all about our plan to travel in a northwesterly direction to Vinland. They caution us about the whereabouts of the heavy ice floes and candidly warn us to avoid the *skraelings* at all costs.

"Leif told me something similar," is all I say. "I am not afraid to meet up with the Red Men, but I understand the need to be wary."

After one moon cycle has come and gone, our impatience builds. Ulf and his crew are still missing and they have not sent word. Finnbogi and Helgi begin to wonder if Ulf misunderstood the message and set sail for Vinland's shores without waiting for our ship. One night, as we are lounging around an outdoor fire that emits little warmth, Logatha and Finnbogi begin talking earnestly about what we should do.

"Summer is passing," Finnbogi says as he untangles himself from his wife's embrace. He sits up tall and stretches out his muscled legs as I poke the fire with my roasting stick. "We've waited long enough for Ulf's ship to come. It may be best to collect our things and leave this place so that we arrive in Leifsbidur in time to prepare for winter."

Logatha inches closer to Finnbogi so that she can lean her head against his shoulder. I watch their display of tenderness through the hazy campfire smoke that snakes into the sky, trying to touch the midnight sun.

"What say you, Freydis? Should we continue on to Vinland without Ulf?" Finnbogi asks. I stare into the blazing fire that pops and sizzles and throws out sparks.

"It seems strange that he has been delayed so long."

"That scoundrel abandoned us," Logatha laughs uneasily.

"I hate the thought that Ulf's ship may be lost," I sigh. For a moment Finnbogi is silent as he fingers Logatha's fine-boned hand.

"I'll tell the others that the wait is done. Tomorrow will be our last day here on Greenland's shores." He looks troubled by the decision, as if he is loath to think about abandoning his people and making the wrong choice.

After he leaves, Logatha and I sit around the fire and talk some more about the missing helmsman, about our fate, about all the comforts we so desperately miss. Despite the fire, the bugs are bad. A mosquito lands on me and I swat at it. When I look down, there is a streak of blood smeared across my palm. In the silence, the fire crackles and pops as Logatha adjusts her furs. Her face is a rosy glow in the firelight.

"I am with child," she murmurs softly. I am so pleased for her that my throat chokes up. Immediately I think of carving a protection rune for her on a whalebone I saw sitting on the beach.

"Does Finnbogi know?" I manage with a smile. She nods her head. Unexpectedly, my eyes begin to tear and she reaches out to grab my hand. I squeeze it and feel her callouses.

"These are early days, but we are blessed. Praise Freyja, the Great Mother, the Giving One! I never thought this day would come. Oh, Freydis, how I hope for a boy to carry on Finnbogi's name."

"Finnbogi would like that very much," I say with another wobbly smile, thinking back to when I myself was thick with child. I remember the kicks, the swollen nipples, the bone-wrenching pain. In the end I had nothing but scars from Thorvard's fists.

Logatha gently brings me back. She asks me questions about giving birth. I tell her how it was for me. I walk her through the long months ahead: the surprises, the hardships, and the pain.

We talk like squawking geese, gobbling up each other's story threads, until it grows late and the midnight sun sinks into the western sky. When the fire starts fizzling out, I gaze out across the glassy sea, grateful that the gods have brought us together, amazed that an Icelander and a Greenlander have been forged into friends.

～

In the morning, the sun skips across the water, twinkling brightly in the cool breeze. Finnbogi and Helgi instruct their oarsmen to row us out to open waters, and Greenland fades into a misty haze of rocky outcrops, bleak mountain peaks, and glacier fjords. At first the bobbing of the ship is tolerable, but after endless hours of seeing nothing but greyish-blue water melding into the flat blue skies, I grow bored.

For days we travel in favorable winds before catching sight of land. As the seagulls circle around the mast, the crew cheers wildly and I allow myself a crooked smile. There are hundreds of seabirds soaring over cliffs silhouetted black against the setting sun, a hazy orange-red orb reflected in the glassy sea. Finnbogi advises that we set down anchor for the night just offshore to avoid having to navigate the rocks when the crew is tired.

That night I dream of red-faced *skraelings* capturing and burning me alive. I watch them eating my roasted flesh and crunching on my brittle bones, smiling at me with Thorvard's face. I wake gasping. My throat is parched and my back is drenched in sweat. In the dim light cast from the rising sun yawning hazy shades of purplish pink along the horizon, I study the silhouetted forms of the sleeping Norsemen sprawled across the deck. Olaf Goðthjælpsen, the blacksmith, is keeping watch with his back to me. Ignoring him, I breathe in the smell of the ocean air to clear my head.

Just as I am stretching widely to unkink the muscles in my legs, I hear an ethereal noise: a puff of air that bounces melodically across the sea followed by another bloated whoof that quickly fades into the quiet. Standing, I see nothing but an endless stretch of blue in the black pre-dawn light until I move to the gunwales and peer overboard. The ocean is so calm that I can see my reflection shimmying. For a long time, I stand peering across the water waiting to hear another swish of air. By the time it comes, the others are stirring.

"Look, o'er yonder," Logatha whispers. I see nothing. A moment later she points to a patch of sea that sparkles in the rising sun.

"We are in whale feeding grounds," I murmur breathlessly. Unknowingly, Olaf steps in front of me and blocks my view just as two of the gentle giants pop up to feed on krill. I wiggle underneath his arm and see them slip beneath the depths with their tails flicking water and curving gracefully, as if waving, right before they dive down deep.

"They are so near to land," Finnbogi mumbles from the helm.

Again, we hear a deep, drawn-out puff of air that quickly fades into silence. It is so strange and mysterious that a shiver runs through me. A host of gods must be orchestrating this ocean concert for the mermaids and the selkies. Wildly I look around, searching for those seals in the water that can take on a human form, but I see nothing – just the water, the endless blue of it.

"Not even the best cowhorn player can puff out air like that," Logatha sighs as she comes up behind me and hooks herself into my arm for warmth. Silently we watch the whales pass by our ship. Their barnacled backs rise gracefully out of the water before they slip into the depths.

When the sun finally breaks over the horizon, Finnbogi orders the crew to raise the anchor. It is a highly valued iron-bound wooden shank brought from Iceland with two large rings to accommodate the cable lines. Just as Birger tries to lift it up, one of the lines breaks and the anchor drops.

"You incompetent, short-witted fool!" Finnbogi yells.

Birger struggles to hold onto the one good line, but his eyebrows arch and his eyes grow wide.

"Turkeys have more brains than you," Finnbogi spits as he pushes past a group of stunned Norseman so that he can get to Birger. His tone commands authority and I pull back instinctively. Amidst the commotion on the deck, my eyes find Logatha. Her face is white.

"Swine's piss! Pull it up!" Finnbogi continues in a rage. "Call on Thor for strength and use your muscles, man! Haul it up before the anchor sinks!"

"If we yank on it, the remaining line will snap," some lippy sailor shouts over many heads. Finnbogi's face turns wild.

"Are you blind as bats? We need that anchor back right now, you flittering moths. If that anchor sinks, it will be lost forever in Njörd's underworld. By Óðinn's beard, I won't allow any sea god to rob me of that iron treasure. I need a volunteer to dive down deep and figure out where the line is snagged."

Logatha reaches for her husband's arm but Finnbogi shrugs her off. His gesture guts me, and I am suddenly drinking poison and living through another of Thorvard's fits, remembering that he struck me when his mood was black.

"That anchor was not cheap to make," Finnbogi rants as

he grabs a coil of hemp rope with his other hand. He cusses loudly as a sudden breeze rips alongside the hull. I jump, feeling startled and disoriented.

"I need someone strong to pull it up," Finnbogi barks as he looks around.

"I'll dive for it," Snorri the Greenlander says. Grinning widely, he pushes his way through the gathering crowd and marches over to the gunwale, and peers way down.

"By Óðinn's beard, the water will be very cold, but I haven't had my morning swim yet," he quips as he disrobes.

In silence we watch him take the plunge. As the ripples from his entry point spread out, I find myself staring at the bubbles that dot the surface of the sea.

For a long time, nothing happens. The water stills. The Norsemen freeze. An instant later, Finnbogi transfers his position on the line to another man and strips off his shirt to reveal a hairless chest, goose-pimpled in the freezing cold.

"Gods' bread, you can't go too. It's too dangerous," Logatha groans as she tries to hold her husband back. Finnbogi will have none of it.

Just then Snorri resurfaces, holding up the anchor with water sluicing down his hairy arms. The crew cheers and whistles, and Finnbogi laughs, but he gets distracted when Groa pushes past. After she wraps her shivering husband in a warm fur hide, someone gives him a drink of ale. He takes a gulp just as Finnbogi smacks him good-naturedly on the back.

"The blasted thing almost fell, but I got it back," Snorri

says through chattering teeth with a steady stream of water dripping down his face.

"You did it, man," Finnbogi says, but he can't stop grinning from ear to ear. Without waiting, the helmsman turns from us to go supervise the Norsemen who are working hard to reattach the line.

"I'll make an offering to the gods when we arrive in Leifsbidur," I say to Logatha. "I'll thank them for making Snorri brave enough to make the dive."

She rubs her stomach. "I'm just glad that the sea god didn't have it out for me. The ocean could have stolen everything. Truly, Snorri should be honored for his courage and his strength."

I release a bloated sigh. I had once hoped to marry such a man.

Chapter Fifteen

FOG FINGERS

With the anchor raised, the ship is easy to turn around. Eventually we make our way towards the shore where the mountainous cliffs dwarf our ship. Finnbogi seems certain that we have arrived in Helluland, the place of rock that Leif so aptly named. He begins to look for a place to land as the longboat pitches in the ocean swells, but the rock walls are a barrier and there are large glaciers covering the highlands that spread out to sea.

"Are you certain there is no estuary or beach that will comfortably hold the longboat's keel?" Logatha asks from her barrel perch as I tilt my head back and look way up into the massive cliffs.

"I can't see one," Finnbogi mutters as he scans the rockface up ahead. "In truth, it looks as though there is no land on this stone slab to explore."

Unless we climb a *rôst* or more into the sky, I grumble in my head.

"For all we know this chunk of land marks the

beginnings of *bifröst*. It is strange that this would be the site of that burning rainbow bridge that could lead us all from Midgard to Asgard. Me, I'd like to see where the gods reside," Gunnar says to Egil, a Norseman with a missing tooth.

"Too bad the cliffs are too high. We could climb and take a look," Snorri says. For a moment the crew is quiet.

"Óðinn's Asgard is not a place for me quite yet," Finnbogi announces in a booming voice that echoes against the jagged mountain scarp that flanks our ship.

As the men stand around debating what to do, Logatha shivers. Sidling up to her, I wrap my arms around her shoulders to give her warmth.

"I was hoping to get off this cursed longboat and stretch my legs," she says as a yawn scoops up her words. "This little one inside of me does not like the sea. I feel so sick."

"The sickness eventually passes," I say. Just ahead, the seabirds are swerving wildly in the wind.

"Oh gods, I crave wild game that has been slowly smoked over an outdoor fire," Logatha continues.

"Me too," I say. "I wish I could follow a moraine into some tarn where I could wash my feet."

The tinkle of Logatha's soft laughter pings off the rocks. "Remember the hot pools?" she says longingly. The memories of Faðir's farm come unbidden. I close my eyes.

"I didn't mean to upset you." The waves are slapping against the strakes.

"I'm thinking about Thorvard."

"He is not your husband anymore."

"*Neinn*, he will always be my husband. He is just not here."

"May Hlin, the goddess of protection, keep you safe."

"Hlin married a mortal man for love, renouncing her Aesir birthright and that of her sea mother Rán. I have never loved a man and I will never renounce my birthright. I am an Eiriksdöttir who is beginning to think that I am not in need of the gods. Worshiping them never seems to help."

Logatha is silent as she points to a bird's nest stuffed into a crevice between two rock walls. "When we next hit landfall, I'll offer sacrifice on your behalf," she says.

I turn my head away from her.

"It is important not to anger them."

"May Finnbogi help us find a route that will lead us all to sandy shores," I say carefully as I glance at her. "May you give birth to a healthy bairn who has Óðinn's wisdom and the strength of Thor."

"I hope my bairn will be as loyal as his mother's dearest friend," Logatha announces to the air.

From the bow, Finnbogi orders the oarsmen to stop rowing. A dense white mist is swirling around the ship and slinking across the riveted planks. I draw my mantle closed.

"Stop the ship," Finnbogi orders. A hush falls over the entire crew as we strain our eyes to look for blocks of ice with fragile dendritic arms floating past. The sea is too calm and flat, and the fog is making it hard to see. In front of me, two Norsemen are working to bail out water from the bilge.

"Helgi," Finnbogi calls when we are almost on top of the other helmsman's stern. The fog is growing thicker, shrouding everything in mist.

The two longboats pull alongside and in the fading light I catch a glimpse of Helgi's face. He is a thin man, tall in stature like his brother, with a commanding voice.

"Brother, if I could use my sword, I swear to you that the brewer of fog would meet his end."

"Helgi, you lack the power and the strength to fight against this killer of ships. You must go slowly," Finnbogi replies, but he sounds agitated and he can't stand still.

The hair on my arms rises. I imagine hitting a tilted block of ice with creviced walls, a mountainous cliff of pure white ice. I know that the massive ice carvings can be larger than Helluland's rocky cliffs. I've seen them from a distance.

"Should we anchor here?" Finnbogi asks as the longboat bobs up and down in the gentle swells.

"Not here. We are too close to the rocks, and the water seems to be very deep," Helgi replies as he looks around.

"The fog makes it difficult to determine what lies ahead," Finnbogi frets.

"I think we should keep going and see what the sea goddess has in store for us."

"I fear her ire. Just look at the fog closing in."

"Be strong, brother. We have been in situations like this before."

At that, Helgi moves back to his position at the helm and gives orders for his oarsmen to pull away. To my relief, Finnbogi is as cautious as he is vigilant. He is slow to follow Helgi's longboat and he navigates the dangers of the sea like a seasoned sailor who has witnessed shipwrecks and handled fog.

Helgi pushes on, and we soon lose sight of him. Then a shout from the watchmen warns us that there are rocks ahead.

"There are too many dangers in the dark," Logatha says in a worried voice as she joins Finnbogi at the helm. "By Óðinn's eye, I think it might be too risky to carry on."

"Nonsense, woman. It seems like the mist is clearing, and Helgi has owl eyes."

The bitter cold rises up from the frigid sea and I shiver as the mist swirls around my feet. I look around and all I see is an ethereal world of white that swallows everything in sight. The fog is moving closer, looming for as far as the eye can see. Soon it will suffocate. I can just make out Logatha clinging to her husband's arm.

"These waters could be studded with turreted blocks of ice," Logatha whines.

"We can travel slowly," Finnbogi reassures. "I will post lookouts through the night."

"The ocean has been known to sever brother from brother," Logatha warns.

"We could go back and try to find a place to land on that rock of an island called Helluland."

"I am not going back there," Logatha mutters. "Gods' bread, I don't have a good feeling about all of this."

"Hush, woman," Finnbogi pleads. He nods for me to come and take his wife away, and I step forwards and tug her gently on the arm.

"Come," I whisper as I watch my breath fog swirling in the mist. "Let Finnbogi do his work so he can guide us to safer waters."

For half the night we travel at a slow but steady pace under a curtain of heavy fog. When the mist finally lifts, I see the sea rising to meet the nighttime sky, black on black. There is no horizon, just a sea of twinkling stars reflected on the surface of the sea.

Huddled next to Logatha for extra warmth, I listen to the water slipping off the heavy oars in the quiet stillness of a frigid night in the middle of the open ocean. Finnbogi has told us all to look for ice, but it is like looking for a giant's grain of salt sprinkled in a bowl of soup.

Sometime in the wee hours of morning, I fall into a restless sleep and travel to another land of ice and fog, a place where only the frost giants live. I conjure the mist to hide me in a thick white veil, and for a moment all is quiet. Then, out of the stillness, I register the sound of panicked men.

"Bring to! Bring to! Heave astern!"

Groggily I stir awake just as the lookout blasts his cowhorn. Instantly, the men spring up. There is ordered chaos on the deck.

"Hard rudder to starboard!" a Norseman yells.

"Avast! Avast!"

"In Óðinn's name, what is happening here?" I ask. Beside me, Logatha's face looks white.

"Helgi's ship is bilged," she says through quivering lips. "By the sounds of it, a large chunk of ice scraped against the wooden strakes beneath the waterline. Helgi's lookouts failed to see it in the dark."

In the dim grey light that marks the coldest time before the break of dawn, I peer across the water and see the hazy outline of Helgi's longboat stopped directly in front of us.

"Bear away! Bear away, boys!" Finnbogi shouts. "We don't want to gain the wind on her."

The oarsmen bring the ship up short. Ahead of us we see Helgi's men silhouetted black against a lavender-colored sky at the break of dawn, trying to force their vessel to list to the starboard side. Then we hear their anxious shouts, their panicked voices, the baying of an agitated cow.

"It sounds as though their sails are hanging sideways all fouled in the lines," Gunnar says as he sidles up next to us.

"I will row out to see what happened. Who will come?" Finnbogi asks. I help Logatha adjust her sealskins, then I grab her mittened hand.

Finnbogi and Gunnar depart in a small rowboat while the rest of us return to worrying. We hear panicked bleats and bellows, shouts and groans, the splash of a heavy barrel thrown overboard. Impatiently we wait for someone to bring us news. In the pre-dawn light, I lean over the gunwales, but the other ship is too far away and it is still not light enough to make out anything clearly. When I turn back, Logatha is staring out across the sea.

"Please forgive me." My voice comes out all rattled.

"For what?" she asks.

I take a breath and see the dark smudge of a rowboat coming towards us from the direction of Helgi's ship. "For not believing in the gods," I breathe.

Chapter Sixteen

WORM MEAT

"**R**eady about. You lot there, lend a hand and belay the ropes," Finnbogi orders as his boat pulls alongside the ship. His face is smeared with streaks of mud illuminated by the first sunrays breaking over the horizon.

"What happened?" Gunnar shouts.

"An iceberg ripped through the ribs of my brother's longboat. Helgi's ship is going down into Rán's coral caves," he says with his face upturned. "The sea goddess was lurking near that underwater ice mountain up ahead, glowering with her grasping fingers. She enticed my brother to bring his ship her way, hoping to draw him down into her cheerless realm with her nets, but I won't let her take Helgi or his men. We need to send this rowboat back to pick up the remaining crew."

Snorri steps forwards when he hears the news. "Make way, you sheep-fuckers," he says gruffly, taking charge.

At his command, the Icelanders scramble to throw down ropes and clear an area big enough to accommodate another crew. The deck becomes a moving mass of bodies as gear is moved and ropes are coiled. Snorri can't stop bellowing.

"Bring ale!" Logatha yells as she scrambles to help the first batch of men on board. They look haggard, shocked, and frozen stiff. I give them furs and heated stones. Within minutes we are waving Finnbogi off again.

"Thor, give us strength. We might be forced to break bulk to make room for Helgi's crew," Asta says as she clamps my arm.

"We won't be throwing no supplies overboard," Snorri growls as he crooks his finger and motions to a passing thrall. He glares at us. "Summer is almost halfway gone. We'll be lucky if we arrive in Vinland in time to hunt. We can't afford to throw nothin' overboard."

Across the water, a cow is bellowing in distress. "What will happen to the livestock?" Logatha frets as she approaches us carrying a load of furs for Helgi's men.

"We can't accommodate any more animals. Our hold is full," Asta mutters as she reaches out to help with the furs.

"Then someone will have to kill the cow," I say simply, but there is a feeling of betrayal, as if I've murdered the beast myself.

It takes most of the morning to deal with the ship and relocate the men. In the end, we lose half the sheep. Helgi is heartbroken as he watches the sternpost of his ship slowly slipping into the ice-cold depths of a watery grave. Feeling gutted, I watch him struggle to control his grief. When I see him shut his eyes and cover his face with his hands, I need to look away. Helgi is leaving behind his heart's passion, his life's work. The ship is the total sum of what he is worth. He loses it to Rán who swallows it whole as it spirals down. She gets the ship. We get the crew. Our decks are crowded; our hold, too full.

"The poor man," Logatha remarks when we find ourselves standing alone at the stern.

I feel the stirrings of a hot, hard rage begin to coil around my heart. Loss has become so familiar that Helgi's situation is nothing new. I have become a hardened shell who now shares space with a broken man. When he withdraws, I cannot bring myself to approach him in his misery. I cannot bear to feel the cold daggers of it. It is too familiar. Too painful for me to watch.

For two more days, we sail under cloudy skies, enduring the rhythmic waves pitching up and then rolling down, spraying mist and churning up white sea-foam in the choppy waters. There are no more stops until we hit the coast of a land that is flat and forested, sloping gently seaward with many white sand beaches.

"This must be Markland," Logatha sighs. There are dark circles underneath her eyes. Finnbogi orders the oarsmen to break the rhythm that they've set down.

"Tomorrow, we will go ashore and find a spot where our cows and sheep can graze," he announces in a booming voice that cuts through the excited chatter. He does not announce that going ashore is essential because our provisions are running low now that there are double the mouths to feed onboard.

The shipbuilder, Sven Forkbeard, seems pleased by what he sees. "Look at all those trees," he murmurs as his face lights up and his whiskered mouth breaks into an exuberant smile. "With one tree alone, I could make a mast for a massive ship. By the gods, it will take no time to rebuild the longboat that Helgi lost."

Helgi barely glances up.

"There will be timber when we arrive on Vinland's shores," Finnbogi says, but his voice reveals the strain of recent days.

"I wonder why my brother didn't build his longhouse here on these wondrous beaches," I muse almost inaudibly.

"Leif the Lucky likes to take chances in everything he does, including leading expeditions across the northern sea," Snorri says. "He is the kind of man who never sits still. When it comes to explorin', he is never satiated. I'm sure he'd brew some wind and smite the sea just so he could continue to go in search of land."

I release a tiny laugh. "My brother certainly can be bullheaded," I admit, "but in the end, it is about the stories. Truly, he is someone who lives to tell the tale."

"He also likes to make a profit," Finnbogi says as he slides his eyes my way. The crew goes silent.

"He is a Greenlander," is all I say.

The next day we go ashore and find dew on the grass that we collect in our hands to drink. Logatha tells me that she has never tasted anything so sweet. Even the sheep seem to bleat more loudly when we send them out to graze.

That night as we sit around the blazing fire where the sparks rise to touch the emerging stars, I catch Sven Forkbeard studying the silhouetted spruce boughs swaying back and forth as if they are worshiping the gods.

"I want to make a sacrifice," Logatha whispers softly. "I am concerned about the safety of my unborn child."

"Why?" I ask, feeling scared. "Are you unwell?"

"I have lost a little blood," she says.

I go to comfort her, but she pulls back. The firelight skips across her face.

"Don't worry, Freydis, it is nothing," she says as she struggles up. "I just thought that I should pay homage to the gods and give them sacrifice. I was hoping that you would come with me."

I nod. "Of course I'll come, but perhaps we should find Groa and ask her to come along as well."

She shakes her head and turns from me, and I follow her up the beach to where a lean-to has been constructed. She has placed her sleeping hides there beside a simple stone altar holding three wooden statues. The first is Thor, god of thunder, god of warfare, and god of strength. The second is Óðinn, the supreme deity, the all-faðir, the giver of wisdom, the all-seeing one-eyed master who guards our fates. The third is Freyr, the god of fertility and prosperity, the god of sunshine and fair weather, the god of peace and good harvest.

Where were these gods when I needed them? Why

didn't they protect me from Thorvard's fists? Logatha's sacrifices are pointless, but who am I to tell her what to do?

Logatha begins the ritual by praying to each god in turn. I listen respectfully and extend my hand when it is time, knowing what is coming. Still, I wince when she uses her dagger to slice open my outstretched palm. After I drip my blood into a flask that holds a concoction of bitter herbs, she does the same. Then we light a fire and watch the smoke rising, but I am as jittery as a jellyfish.

We stay in Markland for about a week in fine weather. A burst of late-summer sun kisses my wind-burned face as I work with the women to scoop up fish just offshore. Meanwhile, the men go out to try their luck at hunting. Praise the gods, they are successful. They bring home deer and caribou and rabbit, and we set to drying and smoking the meat. Summer is drawing to a close and it is the start of corn-cutting month when the air turns cooler as soon as the sun begins to set.

When Finnbogi finally gives the order to pack up camp, Logatha isn't feeling well. She tells me that she is cramping, but there is nothing I can do about it. To distract myself from worrying, I assist with the reloading of the ship. We now have over sixty men, two cows, some woolly sheep and some sickly-looking, squeamish goats.

For two whole days we sail in a northeasterly wind under a clear blue sky before we spot Leifsbidur on a Thor's day in mid-afternoon. Throwing my arms into the air, I release a wild whoop as soon as I catch sight of a longhouse nestled amongst the shoreline grasses, set beside some rolling hills. Even Snorri smiles when he sees my exuberance. Breathing in the smell of land, I peruse the browns and yellows and golden flecks popping up amidst the green.

"Look!" Finnbogi says, pointing. "Ulf's longboat reached Leifsbidur ahead of us." I follow his finger and see the mast of a second longboat anchored in an estuary down the beach.

"Thank the gods Ulf and his crew made it here safely," Logatha exclaims from her perch on a bed of furs. She is gaunt and sickly looking; her cheeks are the color of the grey sea.

"That longboat down the beach looks familiar. Its single sail is furled, and one of its masts is unstopped," Helgi mutters through his teeth. He is a different man without his ship.

"Those Greenlanders must have arrived some time ago," Finnbogi puffs as he squints his eyes and braces himself against the wind. He is looking haggard and old. Forsooth, this voyage has taken its toll.

"We should move our ship in the direction of that stream over there," one of the seasoned sailors calls out. "Leif said the area is teeming with salmon." He points, and I scan the sedge meadows which stretch into green low-lying shrubs; behind them is a line of trees far off in the distance.

"Does it stay green like this even in winter?" Logatha asks incredulously as she struggles to stand on wobbly legs.

Finnbogi shrugs. "We will explore it," he says, but he is distracted.

The ship makes its way past a rocky mountain that marks

the entrance to the bay and I follow Finnbogi's gaze up the coast to where the other longboat sits, half-hidden behind a point of land. There is something in the helmsman's look that rattles me. I sidestep barrels and crates and push my way through the Norsemen until I make it to the helm.

"Freydis, do you know the markings on that ship?" Finnbogi asks. His voice sounds strange. I shake my head.

"That ship heralds trouble," Helgi spits as he comes to stand behind his brother.

"Trouble?" I repeat.

"That's not Ulf's ship," Snorri announces.

"Whose ship is it then?" I ask uneasily.

"It is your brother's ship. That's the ship he sailed to Vinland's shores. The last we saw of it, it was anchored in Eiriksfjord."

Finnbogi runs his massive hands down his face and shakes his head.

"My brother's ship?" I ask. "But he stayed behind in Brattahlíð."

"By Óðinn's beard, that ship was in his harbour when we left Greenland at the beginning of the month of *sólmánuður*," Finnbogi mutters. "Either your brother is here, or his ship is being used by someone else. Is it possible that Thorvard outran us in your brother's ship?"

I stare at Finnbogi. Waves of fear peak then break. It isn't possible. It can't be.

"Thor be with us, that isn't Leif," Logatha says, pointing. "Look."

Thorvard is standing on the shore with his legs spread

wide apart and his arms crossed, waiting. I can't even see his face but I feel him fondling me, enticing the ship to come closer, reeling us in with his net like a fisherman would snag a fish for dinner.

"That horse cock beat us here," Helgi exclaims.

Just then Thorvard turns and wanders back up the rocky beach. I had hoped to escape him and rid myself of his abuse, but once again he has outsmarted me. How is it that this bloodsucker always finds me?

My vision blurs. I reach out for Logatha with outstretched arms, hoping she will be there to hold me up. In a daze, I feel my head roll back and my hands flail out as I start to fall, but at the last moment I catch myself and stumble just before I hit the deck. From somewhere distant, a hungry seagull screams.

"Tack is free!" Sven yells as someone behind him turns the crossbar in the foreship to the other side so it is ready to receive the tack to turn the boat. Sven's face is a blur.

"We can't let Thorvard have her," Logatha says as if through water.

"I assure you, wife, I'll not let that happen." Finnbogi's lips are moving but I can't seem to catch the rest of what he is saying.

"Give me the sword that hangs from your belt," I mumble, all wool-headed. "I wish to run it through my husband's heart."

"Tack set," someone calls.

"Cool your blood, Freydis," Helgi mutters as he begins to trim the line. "Thorvard will expect us to come out fighting. We must devise a better plan." He curses as he bends his back into his work.

"Give me your shield and sword. I'll kill the bastard straightaway!"

"You'll ruin your reputation," Logatha cautions as she rubs her tummy as if in a trance. "They will call you a murderer and banish you when we get back to Greenland's shores."

"We are far away from Greenland," I remind my friend.

"I'll avenge you, Freydis," Helgi mutters as he continues to prepare the ship to come into shore. "Don't think you have to face Thorvard on your own." He flicks a sideways glance and it seems as though he is different, as though he is a man reborn again after losing all.

"If that son of a bitch is bold enough to follow us to Vinland's shores," Finnbogi says as he grabs hold of the rudder stick, "he should be bold enough to accept my challenge to a duel."

"*Neinn!*" Logatha spits out angrily. "I'll not lose my husband at Thorvard's hands."

"Hush now, wife. Do you not believe that I am capable of squelching such a worm?"

Logatha's eyes pop wide.

"Stop this nonsense. All of you. I am Freydis Eiriksdóttir, trained by the great swordsman Ivor of Gardar. I will defend myself and fight my husband, but I need a weapon. Give me your leg biter, I say!"

"You can't face him yourself," some Norseman says.

"Begone if you are not deathless! By Óðinn's missing eye, I'll smite any man down who tries to hold me back."

Helgi unbuckles his belt which holds his sword. Then he climbs over the heads of several men to retrieve his scuffed shield which he brings to me. When he hands over all his fighting gear, I bob my head to mark my gratitude.

"Thorvard of Gardar is a snake. We must make him bleed," Helgi sniffs. "He is a fattened worm who should be squished. Those of you who are not needed to man the ship, take up your swords and shields and be ready to go to battle against that thief. Freydis Eiriksdóttir will lead us out and make him bleed."

In the chaos that follows, I gather up my fighting men and bellow out orders and words of encouragement as the ship pulls into the bay. In the distance, the settlement of Leifsbidur looks deserted.

I study the faces of the Greenlanders, before my eyes move to the dragon carving that marks the helm. Finnbogi is gazing at the beach, but Logatha is not with him. She has disappeared.

As soon as Finnbogi's crew rows us into shore, I jump out in the shallows and feel the icy water clawing at my legs. I have thirty-five Greenlanders following me with Helgi and his crew bringing up the rear.

Leifsbidur is a dreary place with an abandoned yard. To my surprise, Thorvard has been using the longhouse, the byre, and the smithy that my brother built. A fresh pile of dung lies in the middle of my path. Just ahead there are two sleepy sheep.

"Where are you hiding, you Loki ass-kisser?" I shout. It is so quiet that I consider unsheathing Helgi's sword. Instead I raise my arm and flick my wrist to signal my men to follow.

"Be careful, Freydis," Helgi cautions as he advances from the back.

With sweaty palms, I grit my teeth and try to close off thought, but there is hatred burning in my gut. How did Thorvard arrive here first? Where is Ivor, his right-hand man? How about my brother? Where was he in all of this?

I make my way towards the longhouse, stepping carefully over puddles of water left by rain. Just as I go to lift the latch, the door flies open, and Thorvard steps out dressed in all his finery. His massive frame fills the doorway so I can't see what lies beyond.

"Why did you put your belongings into my brother's longhouses?" I ask disdainfully. "Leif lent me the longhouse, and he said nothing about sharing it with the likes of you and your Greenlanders. Get out, you dog!"

Thorvard turns the order over in his head and sucks on it like someone would suck on a blade of grass. "Ach, Freydis, I will never be a match for your ill-will," he eventually says as he lifts his chin and sizes up my fighting men. I draw my sword.

"Where is Ivor?" I ask boldly.

Thorvard spits a wad of phlegm at my feet. "Freydis, your actions vex me."

"I won't ask again about Ivor's whereabouts."

Thorvard sniffs. "Ivor is my trusted man, and he is not here. I left him behind to manage the running of my farm.

Unlike some, he is an honest member of my household who shows me loyalty and does what he is told."

Thorvard glares at me. I throw a tiny smile.

"When I return, I'll honor him," Thorvard continues, eyeing me with his snake-like eyes.

"Indeed you shall," I smirk.

Thorvard's face turns cold. "Wife, I am not pleased that your brother gave you permission to sail to Vinland without my consent. Swine's piss! I am your husband, and you dishonored me. Your brother should not have allowed you to go anywhere with Finnbogi and his good-for-nothing brother. They are Icelanders and all they do is cheat and steal."

I can hear the rumbling behind my back, the hiss of agitated men. "Thorvard, I have enjoyed being rid of you."

"Come now, Freydis," he says as he glances behind me. "I think it is wise that we be friends."

My men unsheathe their swords, and the sound of dozens of weapons clinking and clanking, of wooden shields locking together, of feet shuffling into place, brightens my mood. I allow myself a tiny smile.

"What a display of force you make, my shieldmaiden wife," Thorvard says as he pulls out his pocket knife to clean underneath his nails.

"If you don't leave, I'll give the order to attack," I say evenly. "Now take your men and leave my family's property."

"I am your husband. You can't tell me to leave."

"Get out!"

"You little wench, are you mad? The Icelanders are as good to you as seagulls' shit."

There is a burst of noise as Thorvard's Greenlanders suddenly come pouring out of the longhouse with their weapons drawn. Instantly, I back away. By my count, Thorvard only has thirty Greenlanders backing him whereas I have thirty-five.

"Freydis, this is nonsense. Think twice about what you are about to do. You are my wife, and I order you to tell your men to sheathe their swords," Thorvard shouts in a threatening voice.

I pause to take in air. "Am I your wife, your property, or your slave?"

Thorvard's men chuckle uncomfortably.

"Ever since your *faðir* married you off to me, you've been difficult," Thorvard sneers.

"And you've been a swine. How dare you abuse me behind closed doors! How dare you cheat me and steal my land!"

"Hold your tongue, Freydis Eiriksdöttir!" Thorvard's face turns red. His hunting eye begins to twitch. "According to the Althing laws, I have a right to oversee my wife's property no matter where she is or where it lies."

"The laws of Greenland mean nothing here in Vinland," I yell. Raising my shield, I stand my ground to address Thorvard's men. "Here in Leifsbidur, let it be known that I answer to no man. All of you must leave my brother's house or I'll cleave you in half and feed you to the ravens and the wolves."

Thorvard blinks. I stare at him unwaveringly and aim

my sword directly at his heart. For a moment, he goes still. Then he wipes his muscled forearm across his face and turns away to retrieve his sword. It is a weapon I recognize all too well. It is the bridal gift I gave him when I was a foolish hen.

Behind me, footfalls shuffle through the grass. "Leave them alone, Freydis," Logatha whispers in my ear. "Don't foolishly challenge Thorvard to a duel. It could go badly for you if your men are killed."

I shrug my shoulders.

"He is nothing to us, Freydis," Logatha continues in a desperate voice. "There will be blood spilled at your expense and in the end, that piece of dung will force you back to the marriage bed."

"He cannot have me, and he cannot take my brother's longhouse," I mutter without breaking eye contact with Thorvard of Gardar, but I feel the urge to shake her hard and make her understand that I am a different woman now that I have shielded up.

"Let's find another place on Vinland's shores to make our camp," Logatha pleads, but her words scratch like thorns.

"I'll not stand down and let him win. Today I will do my *faðir* proud when I carve Thorvard into worm meat. By sundown, you will see his heart stuck onto a stake."

Behind me there is silence. Dead silence. Without turning, I raise my hand and give the signal, and Helgi hollers.

The fight is on.

Chapter Seventeen

CORPSE-SCORERS

My battle-hungry Greenlanders emit a *vyking* roar, a cheer that is so loud it scares off a flock of birds. The black winged creatures rise from a nearby field, their squawks and screeches mingling with the rumble of charging feet, the clink of swords. I catch one last glance of Thorvard as the first wave of charging men swallows him. With brandished swords, the men begin to fight like dogs and grunt like pigs. I take a breath, reveling in the feel of the sword in my hand.

Drawing on instinct, I am shielded from the biting blades so that I easily deflect a blow. Shivering, there is a moment of pure panic, a moment when I hear Ivor's voice inside my head encouraging me to shift my shoulders to avoid getting jabbed. With a sudden surge of strength, I duck and narrowly escape getting nicked in the shoulder, only vaguely aware of the sweat falling into my eyes as I flick my hair back to better see, to better dodge another sword.

I go to plunge my sword into someone's chest and all noise stops. A bloodthirsty drive pulses through my thrumming veins as my vision narrows, my thinking slows.

I have killed a man. My first.

I work in a breath, fighting to remember the innocence of youth, the hot springs I enjoyed on Faðir's farm.

I hear a gasp, a grunt, a muffled shout, a burst of noise, as though I am resurfacing after plunging into the darkness of a cold, deep lake. Thorvard has stolen my youth, my life, the meekness that I used to have. I wrench my sword out of the Norseman's chest and feel nothing but the ridges of the hilt and the cold, hard metal in my palm.

It is only when I stop to remove the blood splatters from my face after killing two more of Thorvard's men that I catch a glimpse of Finnbogi, who is fighting on the outskirts of the skirmish near the door of the longhouse, fiercely trying to take down one of Thorvard's trolls. His sword arm is slashed and bleeding, and he looks apoplectic as he wields his sword.

Just then we hear an ear-splitting scream, a cry so terrified and panic-stricken that my attention is immediately riveted back to the longhouse door where Logatha is struggling to untangle herself from Thorvard's grip. He has her at knife point and her pregnant belly is sticking out.

"Logatha!" I shout as I try to plough my way through the throngs of men.

"Help me!" she cries as Thorvard violently yanks her inside the blackened maw out of sight. There is another chilling shriek followed by a violent thud as someone's sword finds my shield. With a forward lunge, I jab my sword and aim to kill. In an instant, my rival falls.

I feel flushed. Alive. Forever changed.

Snagging a breath, I collect myself and try to fight my way towards the longhouse, but it is all I can do to push my way through men who snarl and grunt as they attempt to deliver vicious blows. Someone grabs my hair, but with a twist I get away, leaving a fistful of red locks behind.

"Come bite my sword, you corpse-scorers who drink the mead from bloody wounds!" My throat chokes out the battle cry as I push my way forwards with all my strength, wielding my sword as I fight my way to the longhouse door.

"I am ready for you, you bold sword-swinger," I yell as I stagger forwards, wincing when I hear another agonizing cry. With caution, I follow the scuffling sounds, the whimpering moans, the heavy grunts. Thorvard releases a string of nasty curses, and Logatha screams again. Then all goes still.

When my vision finally adjusts to the dark interior, it is not Logatha whom I see first but Finnbogi. The helmsman is bleeding profusely from the arm and blood is streaming down his wrist and dripping in big, fat blobs onto the floor.

"Get your hands off my wife," he spits as he struggles to hold his sword arm up. Thorvard releases a baleful laugh.

"Freydis, have you come to watch me 'abuse' your friend?" he asks.

I raise my sword and spit.

"Oh Freydis," Thorvard continues, his voice silkily low. "Tell these Icelanders that you are to blame for all the deaths they face today. For shame, lives have been lost because of you. What will we tell your brother Leif?"

"Nothing. I won't tell him anything. I'm not going back to Greenland. I never will!"

With a flick of his wrist, Thorvard uses his knife to nick the whiteness of Logatha's throat and draw a thin line of blood.

"Please don't," I beg, just as Finnbogi attempts to lunge.

Thorvard is too quick. He throws his knife and the blade narrowly misses Finnbogi's chest before I rush at Thorvard with my sword, pointing the tip at his chest. Just before I reach him, he grabs Logatha by the neck and begins to squeeze, and my blade narrowly misses stabbing her in the chest. With a jolt I stop and back away, shivering and gripping my sword hilt so firmly that my knuckles all turn white. Logatha is struggling hard to breathe, gurgling a pathetic noise in her efforts to say Finnbogi's name. There is a purplish tinge moving up her neck into her jaw and spreading quickly into her mottled face.

"Stop!" Finnbogi shouts.

"Drop your weapons to the ground," Thorvard orders in a voice that chills.

Finnbogi throws his sword. I do the same. A moment later Thorvard releases his vice-like grip with an evil smirk and Logatha doubles up, gagging and choking, half-crying as she gargles air.

"Freydis, how is it that you are friends with this helmsman and his pregnant wife?" Thorvard begins in an oily tone as he grasps Logatha's wrists and twists them behind her back. He yanks her into the shadows. I can barely see the two of them. "Help me understand why you, in your fortunes tender, have chosen to do business with a group of Icelanders? Where is your loyalty, my Greenlander wife? Have you sold your soul to this sorry lot? Finnbogi needed you to feed his men and outfit his ship. I suppose he also asked for goods to trade so that he could barter with the *skraelings*. Forsooth, he is using you, my foolish wife." He takes a breath and I hear the whistle of it climbing up his nose. "As soon as you return to Brattahlíð, Finnbogi will cheat you out of any deal you've made with him. Think on it. He is Icelandic and they always cheat."

Finnbogi is staring straight ahead at his fear-crazed wife. I glance between the two of them.

"Perhaps you sailed with Finnbogi to keep him warm? Perhaps you please him in ways his pregnant wife cannot? Perhaps you lie with him and he screws you like he would a ewe?"

The insinuation is insulting. Thorvard pushes Logatha into the light.

"Let go of her or I'll kill you," Finnbogi whispers in a seething voice. There is a throbbing vein in his neck popping out.

A low, grinding chuckle erupts from Thorvard's throat. In the shadows, I reach for my hidden knife with sweaty hands, wishing I was gripping the sword's hilt just above the quillon block.

"You are a snake who doesn't deserve an honorable death," Finnbogi says as he jabs his finger into the smoky air.

"You talk of honor?" Thorvard snaps. "By Óðinn's

beard, you are a sly and cunning fox who stole my wife! You should have asked before taking Freydis to your bed. I would have given her to you willingly. She is a barren wench."

"Let go of Logatha," I say so quietly that both men turn. Aiming the tip of my knife directly at Thorvard's throat, I close one eye and focus on my mark with an aim to kill. Thorvard knows what I can do. He has seen me practicing in his yard.

Outside, the victors release an ear-splitting cheer. In the cloud of dust floating in through the open door, some men run past. I hold my mark.

"Thorvard, you have lost. Your men are abandoning you," Finnbogi jeers as he retrieves a smaller dagger from his belt. From where I stand, I see drops of perspiration on Finnbogi's brow and sweat beading on his upper lip. Like me, he is looking for the right moment to thrust his weapon into Thorvard's chest, but he hesitates because Logatha's body is in the way.

An instant later, Thorvard releases a rebel's cry and unexpectedly gives Logatha a violent shove. With widened eyes and a little gasp, she flies towards the pointed end of Finnbogi's blade. Instantly, Finnbogi throws the weapon against the wall and leans forwards to catch her, but she stumbles unexpectedly. With a terrible shriek, she stretches out her arms to brace herself from the fall, but she can't quite manage. There is a wooden table directly in her path which she crashes into with such force that she somersaults through the air, landing on her back with a heavy thud.

Finnbogi wastes no time. He runs to her. Just as he is

crouching down, Thorvard tries to slip out the door, but I am fast. In a whirl, I lunge and plunge my knife through my husband's leather vest and pull down hard. Immediately, the gash spurts blood.

"Pray for deliverance, Freydis Eiríksdóttir," Thorvard shouts as he scrambles to right himself and join a group of battle-weary Greenlanders retreating down the path. I try to grab him, but I grasp only air. Bracing myself against the lintel post, I watch him run away and will my heaving chest to slow. My calves are shaking; a knuckle bleeds.

I am about to cup my hands around my mouth and yell for help when I hear the faintest of moans behind my back. Scanning the floor, my eyes bounce off overturned furniture and broken earthenware before I spot Logatha lying in a crumpled heap by the hearth.

"Sit up, my love," Finnbogi breaths. "Thor, the lord of strength gave us vigor to brave the enemy and we prevailed. Sweet woman, hush. Thorvard of Gardar is gone."

"There is too much blood," Logatha cries as she attempts to turn onto her side.

Outside, I hear the groans of dying men. Through the open door, I see Helgi leading a group of bedraggled Norsemen through the yard, taking stock of who has died and who still lives. There are Icelanders and Greenlanders strewn across the trampled field, men bleeding out as the crows sweep low. Wearily, I fall back against the sod wall.

"The shipbuilder is dead," someone yells.

"The blacksmith has a cleaver in his back."

My heart skips a beat. Sven was our only shipbuilder, a

man whom we could not afford to lose. In misery, I suck in air, listening to Logatha's wretched groans.

"I am here," I say softly as I scramble up and go to her, forgetting the deaths and injuries. Finnbogi shoots me an anxious look. There is sweat mixed in with blood trickling down Logatha's pasty brow. I wipe her forehead with my sleeve. With a gentle touch, I brush her hair off her face. Her whimpers fade when she sees my face.

"Thank the gods, you're safe," she rasps as she grabs my hand. Her fingers are as cold as ice. There is a mess of blood smeared all over her apron dress.

"I can't bear weight on my left foot. What is worse, I am cramping up."

"I think she fell against the child," Finnbogi says as he continues to tend to all her injuries. "By Thor's hammer, I'll hack off all of Thorvard's limbs and slowly feed them to the gulls if something happens to my wife."

Logatha blanches as she struggles to sit up. "Get me rags, Freydis," she cries desperately. "The bairn is coming! I can feel it crown. By the gods, my water broke. Please, sister, I need some help."

"It is too soon," I groan as Finnbogi and I attempt to lift her up.

"The bairn is coming," she sobs again.

I stare at her knowing what I need to do, but my thoughts begin to whirlwind into a dark and dangerous place, and my legs freeze up. Finnbogi shouts to wake me up, and without another word I turn and stumble out the door.

In the yard, the dead bodies are lying in bloodied heaps.

Swarms of flies are hovering over the fallen forms and vultures are picking at the blood-soaked flesh and crows are hopping around the corpses releasing ear-splitting caws. Gagging, I hold my nose against the smell of blood and gore. Snorri is tending to the wounds of some of my injured men. The Greenlander Arvid has lost his hand. Jerrik's side is oozing blood. Other men moan and struggle to take in air, their sliced-up throats emitting pathetic sounds. An axe sticks out of someone's head.

The first woman I meet as I pick my way across the field is Asta. I grab her arm. "Logatha is in labour. She needs your help."

"She'll not survive it. It is too early," Asta frets. Her eyes look haunted. She looks half-alive.

"Try to assist in any way you can," I manage as I drag her back to the longhouse. "I'll try to find Groa. Isn't she known for her midwifery skills?"

"Groa will be hard pressed to leave her post," Asta chokes. She can't bring herself to look at me. "She is attending to the wounds of all the men who fought to defend your honor and protect your life."

"I need to find her," is all I say as I try to steady my shaking hands.

"Good luck to you, then. I last saw her stitching up Olvir's knee."

When at last I find her, Groa is working on one of my Greenlanders and I am forced to wait. I glance over my shoulder, and Groa commands me to lend a hand. Afterwards, I escort her through the churned-up yard where the smell of burning flesh from the cremation fires

234

causes my eyes to water and my throat to close. With effort I close off feelings and trudge past bodies without looking down. Groa scrambles to keep up with me. As we walk, she predicts that Logatha's labour will be very long.

As soon as we arrive back at the longhouse, Asta emerges from the shadows.

"The bairn is dead and Logatha isn't faring well," she murmurs as I push past. On the ground beside Logatha, I see a pool of blood and fibrous strings and a wee fairy-fish all curled up. By the gods, this is all my fault.

Logatha gives a little moan. Her eyes are closed. Shivering, I reach for her hand, but then I pull back, recalling my own ordeal – the pain, the grief, the suffering.

Logatha stirs again and I go still. There are children's voices inside my head – babies crying, little ones yelling excitedly. I see our bairns linked together like their mothers are, forever friends, the light shining down on their little heads. The vision shimmers, sparks then flares and fizzles out.

Logatha's face looks pale in the late afternoon light creeping inside the door, stretching into the shadows. For a moment I worry that she is dead, but then I catch the slight rise and fall of her chest, and I make the decision to let her rest.

When I emerge from the longhouse, Asta and Groa are waiting for me in the yard.

"It started off slowly but then it became painful for her very fast," Asta mumbles as she bats away a swarm of flies. I hang my head. The guilt weighs me down like a ballast rock. The bards will say that I was to blame, that I stirred up trouble between the Icelanders and the Greenlanders. They will say that I challenged Thorvard of Gardar to a duel. They will call me an unfaithful wife.

"Logatha passed a lot of blood before the contractions eased and the bairn slid out," Asta blubbers, talking as if I'm not there. Her face is backlit by the setting sun. "Sadly, the wee thing was just too small to fight to take in air." She bites the side of her trembling lip.

"When Logatha wakes, she will be sick with grief," Groa whispers quietly. She shakes her head. "How tragic that she lost her firstborn child."

"Her back will feel like it is on fire."

"Finnbogi will need to be consoled," I sigh as I wrap my arms around my body and flick a glance out to sea. I take a breath. "Did Logatha even get to see her bairn?"

"*Neinn*," Asta says. A shiver of wind whisks through the yard. "There was nothing to see in that bloody mess."

"Where is Finnbogi?"

"Gone," Asta murmurs. "He left when he learned his bairn was dead."

Registering the staccato buzz of a single fly whizzing wildly around our heads, I follow it for a few moments before it lands. Then I swat at it. To my surprise, I squash the thing. In that moment, I make a vow to avenge my friends by tracking Thorvard down. I'll go in search of him as soon as I have regained the power in my battle arm. Until that day, I will curse his name and flog myself and blame myself for everything.

Chapter Eighteen

THESE MOMENTS OF RECKONING

A fter the skirmish that cost the Greenlanders twenty lives and the Icelanders five, I busy myself preparing for the long winter months ahead. The deaths of the master shipbuilder, Sven, and our blacksmith, Olaf Goðthjælpsen, are our greatest losses, but I will miss them all – the men who were loyal to Faðir's house, those who were loyal to Helgi and Finnbogi, and even some of those who were loyal to Thorvard of Gardar. I knew them all.

After we send their bodies out to sea on burning barges that the men construct from the wealth of trees surrounding the settlement, some of the men go out hunting while others stay behind to put the settlement of Leifsbidur back in order. Groa and Asta try to comfort me, but I shrug them off. Logatha avoids me completely.

We find no corn to cut during the month of *kornskurðarmánuður*, but there is a stream teeming with salmon that runs through the settlement. The fish are so plentiful that all we have to do is reach in and scoop them out. Afterwards we smoke and dry the fish while Helgi and his men go out again for caribou. On their return, they bring back butchered meat and a large and magnificent caribou rack, all heavy with branching forks that takes two men to lift. Using wood ash and animal lard to cure the hides, I sink myself into the work, trying to ignore everything.

Then the weather quickly turns. One morning we awake to a yard thick with frost, and I go outside without any shoes to gather chicken eggs. I like the feel of the cold, silky grass slipping in between my toes but the Icelanders chastise me for not wearing boots. I tell them not to worry and they laugh at me.

As for Logatha and Finnbogi, everyone tells me that they continue to grieve the loss of their firstborn child, and the more they gossip, the worse I feel. One day, as I am stacking cords of wood, Logatha comes out to meet me.

"How do you like it here?" she asks.

"I think the land has much to offer," I reply, glancing up. She is staring across the open fields.

"Freydis, I've been meaning to speak with you." Her voice breaks off. I take a breath.

"Logatha, I did wrong by you."

"You are blameless, Freydis." She bends down and plucks out a blade of grass. The tide is coming in; the wind is cold. "Finnbogi and I are sad to have lost our child, but it is not your fault."

"I feel it is," I interrupt. I bite my cheeks.

"It is Thorvard's fault." A rush of wind snatches up her words. "He sliced at me with his sword. He pushed me hard and threw me down. By Óðinn's beard, your bastard husband killed my child."

Above our heads, a flock of geese is flying south. Their noisy honks herald change. Logatha stares up at them, blinking rapidly.

"Finnbogi vows to avenge us both," she says as the autumn sun flares a brilliant red and gold. "My noble husband will challenge Thorvard to a duel in order to restore your honor and make him accountable for our loss. After he wins, he will expose your husband and condemn him for his abusive ways."

Logatha sets her jaw. She looks at me as the wind whistles down the beach. "Finnbogi promised that he will be your witness when you seek divorce."

Through a mist, I bow my head.

"I just want you to win your freedom back so that your husband can't touch you anymore," she whispers earnestly.

The tide is coming in, the waves are crashing into shore, and the seagulls are diving low for fish.

"Thorvard of Gardar is no longer my husband. He is dead to me." The wind flings my words out to sea.

"We will consider you a widow then," Logatha murmurs. In front of us a salty spray rises with the ocean swells. Logatha turns. She clasps her hands around my ugly ones. "I have come to terms with the loss of my wee, sweet bairn," she murmurs into the wailing wind. The gulls swoop low over the cresting waves.

"If I know Finnbogi, he'll make Thorvard pay."

"He will seek justice for the two of us."

She stands and I study her profile, recognizing that she

is the sister I never had and the friend I've wanted my whole life.

"There is no justice," I finally say.

In the distance, a seagull screams.

~

As the days grow shorter, I work hard to forgive myself while Logatha treats me no differently than she did before. We are inseparable as we do our chores. We clean the longhouse and stack the firewood. Then we set up a women's room. After hauling in supplies and setting up the loom that Asta brought, we spot several critters living in the longhouse posts. We smoke them out and set down traps, and soon we have won back the place and found our peace. One day Logatha asks if anyone has seen or heard from Thorvard's men.

"I saw the lot of 'em hiking up the coast, taking goods from his ship into the bush," Snorri says as he sharpens his axe blade against a whetstone.

"The Greenlanders are hiding out inside a nearby cave," Gunnar sniffs.

"*Neinn*. The *skraelings* ate Thorvard whole and spat him out into the sea," Egil huffs.

Finnbogi attempts to assess the reliability of these reports before squelching rumours that Thorvard is plotting to attack again. Then he orders us to keep busy in preparation for *skammdegi*, the darkest and coldest months of the year.

Life in Leifsbidur settles into a grueling routine. The

seasons change. Brilliant colors drape the rugged hills, and the longhouse turf turns yellow-brown while the mosses and lichen splotch brilliant tufts of rusty red. The partridgeberries, squashberries, and cloudberries ripen, and we harvest them, reveling in the sweetness of their taste, pinching them off so that our hands stay constantly sticky with the berry juice. Then we shear the sheep and cut and dry grass for hay. Everyone is busy. The blacksmith's son offers to train Gunnar, and the two of them put the smithy to good use, but he is like his *faðir* and his *faðir* before him. He insists on keeping the door to the smithy tightly shut while he is working hard to fashion us some iron goods.

One day I make the decision to wander into the barren, windswept hills, where I find a deer path leading to the beach. Sidestepping bulbous strands of seaweed thick with sandflies, I try to clear my head as I search for the barnacled mussels hidden in the rocky sand, hoping to harvest some for the Feast of Haustblót. The tide is out and I find my peace listening to the waves swishing into shore and the seagulls squawking overhead.

Before I know it, I have wandered far away from Leifsbidur. Glancing down the beach, I spot the settlement lying half-hidden behind the knolls. Leifsbidur looks like a place of ghosts. The byre is a tiny dot and I can just make out the turf ceiling of the longhouse against the backdrop of a silvered grey and dreary sky.

Just then a gush of water squirts up high from a sand mound that marks a mussel cache. Crouching low, I work my fingers into the sand to retrieve the black barnacled treasure. When I look up, four faces peek out at me through the grass. Startled, I release a little yelp as my hands lock onto the mussel shell and the scythe-sharp edge cuts into me.

"For the love of Thor," I mutter underneath my breath.

The *skraeling* children with their fearsome scowls and their large brown eyes do not flinch. Their little faces, smudged with berry juice, look sober as they stare at my basket full of mussels, eying the shellfish hungrily. The tallest has plaited hair with an eagle's feather sticking out. The smallest wears a hawk's lure on a band that rims his half-shaved scalp.

"Góðan dag," I say, keeping my voice tone low and soothing even though I shake inside.

When Hawk's Lure stands up fully in the grass, his bare flawless chest reflects red greasepaint. *He should eat some meat*, I think. *Oh gods, I hope he won't eat me. I won't allow myself to be chewed by that little man.*

Hawk's Lure's sinewy body looks very strong. He is an intimidating man-child whose warrior demeanour, cradled in boyhood bravery, dispenses fear. A moment later I hear a warbler's call – an unnatural, unnerving sound. My legs lock up and I strain my eyes to look past the little band of *skraelings*, but I see nothing moving in the grass. Cold shivers beetle through me as the children's searching eyes rake over me. Just then, a second warbling trill comes tumbling through the nippy air.

With a surge of panic, I scramble to gather up the reed basket that holds my mussel catch, keeping my eyes fixed straight ahead as I slowly begin to back away. A third call comes. One of the warrior children returns a loud, sharp whistle, and suddenly the grasses part to reveal a group of *skraeling* women wearing skins that have been dyed with red ochre.

The first spits out a word in her own language, clawing for her little one. Another quickly scoops up an infant from the sand. She is of willowy build with a raven-black braid trailing to her hips and a carrier made out of birchbark scuffed a rosy red in which there lies a sleeping child. A third carries a pointed spear. The shaft alone is as tall as me.

For a long moment, we stare each other down. Then Spear Mamma speaks to the children but her words sound so harsh that the seagulls perched on a nearby piece of driftwood suddenly take off in flight.

Moving slowly, I start to back away until a sudden movement distracts me and my basket slips out of my sweaty hands. Hawk's Lure points excitedly. To shut him up, I gesture to the mound of shellfish that has taken me so long to pick.

"I'm gathering them to eat," I say carefully, feeling alive to every noise, to every movement along the beach. Hawk's Lure and the other children begin to close the gap between us and I step back. Glancing over their shoulders, I see movement as a group of Red Men suddenly emerge from a patch of grass that lines the beach. Gutted, I make a gurgling noise attempting to clear my throat, but no words come out. My tongue is frozen; my mouth is dry.

Out of the corner of my eye, Spear Mamma smiles at me with her perfect teeth. Instinctively, I lean down and grab a mussel and hold it out as an offering. Instantly Hawk's Lure darts forwards and scoops it up before he dashes back into the tangled grasses where he disappears.

"There are more mussels all along this stretch," I manage, knowing that my quivering voice betrays my fear.

I have barely finished speaking when I hear a harsh, undulating cry that marks the arrival of two more *skraeling* warriors who are heavily adorned with red greasepaint. They are barefoot and their chiselled chests are painted red. When they see me, the taller of the two pulls out an arrow from the quiver on his back. Without waiting for him to nock it, I leave the basket, gather up my skirts, and run.

As I scramble up the bank, I brace myself to receive an arrow in the back, but nothing happens as I slip into the maze of tall reeds and grasses that lines the shore. Squatting low, I continue to push my way through the thistles that scratch my arms and cut my shins, panting heavily and swearing underneath my breath. The bugs are bad and there is no path, but I use the position of the sun to steer me back towards Leifsbidur, half-stumbling as I scramble to get away, panicking when I look back.

By the time I reach the well-worn path leading back to Leifsbidur, my heart is beating so loudly that all I hear is the thud of it as I suck in air and swallow bugs. There are mosquito bites welting on my ankles and the itch is fierce, but I push myself to keep running as I draw in air. By Óðinn's beard, how could I have been such a fool?

Up ahead, I hear someone shouting frantically. When I look up, Finnbogi is coming towards me from the direction of a nearby bog.

"Freydis, where have you been?" he pants as he runs up

to me. "Logatha is beside herself. Someone saw you wandering too far up the beach." He stops abruptly when he sees my face. "How now? Have you seen a ghost?"

"There are Red Men behind me," I gasp as I wipe my sleeve across my sweaty face.

"*Skraelings*? Where are they? Are they close to the settlement?"

"*Neinn*. They stole my shellfish. It seems as though their purpose is to gather food." I try to catch my breath as Finnbogi scans the terrain behind me.

"Freydis, you should not have been out here on your own. The *skraelings* are unpredictable. They have been known to carry women off, to kidnap them and make them into thralls."

"They have been known to do things worse than that," I sputter as I double over, panting heavily. When my breathing slows, I lift my head. "My brother warned me about them, but he also said they were motivated to trade furs for tools."

Finnbogi's eyes are fixed on the distant boglands rimmed by a copse of alders. "This is true, but the *skraelings* brought their trading goods into Leifsbidur. Your brother did not go out to them."

"I see," I say miserably. A headache throbs.

"Let this be a lesson," Finnbogi warns. "You must never leave the settlement of Leifsbidur on your own again. It is just not safe. Both Logatha and I were worried sick."

"Don't tell Logatha that I've been wandering the beach alone," I plead in a desperate voice. My guilt – a coiled-up snake – wraps itself around my throat.

"I won't speak to her about this, but mark these words: if you respect us both, you will never wander off by yourself again."

His warning is said with kindness, but the words still sting. All I wanted was to walk alone to explore the land and smell the air. I feel like I am a prisoner of Leifsbidur, forced to do only women's work. Instead of spinning wool and mending cloth, I yearn to try my hand at dressing a caribou and killing deer.

"I want to go out hunting with the men before the snowstorms come," I manage as I study him.

"'Tis is not proper," Finnbogi says in a clipped voice. He looks at me, studying me with his blue ice-chip eyes.

"Please, Finnbogi. I feel as though I have been a burden. Now that I have rid myself of Thorvard of Gardar, I would like to earn my keep. Besides, it is my fault that some of your Icelanders lost their lives. The battle you fought against my husband was one I should have endured alone."

He grunts dismissively, and I peer into his tired face.

"Please, Finnbogi," I try again. "I know I have good hunter instincts and a keen eye. I can paunch the kill, and I am strong enough to use my knife and peel back the fur. Many a time I have stripped the pelts off the carcass and deboned the meat all by myself. If only the huntsmen would agree to take me out with them, I could prove my worth."

"Therein lies the problem," Finnbogi interrupts. He clears his throat. When he continues, a flush of color moves into his neck. "The huntsmen miss their womenfolk. You would be easy prey for them."

"Easy prey?" I repeat.

Finnbogi throws me an awkward and embarrassed look. "If I send you out alone to hunt, I cannot guarantee your chastity."

"I'll let no man abuse me," I say irritably. "I'm done with that! The next man who comes near me will meet a ghastly fate!"

He tries to hush me but I shake him off. All around us, the rustling grasses shiver in the windy gusts.

"I'll run my dagger through the heart of any man who tries to do me harm. I'll chop off his hands and kick his balls and show him what I am all about. I'm done being treated like a dog. I'm done spreading my legs for any man." Finnbogi takes a step towards me. I lift my hand and my brow contorts into an angry scowl. I feel a flush of heat slowly moving into my cheeks. "By the gods, I'll cleave in half any man who dares to touch me against my will! I've killed before, and I am prepared to kill again."

"I've tried my best to protect you, Freydis Eiriksdöttir," Finnbogi says, "but I also know that you are strong and fierce and capable without my help. Forsooth, I've seen you wield your sword and slice through several Norsemen's backs."

"Please, Finnbogi," I beg. "I want to go out hunting with your men."

"You are a stubborn woman, Freydis Eiriksdöttir."

"Does that mean you will let me go?"

He waves me off. "I'll let you go, but please know this: I only warn you because I care."

"I am grateful that you look out for me," I say, throwing him a little smile.

"Ivor the Keen is taking a group out hunting just before *gormánuður* begins. The weather is growing colder, and the men won't risk an overnight trip in case it snows. I'll tell them that you would like to join their hunting party. You will have to be careful, Freydis. My men are unpredictable. They are raider types who have brutalized defenseless maidens not quite as strong or as well-skilled as you. Only Ivor and Snorri and Gudbrand can be trusted. Stay close to them and avoid the Red Men at all costs. I don't want to hear that you were being difficult."

"Difficult?" I ask, my annoyance cresting in my voice.

"Stubborn," he clarifies. Finnbogi twists his neck once more to scan the trail that skirts the bogs. "Logatha will not like it that I allowed you to go off hunting with the men," he says as he reaches up to rub the stubble of his beard.

"I'll tell Logatha about my hunting plans myself," I reply irritably. "She understands that the will to explore is in my blood."

Finnbogi gives a little laugh just as another flock of honking geese flies past. "If I know you, you'll tell her more than that," he says. "Just please watch yourself. There are dangers lurking everywhere."

Two days later when I find Logatha working hard to salt a catch of cod, I breathe in deeply and tell her all about what I intend to do. She clucks her tongue.

"You are a fool for wanting to take up your bow and arrow and do men's work."

"Logatha, I am desperate to explore the hills and wander

out into the boglands where the autumn foliage is turning colors and the air is sweet and crisp."

"You get that here," she says impatiently.

"It's not the same."

She glances up from her work. "Be on guard for *skraelings*. Ivor says he spotted some lurking around our settlement the other day."

"I'll be vigilant," I promise. She waves me off.

"I'll tell Ivor the Keen to keep his eye on you."

But Ivor the Keen isn't pleased when he learns of my intention to come along. He complains that, as a woman, I won't be able to keep up with all the men. What is worse, he is not alone in his opinion. I catch a few of the Icelanders making snide remarks. Some even slip in a few lewd jokes. After two days of this, I tell the men that I am Leif the Lucky's sister and that they answer to me and to no one else. Then I threaten to turn them out of my brother's longhouse for the winter. My tongue-lashing is so severe that the huntsmen slink away and I am left feeling smug. Finally, I have managed to regain control. The men now know that I am in charge.

On the day we leave Leifsbidur to go out hunting, it is blustery but warm for fall. We push our shoulders into the wind and journey inland in search of migrating caribou, deer, and fox. The men ignore me, but I don't care. Reveling in the feel of the warmth on my skin, I lift my face into the sun and savor the freedom of being outside where the leaves are turning and the landscape is a tumble of browns and yellows and splotchy smudges of orange-red.

After crossing over marshy fields, an Icelander by the

name of Harald is the first to spot the telltale signs that there are caribou grazing up ahead.

"Come!" he says excitedly. "Look at these hoof markings in the moss where the lichens have been nibbled down. It is surely a sign that the caribou feasted well."

"There is no evidence that a herd passed through here," a young Icelander with a freckled face whom I hardly know pipes up.

"Look closely, you impatient lout," Harald scolds the lad good-naturedly. "A whole herd could have slipped silently into the woods if their hooves crossed over that mound of rock."

I strain my ears to listen for the sound of snapping branches at the edge of a dark band of spruce, but the woods are eerily silent at this time of day with only the trees creaking overhead. A moment later I spot a trail of scat.

"They are here," I say confidently.

"By Óðinn's beard, we are wasting our time," a tall Norseman with uneven eyebrows huffs. His name is Jerrik, and I never liked him from the start. "I think we should keep going. I doubt a whole herd entered the forest here."

"On the contrary," I say irritably. "Look. The tree branches are all bent and twisted, which marks the spot where several enormous antlers passed into the woods."

"Freydis is determined to target a bull today," someone says in a teasing voice. The men chuckle at my expense and I feel my cheeks heating up. Gathering myself, I stand up tall.

"I want to eat this winter," I retort as I reposition the quiver on my back.

"I'll accompany you into the bush," Harald announces suddenly. Behind him there is grumbling.

"I'll come, too," Ivor the Keen pipes up. He steps forwards with a group of eager hunting types. Very soon, half of us depart to go in search of meat while the other half decide to stay behind and take a nap.

I have barely entered the bush when I spot more hoof prints imbedded in the muddy ground. "They went this way," I shout, throwing the words behind my back. My discovery prompts a gathering, and Harald suggests we all fan out.

As soon as I have crested the top of the next hill, I spot a group of mature stags with massive frames and long, smooth racks. They are grazing beside a bog surrounded by a thicket of stubby black spruce trees. Immediately I nock my arrow, placing my weight carefully and trying not to snap the twigs and brambles underfoot. Then I give the signal – a bird call that trills easily from my lips. The other huntsmen quickly position themselves around the herd. I see them waiting in the bush.

In front of me, the caribou move slowly, grazing as they go. One bull raises its head, its black eyes staring, its antlers so heavy it can barely hold them up. I target that one. As I lift my bow, the caribou's ears perk up. The flies are swarming around its face. The animal blinks. Its eyes are round pools of light.

Slowly and steadily, I take aim and release the shot. Everything around me stops and I follow the arrow's trajectory, listening to the whizz of the shaft as I hold my breath. There is a sudden burst of noise and the caribou goes down on a pile of dead brown leaves beside a copse of balsam firs. The rumble of the retreating caribou stampeding out of the clearing is so sudden that I have to shield my body from the cloud of drifting dust their hooves dredge up.

Just as a joyful cry escapes my lips, I hear an alarming sound. Startled, I turn and freeze as two Red Men with spears pop out from behind a tree. Their eyes are as black as iron ore and their thick, straight hair trails down their broad-shouldered backs. One of them flicks a sideways glance at my kill before turning back to study me. Terror grips my gut as his eyes come to linger on my breasts as though he is a predator deliberately studying his next prey. I slow my thoughts and swallow fear. Then I turn and aim my bow and arrow directly at his chest.

I think of Hawk's Lure. I remember Spear Mamma. Today, these carrion feeders won't unnerve me so easily. Today, I am a huntress. Today, I have found myself.

In the branches behind the *skraelings*' heads, I spot a raven, its feathers starkly black against the white of the silver birch. When it releases a long, rattling croak as it swoops across the forest floor, I am unnerved by the haunting echo of its cry, but I stand my ground.

For a moment I am distracted, but when the other *skraeling* tries to bolt, I release my arrow and it narrowly misses hitting him in the back. The stockier one goes to run, but then he stops, transfixed. The forest is pinging with the sound of the retreating raven's croaks, the echoes bouncing off the tree trunks and then slowly fading into the deep woods silence of the place.

I squint. The shadows shift.

The Red Man smirks. Staring him down, my mind strangely bends with the strain of everything – this place with its pine-tree scent, this unknown land, my unknown fate.

I shiver, falling into a trance almost.

The smell of rotting leaves wafts up from the forest floor and the crisp autumn air nips my cheeks. There is a sudden crunch of branches underfoot.

Standing in front of me, the Red Man tilts his head. For the first time, I notice that he is bare-chested, that his tanned skin is hairless, and that his muscled chest is perfectly contoured. Above his left nipple he sports a large tattoo. The outline of the bird has been shaded in with sleek black lines. The inside has been colored red.

I stare at it.

Red Raven smiles.

Chapter Nineteen

FOREVER HAUNTED

"**H**alt!" I shriek as I nock another arrow. Red Raven darts behind a tree. I cut him off, searching for his friend, a solidly built, beardless, stern-looking brave with a stag-skin loincloth and red-ochred cape that has been thrown over his goose-pimpled shoulders and tied at the waist with a belt. He is struggling to remove his foot from a tangle of tree roots, and he looks distressed. In a throaty tongue, the two exchange a torrent of words before Red Raven turns and points to me. With shaking fingers, I continue to draw my bowstring back.

"The kill is mine!" I shriek, gesturing wildly at the fallen caribou with my head. The mosquitoes hum around my head. I glance around, looking for Ivor the Keen and his men but the woods are still. Through the jumble of leafless trees I think I see movement, but when I look again, nothing stirs. In the silence, I can't seem to shake the feeling that there is an unnatural spirit presence lurking in this place of creaking trees screeching out their haunting twig tunes.

When Red Raven conducts another predatory evaluation of my bones, my stomach sours.

"Get back," I shout as my knees begin to buckle. I can feel sweat dripping down my back. Red Raven looks past me at the fallen bull and mumbles reverently, his mutterings rumbling up from somewhere deep inside his chest. An instant later he slowly begins to move towards me with a cautious hand outstretched. His toes rustle the fallen leaves. The crunch of them reminds me of brittle bones.

Something moves in the mound of leaves. When a little bird scratches through the dead brown pile, Red Raven stops and stares. For a moment, all goes still. Then his eyes slowly wander up and come to rest on my red hair. Without a word, he dares to take another step forwards on his hunter's feet, taking care not to do anything too sudden to startle me.

The arrow in my hand feels too heavy and I am suddenly aware that I am very cold. With effort, I focus in on Red Raven's bird tattoo, but my thoughts are as slow as dripping sap, and my leg muscles feel like tangled kelp. When Red Raven suddenly stops and draws forth a strange-looking object, my eyes go wide. It looks like a catapult.

Instantaneously, I turn and bolt. Sheer panic makes me dodge the low-lying shrubs that scratch my shins and cut through my skin. A pulse is throbbing in my throat, a drum is pounding in my head. Wheezing, I push myself to run without looking back as the goosebumps pop and I swallow bugs.

By the time I reach the clearing where I had left the Icelanders lounging in the autumn sun, the stitch in my side is so intense that I double over and suck in air. When I see my legs – the scrapes dripping blood surrounded by patches of spruce gum that I can't rub off – I fall into a vicious rage.

"On your feet, you lazy louts!"

Ivor's men barely stir. I limp towards the group of them and kick Jerrik with my foot. "Get up, you lily-livered huntsman! There are red-faced *skraelings* in the woods."

My warning spreads like wildfire and the men jump up, scrambling to shoulder their weapons and gather up their gear. Just then Ivor the Keen emerges from the woods in the company of the other men. His skin is flushed and he looks rattled, as if he has seen a ghost. I glance at him sharply.

"Why did you run away from such worthless Red Men, strong warriors that you are?"

Ivor the Keen stares at me. "How did you make it here ahead of us?" he gasps.

"It seems likely that the *skraelings* will steal my caribou racks and all that meat. We need to go back for it."

"Calm yourself, Freydis," Ivor the Keen whispers as he brings his index finger to his lips. "The *skraelings* have weapons, and we are not prepared to fight them off. May the gods decide the time for battle. Today we are only here to hunt."

"Then hunt we shall," I spit. "I have shot and killed a bull today. The antlers alone would give our people many tools. That luscious hide would be a treasured gift. Think on it, I beg of you! Send your men back into the bush to retrieve the caribou that I have downed."

"*Neinn*, it is too dangerous. The *skraelings* are unpredictable. They could bring us trouble."

"Then let me have a sword," I blurt. "I think I could fight them better than any of you."

"*Neinn*, be still, woman," Ivor the Keen snarls in a fierce whisper as he steps forwards and takes me firmly by the arm. "The men are packed and ready to return to Leifsbidur. You will not reprimand them for exercising good judgment and deciding to leave without a fight. Besides, Finnbogi asked me to watch over you, and I'll do just that. Now listen up, you will leave this place or I'll be forced to tie you up and drag you home behind me."

For a moment, I simply stare at him. Then I quickly yank my arm away. I feel like biting him like a wolverine, but instead I emit an injured huff. "I'll not go anywhere until I retrieve my kill."

"It was a good shot, a fine shot," one of the men pipes up. "You downed a caribou with the largest rack I've ever seen. You should be pleased with yourself, Freydis Eiriksdöttir. Your *faðir* would be very proud."

"If you feel that way, then come back with me for the caribou," I challenge him in a haughty voice. Fear nests around his eyes. He takes a careful step back from me.

"You gutless worm," I say disgustedly.

"Come now, Freydis. You are a headstrong woman who doesn't see the dangers of facing Red Men in the bush when we are not prepared." Harald the Bald is trying to be gentle as he relieves Ivor of the care of me, but my blood is boiling. I can feel my temples throbbing and the heat rising in my cheeks.

"We will leave you here if you refuse to return to Leifsbidur," Ivor the Keen says stiffly as he motions to a runner to go and scout ahead. I am so frustrated that I am vibrating like a leaf in an autumn wind. Miserably, I know my only option is to follow the men out or be captured by the Red Men with their troll-like fingers that strum bows like gods strum lyres.

The trek back to Leifsbidur is long and hard as we circle around the muddy bogs and cross through shallow marshes surrounded by dense clusters of tuckamore. I am surly around Ivor the Keen who maintains his silence as he walks beside me looking grim. The other men are watchful with swiveling heads like the great grey owl as we travel into a lee of thick birch and poplar trees. When we wind our way around the marshes harboring migrating ducks and honking geese, we encounter no one, and I stay silent, but my resentment breaks into shards of bitterness that I flick at Ivor the Keen and his men.

By the time we arrive back in Leifsbidur, my mood is completely foul. I give Ivor the Keen the cold shoulder and refuse to take my supper in the hall with the men. Instead I find a stoop where I can be alone and sulk. For a long while I sit listening to the waves pummeling the shore and watching the swells crashing violently against the rocks, churning up a white frothy foam. In the distance, the sound of the laughing Norsemen who are eating their fill spills out from the great room, and I can't help but think about how much I hate them all. My stomach sours.

It is Logatha who comes outside to find me. Without saying anything, I know she has heard about my trophy kill.

We sit together until the shadows of a harvest moon start to lengthen and the evening chill begins to creep underneath our furs.

"Soon we will be living in darkness for most of the day," Logatha sighs. Her breath rises in plumes of mist. I say nothing but think to myself that she is wrong, based on what Leif has told me about Vinland winters.

"It is cold out here, Freydis. We should go inside," Logatha says as she huddles close to me for extra warmth.

"I'll not join that sorry lot. They are lazy hunters, all of them."

Logatha shivers as she clings to me. "I am happy that Ivor the Keen brought you safely home," she sighs. Her words are whisked away by the rising wind. "I don't trust those red-faced *skraelings* with their animal hides that barely cover their private parts. If you had stayed to pelt out that caribou, the *skraelings* would have fought you for the racks. The huntsmen tell me that they were very large."

I shrug my shoulders and lift my chin. "My hunting efforts were all for naught."

"There will be other opportunities, Freydis," Logatha murmurs. She rests her head against my arm and we sit together in silence until the stars come out, winking as if to mock me.

"Ivor the Keen is spineless," I grump.

"He is level-headed and Finnbogi trusts him. Now let it be or you will be haunted by it, and that will never do."

She is right. I am haunted by it. I can't let it go. The racks were worth their weight in gold.

A few days later, I wake to a woollen grey sky that

smells of rain. When the stormclouds finally break, the rain does not let up, and it storms for days. Even walking between the longhouse and the byre is miserable in the icy rain. Then the fierce winds come swirling into the settlement, churning up the raging seas. Everyone wants to stay inside, and just like that the chance to score another kill is lost.

"We need to move the animals into the longhouse for the winter," Finnbogi mutters as he squats down low to warm himself in front of the roaring fire. A puff of steam rises up from his sodden mantle. "I'll set up a partition behind the loom."

"The animals will keep us warm at night," Logatha smiles with an impish look.

"You and I, we don't need their heat," Finnbogi teases as he eyes his wife. His dimple pops in the firelight.

I stare at them. "We are low on meat," I say with a heavy sigh. "I'd like to try my hand at killing deer to get us through the winter."

"Fie," Logatha says as she glances at Finnbogi with a hidden message I cannot decipher. She rises to turn the capelins that have been set to roast on the scroll iron.

"You worry too much," Finnbogi says in a serious tone.

"It's good to worry," I say defensively. "I think we should send more hunters out before it snows."

"It would be miserable in the wind and rain," Finnbogi says impatiently as he tugs on his tasselled beard. "Besides, we can always set down winter traps."

I feel tingles in my arms and legs. "Perhaps it would be wise to dry more meat just in case." I look down so he does not see my annoyance. "Before the first snowfall comes, I'll go out hunting once again."

There is an awkward silence. Logatha stops her work.

"The men will not go out with you again," Finnbogi says carefully, keeping his eyes downcast. "They say that you are…"

"That I am what?" I snap.

"Too hard to be around."

"Too hard to be around?" I repeat. I can feel my cheeks becoming hot.

"Ivor the Keen is spreading rumours," Logatha adds as she looks at me.

"What kind of rumours?" I ask sharply.

"He has been calling you 'hotheaded' and 'stubborn'. He thinks you are a woman ruled by Loki's whims." Finnbogi sports an embarrassed flush that begins to spread down his neck.

"Why does he debase my name?"

"Because you called the men cowards for failing to face the *skraelings* who scored your kill," Finnbogi replies. He pauses to clear his throat. From the corner of my eye I catch sight of a few of the Icelanders listening in, their curious eyes flitting between the three of us.

"Perhaps I should leave this house and go find somewhere else to live," I say in a bitter tone.

"*Neinn,*" Logatha murmurs quickly as she throws Finnbogi a disapproving look. He looks as serious as someone who is re-stitching wool.

"As you know, most of your Greenlanders have defected to Thorvard's camp," he says, frowning. "Soon it will be said that the Icelanders and the Greenlanders could not get along."

I stand up slowly and turn around to warm my back against the fire.

"Snorri and Gunnar remain the most loyal. They refuse to speak out against you," Finnbogi continues with a heavy sigh.

I rub my temples with my palm and search my memory for the faces I have missed seeing around the fire.

"By Óðinn's beard ! Are you certain my Greenlanders went to Thorvard's camp?"

"Snorri tracked them there two days ago," Logatha says. She pops into view and I watch her fiddling with some wool.

"Freydis, you should know something else," Finnbogi says. I raise an eyebrow. "There is a rumour…"

"What are you saying?" I ask sharply.

"Snorri is an honorable man who is working hard to clear your name," Finnbogi says before he tosses Logatha a desperate look.

"He has managed to convince some of your Greenlanders to stay with us here in Leifsbidur by telling them about the abuse you endured at Thorvard's hands," Logatha finishes.

I feel my brow creasing into a frown. How is it that my shame is being used to ensure the loyalty of my men? I don't need their pity. I don't need anyone if this is all there is. Maybe, just maybe, it would better for me to be alone. Even if I could prove that Thorvard is a snake, they would still judge me as being difficult. There is no escaping him. How is it that they worship him?

I turn my back on Logatha before she notices my stricken face. Someone opens the door and the wind howls fiercely and the woven baskets hanging from the rafters begin to sway. In that moment, I remember and the fear comes slinking back, making my stomach churn. In my head, I hear the timbre of Thorvard's voice, his murmured threats, his heavy footfalls when he gets mad. Then I begin to worry about the consequences of slandering my husband's name. His ghost paws at me, whispering that I'm a stupid fool, belittling me with a gathered string of hurtful words and obscenities.

That night as the Norsemen gather around the hearth, I scrutinize each man's face, attempting to ascertain their loyalty. When my eyes come to rest on Snorri, I see that he is seated beside Groa and that she is with child. As I silently observe their exchange, I feel lonely in the crowded longhouse that my brother built.

A week later when the snowstorms come, we crowd inside the great longhouse with its four large chambers and one great hall and pass the time by singing ballads and playing games and reciting tales. Outside, the storms dump snow which builds in banks outside the longhouse door.

Despite my disappointment in the Greenlanders who have defected to Thorvard's camp, I worry about how they are managing the brutality of the winter storms. Finnbogi assures me that the Greenlanders will survive, but I'm not so sure. It's too damn cold. In secret, I offer sacrifice to the gods, asking them to deliver my men from harm.

"I do not want any more deaths to be blamed on me," I tell Logatha one night as we sit in front of a blazing fire listing to another howling blizzard raging outside our door. "I promised Leif I would look after the Greenlanders."

"The Greenlanders are no longer your responsibility, Freydis."

"Even so," I mutter, squirming uncomfortably in my seat.

"Their safety is no more important than ours," Logatha sputters as she finishes with her drop spindle, the twist crawling up into the fibers that she has drafted out. In front of us, the fire hisses as a log breaks in half.

"The Greenlanders are my people," I whisper quietly as Logatha drops her yarn into a nearby basket and takes up a stick to poke the fire. "Some of the men only came to Leifsbidur because I asked. I would feel responsible if anything happened. I don't want them to suffer."

"They betrayed you," Logatha says, glancing up. "They defected to Thorvard's camp. You must let go of the guilt you carry. Imagine tying it to a rock and throwing it out into the stormy sea." Her eyes look glassy in the firelight; a web of shadows covers half her face.

"I know you hate my Greenlanders," I say eventually. The tattered shawl around her shoulders needs repair. I will take some yarn and stitch it up when the light is better.

"*Neinn*. I hate the Greenlanders for supporting a wife-beater and for backing the murderer who killed my bairn." The resentment builds in her voice.

"Finnbogi will avenge us both," I remind her as the fire crackles noisily. Another log explodes and splits in half, sending a shower of burning sparks into the air. When they land, I quickly snuff them out with my toe. From the opposite end of the longhouse we hear a sudden burst of laughter.

Logatha leans in closely. Her eyes pick their way up to the brooch on my apron dress. "I am afraid that Finnbogi will challenge Thorvard to a duel," she murmurs.

"Finnbogi would surely win the fight," I say.

She nods but her face is pasty white. "I wish someone would stab that bastard in his sleep," she whispers, flushing deeply. I straighten up and brush back my hair with my hand.

"Me too," I breathe.

That night I envy the tender loving that Finnbogi gives to Logatha. Their bodies move together in the far back shadows, and their passionate groans and sighs echo softly through the longhouse. I yearn to have what they have found, to feel what they must feel, to be with a man who is my guardian, but I know that kind of love is beyond my reach. I am sad about it, but I cannot cry. I can't do anything anymore.

Turning my back against the longhouse wall I try to fall asleep, but I stir awake at every noise. Just when I am drifting off, I slide into an ethereal fog and see images of a *skraeling* man. Red Raven has a leering smile.

His eyes – his luminous eyes – are focused hungrily on my hair.

"Get back," I say.

Sometime during that spell of winter lockdown, Logatha becomes pregnant once again.

"It is something to celebrate," I say, feeling genuinely happy for her.

"Freydis, I am scared," she replies.

"It will be different this time around. You must try to eat for two."

"I will eat only after the morning sickness passes and I can stomach food," Logatha says, smiling sweetly. She looks at me and her demeanor suddenly changes. "Freydis," she whispers as she pulls her woollen shawl around her shoulders, "I worry that we will run out of food before the winter ends."

Our eyes lock. I, too, have had that very thought. I know what it is like to run out of food, and I will try to stop that from happening here in Leifsbidur. I take a breath. "There are hunters among us who will brave the storms to bring us meat."

Across the room, I see Grelod stand. She thinks that I have beckoned to her with my flailing arms but I have not. I wave her off impatiently. When I turn back, Logatha is staring at the wall.

"What is wrong, sister?"

"Nothing," she whispers, but I see the nest of crow's-feet wrinkles around her eyes crinkling. I squeeze her hand.

"Worrying is not good for the growing bairn," I say in a gentle voice.

"Even now I feel the sting of gut-wrenching grief when I think of what Thorvard took from me," she mutters. She can't look at me.

My tongue feels thick. "We will not let him steal from us again," I manage eventually.

"*Neinn*," she mumbles with a scowl. "We share a hatred that we can split in two to give us room to smile."

I nod but I can't trust my voice to speak.

"The fear and anger always seem to lessen when I talk to you," she says as she places a warm hand on my shoulder.

"I am sorry about what he did to you," I say. I bite the insides of my cheeks. Logatha's lips tighten.

"I am sorry they made you marry him."

I tilt my chin up to look at her. "I've escaped from his clutches thanks to you and Finnbogi," I say, but my guts are churning and my palms are wet. She grins at me, and the smile is warm and endearing.

In the coming weeks, the winter storms set in and the temperature dips so low that no one dares to venture out. One day, as I am dressing behind a bed curtain in the blackness of an early dawn, I hear Soren Egilson, a red-headed Greenlander who hails from the north, and Snorri, the Icelander, arguing vehemently.

"In the name of Thor, it is time to kill that goat for meat," Soren says crossly. Memories of Brúsi come swirling in, rattling me so much that my pulse picks up.

"Gods' bread, we can't butcher her or we'll lose the herd. She breeds better than all the rest."

Peeking through the curtain, it looks as though Soren and Snorri are the only ones awake.

"That goat hasn't produced milk for days," Soren sniffs.

"Come on, man," Snorri barks. "Use your head! Didn't you feel her abdomen? She is carrying kids."

"We will starve her out and she will lose those baby goats. At least right now she gives us meat."

"Watch your tongue, you shit-bag, or I'll cut it out," Snorri snaps, and I fall back. "We won't be butchering no goat today."

"Who put you in charge?" Soren asks. His tone is sharp.

I take a breath and step out of the shadows. My vision tunnels as I point my finger at Soren's chest. "Hold your tongue! While you reside in my brother's house, I am in charge, and I am of the same mind as Snorri. We will spare the goats."

"I answer to no woman," Soren says defiantly. "Go to Hel, Freydis Eiriksdóttir!

Behind me I hear a rustling noise. "If you refuse to heed her words, then you'll heed mine," Helgi mutters from a darkened corner at the back. He hacks out a wet, phlegmy cough. Glancing at him, I see that his face is pale.

"We will not kill the mother goat," I mutter angrily.

"That goat needs to birth those kids," Snorri barks. "In the meantime, someone needs to go out to find us meat."

"Who will go?" Soren scoffs.

"I'll go," I say quickly.

From the opposite end of the room, Logatha inches her way off a bed platform, dragging a heavy hide behind her. "*Neinn*," she says forcefully. The bulge of her pregnant belly is hidden underneath her furs. "It is too dangerous."

"By the gods, I don't want us to starve to death," I say

pointedly. I purposely don't mention that I long to escape outdoors so I can wander freely in the snow and smell the air instead of the filthy stink from all the men.

"Freydis, you'll freeze to death," Logatha mutters.

"Let the gods direct my path," I sigh, turning back to face the fire. Behind me, Snorri begins to count all the able-bodied men.

"It seems like many of us are too sick to hunt," Helgi grunts.

"They aren't sick," Soren snorts irritably. "They are lazy louts who look for every excuse to get out of doing chores."

"Give me my harpoon," Finnbogi says in a raspy voice as he hoists himself out of bed. He looks so ill that his brother tells him to sit back down. Finnbogi shoves past him and stubbornly makes his way towards the fire.

"One of us should stay behind and guard this place," Helgi snaps. Finnbogi refuses to turn around, and Helgi scowls. "Brother, I'll volunteer to brave the storm. It is best that you stay here with your pregnant wife."

"That is a good plan," I say quickly. Finnbogi plops down wearily on a bench before turning to stare at me with his bloodshot eyes. "Come now, Finnbogi. Let me join Helgi and his men. I am used to tracking in the snow."

"I am game for taking her along," Snorri announces as he circles around the fire. "I have seen the outcome of her marksman's eye. She killed a caribou in the bush, and if she can manage that we need her with us. I am confident that Freydis will prove her worth."

I nod my head as a warmth spreads through me.

That night, another blizzard hits. Then Soren himself

falls ill. His breath comes in rapid bursts and he develops a raspy cough. Soon many others take ill so that only a few of us are left to keep the fires stoked.

"I have hunger pains," Logatha complains one day as we sit together listening to the storm outside. It is a whiteout, and inside the longhouse we can barely tell if it is day or night.

"I'll go out tomorrow to find us food," Finnbogi says. His thin frame is shaking despite the warm sealskin that is draped across his back. There are dark circles around his eyes.

In a flash I visualize Thorvard's greasy lips, a chunk of mutton in his hand.

Logatha tucks her head underneath Finnbogi's chin and his furs meld into hers. The fire flares. Logatha's cheeks are pale and gaunt. Finnbogi's shoulders are trembling and he looks flushed. He can't stop shaking despite the warmth the fire throws. When he tilts his head back and closes his eyes, I stare at him.

"Perhaps it's time to kill a goat," is all I say as I listen to the fire snap.

Chapter Twenty

RED RAVEN

I wake to silence. The blizzard is over but it is bitterly cold and there is a layer of frost covering the table top and a layer of ice on the water pail. The hearth fire is nothing but an orange glow of embers surrounded by the snow of white ashes.

In the shadows the Icelanders sleep late, their snores erupting in sporadic bursts, their coughs purling in their throats. The sickness that Logatha calls *"skyrbjugr"* has begun attacking in full force. Many complain that their limbs are sore. All they do is sleep and cough. I worry that they are marked to enter Helheim soon.

In the dappled grey light of a winter dawn, I make my way towards the door where I unbolt the latch, cringing as the creaky screech shatters the morning peace. Outside, the snow fills the gullies in uneven dips where the river lies somewhere below. All I see is white. Fields of white. Inhaling deeply, I roll my neck and watch my breath coming out in foggy wisps.

"The sun is back," Logatha murmurs softly from the shadows. Startled, I turn. Her soft chuckle sits low inside her chest as she steps forwards and gently takes me by the arm. Together we watch the sunrise tiptoeing across the glittering snow, following a path of sparkles.

"Not even Skaði, that fearless god of winter, would dare to venture outside today. It is too cold." Logatha shivers, hunching her shoulders and folding her arms across her chest. Her cheeks are hollow. She looks too thin.

"Despite the cold, I want to go out hunting," I murmur as I rub her back, resolving to secretly slip some extra rations into her soup to fatten her up in her pregnant state.

"Freydis, I know you are eager to check the traps," Logatha says, huddling closer for extra warmth. "You must take Finnbogi with you when you go."

"Your husband is too sick, Logatha," I say. I glance behind me towards his bed.

"Then take Helgi. I passed his bed platform and he isn't there. He must have risen early to check on things around the yard."

"I'll go find him," I lie easily. "He and I will leave before the others wake."

"I'll pray to Óðinn and to Thor for your safe return," she says. Her eyes emit a strange sadness, a look I dare not own. "Just promise that you will come back by dusk. I wouldn't want you to freeze to death."

"Logatha, you are a mother hen," I tease. I feel my hair come loose from my messy braid. She reaches out and tucks it back.

"Freydis, promise me that you will be safe."

"I will, my friend," I say distractedly. "I'll hunt caribou. Just you wait. I'll bring us back an entire shank of meat to eat tonight."

Logatha claps her hands together and licks her lips. Her gesture is so comical that I begin to chuckle. The laughter feels all buttery and I cherish this woman who has helped me find my peace and restore what I thought was lost. Bending our heads together, we look out across the land at the light bouncing off the mounds of snow and ice.

"I'm not sure you should go," Logatha chirps. We turn away from the open door and she studies me as I begin to gather up my gear.

"The weather is a good omen," I say. I am so famished that the thought of eating roasted mice appeals to me. When I stand, my knees crack.

"Help me get into my coat," I mumble. Logatha plucks the sealskins from my arms and holds the coat out for me. When I slip into it, I feel the softness of the polar-bear fleece that edges the sleeves and lines the hood.

"That coat highlights your red hair," Logatha teases. "You look warm and huntress-like."

I squat and wrench the ties on my leather boots. "Tell Finnbogi goodbye from me," I say, but my voice gets muffled when I go to adjust the quiver on my back.

"May the gods go with you, Freydis," Logatha says quietly.

"Stay indoors today, sister," I reply as I step outside. A whoosh of cold air stings my face as I lean down and begin to strap on my snowshoes and adjust the ties. "Look at the lacy path the ice god prepared for me."

"She never rests," Logatha chuckles softly before she throws me another worried smile.

"I'll be all right," I say, glancing up. Logatha's eyes soften when she sees me staring at her pregnant bump. When I stand, I rub my mittened hands together to generate some extra warmth. "Please get some rest," I say through the layers that are already frosting up around my nose and mouth. "May the gods take care of you both. Please look after Little Bump."

Shivering, she nods. Then she shoos me off as the wind whips through the yard, eddying under the byre's overhang.

I make my way to the end of the longhouse but it is hard going through the snow. Just before I disappear around the corner, I turn around. Logatha is still standing in the open door with her furs wrapped tightly around her gaunt frame. When she sees me, she turns and smiles. Then she lifts her hand and waves.

Helgi is humming in the byre as he pitches apart the frozen hay. For a moment I stand and listen, and then I turn away. At the gate, a crow swoops down and begins to caw as if to encourage me to leave.

I begin to move, reveling in the sound of the ice crackling underfoot as my snowshoes break through the top layer of snow and then sink. The sun is bright but I press forwards across the fields, glancing up at the blue sky before skirting across the frozen river, feeling only a soothing peace.

By mid-morning, I have checked all the traps and killed only one rabbit. After that I can't seem to find any signs of life, but I push myself to keep ploughing through the heavy snow, making my way slowly east, keeping an eye out for any signs of movement in the white. When I stop to adjust my furs, I spot a frozen cobweb on a branch, twinkling and sparkling in the sun, and it occurs to me that I am all alone in the middle of a vast and quiet wilderness.

I whistle like a guillemot and hear the lonely trill come back to me in a hollow echo, loud and discordant. There is a surge of panic and then I fall dejectedly into the snow. My eyes are watering. The world is a blur of white on white. I think of the dangers of the land: the hidden tree wells; the rocks and streams; the sudden drop-offs; the risk of frostbite if I get too cold. It takes a long time to get up again.

When the blinding sun tricks my mind into seeing an animal that isn't there, a curse slips out and the noise disturbs the peace of some lone bird that rises with a noisy squawk. Eventually I drag myself into a cluster of black spruce trees where I narrowly miss getting buried by a shower of snow that slips off the branches at the top. All of a sudden, there is movement in my periphery.

At the far end of the clearing, two majestic deer are slowly picking their way through the snow. When I see them, I immediately think of Logatha in her pregnant state and thank Skaði for the gift. Then I think of Finnbogi, Helgi, Snorri, and all the rest. Groa, Grelod, and Asta too. I can almost taste the venison roasting on the fire.

Keeping the deer in sight, I carefully draw out an arrow, nocking it into place and setting the groove of my first three fingers around the bowstring to create a hook. Then I raise my arm and draw the bowstring back with practiced ease.

Just as I touch the string to the centre of my nose, the stag's ears begin to twitch and it turns its head. I breathe in icy air, feeling the bite, the sting of the freezing cold. An instant later I release the shot.

Behind me there is a whizzing hiss. The twang of another huntsman's bow. In a daze I see a shaft lined with feathers come shooting past, and for a moment I am too shocked to move. When I turn around, three hunters dressed in sealskin furs that are tinted a rosy red are standing directly in front of me. Their fur-clad forms are so bulky that they block out the sun.

"By the gods, you stole my kill!"

One of the hunters throws back his hood and stares at me audaciously. With a staggering jolt, I see my mistake. The hoodless one is covered in red ochre paint with a tattoo scrolling down his cheek.

"What do you want?" I shout, my voice so shrill that another clump of snow on the tree beside me slithers down. The hoodless one devours me as he stares me down. I feel my brow crinkling. He looks familiar. There is a sudden rush of heat, and Leif's voice pings into my thoughts. His baritone is as dry as the brown, dusty autumn leaves:

These *skraelings* are a vicious lot, a band of thieves.

Don't worry, brother. They won't take my spoils so easily.

Striking my breast, I let out a furious battle cry and lose my hood. When my tangled, frosty red hair comes tumbling out, curls and all, the Red Men gasp. Their eyes grow wide. They point at me excitedly.

Keeping one eye on the men, I begin to move towards

the deer carcass that lies half-hidden in a bank of snow. There is sweat running down my neck and back, and I find that I am holding my breath without even realizing it. From this distance the stag looks big and my spirit soars. The shot was clean. My arrow must have killed it almost instantly. Unless...

I suck in frost. What if my shot went wide? I spin around. What if it was the *skraeling's* arrow that took out the deer?

The shrill squawk from a bird flying overhead rings out. Even from this distance, I can see the markings on the Red Men's faces. The black. The red. It makes them look formidable. In that moment, Logatha's ghost touches my shoulder and locks my bones.

You should leave, Freydis. The deer meat is not worth the risk. These Skraelings are a pack of wolves who will kill you for the treasure that your bow and arrow netted. It was a good shot. A fine shot.

I steel my nerves and clench my jaw. In a frenzy I rip my furs open and start pounding on my chest, wailing and shrieking as my curls tumble into my face. The Red Men look up. Their eyes grow wide. Instantly, two of them flee into the woods, but the hoodless one stands his ground. His body stills.

"Stand back," I yell as I shake my mane to hold him off. He seems surprised that I am a woman, but he doesn't move. Tilting my chin into the sky, I release the loudest scream I've managed yet – a shrill, high-pitched screech, an ear-splitting wail that echoes up and down the valley floor. The *skraeling* jumps. His gaping mouth is soundless.

"Get away," I hiss as he looks past me to the fallen deer lying in the snowbank. Keeping his eyes fixed on my prize, he slowly begins to move towards me on a set of snowshoes just like mine. He follows my tracks through the snow so gracefully that he reminds me of a swaying silver birch.

Against my better judgement I let him approach as dissonant sounds begin to slither off his tongue, rolling and building to a peak. The noise marks this place, this no-man's land. It is like he is praying for the fallen deer, honoring it with some strange ritualistic song.

As soon as the hoodless one reaches the animal, he squats beside it to close its eyes. There is such a gentleness about him that I can't make sense of him. Mesmerized, I get caught up listening to the sounds spilling from his mouth, the bubble of them flowing out like the sound of a river washing over rocks.

It dawns on me that it is growing late, that I must work fast to skin out the deer before I lose the sun. Cautiously, I leave the Red Man to himself, but I am vigilant and unnerved to have him in my space, watching me intently, treating me as though I am to be revered. Working quickly, my attention split between the Red Man and the deer, I cut into the belly of the deer and expose the flesh and fat as the steam rises, pluming in the frigid air.

When I am halfway done, I step back and see the gore in the blood-splattered snow: the gristle, the meat, the bone, and the flesh. The red on white. I see it all and miss spotting the hoodless one get up. When he helps himself to a chunk of my de-boned meat, I curse myself. If Finnbogi were here, he would chastise me for letting this red-faced rat steal from me. He would tell me that I've lost my edge, that the trickster god just won the game.

The hunter moves past the chopped-up carcass, past the shanks of bloody meat sticking out of the mucked-up snow. Warily I watch as he circles around me. I grip my knife. I could kill him now and be done with it, but something urges me to let him live. The Red Man who courts dead deer is a curiosity in this unfamiliar place where the animal's spirit seems to linger mystically. Hesitantly I resume my work.

Just as I am beginning to cut the pelt free of the legs, I hear a noise. When I glance up, there is a sleek black raven with a powerful bill soaring high as it catches wind currents. Its blue-black feathered wings with their iridescent sheen catch the light as dusk descends. Suddenly, it soars into an updraft and then it falls, gliding and tilting its wings as it croaks out a loud, irreverent call.

For a moment I just stop and stare. When I finally lower my head, the *skraeling* is staring at me with his eyes as grey as slate. I know those eyes. Those piercing eyes. I search my mind, upturning ghosts before a sudden memory sparks. Oh, curse his bones! Red Raven smiles.

Warily I watch him shake the frozen tingles from his feet. When he snowshoes closer, I am so on edge that I startle when he leans in to help de-bone the deer.

"The kill is mine," I mutter, worrying that I am about to be lured into some kind of trap. He flicks a glance up at me before turning back to his work.

In silence we tear the meat from the sinew, the fat, and the cartilage until there are splotches of blood everywhere –

on my sealskin hides and on the polar-bear fleece that lines my hood, on my hands and in my hair. Taking up a handful of snow in my bloodied hands, I begin scrubbing at the stains while Red Raven cups his mouth and whistles low.

There is a ripple of unease that shoots through me. I twist around. In the ice-blue shadows of a fast-approaching winter dusk, his friends suddenly appear at the edge of the clearing, dragging an empty sled behind them.

Red Raven hacks out a greeting. The words sound harsh and I pull back. He glances at me uneasily and I hate that his eyes look kind. Skraelings aren't supposed to have a smile like that – the one he throws at me, the one he uses when he eyes my hair.

As soon as I start to back away, he tries to stop me with his hand.

"Don't touch me," I say, pulling back as if I'm stung. He turns to his friends and waves his hand, beckoning them closer. Sturdily built, he is a stocky man with straight, broad shoulders and muscular thighs with a strong jaw and smooth, acorn-colored skin sporting a sheen of red. He has a commanding presence about him, but something in the way he looks pulls me into him like sticky tree-sap.

When his friends spot me they stop and stare, and their eyes look scared, but Red Raven seems unperturbed. He talks to them and grins again with his perfect teeth. Then he points to the chunks of meat before he turns his gaze onto me and points to my hair.

My thoughts tunnel into imagined horrors and dangers that I could face – situations in which I can't fight to save myself, situations in which I am tortured while I am still alive. I am rendered helpless by my thoughts as I stare at the dried blood underneath my nails. The temperature is dropping quickly. My fingers and toes feel frozen stiff.

Beside me Red Raven raises his bloodied knife that he has used to help debone the meat and I jump back, shivering, but he doesn't see. When he motions to his friend to lean down and help him finish the task of pulling out the heart, it crosses my mind that I could try to kill them all, but I hold back. I am too malnourished, too fatigued.

When Red Raven finishes cleaning off his knife, he finds my eyes before he jabs himself fiercely in the chest. "Achak," he grunts in a deep baritone.

Tongue-tied, I say nothing. Now that the work is done, it would be easy enough for them to steal my meat and slit my throat and leave me bleeding in the snow. They wouldn't have to know my name.

"It's time to go," I say. Achak tilts his head and looks at me strangely.

I try to tell them that the meat is mine, but one of them points towards the setting sun. I have lost all track of time since entering into this strange dance, this saga with a group of strange *skraeling* men. When I glance towards the sky, I can feel my skin tingling. Soon we will lose the light.

Achak jerks his chin towards his friends. Through gestures I discern that he wants me to follow them.

"Neinn," I say. "I must return to Leifsbidur."

The name triggers recognition in the Red Men's eyes. I watch as they confer amongst themselves. Another surge of panic bubbles up.

"Leifsbidur," I repeat. "It is my home." The Red Men stop their chatter and look at me.

"Leifsbidur," Achak repeats in an accent so thick it is hard for me to decipher the chopped-up sounds. He points behind me to my snowshoe tracks as I gulp in the freezing cold that stings my lungs and exhale a puff of dragon air.

"I need to carry the meat shanks back to my people," I say, gesturing fiercely at the bloody piles as the sun slowly slips behind the hills.

One of Achak's companions jerks his chin at the silver moon on the rise. In the process, his red fox-fur hood falls off his head, revealing a head of luscious obsidian-black hair that reaches past his shoulders.

I have lost precious moments trying to communicate with these red-faced huntsmen whom I don't trust. These *skraeling* men. These carrions who pick my life apart. Achak releases another string of words as I go to hoist my pack on my back. When I turn around, his body blocks my path.

"Let me pass," I say angrily. He doesn't move. He merely points and I follow his finger. It is now too dark to see the trail. My panic swells.

I can't return to Leifsbidur. I won't be able to find my way back home. By Óðinn's beard, I'll freeze to death!

My body shudders as I begin to cough. The hacking brings up a thick mucus phlegm laced with blood. Suddenly I realize that I am burning up. There is sweat beading on my brow. Achak studies me carefully. I look away.

"I must return to Leifsbidur," I repeat. A headache

pounds. Just then, another throat itch bursts into a wretched cough.

The *skraelings* surround me, attempting to cut me off. Achak's cry echoes across the clearing and I shake my head, trying to dislodge the fog and piercing pain. Another cough moves up from my chest and my shoulders shudder violently.

"You can't take my meat," I cough, spluttering uncontrollably.

Achak's brow furrows as the winter sky turns indigo-blue and amethyst and the stars peek out; the opal moon rises, casting silver moonbeams on the white snow. With a stubborn sniff, I toss my hair back and start packing up.

The meat is mine. No *skraeling* will rob me. *Neinn*. Not today.

Chapter Twenty-One

A LONE WOLF HOWLS

Achak shouts at one of the Red Men and he presses forwards through the snow, moving in the direction of the sled. Along the way, he stoops to pick up a shank of meat lying frozen in the snow and I let out a startled yelp. On instinct, I run at him, heedless of the risks.

The other Red Man draws out his skinning knife and points it at me which stops me cold. I feel a desperation swishing through me, eddying into a whirlpool of fear.

"Back away," I shout indignantly. "Twice I've let you *skraelings* take the fruits of my labour. I'll not let that happen anymore."

Knife Man is crouching low over the bloodied chunks of meat. When he stands with his knife in hand, my skin prickles and my knees go weak. Locking eyes on him, I picture his weapon sinking deep into my flesh. Then I see him flensing the skin off my bones. On instinct, I charge without any thought of the consequences. He is caught off guard, and I knock his weapon into the snow.

He is stronger than I thought. Instead of toppling, he pushes hard. Startled, I lose my balance and begin to fall. In the chaos, one of my snowshoes strikes my standing leg. With arms rotating wildly, I try to prevent the fall, but I land with a whoosh in a bank of snow.

Rotating and wrenching muscles, another cough slips out. My natural instinct is to dig in with my feet and thrust forwards, but my snowshoes don't allow for this. Fear fuels my anger and I roll over and get stuck, thrashing wildly as I churn up snow.

Knife Man turns away from me, leaving me to dig my way free on my own. Eventually I struggle up, only to see two of the Red Men scurrying off with my catch, their snowshoes swishing through the snow.

"You thieves!" I yell. The cry breaks into another cough that cracks the peace and echoes through the frosty air. The winter night is cold and clear. In the moonlight, one of the *skraelings* leans forwards and tugs the heavy sled over a mound of snow. The sled jerks forwards and I clench my fists.

You red-faced dog!

In a panic, I stare at the moon's lambent light casting jagged shadows across the patch of blood-splattered snow where Achak stands. He calls to the others. Then he turns and looks at me. Behind his frame, the ring of conical pine trees rises out of a bank of snow in black silhouettes. Achak points and says something I can't understand, but I recognize that I have no choice. I must follow him into the bush or lose the meat. By the gods, I am done being used by forceful men! I am done tolerating these *skraeling* games.

Miserably, I trudge behind him into the white, but my throat is raw, my whole body aches, my temples throb, and my muscles shake. Doggedly I resist the urge to just sit down and fall asleep and freeze to death. Instead, I force my frozen feet to lift up my snowshoes one by one and continue forth, shuffling through the endless banks of snow in the bitter cold.

Far off in the distance a lone wolf begins to howl. Its mournful, unearthly cry originates from the crest of the shadowed hills and echoes through the valley, shattering the stillness with a jolt. As soon as the call fades away and the next one comes, I scuttle quickly through the snow.

When Achak sees me struggling to break a path, he doubles back to wait for me while his companions disappear behind two black tree-sentinels that guard the entrance to the woods. In the darkness, Achak's eyes – two orbs of light – illuminate his entire face. Just then, we hear another doleful cry, an unnerving wolf song that slips into silence as quickly as it came.

It is quite the trek down a winding trail that leads to a snow-house that has been dug into the drifts piled up against a knoll. Achak motions for me to go inside. I feel my body lurch to a sudden stop as I gasp for air, worrying that it is a trap, that the Red Men will tie me up and skin me alive, that they will feed my heart to their dead deer god.

I find my knife and stealthily slip it out. I will kill this Red Man. I will kill them all to save myself from being chewed by Red Men's teeth. I will fight Achak off to survive this place in this godless land where men turn into wolves at night and snowbanks swallow and devour flesh.

Just as I begin to lift my knife, Achak crouches before the entrance to the snow hut and quickly disappears into the snow. Stupefied, I am left standing there all alone as the frigid air picks its way into my lungs. Outside, everything is very still. Looking up, I see a myriad of twinkling stars as I struggle to make sense of everything. A moment later, my chest explodes and I begin to cough uncontrollably.

When I hear the wolves begin to howl again, I turn and scan the trees where nothing stirs, feeling the prickle of a niggling fear wrapping itself around my throat and cutting off my air supply. Trying to suppress another rising cough, I turn around, realizing that I can hardly breathe and that my nose is stuffy; one nostril is already clogged. Not even Logatha knows where I have gone. If only I could tell her about this *skraeling* land of snow and ice and death and fear, a place where – poof! – the Red Men disappear.

Breathing heavily, I glance up at the nighttime sky one more time before taking the plunge and slipping into the snow tunnel that swallowed Achak whole.

When I finally manage to sit up straight, I find myself entombed inside a domed snow-house where the Red Men have lit a cooking fire. To my surprise, the place is warm and comfortable. It is not at all what I expect. The deer meat has been set to roast upon an open fire and one of the Red Men has removed his furs. His deer-hide shirt has been ochred a rosy pinkish red.

I go to chastise them when I see them eating my treasured

meat, but Achak holds up his hand. He bows his head respectfully and through gestures, he lets me know that the *skraelings* are grateful for my hunting gift. Then he hands me a piece of sizzling meat which looks so succulent that I almost faint. A moment later I recoil when I see the dirt and grease and dry specks of blood ground into his calloused hands.

The Red Men laugh. I feel a rush of anger and a spike of impatience needling through me as I begin to hack and cough once more. In my misery, I reach out quickly and snag the meat and stuff it all inside my mouth. Gobbling it down wolfishly I revel in the gamey flavor, but I can hardly swallow it because my throat is raw and very sore.

In a fevered daze, I force myself to finish eating. Then Achak hands me a drink of melted ice water. When I snub him, he leaves me be and inches back to where his companions sit. Quite frankly, I would rather let him see me lick the ice on these snow-house walls than accept another gift from him.

Wearily, I pull my knees up to my chin. I feel too sick to stay awake and listen to the *skraelings'* chipmunk talk. Reluctantly I close my eyes and shake my head through the blur of tears.

When I wake up, it is very quiet and very still. To my surprise, I am all alone inside the hut – but I am still alive. For a moment I sit there not knowing what to do. Then I quickly wriggle up and out, only to discover that the wind is howling and it is snowing hard outside. The Red Men are huddling in a group as the snow swirls around them and the wind gusts wail. I can barely swallow and hardly talk.

My throat feels as though someone has pierced it with a thousand spears.

Glancing up into the grey blizzard-laden sky, I think of Logatha, and Finnbogi, and my kin back home. The memories almost bring me to my knees. By Óðinn's beard, my tracks will be covered in this storm. No one will know where I have gone. They will think I just disappeared.

On impulse, I try to run, but instantly I sink knee-deep into the snow. Glancing up, I am horrified when Achak comes to pull me out. As his snowshoes swish towards me through the swirling snow, I start clambering through the snow drifts, desperately trying to get away. When he catches up, I lean into him and push him hard, and he releases a startled cry as he tumbles backwards into the snow.

With a grunt, I fight to keep myself from sinking lower. In the process I am met with another blast of wind that drives bits of ice into my upturned face.

"I don't need any more help from you," I wail as my voice cracks into a hoarse whisper and my half-coughed words get lost in the blinding snow and howling wind. I try to twist around and change direction but the snow funnels around me.

Struggling to claw myself out, I grow increasingly impatient until I spot Achak making his way back to the snow hut. As the snowflakes whirl around my head, I watch in silence as he dislodges my snowshoes from a mound of ice and then turns to bring them back to me. With a painful gulp, I will my pulse to settle down before the cold air stabs my throat and sends me into another coughing fit.

That afternoon, I begrudgingly trudge behind Achak, who is barely visible in the whiteout as he doggedly works to break a trail in front of me. Blinded by the stinging snow that whips across my burning cheeks, I sweat inside my furs as I follow him through the endless drifts, feeling both hot and cold all at once. Working hard to suppress the thought that all I need is a bit of yarrow or a mustard plaster for my aching chest and my hacking cough, I focus on putting one foot in front of the other and try to squelch the queasy feelings in my gut.

The *skraelings* expertly navigate a path through a forest of silver birch as the snow falls down in blinding sheets and the silver-grey sky turns dark at midday. All around us, the whistling wind buries into my ice-encrusted furs and wildly flings up wisps of blowing snow.

When I lift my head, I see the *skraelings* making their way up a steep bank in single file. *We're not heading in the right direction*, I think. *I need to return to Leifsbidur!*

Up ahead, I see Achak stop and turn even as my body begins to sway. I reach out and clutch a tree to steady the spinning sensations in my head, but when I try to breathe there is a flash of pain and I can't seem to release any sound from my sore throat. Achak calls out for me in the shrieking wind, but I am so sick that I can't shout back.

He doubles back and I try to push him off, but he

catches up my hands in his and before I know it, he is working hard to securely fasten a rope around my waist so that he can pull me behind him like a common thrall tethered to a *skraeling* guard. Groaning, I try to resist him with all my strength, but he speaks to me in his native tongue using soothing sounds as the snowflakes fall, burying everything. Then my mind plays tricks. The Red Man morphs into Finnbogi's form. After that, the game is different, and I give in to him, trusting that he will help guide me through the blinding snow.

The visibility is very poor. We tilt our bodies against the driving snow and push forwards against the screeching wind, but my head throbs and I worry that frostbite is setting in. Achak slips ahead. In the blizzard, I force myself to carry on, to endure the pain, to follow this *skraeling* into a world of white. After a while, I can hardly walk. I slow my pace and feel Achak tugging on the line.

When we finally enter the *skraeling* settlement, the sweat is dripping down my back and my throat is so raw that swallowing is almost impossible. Achak helps me inside a massive tent that has been insulated halfway up with birchbark sheets. The smell of woodsmoke mixes with the smell of pine and grilling meat, but I am too sick to seek comfort from any of this. Feeling dizzy, I sway unsteadily on my feet. Then someone helps remove my furs. Prying hands unwrap the coverings on my legs while someone else tugs fiercely on my snow-encrusted hood. As it falls away, there is a wondrous gasp, an astonished cry. Then a throng of Red Men push in closely and reach out to touch my red hair. Standing beside me, Achak tries to hold them back.

I suck in air and try to jab the crowd for elbow room. My lungs are wheezing and I have no voice. Feeling lightheaded, I stare straight ahead as the crowd makes way for an old woman who has long white hair and toothless gums. She shuffles in closely, and I half smell the odour of bitter herbs rising from her red-fringed hide shawl which displays a zig-zag pattern on the edges accentuated in raised relief with bird quills underneath. I feel myself tensing when she leans in closely to scrutinize my skin and hair. Steeling myself, I let her loop one of my red curls around her bony index finger before she inspects the red strand carefully. Her filmy eyes glance up at me repeatedly.

Unexpectedly, she gives a vicious tug, and I let out a high-pitched squeal. When the old woman holds up a piece of my red hair in her fisted hand, the *skraeling* men begin to laugh. I can hardly believe their audacity.

"May the trolls take you!" I hoarsely yelp.

From somewhere behind me, Achak mumbles something in reply before he steps forth and takes me firmly by the elbow. Then he leads me through the crowd. Still panicked, my eyes flit across a wall of logs daubed with mud. The roof is raised in a conical shape terminating at the top in a small circle where the smoke floats up and out. Along the walls, there are bows and arrows, clubs, stone hatchets, and carrying baskets made of reeds and birchbark. All of the containers have been dyed red and arranged in the neatest manner on shelves and hooks. There is even a string of dried smoked fish hanging from the rafters that I would love to retrieve and eat.

When my fevered eyes fall back down to the *skraeling*

men and women who continue to push in close, I feel too tired and sick to care. Just then the old woman lifts her bony finger into the air. Muttering, she addresses Achak in a harsh, guttural tone that makes my stomach plummet and my heartbeat thrum. There are jolts of pain and waves of heat and sickness all at once. A cough escapes, building wetly before the room goes quiet and no one moves. I am conscious of the weight of the weapons on my belt.

Someone wearing rabbit skins begins to chant and my eyes go wide. I have heard that they sing before they kill their prey and offer sacrifice to their gods. Panicking, I back towards the door, but Achak stops me with his eyes. When he steps towards me, I allow him to untie my wrists but I can't stop shivering. A moment later, the old woman comes to take me by the hand. In a feverish stupor I let her parade me around the fire, but when a fierce-looking man with an animal-tooth necklace points at me, I close my eyes and think of death, swaying unsteadily on my feet.

The hearth fire is suddenly intolerably hot. Someone takes away my furs and I worry about them suddenly taking away my life, but they only sniff at me as though I am a dog. Horrified, I step back into Achak's chest. Just then, another Red Man reaches out to run his fingers through my hair. Achak stops him with his hand.

"Thank you," I say with a scratchy voice. Achak scrutinizes me carefully in the firelight. His eyes have something in them I cannot name, and I turn away, listening to the chatter, feeling the heat in my cheeks.

When Achak offers me a birchbark cup filled with melted ice water, I slug it down. "Red," he says in Norse, pointing to my knotted hair. I nod weakly, gesturing with my thumb to my sore throat.

"I am sick," I rasp. Achak studies me, and I swallow painfully before he half catches, half eases me to the ground.

The fire crackles and sparks, and a brilliant light blazes high behind Achak's head. Fevered, I close my eyes again and listen to the wails of a little one, remembering the longhouse back in Leifsbidur, remembering Logatha in her pregnant state. How I wish that I was home.

Sometime later, Achak wakes me to apply a stinky tree-sap tincture to my chest. At first I squirm and try to slap his hands away, but later I give in and accept his ministrations and drink his tea. It tastes like willow bark or dogwood, but perhaps it is something else. Perhaps they are trying to poison me with their boiled broth that tricks my mind into thinking that the concoction is meant to soothe my throat. In a delirious state I drink it down. I am too sick to care, too sick to struggle, too sick to want to stay alive.

Achak throws handfuls of something into the fire that conjures smoke. Then the old woman appears. Standing behind him, she emits a horrid wail that snakes up my spine and crawls into my ringing ears. I open my mouth to denounce the noise, but my throat is raw and I have no voice.

After that I slip into a restless, foggy daze where I drift in and out of sleep, not knowing whether it is night or day.

The wind still howls and I can hear the sounds of Red Men talking behind my head. I do not know how long I lie there in the tent, but when I finally snap awake, I notice that I have been placed underneath a low-lying, tented frame covered over by a wealth of skins. Beside me there is a pile of heated stones and a water bucket. A small birchbark cup bobs gently in a tree-barked pail. I yearn to reach for it, but it is as though a haze of mist is blinding me. I have no strength, no voice, no will.

From my mat, I warily watch Achak crawl inside my tent to wet the stones. Immediately there is a whoosh of steam that engulfs me, shrouding me in a soothing mist. I breathe in the vapors, relishing the feel of the glorious heat. When the rocks grow cold and there is no more steam, I doze again.

When next I wake, my fever is gone, and the vapor tent has been removed. The place seems empty until I hear the *skraelings'* throats chopping words and grunting sounds that I can't understand. I do not move. I make no noise. Looking up, I think about how to best escape this *skraeling* lair until I register the sound of pelting ice hitting the tent in the howling blizzard outside.

In the dim light right above my head, there is a huge set of caribou racks, brown and fresh, swaying gently back and forth. I count the points and feel a sudden rush of cold in my bones as the hairs rise on the nape of my neck. In that moment it all comes back. My trophy prize and the loss of it. A man with a smooth, red face and a tattooed chest. The raven tattoo etched in red.

"You bloody thief!" I say.

Chapter Twenty-Two

MOVING PINECONES

I endure another high fever that attacks in the middle of the night, leaving me freezing cold then burning hot. Barely conscious, I wince when I see someone bending over me until I realize it is only Achak. Then I sleep. When I wake, Achak is sitting cross-legged on the floor with a carving tool in hand. An instant later – or so it seems – his face pushes in close to mine, and he dabs my forehead with a cold, wet bundle filled with chunks of ice.

Drifting in and out, I hear him conferring with the old woman in the guttural language of his tribe. Strangely, I am not afraid of him, even though I suffer nightmares where giant red-faced men with fangs for teeth eat my body while I am still alive.

I am almost certain that *mörsugur*, the intestinal fat-sucking month, has come and gone when my fever finally breaks, but my cough is bad and my muscles ache, and I have no energy to get out of bed. Dismally, I try to calculate how long I have been gone from Leifsbidur, knowing that Logatha will be worried sick. She will think I froze to death.

My cough turns wet. As I lie in bed, I study the comings and goings of the tribe, the way the women like to soften the hides before they sew, the way they smoke and dry their salmon and mix their dried berries in the seal fat. When Achak leans in closely to listen to my rasping lungs, I let him touch me, but I still don't like it when he lifts my head and forces me to drink his tea. The concoction soothes my throat but it tastes foul. He makes me drink it anyway as he eyes the puckered flesh around my raised and bumpy scars where the skin is white.

I finally recover well enough to get up. As I lower myself to sit cross-legged in front of their fire, I make sure to keep my chin held high and my shoulders square, taking care that all should see my coiled, red hair. The old woman is wiser than she looks. As she takes up one of my curls in her gnarled hands, she fixes me with her sharp eyes. I try to pull away, but she flashes me a toothless grin. Then she turns to Achak and mutters something. He throws a careful smile but I stare him down, waiting for his face to sober up and his large, round eyes to go blank.

That evening, the old woman makes me sit with her when her people gather around the fire. The group is small – two families, as far as I can tell. Just as they are about to eat, the tent flap opens and the wind blows in another group. There are men and women wrapped in fox fur and a little baby strapped in a birchbark carrier on a young woman's back. All their garments have been dusted red, but they smell like Norsemen with their fish-smoke scent. It is a smell I have not forgotten. I never will.

When all are seated, I glance around the fire at the glowing faces, knowing I am an outsider with different skin and different hair and a different kind of dress. Their language is incomprehensible – just a jumble of noises, a mix of harsh, throaty sounds. Hearing their conversations makes me miss my kin. I am stranded and there is little chance that I will be able to return to Leifsbidur if the blizzards don't let up.

Across the fire, Achak is sitting beside a hunter with a harsh, intimidating face. The Red Man has long, black hair and a streak of war paint smeared across his cheeks. When he looks at me, his eyes spark fire. I prickle, and then I take offense.

The old woman remains seated in a cross-legged position on the floor. She snaps at him, and his face hardens and his eyes go blank. I avert my eyes just before another blast of smoke from the cooking fire hits me squarely in the face. The children squeal and run away, and a mother curses as she flaps her arms around wildly in an effort to bat the smoke away from her little girl who can barely walk. The child's eyes well up and she begins to cry.

A girl with braids and a necklace of colored shells is the first to approach me. Warily I watch as she tiptoes close. Her long, thin fingers make shadows on the walls in the firelight and her curious eyes are like large pools of dancing light. Just as she is about to touch me, the sour-faced hunter snarls at her to frighten her and the little girl scurries away with a shriek. The old woman cackles.

Achak does not look up. He continues carving with his knife.

When the old woman goes to pinch my cheeks, I snap at her. She pretends not to hear me and continues chortling, her laughter rising with the smoke. The children are left to go unchecked, and in their excitement they try to get close enough to touch my hair.

"You should swat them for their disrespect," I say, trying to draw back.

With an encouraging pat, the old woman pushes a little boy in close to me. He reaches out to touch my cheeks and I attempt to turn away, but the old woman guides him forwards, nattering away as the tassels on her dress, with their little shells and rocks jiggling from the fringes, tinkle so wildly that I get distracted and miss seeing the other children fanning out behind me. All of a sudden, their hands reach forwards to pull and tug at my red curls.

"Stop that, now," I say, jumping when a little girl gives a vicious tug. I hate their groping hands, their tiny touches, their curiosity. I am a novelty who is on display.

When it becomes too much, I hiss at them to no avail. Beside me the *skraelings* begin to talk amongst themselves in a cacophony of harsh and boisterous sounds. Then I hear the strangest noise coming from behind my back. It sounds like someone is shearing sheep.

Twisting around, I catch sight of another boy slinking off with an impish smile, holding something red in his bony fist. With a sharp intake of breath, I reach behind my head and feel the missing patch of hair that the boy hacked off as the other children continue to push in closely.

"You little snake!" I curse in startled disbelief as I lunge for him. Out of nowhere, a pair of strong arms holds me down. With wolverine strength, I push up hard and the children around me go flying as they get tossed. As soon as I struggle up, I come face to face with Achak.

"What in gods' name did that boy do to me?" I shout. Mortified, I clutch the back of my head and turn to show him the missing piece.

Just then, some bird sweeps past my head, and I begin to swear and flail as Achak reaches forwards and tries to calm me down. Beside us, the old woman nets the children in her arms. Her fancy fringes rattle softly when she suddenly trips the boy who sliced off my hair. Wriggling, he tries to scramble away from her, but as soon as he rights himself, the old woman taps him with her walking stick and he goes still.

The hearth fire flares. In the silence, the old woman begins to chastise the boy in front of the entire tribe. By Óðinn's beard, if he were mine I would whip him hard for what he did.

As I sit back down, the old woman demands that the boy release the chunk of hair he stole from me. When I reach back to touch the bristles of my hacked off hair, my anger flares.

The rebellious boy with his fiery eyes slinks forwards showing no remorse. I hate the fact that he looks so smug. He will grow up to be like all the rest – a man who takes from women without asking first.

It is Achak who forces open the boy's balled-up fist. When the hair drops out, the old woman clucks her tongue at him. I feel like pouncing, I am so vexed. After this, I will be afraid to go to sleep in this savage tent where little men are allowed to steal locks of hair.

Achak cuffs the boy on the back of the head and there is a quick exchange between two groups of men. They call the boy Abooksigun. It must mean "The Sneaky One". By the gods, they should beat him for his disrespect, but they do not. Instead they banish him from the tent without a meal. I watch him leave. Beside me the old woman tucks the clump of hair – my hair – inside her pouch.

She pushes her snowy-white hair over her shoulder and adjusts her shawl before she points to the chunks of roasted meat, encouraging me to eat. In the flickering firelight, her face is a map of wrinkles but her eyes are young and alive. She tugs on my sleeve before reaching out and snatching up the meat chunk, but I snub her and refuse to eat. In response, the old woman tsks and shakes her head as she stares at the dishes that have been prepared: the root vegetables, the nuts, the meat, the fish. A moment later, she helps herself to the food that I reject, and I have to listen as she slurps the bones and sucks on the grizzled fat with her toothless gums. The sound is so irksome that I try to inch away. From across the fire, Achak's eyes meet mine, and it is as though he is warning me to be respectful, to watch my step in the presence of the grandmother whom they all revere.

When at last the meal is done, someone begins to beat a drum and the singers start up with an eerie wail that crescendos before dropping low and rising again to a shrieking pitch. In front of us, the fire throws out sparks and the hunter with the war paint streaked across his face stands up and begins to dance. Tucking myself back against the wall, I watch as the hunger pains rip through my gut. Still I refuse to eat. Even when they place a reed basket full of dried salmon at my feet, I stubbornly reject the offering. I will not eat their fish or caribou. I will not give them the satisfaction. They will learn to treat me like a goddess because of the color of my hair. I'll make them think I don't need their food. After tonight, I'll expect respect.

As the night wears on and the old woman instructs the *skraelings* to dance for me, I think of Asta and Grelod and Snorri and Gunnar and Finnbogi and Helgi, too. Logatha I miss most of all. It feels strange to be inside this family tent where I am surrounded and yet I am alone, dying like a flapping fish, struggling in the fight for one last breath.

Achak sits across the fire talking with an older man. His face looks animated; his smile reveals a set of perfect teeth. Yet there is nothing perfect about him. His shoulders are broad, and he is slightly taller and stockier than the other men. His black hair trails to his shoulders, loose and flowing and bone-straight with one lone braid ornately decorated with seashells gathering hair together at the side. There are red ochre markings caressing his cheeks, and his face is clean-shaven. Some would call him handsome. I would not, although his eyes hold something mysterious – a light of sorts.

Turning my head towards the door, I try to recall Logatha's face. Her sweet, gentle smile. I pray that her bairn is safe. That she isn't starving. Oh gods, I hope she isn't sick.

The *skraeling* longhouse is uncomfortably hot and I shed

my furs. Inside my head, Finnbogi's voice cautions me to be careful before he whispers that I am a disappointment, that I have failed Logatha most of all. I feel the prick of tears and a lump rising in my throat. My movement draws a curious eye. Achak ignores the hunter at his side and stares at me. Beside me the old woman is fast asleep.

Without hesitating, I scramble up and make my way towards the entrance of the tent and peek outside. No one stops me. The banks of snow look to be about ten feet high. It is snowing heavily and very cold. Somewhere out there lies the settlement of Leifsbidur. I must go back. I must check to see that my kin are safe.

Achak startles me when he sneaks up behind me and shuts the door. When I turn around, he studies me before offering me a piece of meat. My eyes meet his. Hesitating, I accept his offering knowing that the only way I will be able to leave this place is if I have built back my strength.

"Where is my coat?" I ask overtop all the noise. I gesture to the furs a female wears and rub my arms as if I am cold. For a moment, Achak looks confused before his face breaks out into a smile. Then he turns and points to a hook where my sealskins with the polar-bear collar are hanging all splattered with specks of dried blood and mud.

"What about my spear, my bow and arrows, and my gear?" I try. Instinctively I point to the weapons hanging around the room. Achak frowns before looking up.

"I want to go back to Leifsbidur," I say boldly, hoping he will understand. His eyes find my face. He throws a little shrug.

"I need my leggings and my weapons, too." The tears

come unbidden and I swallow, feeling the lump building in my throat, feeling embarrassed that this Red Man should see me cry. His eyes work their way down the scar that runs the length of my cheek bone to my mouth. I hate him for staring at it.

"Can you help me return to Leifsbidur?" I ask.

Achak's gaze homes in on my missing lock of hair. I wish I could tell him that Logatha is waiting for me and that the settlement of Leifsbidur needs me back.

Someone thwacks the caribou-hide drum and an undulating voice begins to chant as another group of Red Men stand up to dance. Their fluid, bending forms replicate the movement of swaying grass.

Directly across from me sits a woman nursing her infant with bare breasts exposed. The bairn's little hands wiggle up against the mother's breast. A moment later, Achak tugs on my arm and points to a collection of pinecones that he has quickly placed beside me. Then he points to another collection he has placed in front of his own feet. Leaning down, I watch him pluck a pinecone from my pile. Slowly he pushes it towards his own pile. The pinecone message doesn't make sense. I shake my head.

"Leifsbidur," he manages awkwardly as he points to the pinecones by my feet. He plucks another single cone from my pile and points to me. Then he moves this pinecone to his pile. In a flash, I see the meaning of his game. Gingerly, I reach over and pick the most recently moved pinecone up.

"I want to return to Leifsbidur," is all I say as I gently place the pinecone back in my pile. Without looking up, Achak shakes his head and reaches forwards to retrieve a piece of rabbit fur that is soft and white. He startles me when he grabs my pinecone and throws it roughly on the ground. Then he takes the rabbit fur and throws it over top of the pinecone while muttering *skraeling* words and pointing to the snow outside. A moment later, he picks up a stone and grinds it into the rabbit fur to crush the pinecone underneath.

The meaning of the message is clear enough. The falling snow will cover me and I will die. Behind us the Red Men's drums go wild. Achak sighs deeply. He looks at me with lugubrious eyes before he begins picking off pinecone remnants from his pants.

"Home," I mutter. "I need to go home." As I go to turn from him, Achak stops me. His hand is warm. I brace myself, looking down, but his touch is gentle. He points to the bed depression full of furs where they make me sleep. Then he points at me and his eyes fall shut. For a moment I just stare at him, breathing in the smell of the aromatic woodsmoke, listening to the noises around us – the sounds of the beating drums, the sounds of laugher, the sounds of the tribal gathering at its peak in this *skraeling* longhouse with its roaring fire.

There is a tingling feeling in my arm. I glance at this man who muttered prayers over the deer I killed, who kept me alive, and who gave me willow bark tea. My eyes stay fixed on his long, dark eyelashes flickering like a butterfly before my gaze falls to his crooked nose and the redness of his smooth, angular cheeks and the kindness of his gentle smile.

When I stir awake at the break of dawn, the snow has stopped but it is freezing cold and I can see my breath. After rolling up the hide that covers me, I tiptoe towards the firepit that is filled with snow-white ash. In the shadows by a pile of hides, I spot one of the reed baskets but there are no fish left inside. Swearing underneath my breath, I scan the tent. The sleeping forms look comfortable tucked into nooks and crannies and cedar-lined dugouts carved into the ground.

Groping frantically in the faint light of an early dawn, I am startled by the sound of men's voices in the yard as I am reaching down to steal someone's boots. In a panic I throw a glance at the door. All is quiet in the tent.

Without making noise, I pick my way to the door before I crack it open and peek outside. Achak is standing in the snow, all wrapped up in his sealskins, his breath pluming puffs of mist into the frosty air. He is talking with the sour-faced *skraeling* who doesn't like me, and their voices drift towards me in a hushed rumble. . Achak's hunting spear is strapped securely to his back and he is helping his friend tie a rope on a sled. In the distance behind the snow-covered trees, the horizon is a smudge of orange as the sun begins spilling beams of light into the ice-blue winter sky where the oval moon still lurks, as if reluctant to fade away.

Without blinking, I rip my furs off the hook and look around the tent to see where the Red Men stashed my gear. I can't see my weapons anywhere. Cursing underneath my breath, I tiptoe around the longhouse, trying not to make any noise as I pick up items I think I'll need and stash them in the pockets of my coat.

The old woman is cuddled against a little girl, snoring loudly with her white hair curtaining her face from view. In another shallow cradle in the ground, I notice a boy stirring. When I look down, I spot the thief, Abooksigun. His face is barely visible underneath his furs. Someone must have allowed him to return to the tent late last night after the feast was done.

Glancing down at the boy's sleeping form, I am tempted to hack off his braid before I go, but I resist the urge. Disturbing the peace inside this tent would only serve to disadvantage me.

Someone behind me stirs and my heart stops. For a moment, I freeze. Outside, I hear the voices fading as a crow begins to caw. The sound jets me out of a frozen place. With stealth, I leap across the firepit and make my way towards the door without waking anyone. When I step outside into the quiet yard, I breathe in sharply when I'm hit with a sudden blast of cold.

The men are gone. I see their tracks looping around a circle of conical huts. One structure has a smoke hole that spews out greyish plumes into the pale blue sky. I avoid that tent and try to make it across the yard, but I do not manage to get too far before I sink into a mound of snow.

"Shit," I mutter into the air, and the crow caws again as if offended. Grunting, I fight to struggle free before I am forced to double back. I spot a pair of snowshoes leaning against the old woman's tent, but just as I am working to dig them out of the ice with my mittened hands, an explosion of noise comes from inside the tent. Abooksigun's voice cracks the air, rising up in a thin, high pitch before falling into a rich blend of sonorous sound.

Carefully I unkink my fingers and start digging fast. When I finally free the snowshoes and put them on, I waste no time leaving the settlement. Already I am crazed with thirst, but there is a desperation whirling through my bones, an eagerness to join the hunters before I lose their trail.

The fields are blanketed with white and the land is ghostly silent and deathly still as I forge my way through the snow, doggedly following in the Red Men's tracks that thread through a forest of snow-capped tuckamore before circling a marsh where a patch of brittle brown cattails are sticking out. Then I follow the tracks leading into the hills where the windswept drifts are very large.

I make steady progress all morning, moving inland across a bleak landscape. Then the snowshoe tracks peter off in a patch of ice running the length of a lake that slivers through a canyon.

I cannot think. My toes and fingers are far too numb and my nose is cold. Just then, an icy blast of wind blows a dusting of snow in my face causing my eyes to well up and my lashes to freeze. Shivering, I rub my hands together to generate a little warmth. Up ahead, there is a snow-capped peak that will give me a view of the valley below. Hopefully I will be able to spot the men.

With effort, I push myself to carry on. When I reach a large spruce tree that lies directly in my path, I find the frozen carcass of a caribou lying in its tree well. Its eyes are open and its death stare beckons me to jump into the hole and lie with it. The thought frightens me. I back away and lose my balance, falling softly in the snow.

Black thoughts come unbidden, sneaky, and instantaneous. If I could just fall asleep and ignore the bite of the bitter cold,, I'd wake refreshed. The desire to just give up gnaws at me, itching fiercely, tugging hard. From far away I hear Finnbogi's voice.

Get up, he shouts. *You have to move!*

I blink three times and will my body to find the strength to struggle up. There is nothing in this frozen wasteland, this godless place where I am alone. All I have is one pathetic knife and one hunting spear. I was a stupid fool for leaving the *skraeling* camp without all my gear. I don't even have enough food and water to get through the day.

I feel a surge of panic as I scoop up snow and start to suck. The liquid soothes me as I stare across the land, taking in the vastness, the utter emptiness and loneliness of it.

"Achak!" I call out into the stillness. He doesn't answer. No one does. *"Achak!"* I scream again. My cry echoes in the wilderness, fading into nothingness. The silence is absolute in all this snow. When I look back and see the crooked snowshoe trail that marks my passage up the bank, I am overcome and terrified by the silence of the place.

In the chilly air, the shivers come. I have been a fool. Logatha needed me to come back to her. I was bound to her, to all of them. Even now, I see their faces around the fire.

A resolve sets in – a survival instinct that makes me struggle up. In front of me, there is a craggy bank of treacherous rocks that borders a frozen lake. At the top, a blast of icy wind hits me squarely in the face. Miserably, I gather my furs against my chin before looking out across the land where I see only a sea of white broken by clumps of snow-covered trees. The landscape is a dreary wide-open space, a land of white where the silence ... the silence screams.

A shiver of movement rattles me before I realize it is only birds. Then my thoughts slow like a trickle of tree sap, and I suddenly realize I could die out here. Oh gods, what if another blizzard comes? For a moment I am tempted to go back to Achak's tent, but then I square my shoulders and set my jaw. I need to try for Leifsbidur. I made a promise to Logatha.

As I begin to inch my way down the slope, my snowshoes hit an icy patch and I lose my footing and begin to slide. Trying to break my fall, my arms flail wildly and my ankle twists. Horrified, I release an ear-splitting scream as my body picks up speed and careens towards the ledge that drops off steeply to the lake below. There is blinding panic that cuts off air when I realize there are no bushes to break my fall and no rocks sticking up to stop me sliding over the precipice. In a terrifying whirl, I howl again before suddenly careening over the bank and dropping suddenly, falling with my legs and arms outstretched. My spear dislodges from my pack, and in my periphery, I watch it fall to the lake below as I try to brace myself for the fall.

There is a flash of light as I land with a heavy thud in a mound of snow on a rocky ledge. Immediately, there is searing shoulder and ankle pain. Willing myself to stay alert, I attempt to quell the hysteria rising in my chest as I try to shift my body and move my arm.

The wind emits an eerie moan. Turning my head, I catch a glimpse of where I am lying on a rocky ledge that is jutting out of a cliff overlooking a frozen lake. My breath catches. I have narrowly missed falling to the lake below where I would have met my death. The relief washes through me before the panic peaks. By the gods, no one knows I am stranded here. No one knows I am injured and all alone. Surely, I will die out here.

For the remainder of the afternoon I lie there staring up at the ice-blue sky waiting for the freezing cold to put me to sleep and stop the pain. In the silence, just as my eyes begin to close, I hear a faint noise coming from up above. With my good arm, I shield my eyes against the winter sun and look way up, wincing when I spot clumps of snow and ice and bits of dirt dropping from the rockface up above. The particles slip past me as they pick up speed.

"Down here!" The words slip out in a puff of fog as a sharp and agonizing pain shoots down my leg. Moaning, I try to lift my head to better see the top of the snow-covered ridge. On the upper banks, a face appears. Squinting against the winter sun, I think I see Achak in his sealskin furs, but when I look again, Abooksigun is on his stomach peering down. He smiles mischievously and flashes teeth.

I blink again.

For the love of Loki, that little thief has followed me.

Chapter Twenty-Three

WIND MURMURS

"S top!"

I inhale the icy air, panicking as Abooksigun inches closer to the edge. His movements send an avalanche of powdery snow plummeting soundlessly down the cliff. "Don't come any closer. It's too dangerous." An instant later, he disappears.

I try to sit but a sharp current of pain jolts through my ankle and shoots up my leg, causing me to slink back down. I hear a click then a pop. Wincing, I try to adjust my position, shivering when a cold updraft swells from the lake below.

"Abooksigun!"

The white mist from my breath hovers in the chilly air before disappearing in feathery wisps. Just then, another shout mingles with the sound of a raven's croak as the heat slowly leaches from me and the cold creeps down my back. In the swirling mist, the ethereal whispers breathe life back into me.

Don't be scared. You've suffered worse than this.

Logatha's singsong voice pings off the rocks. The melody of her wind murmurs carries me in a rhythmic trance into the sky. Through a rippling haze, I see her face as she comes to me on one of Óðinn's black-feathered birds with its beady eyes and smooth, curved beak. Her image flickers, sparkles, breathes. In pain, I try to shake the cobwebs from my head, bracing myself as I endure another surge of stabbing pain.

By the gods, you'll make it through. I'll offer sacrifice to the gods. Logatha's words are carried into the stillness, released on a breath of wind.

It's what you do. It's who you are, I reply in a hoarse whisper that escapes in wispy puffs.

She mops the perspiration off my brow. *I have waited long for you to return to us, Freydis Eiriksdóttir. Where are you, sister?*

I try to struggle up. *I can't come to you,* I sputter, but her ears seem plugged. *My ankle is broken and I can't walk.*

Logatha's life force mixes in with the icy fog breaths I push out. I have made her cry. I know it. I try to reach for her, but the pain is so intense that I have to drop my arm. Every bone in my body hurts. I feel the cold of everything.

Logatha inches backwards along the ledge. An instant later, she takes a step out into thin air and my heart jumps while my breath ladders up my nose. She doesn't fall. In the hazy light, a raven scoops her up on its black-feathered wings, carrying her away into the ball of sun where she disappears into the blinding light.

In the distance I hear a raven croak, and I think I see a

small black dot being swallowed by the brilliant sun. The sunset flares. The noise of flapping wings brushes past in a gust of wind and then a snowy powder rains down and my memories smudge.

I am lying on a ledge.

I am freezing cold.

My body hurts.

With a sob gathering in my throat, I discover that there is no raven and no Logatha. No blinding light. No wind. Just snow and ice and frostbite setting in. Peering up the side of the massive cliff, I feel the cold air claim my bones and a chunk of snow moving down my boot.

I will die out here.

Wincing, I try to shift my weight. Using my good arm to draw my furs around my face, the pain flares again and I draw a breath that sears my lungs. The boy has left. He might not return. He must be Loki in disguise. Or worse. Perhaps I forged him out of fear, out of hunger and burning pain.

As I am clawing at my ankle with my frozen fingers, there is another jolt of agonizing pain. I gasp and my cry travels the length of the frozen lake. Then I lie still, waiting for the cold-loving Ullr to come for me after he glides around the world, covering the land in ice and snow. There again, Skaði, the bowhunting snow goddess, might claim me first.

Time crawls. My will to live begins fading fast. In the cold shadows of the rockface, the thought of rolling over the ledge appeals to me. The thought pops in and out. Faðir's face takes form and crystallizes in the mist. He died of sickness, which prevented him from entering Valhalla's gates. He would want something more for me.

With grim determination, I force myself to inch my body off the ground without looking down. Far off in the distance I hear a flock of birds coming towards me, their cries thin and shrill. It is almost as though they are mocking me. The sound pings off the cliff walls, and in distance a man shouts. His muffled cry flutters down from the bank above.

Peering up, I see nothing but ice clinging to the rockface in lacy frost patterns, a patch of snow hanging from an upper ledge where a lone tree grows. My head is pounding; my back is cold; my eyes start brimming with big, fat tears. An instant later the boy's face appears. Shielding my eyes with my hand, I try to determine if he is real.

In a whirl of movement, Abooksigun stands and waves. I feel strangely peaceful, strangely calm. He has brought Achak and two other men. Their faces are wrapped in sealskin furs.

High above me on a sturdy perch, Achak motions for me to shimmy closer to the rocks where they attempt to drop a rope. The ridge is steep, the drop-off sudden and treacherous. It will be a grueling feat for the Red Men to rescue me when my shoulder is useless and I can't walk.

I yell up, pointing wildly to my foot that is twisted, misshapen, and very sore. Achak seems to understand. A moment later his face disappears. Peeking over my shoulder, I look down and my stomach falls. The lake lies far below. If I fell, I would surely die. A rush of fear knocks the wind right out of me. I would rather face the rock wall than peer down into the nothingness.

The hunters leave me waiting for far too long. When Achak finally reappears, he helps lower Abooksigun down to me, monitoring the boy's body as it twists and turns and spins wildly in the air.

Stretching out my good arm to grab his hand, Abooksigun tries to reach for me, but the sudden movement steals my breath away and I bite down hard and cut my tongue. Abooksigun is oblivious until he sees my fear-crazed face. Then his forehead crinkles into a frown. His eyes are chocolate-brown and bordered by lashes that are long and dark and thick and curled, the frost on them glittering as he paws his face. When he swings towards me, I see his determination mixed with an unexpected strength.

"My ankle is twisted or badly broken, I can't tell," I say, knowing it is impossible for him to understand. Abooksigun quickly secures me to a second rope without untying himself from the initial line. Then he leans down to inspect my foot. Reaching underneath his furs, he pulls out a piece of softened hide and starts using it to wrap my ankle. I point to the leggings he is wearing.

"Did you rip off a piece of your hides to help bandage my foot?"

He mutters something in his native tongue.

"This was Achak's, then?" I sputter when I hear Abooksigun say the hunter's name. The boy's face cracks a grin and he nods before motioning for me to extend my arm.

I endure his ministrations in agony, clenching my teeth and stifling a painful moan when he yanks the wrappings too tightly. When he goes to touch my shoulder I jerk back, and my sudden movement dislodges a chunk of ice that plummets to the lake below.

Abooksigun pulls back from me and eyes me hard. Then he signals to the men to lift me up.

"You have redeemed yourself," I say earnestly. When he sees me clasp my good hand to my heart in a gesture of gratitude, he bows his head in deference.

Peering up, I shiver. Achak is at the top looking down. At that moment the rope falls down, and Abooksigun takes my mittened hand and helps me grab it. My other arm is useless – a dangling stump.

They hoist me up. At the top, strong hands reach out and pull me up and over the icy ledge. A moment later I find myself lying on my back, staring up at Achak's face. The huntsman chokes out some words, addressing me in a clipped, harsh tone.

"I don't understand," I say, squinting up at him.

He turns away but in moments he is back. In his hand he has a piece of wood that he tries to place in my mouth. There is a sudden surge of fear. Cringing, I clamp my lips shut and try to twist away. The movement jars my injuries and I cry out in pain.

Askook scowls as he leans over me, blocking out the winter sun, and the memories come shimmying through me, unbidden. I am robbed of breath when I catch a glimpse of Thorvard's profile bathed in sun. He is leaning over me, sticking his fingers in my mouth.

"Stop it!" I spit, batting at the air, half-choking on the words as a sob erupts.

Achak jumps. He points to his shoulder, points to mine.

I shake my head. I can't speak his language, and he can't speak mine.

A moment later, he straightens up and I focus on his glorious teeth that look like floating chunks of ocean ice, willing the rhythmic thunk of my heart to slow. A moment later, he motions for me to watch him closely, and I scoop up a breath and almost gag when I see him insert the woodchip between his teeth and bite down hard.

Shaking my head again, I try to communicate that I am in too much pain for this stupid game. I won't make myself vulnerable in the hands of any *skraeling* man.

The others retrieve Abooksigun from the ledge below and then huddle together at my feet. The boy looks relieved as he natters away in his boy-man voice. Beside him stands a Red Man with soft, serious eyes. They call him "Nashushuk". His face looks kind.

Nashushuk comes to kneel beside me in the snow. Slowly, he takes his mittens off. "What are you doing?" I ask, eyeing him suspiciously. He ignores me. There is a stench of fish and smoke wafting off his furs. When he leans forwards, he too tries to coax me to place the piece of bark into my mouth. Miserably I look at him, knowing there is no point in trying to explain myself. Then I close myself off to everyone, to everything.

Nashushuk glances at Achak who stands as still as stone. Achak looks cross. He won't look at me. Just before he trundles through the churned-up snow with the winter sun bouncing off his fur-clad back, he throws a scowl at Nashushuk, and the words slipping off his tongue sound harsh and mean. Then he picks up his axe and moves in the direction of his other friend who is removing a caribou carcass from the sleigh. When Achak addresses him, I catch his name. Askook. He is a tall, austere-looking hunter-type with long black hair flowing down his back and red tattoos scrolling down one cheek.

Abooksigun glances quickly at the men before he comes closer to me and places the rejected wood piece in his mouth. Numbly I watch him bite down hard but this time he simultaneously pretends to twist his shoulder into place. All at once I see the plan. They want to pop my shoulder back into place. Placing my good elbow across my eyes, I breathe in deeply and then beckon to the boy. A moment later I am tasting wood.

By the time my shoulder has been reset and bound, Askook has prepared the sled to receive me. In a foggy haze, I let them transfer me without crying out, but my shoulder is in agony and I almost vomit from the pain when they lower me onto the sled.

Abooksigun is immediately at my side, dropping ice into my mouth. Behind him, I catch a glimpse of the caribou carcass in the snow and I feel guilty for making them leave their hard-earned prize behind.

Instead of meat, they will bring me home in their sled tonight.

We travel back to the *skraeling* settlement with the moon reflecting off the snow, and the huntsmen ignore me – all except Abooksigun. I almost resent him for his nattering.

Listening to the sled gently swishing through the snow, I fade in and out, smarting from the vicious pain.

When, at last, the circle of brightly lit *skraeling* longhouses come into view as a beacon of hope in the freezing cold, Abooksigun points excitedly. His pearly-white teeth glow eerily in the dark. When I look up, there are millions of stars overhead, twinkling in the frosty night.

As soon as the sled slides to a stop, there is a jolt of pain. Abooksigun quickly bends down to check on me. When he sees me pawing at my face, he exchanges the hide covering around my nose and mouth for one that isn't matted with frost and ice. Just ahead, there are wisps of smoke snaking into the air from the *skraeling* dwellings, and as I follow the smoke with my eyes, Achak fires off a series of short, sharp words. When the grumpy one, Askook, replies, I have the distinct impression that he is blaming me for losing the caribou. There is a sudden surge of guilt. I know the pain of his disappointment. I know this loss.

As soon as we reach the old woman's longhouse, Askook abandons us. His black silhouette – a tall, straight stick that melds into the shadows cast by a line of silver birch – moves quickly towards the tent at the far end of the clearing where a blood moon hangs suspended in the sky.

In the eerie quiet, Achak flicks a glance at me as he passes by and I try to smile up at him. To my surprise, he ignores me when he addresses Abooksigun in a serious tone. The boy chirps back but the conversation – the inflections and intonations – seem all wrong to me. A moment later the boy scurries off and Achak returns to help

Nashushuk haul me into the family dwelling I thought I'd never see again.

When the old woman sees my injuries, she instructs the men to move me to her bed of furs. There she unwraps my leggings and peeks underneath the dressing. It must be bad. The smooth skin on her forehead wrinkles into knots and she spits at a group of *skraeling* women who gather round. As soon as she turns, I look down and see my swollen, twisted foot that is red and blotchy and twice its normal size.

The old woman uses her gnarled fingers to scoop out salve that she works into my injured foot. The pine stench is bad, but almost immediately I feel the tincture's soothing warmth. Then she turns her attention to my wrist, my shoulder, and my arm.

When my ordeal is over and the women have splinted my foot and wrapped and iced my other injuries I try to sleep, but I can't get comfortable in the bed of cedar that lines the bottom of the old woman's sleeping hole. I close my eyes and try to slow my breathing, but the pain is too intense. I cannot sleep.

One by one, the Red Men leave the hearth fire to go to bed. In the silence, I turn my body towards the birchbark walls and cringe when the pain flares. Just then, I feel the heat of someone behind my back, and I hold my body very still. Without a word, Achak tucks the furs around my back.

The next morning, I notice that someone has placed two circles beside my bed. One is made up of acorns that have been painted red. The other is a circle of pinecones, but the loop is missing a pinecone to complete the loop. I don't see the significance until I notice that a small, misshapen pinecone has been placed in the center of the red acorns. Then my tears well up. He is trying to tell me that his tribe is circling around me to offer their protection while I heal.

Glancing up at the drying fish dangling from the rafters, I see the work these *skraelings* do to survive all winter long and realize that they are not so unlike my people. Furs and skins hang on the walls. Tools and weapons hang from posts. The smell of woodsmoke mingles with the smell of cooking meat. On the ground, there are birchbark containers full of drying herbs and root vegetables.

I lay my arm across my brow, trying to blot out the pain of everything. At least I am safe among these people in this tribe. I should feel at ease knowing that it doesn't matter where I sleep as long as I have a bed. Beothuk. Norse. All of us are just desperate to survive these winter storms in this wretched wilderness.

When Askook enters the heated dwelling that afternoon, he brings with him a blast of cold. As he is tugging off his furs, I admire the leggings that he is wearing with spruce root stitching along the seams. The root is shiny and white and contrasts nicely with his ochre-red pants.

Askook barks at Achak when he sees me lying in the old woman's bed. To my surprise, Achak chuckles and the old woman smiles her toothless grin. Then Achak stands and offers Askook a seat by the smoking fire. They talk briefly amongst themselves, and I grow weary from watching their muscled shoulders rippling underneath their fine stag-skin shirts.

Askook stays late to visit with Achak, Nashushuk, and some other men. When he shakes his fists good-naturedly at Abooksigun, the man-child glances at me quickly before he says something which makes the other hunters laugh. Then Askook's voice climbs to a dangerous peak. His demeanour reminds me of my former life when I allowed Thorvard to rule my moods, to usurp my thoughts, and rob me of almost everything. I won't have that anymore. I can't. Not here. Not in this place where I have the chance to be someone new. I know the *skraelings* love the color of my hair. I hope to be revered for it.

As the shadows shift I move in and out of sleep, trying to get comfortable. When Askook is about to leave, he passes by my bed and glances at me with his stone-cold eyes in an effort to intimidate. If I were whole, I would spring up like a wolverine, scratch his eyes out, and bite his hand.

Achak steps between us, blocking the huntsman from my view. The old woman says something in her guttural language and shakes her head. When she raps Askook on the back of his legs with her walking stick, she mutters something underneath her breath and he talks back.

From underneath my furs, I feel a little smile forming when Askook suddenly glares at me. In a huff he leaves the tent, throwing open the door so wide that a rush of cold air slips inside, making us all shiver. The old woman grunts. Achak slides a look her way and Nashushuk coughs out a bunch of words.

In the shadows cast by the flickering fire, Achak reaches down to adjusts the pell-mell furs that I've stirred up, and the smell of him lingers in my nose and hair; the warmth of him lingers everywhere.

I catch his eyes, the glint of them, silver-flecked. On the edges of memory, floating in the shadowed labyrinth, Logatha haunts me.

Shame on you! Watch your step and beware, sister. The Red Men will only disappoint. Just remember that you are Norse and they are not. Do not succumb to their skraeling *games. Do not let them seduce you. Remember, your only job is to concentrate on getting well.*

Chapter Twenty-Four

WHEN GOOSE PIMPLES RISE

The blizzards howl for weeks on end and I am bed-ridden because of my blasted leg. In the dead of winter, the *skraeling* longhouse is a busy place with families coming and going. The old woman seems to be in charge. She is always welcoming her people in and encouraging them to sit with her around the fire. Her wizened face is cobwebbed by wrinkles but her eyes are bright and she treats me like I should be worshiped and revered. To my delight, she often sends little gifts: smoked salmon wrapped in dried seaweed, a little shell, a shiny piece of rock, a raven's feather that is a blend of bluish-purple and black.

Lying in the old woman's earth cradle, I watch everyone as Achak tends to me. He is my guardian – a huntsman turned healer. I sometimes wonder if he has been assigned to watch over me and guard me so I don't try to get away.

In his free time, Achak sits by the blazing fire with a chiseling tool in hand, concentrating on etching patterns into bone. He likes to carve. I like to watch him, lying cozied underneath my furs.

Unbelievably – especially in this Red Man's tent where everything is uniquely strange yet simultaneously familiar – the men are helpful. They cook. They sew. They even care for the young ones while their women work. I wonder that they are not ashamed.

One afternoon when my ankle is particularly stiff and sore, I motion to Achak to bring me water in a birchbark cup. Immediately he understands. Not only does he bring the drink, but he tips the cup so that I can swallow more easily without using my injured shoulder which has been bound up tightly in a sling. I take two giant gulps before Achak gently cautions me to slow down. In the process his fingers unexpectedly brush against the back of mine. Startled, I pull back and swallow wrongly which triggers another coughing fit.

Achak leans forwards to tap my back. His shirt is loose. I catch a glimpse of the red raven tattoo on his muscled chest. In that moment, my coughing stops and I avert my eyes; I feel myself begin to blush. What am I becoming in this *skraeling* place where Loki tricks me into seeing men who truly care?

Achak sits up straight and studies me. I hate that his gentle eyes display concern. I drop my chin. Even if I had the words, I doubt he would understand. He is a hunter who likes to kill. I turn my face into the wall.

Over the next few weeks I try to walk, but I am so hesitant to put weight on my ankle that I feel as dependent as a newborn fawn. Achak offers me his shoulder and I lean on him when the old woman makes us circle around their house – a dwelling they call a *mamateek*. It is an impressive structure about ten feet wide with six sides and earthen walls covered over with skins and birchbark with poles starting at the forest floor and meeting all together at the roof. Grandmother likes to sit in the middle where they make their fire. She watches me walk around the firepit, but other than that she won't let me do anything and I grow bored.

From my perch in the old woman's sleeping hollow, I memorize the *skraelings'* routines, learning what makes them angry and what makes them laugh. I even try to learn their words. My efforts are met with stares and a round of laughs. Abooksigun teases me most of all, but somehow I no longer mind. He has earned the right.

My presence in the old woman's tent and my mispronunciations of the Red Men's words stir up trouble when Askook comes. He is friends with Achak but he doesn't like me, I can tell. When he scowls at me, memories of Thorvard of Gardar come flooding back and I withdraw into the shadows, feeling as though I am a skunk, as though I am someone as worthless as a grain of sand.

When I am well enough to get out of bed for good, the old woman invites me to take the seat of honor around the fire, but I offer it up to Askook, hoping to avert trouble. It means nothing to me and from Askook's look I can tell it means everything to him. The hunter lifts his chin with the air of a proud man and I remain silent, remembering the promise I've made to myself. I will no longer give away my power or allow myself to tolerate any man's grumblings. I have toughened up.

As winter settles in, the snowbanks grow even deeper but the tribe makes the best of it with their storytelling, music, and dancing. When the drummers pound their drums and sing in undulating voices that rise in cedar smoke, grandmother seems to be at her happiest.

During the day, the women like to sit around the fire crafting shell-bead necklaces and sewing clothing out of hides while the men fix their tools and carve etchings into wood and bone. Then the weather clears and the hunters go out on several occasions to look for meat. Achak's hunting eye must be keen. He brings back rabbit, fox, marten, caribou, and deer, and when he has finished attending to the meat, he brings me ice wrapped in a piece of hide to use as a cold compress to soothe my foot and shoulder pain.

Several weeks pass. One morning I wake to a quiet, empty *mamateek*. The air smells fresh and there is no wind, just sunshine spilling through the smoke hole and cutting through the haze and tickling the cobwebs in the corners. In the filmy light, Achak stops his carving and looks up. His pitch-black hair is haloed by a sudden beam of light.

Lazily I stretch before easing myself out of bed. My ankle still looks deformed and I feel too scared to walk on it without support. Achak grins broadly when he sees me. For a moment, I hold his eye before glancing in the direction of the door.

"Where did the others go?" I ask a little shakily.

Achak lets me know with gestures that the men have

gone to check the traps and the women have gone to gather wood.

"Don't wait for me," I mumble as I motion for him to go outside. "The fresh air would be good for you."

His eyes flit towards the door. A moment later he jumps up and scampers out the door, moving as smoothly as a huntsman slipping through the bush. For a few moments I am alone, nurtured by the quiet whispers of the *mamateek* and the sudden sense of unbridled peace. When Achak sticks his head back inside, no words pass between us and yet we speak.

He gestures for me to come outside.

I point to my ankle. "I'm still too sore and weak."

Achak grins. As fast as a rabbit, he makes his way towards my bed, leans down, and scoops me up. Startled, I inhale sharply, and he staggers a little as he shifts my weight in his arms. Without thinking, I wrap my arms around his neck and tuck myself in close to his tattooed chest. Then, in a few quick strides, he carries me outside into the glorious sun. Instantly, I am rendered blind.

One lone bird perched on top of a mound of snow begins to chirp. It tilts its little head back and forth, studying us for a moment before it begins to hop around in the melting snow. The sun licks my face deliciously, but without a coat the cold sets in, birthing goose pimples on my skin. Achak jerks his chin in the direction of a pair of hawks soaring high above our heads. Their majestic wingspans and white bald heads are clearly visible in the clear blue sky.

Shivering, I draw myself in close to him to benefit from

his body heat. Achak looks down. Our eyes connect. Then he takes one final breath and turns to go back inside. I am aware that I am a skeleton – a mere whisper of what I once was – when he easily carries me through the doorway.

Inside the stuffy room, it is dim and smoky. Achak gently lays me down on my bed of furs, taking special care to cover me. The bear skin tickles. I swat at it. My reaction draws an easy grin.

"Why do you keep your face so red?" I murmur.

He searches my eyes before he mimes batting bugs away. When I look confused, he mimes lathering up his face and then waiting for a bug to land on him before he squishes it before it bites.

"You mix the ochre with fat and smear it all over your skin to keep the insects from biting you?" I laugh.

Achak smiles. Breathing hard, he hesitates. I choke back fear and force myself to stay still as he leans in close and lifts a lock of my red hair. Then he smiles at me reverently.

My senses are pinging. I have a tingling sensation in my chest that travels up my neck when I catch a whiff of cooking smoke, whittled pine, fresh outdoor air, and melting snow wafting off his hides.

With care, Achak moves his hand towards my cheek and I let him caress the scar that runs from my nose to my ears. Sweet Freyja, it takes great effort not to blink. Memories of the abuse that I endured pop up and I kill them quickly, piercing them with my hidden sword by remembering Achak's kindness when I was ill. He tended to my broken bones. I drank in the smell of his berry-perfumed tea and his fresh pine-smelling poultices.

Achak stares at me. After a long moment of trying to still my thoughts, I get lost again in his handsome scent, a mixture of woodsmoke, herbs, earth, and snow. In that moment, I come alive and find my smiling self, that piece of me that I had lost. Once Logatha was the one to help me find that gem. Oh gods, what would she think of me in this place?

Trembling, I let Achak take me in his arms. I love his lips, his chin, his throat, the red lines scrolling across his cheeks. As he traces his finger down my neck, I throw my head back and begin to laugh, feeling his tickles, reveling in the warmth of his gentle touch. Then, with caution, I let myself relax, bracing myself so I don't drift into another time where the dark memories lurk.

Achak's skin is rough. Nervously, I begin to entwine my fingers into his. In response he mumbles softly in his own tongue. I feel the heat of him, marveling when I suddenly feel the spark of skin tingles. I take a jagged breath. He takes one too and his eyes flash with a lustre more brilliant than the springtime sun dancing across a frost-covered meadow.

"You never asked my name," I whisper, blinking twice. I tap my chest. "I am Freydis. Freydis Eiriksdöttir. Freydis of the Norsemen's tribe."

"Freydis..." He releases my name as though murmuring a hallowed prayer. It is not at all what I expect.

"You are Achak," I say quietly as I stare into his large grey eyes.

"Achak." He sweeps his arms around the room. "Beothuk."

"You are Achak of the Beothuk tribe?"

He grins. With his free hand, he tentatively reaches out to touch my hair.

"Red," he says with difficulty. I feel a rush of heat in my cheeks.

"My hair has always been like this – curled in ringlets and wildly red," I whisper, certain he doesn't understand. "I am the only one who has my *faðir's* hair. My brother Leif is not like me. He has raven-colored hair like Mother's. Leif is…"

Achak's eyes light up and he smiles at me with his perfect teeth. "Leif. Red *vyking*?" he repeats incredulously. He lifts his hand to approximate my brother's height.

"*Já,*" I say, laughing at the way he pronounces his words in Norse.

"Furs. *Vykings*. Trade." He waves his arm around the tent. "Beothuk tribe."

I am so shocked that he knows some Norse that tears well up. I snatch a breath.

"You knew my brother?" My voice is tremulous; I am so proud.

"*Já,*" Achak replies, trying to copy the way I pronounce the word. The sound bounces across the empty room. For a moment we laugh together before a comfortable silence settles between us.

"The others will be returning soon," I finally say as I try to convey the message without using words. Achak slowly shakes his head. A look of amusement creeps into the crease lines that edge his eyes.

"Beothuk… hun… hunt," he manages quietly.

I study his mouth. My heart is beating very fast. Tentatively I reach out and touch his cheeks but his red tattoo barely smudges underneath my thumb.

His gaze wanders across my face as the rumble of a low-pitched, mirthful sound begins to erupt from somewhere deep inside his chest. My fingers stop and he reaches up and cups my hand. His eyes take me in. After a moment, I extract my hand and with my index finger I begin tracing a line down his handsome cheek. When he throws a tiny smile, I continue moving my finger down his neck and down his smoothly contoured chest where the red raven tattoo sits above his left nipple.

Slowly his body moves into mine. With a jolt, I roll back onto the bed of furs and feel the warmth of his gentle hands tentatively reaching out to caress my skin. Hesitantly he comes towards me once again. His eyes pull me in and I let him kiss my neck, reveling in the feel of him.

We come together, quivering with the same desire, a hot passion rising like a building wave. I lose myself in the feel of him, tingling as though I am sipping wine, marveling at the feelings that I have always wanted but never known.

Achak carefully moves his body on top of mine and I hold his kiss, feeling the dizziness of the moment and the relief that he knows my injuries, that he knows where he can put his weight. For a moment I curse Thorvard's name just as Achak whispers mine. Then there are pleasure sparks and I try to still the thunder in my chest and ease the tingles exploding everywhere.

Achak's eyes caress my lips but then he stops. Slowly, he tilts his face to the side and studies me as though hesitating.

He points to me. Then he lays his hand on his heart. In the silence, a single tear drips from my eye and he reaches forwards to brush it off. It is enough. He sees me with his gentleness.

There are a thousand prickles in my fingers and in my toes as the warmth of him slides up against my skin. My heart explodes and I draw him closer, feeling the muscles in his back, grabbing lower, sighing with a longing ache.

Slowly, his hands begin to work their way up my thighs and hips, and we fall into kissing as though we are two mating birds sharing the magic of our warbles. Groaning, he cups my breasts and I grip the back of his thick, warm neck to keep his lips on mine while I pull him close. With more tender kisses, he lets me know that he likes the color of my red hair, which makes me laugh. Then I throw caution to the wind and slip my tongue inside his mouth.

The passion flares and I work his shirt off with my good arm. His chest is smooth. His skin is warm. Tentatively, I reach out and touch his raven tattoo with my eager thumb, tracing around the contours, poking the edge of my nail into the outline of the black feathers, all the way to the tips of them. Just then, Achak throws a lovesick grin my way and I think my heart will surely burst. With gentle hands he grips my body and draws me in, and I revel in the feel of him as he slowly moves my legs apart.

I am so eager that I gasp when he enters me. As I arch my back, our bodies come together and he pleasures me in such a way I have never experienced. When he lowers his forehead into the furs, I feel my heart beating wildly, his chest moving up and down. How is it that it can feel like this?

Achak whispers in a low voice and I toss a smile. This language takes no effort to understand. One more time he kisses me deeply and then we lie back, exhausted and content. I lie snuggled underneath his chin with my naked body pressed into his. Achak finds each of my scars one by one and gently caresses them with his calloused finger.

"This one was when Thorvard threw me down," I say, feeling an embarrassed flush move up my neck even though the words mean nothing to Achak's ears. "And this one was when he pushed me hard and I fell against the counting table."

Achak gives each scar a kiss. His lips are gentle. When my eyes well up, he shushes me with a string of words, guttural yet magical, the soft harshness of them pleasurable to my listening ear. Just then, a log splits apart and shoots out sparks in the firepit. When Achak untangles his body from mine to see to it, I follow his naked form around the room and admire the way his muscles move. When he finds his loincloth – a skimpy garment made of well-worn hides with patched-up holes – I try not to stare, but I promise myself that I will make him a new one when I can.

"*Oosuck*," Achak says, pointing to me as he throws a crooked grin. I prop my good elbow up on the bed of furs and shake my head in an effort to communicate that I don't understand. He points to himself. He points to me.

"*Oosuck*," I laugh teasingly. "Am I your wife?" He cocks his head and smiles at me.

"Now I am Freydis of the Beothuk tribe?"

He pauses. The laughter drains from his eyes and face.

"Great Wolf will be angry?" I ask, feeling the sudden weight of everything. I make a fist and point upwards. I don't know what they call their gods. "Great Wolf" is a guess that is not quite right. Achak frowns.

"Freydis." He gestures to his heart then points to me. "Achak." When he smiles, my fear melts away.

He comes back to me and we kiss some more, and the yearning for him starts again. Praise Freyja, the owner of *brísingamen*, the gleaming necklace, who rides her chariot pulled by cats across the sky wearing her cloak of falcon feathers. The goddess of love has heard my prayers in this unlikely place, in this *skraeling* tent that smells of smoke and hides and aspen logs.

When the others finally return to the *mamateek* at dusk, they bring fresh venison. The other *oosucks* roast the meat charcoal black, and I don't get up until the fire hisses and the fat starts dripping down the roasting sticks. Even though I am ravenous, I can't stop staring at Achak's hair and his hunter's build. When he talks, I listen to the inflection of his voice and savor the sound of his rhythmic speech. The music of it unlocks the chains around my heart.

That night, Achak and I lie together on his bed of furs in the presence of the men and women of his tribe. They barely pay attention to what we do even when the moans escape from Achak's throat. As the fire flickers across the markings on his chest, his raven tattoo almost seems to come alive, and I blink and smile and kiss and groan. In response, Achak whispers wondrous words – words that land like dandelion fluff, tickling my ears with their wonderfully strange rhythms.

In the dark, I shiver, knowing that if I could make him understand, he would mend the bruises and stop up the blood leaking from my broken heart.

One night, as the moonbeams stream through the open smoke hole illuminating our red-white flesh moving together as we make love, I look deeply into Achak's eyes and see myself as someone undeserving of his tender touch. I worry that I will never be good enough, that my red hair is no match for some other girl's Beothuk skin, that Achak will tire of me and go off to hunt and leave me here to sleep alone.

Our fervent kisses are long and hard, our pulses quick, our heartbeats loud. Just as I am falling into a sticky cobweb that holds me hostage in a place of uncertainty, Achak's loving lifts me up. He has an uncanny way of honoring me with his hands and convincing me that I am worth more than just the red color of my hair.

That night my dreams are strange. The Beothuk moon god comes to bless our union while the god Freyja opens doors. Then the raven comes sweeping low across the sky as if attempting to hide us with its molten feathers in order to protect us from the hungry predators that are waiting in the shadows. I bolt awake. Achak stirs beside me and pulls me closer before he comforts me with a string of Beothuk words. Then he kisses me with his Beothuk mouth.

In the coming days, Achak's people accept me as though the two of us were meant to be. I am convinced they think I seduced him with my red hair. As for the old woman, she smiles at us with her toothless gums before nattering away at Achak who bows his head respectfully. Her only insistence is that I try to eat, that I try to laugh, that I sit cross-legged beside her when she takes her seat around the fire. It is almost as though I have morphed into someone I no longer know.

It is women's month back in Greenland – that time of year when Norsemen celebrate the Feast of Góablót by taking special care of their wives. The feast has never meant too much to me, but now I understand why the day is marked. It seems like Achak celebrates this feast day all year long. He treats me as though I am an honored wife, a special *oosuck*, a treasured gift. If truth be told, he dotes on me.

By the time the spring thaws come, Achak's people have made a special place for me around their fire, and I am beginning to understand a few Beothuk words. One of the young women of the tribe is trying to teach me the Beothuk creation stories while Nashushuk has taken it upon himself to try to tell me, through gestures, about the Great Spirit they revere. Their *skald* makes me feel at home in their *mamateek*, even though he is accompanied by a drummer's beat instead of a lyre and narrating in a language I can't understand. If Logatha were here, I would tell her that they are like us ... and yet they're not. Their *mamateeks* are just like our longhouses, but they sing too much when they beat their drums.

One night, I shift uncomfortably in my seat, knowing that Logatha will fault me for all that has happened and that she will blame me for staying in this Beothuk village with these men and women who are not my kin. She will shame me openly. I can't imagine what I'll do then.

I get up in silence, searching for a drinking cup. Standing in the shadows, I remember the Norse drinking horns all lined up perfectly on the longhouse shelves back in Leifsbidur. The thought niggles. I begin to tremble and my knees go weak. A moment later, I feel Achak's arms slipping around my waist, his nose nuzzling at my neck. The darkness closes around us and I take a breath and give in to him. I can't seem to get enough of him.

Two more weeks come and go, bringing spring storms that violently shake the rafters and rattle the birchbark walls as the snow and ice pelt down, tinkling wildly as the wind gusts roar. Indoors, the fire is cozy and warm, and I spend my time sewing hides and worrying about the fate of my Icelandic friends.

As soon as the storm lets up, I ask Achak to escort me back to Leifsbidur. He tries to tell me that the route is impassable at this time of year but I shrug him off.

"I must go back," I say.

"Great One will give a sign," Achak reassures. His voice sounds gruff.

"My people might be dead by then."

"Hush, *oosuck*! Release guilt to smoke."

Logatha's face is so crystal clear that it is like she is sitting beside me. Outside, there is commotion in the yard sparked by two crows fighting. Abooksigun stands up quickly and goes to check. As he is leaving, Achak turns to me and tries to speak in Norse.

"Little Fox says snows stop. We go." He points to Nashushuk and Askook. "Friends come. The boy – Abooksigun – takes journey, too. We make trade with Norsemen."

"We'll take the canoe when the sea ice melts?" I ask to clarify.

Achak nods.

"It will be too late if we have to wait for the ice to melt."

"Snowbanks are…" He lifts his arms to show their height.

"Too big?" I finish.

Nashushuk grunts from across the tent and I slide my eyes in his direction. I like this Red Man. He seems to understand that I feel responsible for the welfare of my kin. Staring at him, I think of the dangers I would have to face on my trek back home. The tree wells are likely very deep and the path will be poorly marked; there is probably flooding at this time of year. Worse yet, there are unstable cornices hanging over unseen rocks.

"As soon as we can, we need to leave," I manage, glancing at the two of them.

Nashushuk brings forth a load of wood to restoke the fire. On his way past, a pinecone slips from the pile. When it hits the ground, the damn thing rolls, and I accidentally step on it and crush it into a misshapen blob. Wincing, I swear when I notice that a prickly part full of tree sap has become lodged into the sole of my foot. When I go to pluck it out, my foot starts to bleed.

The next day the black, sticky sap residue is still there. Try as I might, I can't seem to rub it off. In that moment, I am reminded of broken pinecone circles and my obligation to return to Leifsbidur to make the circle whole.

For one whole month I am forced to wait. I feel guilty for experiencing joy in the Beothuk tent. I feel guilty for being Achak's lover, considering that I am Norse. I even feel guilty for rejoicing in the fact that spring is late. It means I can wake up next to Achak every day and I don't have to worry about traveling back to Leifsbidur.

But guilt takes its toll. For days on end my stomach lurches and I can hardly eat. Even Achak is concerned for me. He melts fresh snow and boils it to make dogwood tea that is known to help with stomach cramps but nothing works. Every morning when I first wake up and catch a whiff of roasting winter flounder and seal-oil broth, I throw up. Then at night when the smoke is thick I feel like gagging and my stomach roils.

I can't stop worrying until I discover why I feel so ill. Then my lips slip into a ready smile. There is newfound joy, a burst of hope.

On the day Achak asks to braid my hair, I make up my mind to disclose the secret. In a rush as powerful as a waterfall spilling over a mountain ledge, I gather my courage and begin to speak.

"I am with child," I say in Norse. My lips are quivering and I cannot suppress a growing smile. Achak continues to work my braids. Turning a little in my seat, I feel compelled to repeat myself. This time I try speaking in the Beothuk tongue.

Achak drops his hands. The braid partially unravels as he pulls back and stares at me. For a moment I hold my breath, watching his silhouette flickering in the firelight. He blinks and I see his smile, a smile that fills my eyes with tears. A moment later I find myself wrapped up tightly in his arms as he holds me closely against his chest. When his lips begin to caress my neck, I peek down his shirt and his raven tattoo blinks at me.

"The Great Creator will give Raven a *döttir*," Achak predicts.

"I will bear you sons," I tease with a sudden swelling in my chest. I pull back and gaze up into his glassy eyes. His voice catches.

"You will give me a little acorn," is all he says.

Chapter Twenty-Five

SPIRIT WALKERS

With the onset of spring, the days start to lengthen and I begin to feel my body changing and a tenderness in my breasts. Achak is particularly attentive in the evenings when I am so fatigued. He wipes my brow and whispers loving words – the kind of words I have longed to hear. Then he rubs my swollen feet and gives me a soothing tea to sip. Later, when the moon shines down, we come together in the dark and love each other tenderly.

One day, as the melting snow drips steadily outside our tent and the icicles tinkle precariously in the wind, Achak sneaks up behind me and throws his arms around my waist. When I stop laughing, he hands me an ornately carved red wooden box. I marvel at the workmanship. With shaking hands I gently open the birchbark lid. There, cushioned in a bed of moss, I find two earrings made from caribou bones painted red. Etched into the bone are precisely mirrored images, each of two ravens with their wings spread out as they soar across a moonlit sky. The design is intricate and ornate. It is the most beautiful carving I have ever seen.

"Did you make these from the caribou antlers you stole from me?" I ask, swallowing deeply to stop the emotions from bubbling up.

He grins and takes the box from me. Slowly and carefully he draws the earrings out. Tilting my head back, I sit very still so he can fit the treasures into my lobes. When he is done, he stares at me. There is a dimple carving its way into his cheek that I have never noticed, never kissed.

"The earrings are beautiful," I murmur.

He takes up my hand and places it against his lips. "Ravens play," he says.

I nod. The dangling earrings bob up and down, brushing against my cheek and my chin.

"I have nothing to give you in return," I say. Achak shrugs and I catch another whiff of his handsome smell. I love his smell.

"You give me *döttir*," he says in broken Norse. He lowers his eyes and glances at my belly where our child grows, and I release a ready laugh.

"The child will make us happy."

"Achak of the Beothuk tribe is happy inside this tent," he croons. I cock my head. Behind us, we hear grandmother cough. "See moon?" he says as he points to the earrings. I take one out and stare at it. There is a tiny circle above one raven, a tiny dot that gives off lines of light.

"When I see the moon, I will think of *oosuck*," Achak says as if embarrassed. "When you look at the moon, you

344

must think of me." He looks so serious, I feel myself frowning.

"I think of you always."

"Listen to the spirits: the air, the water, the fire, the earth. They tell us things. They tell me now to watch the moon."

"Why?" I ask.

His voice dips low. "*Oosuck*, when our moccasins follow different paths, both of us will have the moon. We will be together if we look up and share the moon."

"I will never be apart from you," I protest. Outside, I hear the songbirds chirping excitedly in the yard.

"When you go hunt caribou, you will leave me," Achak breathes against my ear.

"Each time I have gone out hunting for caribou, I have found you," I reply in a teasing tone. I feel confused. He pulls away. I bring my fingers up to trace the red markings on his cheek.

"You go hunt. I go carve," Achak says with a simple shrug. I smile again. My index finger slowly moves down his chin towards his throat and chest. Moving lower, I circle his raven tattoo with my nail and he smiles a lopsided grin before his eyelids fall shut.

"Our bairn will grow up with a noble *faðir*," I proclaim. Achak flicks open one eye before he cracks another smile. Then he studies me with a sober expression on his face.

"The geese return. Listen. They honk," he says uneasily when we hear them flying overhead.

"Spring is here," I whisper softly. I keep my voice steady, my face calm.

"*Oosuck* must want to leave?"

"Is it time to return to Leifsbidur?" I turn my head towards the tent flap where the mosquitoes like to lurk right outside the door. Achak makes an injured noise. When he stands, he begins to pace. I take in the hardened beauty of his face that has lived and risked and fought hard to love.

"Nashushuk speaks. He says there is no more snow on the trails. The path to Leifsbidur is clear."

"My people need me. It's time to leave."

"The raven visits me in sleep," Achak groans. "The spirits speak." It seems like he is searching hard to find a word. I am suddenly distracted by the ripple of activity underneath my furs. Gasping delightedly, I reach out for Achak's hand and pull him closer to feel the magic of our child.

"Already he is strong and brave," I say energetically as I search Achak's face. From across the *mamateek* grandmother senses our excitement and comes to us. Her wrinkled face is a map of lines. She takes the fox collar that she is wearing and draws it tightly closed around her neck.

"Red hair leaves?" she rasps.

"*Já*," I say. I feel a rush of gratitude bubbling up. Before meeting her, I was an ugly caterpillar trapped inside a drab cocoon.

"May your moccasins go in peace," grandmother gushes in the Beothuk tongue. I bow my head respectfully. "Songbird will make new *mukluks*. You must walk. The ocean ice is still too thick to take a canoe."

Achak glances at my pregnant belly and my swollen feet. "Is your ankle strong enough to make the trek?"

"I managed before without your help," I reply.

"I will carve a walking stick," Achak says. He looks worried. For a moment grandmother studies my pregnant belly before she grabs hold of Achak's arm and speaks so fast that I can't comprehend her Beothuk words.

"Grandmother says to rest your feet. It is not good for you to go out hunting anymore."

I feel an easy grin moving into the corners of my mouth. Achak sees it too.

"Be careful, *oosuck*," he says to me in Norse. "I think she wants to keep you here."

I turn towards the other men in the tent. "Grandmother wants Achak to carry me to Leifsbidur," I say as loudly as I can, trying to suppress a growing smile. Nashushuk and Abooksigun begin to laugh. Askook stares into the fire.

"Your white bones are too weak to make the hike back to Leifsbidur," the hunter grunts. I glance at him.

"Askook will carry dried fish back to your people," Achak says in a gentle voice. "Nashushuk and Megedagik want to come as well. They will hunt along the way."

"I will come to offer you protection," Abooksigun chirps. His boy-man bravado makes me grin. If he were Norse, he would rival Loki, the trickster god.

"Grandmother says I may need some brave huntsmen to help me find my way back," I announce.

Askook's eyes meet mine. There is something about him I don't like.

❧

That night, as Achak and I sit around the cooking fire, I lean into him as he inspects his carving piece. When he puts it down and starts with another chore, I take a breath.

"Why does Askook have to come with us?"

"Askook wants to hunt," he says as he begins knapping an arrowhead. After he is done, he examines it carefully in the firelight. A moment later, he begins to grind away the edges to make them sharp.

"He should stay behind," I say.

"Askook has long been our friend," Achak says without glancing up.

"I don't care," I pout. "He doesn't like me, and I don't trust him."

For a moment Achak stares into the fire. Then he takes up the arrowhead in his hand and leans into the fire to better see. "Askook does not give trust away too easily," he says. Leaning back, he reaches over me for a tool.

"One needs to earn my trust, too," I say.

Achak keeps his shoulders bent into his work. "It is not you, *oosuck*. Askook does not trust Abooksigun. It is hard to let little owls leave the nest without watching over them. Askook wants to come to keep his eye on Abooksigun."

I release a heavy sigh.

"The trek will be long. Great Spirit will watch over us."

"Óðinn will guide me home," I say.

"The walk is far."

"I would walk to the ends of the earth for my kin."

"The walk to Leifsbidur will be tough enough."

The fire leaps before dying down into orange ribbons of

flickering light. I stare into the glowing embers and get lost in them.

"I shall be glad to see my friends," I sigh.

Achak glances up. His eyes meet mine. "The winds will guide you home, and your people will be surprised to see you," he says in the Beothuk tongue.

At least that is what I think he says.

On the night before we leave, the Beothuk honor me with a feast. I have grown to love and trust them. Forsooth, I have learned.

Grandmother is the hardest person to leave behind. She cracks a toothless grin as she pats my cheeks and strokes my hair. Then she touches my belly and whispers a Beothuk prayer. When she hands me a new pair of *mukluks*, my eyes well up. I tell her that she has been more than kind and welcoming. I tell her this in Beothuk, and she smiles again.

Askook is eager to leave at the break of dawn. As we are packing up, he irks me with his stern, judgmental tone, his scowls, his standoffishness, and his arrogance. When Askook starts his grumbling, Achak takes me by the arm and tries to steer me away from him, but he follows us.

"Trekking back to Leifsbidur in spring is not easy. Your *oosuck* should stay behind," he says.

"She comes with me," Achak replies.

"Paw," he says.

I look between them, feeling terrified. Achak reaches out

and touches my face tenderly before he makes me take up my walking stick.

In the end, it is not my ankle but my shoulder that causes me so much pain. I often ask to stop to rest, and the men honor my request. In the bush, the bugs are bad. Despite the red ochre paint mixed with grease that Achak slathers on my face and arms, the mosquitoes swarm us and soon there are ugly welts swelling on almost every part of me. Achak tells me not to scratch, but I do so anyway behind his back. Later, when the other men go off hunting, Achak stays with me and rubs my swollen feet while the mosquitoes continue humming above our heads.

Two days into our journey we encounter a bank of snow that blocks our path. This forces us to backtrack and find a different route around a marsh that is still iced over in some spots. The surrounding marshlands are edged by an uneven ring of new-growth trees which makes the route almost impassable. Eventually we find our way by dodging a muddy creek and making our way up a hill where it is cold, but the snow is gone.

That evening we camp under the twinkling stars beside an open fire next to the wide expanse of open sea. Even though I snuggle close to Achak, I can't get comfortable. I think of Logatha and Finnbogi and worry about what they will say about my pregnancy.

"The Great One will set things right," Achak says as he struggles to keep the fire going. The campfire smokes from the wet wood we have been forced to use.

"My friends will not know me anymore," I say, looking

up into the nighttime sky where the stars are blinking like thousands of accusatory eyes.

"Be still, *oosuck*," Achak whispers as he too looks up. From somewhere distant, we hear a screeching owl.

"How can I be still? They will wonder why I stayed away for so long."

"I am beside you," Achak murmurs, but his voice sounds tired.

That night, my sleep is poor. The baby is restless. I feel its little legs kicking me repeatedly in the ribs. Not only that, but my shoulder aches. The next morning, and the morning after that, I am grumpy and miserable as I follow the men navigating a path into the wilderness.

On the fourth day, we hike all morning and finally arrive in Leifsbidur late in the afternoon. Everything is quiet in the yard. We pass the smithy with the forge unlit and the door flapping open and closed in the wind. The entire settlement is a haunted place where the seagulls squawk and then skirr away.

I am about ready to enter the main longhouse when Achak reaches out and pulls me back.

"What's wrong?" I ask.

"Ravens," he says pointing skyward to where two black birds soar. Glancing up I watch them circling as they catch the wind currents.

"Something isn't right," I say. The baby shifts underneath my ribs.

Achak's strong arms pull me against his smoky hides just as the wind picks up. In the ditch, the crocuses with their purple petals peeking out of a dirty patch of snow have just started blooming.

"*Oosuck*, you must go inside alone," he says as he points to the longhouse door.

"*Neinn*," I say. I hear the fear in my voice. "You must come too."

He shakes his head. I catch a glimpse of the other Beothuk who are looking around the yard. Abooksigun is out by the bog-iron pit while Nashushuk and Askook are heading in the direction of the pit house and the byre.

"Watch for men who take the shape of fox," Achak whispers softly in my ear. He scans the yard before pushing me gently towards the door. I hesitate before turning back. There is a strange softness in his eyes. For a moment, I feel myself between worlds.

"Kiss me again," I murmur as I turn to him. Achak stands very straight. Carefully, he scans the yard before he pulls me into a tight embrace. His kiss is just as intense as it is long.

"*Oosuck*, you must go," he says as he attempts to pull away from me. His baritone dips low. There is something in his eyes that stirs up fear. I hold his gaze. Even as his arms gently try to push me away, he kisses me tenderly once again.

"I don't want to leave you," I whisper in his ear.

"It is time for my pinecone to leave the safety of the circle," he says with a careful smile. The Beothuk words slip easily from his tongue. For a long moment I stand there watching the wind tussling his long black hair. Then he turns. In two quick strides, he rounds a bend.

I am halfway to the longhouse when I look behind me one last time. Achak is gone. The baby kicks. My throat chokes up.

When I try the latch on the longhouse door it opens easily and I barge inside. As soon as I enter, I am blasted with the stench of sickness, the smell of rot. Instantly my hand shoots up to cover my nose and mouth.

"Logatha?" I call out uncertainly. From the shadows comes a faint, weak voice.

"I am here," she says as the door slams shut.

"Which bed platform?" I ask as I begin to search the shadows. In my haste, I tug at the bed curtains and hold my nose because the stench of sickness is vile and it sticks to me. The bed chambers are either empty or full of sick, haggard-looking Icelanders whom I hardly recognize.

In a darkened corner at the back, Logatha is half sitting up, but her eyes are closed. She is gaunt and pale and the mound of her belly is not large enough considering that she is almost due. Beside her on the bed of matted furs lies Asta. Startled, I step back in shock. Asta is also pregnant, but she looks very sick.

In a few quick strides, I am across the room and leaning down to check her pulse. Her limp arm is slick with sweat and she is burning up with fever. At the far end of the bed, Logatha's bloodshot stare is blank. Her hair, once lustrous, is a dull and stringy mess of greasy tangles that would take days to comb out.

"Art thou a ghost?" she mutters in a garbled rasp as her chapped lips begin to bleed.

"*Neinn*, sister! It is me, Freydis."

"Freydis?" Logatha parrots in a shaky voice. "Freydis Eiriksdöttir? Art thou dead?"

"*Neinn*, sister. I am very much alive," I say, but my lips are quivering and my palms are wet. Logatha is all skin and bones. To look at her is to see the walking dead.

"What fiend is this coming towards me in my house?" she yells with sudden energy. There is a fierceness in her sunken eyes.

"Logatha, I have returned to Leifsbidur."

"Get out, you skin-changer!" She releases the words like a panting dog before she shoots up on her knees and snarls and bares her teeth.

"It is me, Logatha," I say in shock, feeling suddenly wary as I draw back.

"You affect my mind by illusion and madness, you practitioner of *seiðr*," she spits.

"I am not here because of black magic," I say defensively. "I was waylaid by a snowstorm and then some hunters from a Beothuk tribe found me in the bush and rescued me. These *skraeling*s took me back to their village where I fell ill."

"You are a changeling who looks just like my friend. By Óðinn's beard, I have started my journey to the realm of the dead. Do not come closer, spirit." Logatha's mouth froths foam as she madly bats her arms against her head. When I go to grab for her, she shrieks so loudly that Asta stirs in her delirium.

"Freydis is long since dead," Logatha continues in an agitated trance. "She wandered off and died while hunting. That was many moons ago."

She looks half-starved and half-possessed. When she begins to shake her fists and snarl, I glance towards the door.

"I didn't forget you, Logatha," I sputter. "You can't see how it was for me."

"I can't see because you use *seiðr* illusion magic. You witch! Get out, I say!" Her eyes dart troll-like from side to side, and I suddenly worry that she will lunge.

"Where are the others?"

"I had six sisters but they all died," Logatha rants wildly. I am confused. Asta is lying beside her. She is barely breathing but still alive.

"Where is Snorri?" I ask as I look around.

"Hunting," is all she says.

"How about Finnbogi? Where is he?" I grip my knife unsteadily.

For a moment she stops and just looks at me. Then she releases a blood-chilling scream that makes my body freeze and the hair on my arms stand up. My terror grows when her high-pitched moan becomes ferocious and inarticulate and she begins to rock her body back and forth.

Just as I am about to muster up enough courage to approach again, Logatha releases a torrent of animalistic sobs. When she twists around, she points at me with an accusatory finger.

"Finnbogi paid too great a price to clear your name," she yells hysterically.

I shake my head, confused, knowing that she is a broken woman who is very ill. "What madness is this? Where is he?"

"Dead," she says.

"Dead?" I gasp. Her words gut me like a hunting knife. "How?"

Logatha raises her head. Spit mixed in with tears and a string of snot is dripping down her chin. "You deserted us! May Thor smite you down!"

"Calm yourself, Logatha," I plead in a desperate voice.

"You abandoned our people during a time of need," she rants, ignoring me. "Others relied on you to bring back food. When you didn't return, many starved to death. We barely managed to save two sheep. Alas, our Icelanders did not meet an honorable death here in Leifsbidur. *Neinn*. They died of sickness in their beds. You robbed them of Valhalla's feast."

"Their sickness was not my fault!"

"Finnbogi went out to look for you. He searched and searched. He looked for you in the endless storms." Her voice sounds shrill.

"Surely Finnbogi didn't get lost in a blizzard and freeze to death?" It feels as though someone is trying to stop up my nose and mouth with snow.

"*Neinn*," Logatha spits. She lunges as she yells my name. I easily dodge her fists.

"Freydis Eiriksdöttir, you cursed our house," Logatha screams hysterically before she trips and falls. I grab for her, pinching air and cringing when she narrowly misses falling on Asta who is lying on the bed, curled up in a fevered state.

"I tried to bring back meat," I say miserably as soon as I right myself.

"My husband lost his life for you." Her ragged breath catches on the words. I gape at her and see the light leeching out of her dull, half-dead eyes.

"I am not to blame."

"Finnbogi died at Thorvard's hands." Her voice drops low. "My husband challenged him to a duel. They fought a *hólmgang* to defend your honor. Finnbogi demanded blood vengeance to make up for the way Thorvard insulted and abused you, but my husband lost his life in the duel. He was not fast enough when Thorvard drew his sword. Did you know that Finnbogi was very ill?"

"He lost?" I whimper.

"He lost his head. Thorvard lopped it off with his gilded sword. By the gods, he made me watch."

"Great Thor," I cry, but Logatha continues talking over me.

"Get out, you homewrecker! You come into this house and play with my weakened mind using your *seiðr* illusion magic to make yourself appear alive. You are too late. You are a witch who stole my husband's life!"

"Believe you me, I am not a witch. Look at me, Logatha. I am very much alive!"

"You are a spirit walker. Get out, I say!" She is beginning to sound like a person who is *mar-ridden*, not all there. "Freydis Eiriksdóttir would not have let us starve to death." She tilts her head back, leaning against the longhouse wall. "She would not have abandoned her people in a time of need. She would not have let my husband die."

She looks past me and her eyes are glassy as they scan the room. When she shifts her gaze back to me, she shoots up tall and begins to wail. Her sobs crescendo to a peak as her bare feet get tangled in a mess of jumbled sleeping furs.

"Finnbogi fought for me?" I say when my thoughts finally work it through. "To avenge the abuse that I endured? When?"

"Finnbogi died at Thorvard's hands last Saturn's day," she sobs. "It was your fault."

"I'm sorry," I say, letting the words snake out, feeling the stinging poison of them as I hang my head, wincing.

Chapter Twenty-Six

I HAVE THE MOON

I have barely blinked when I hear a tremendous battle cry coming from the yard. There is a warning shout and a heavy thump. On impulse I run outside only to see Abooksigun lying face down in a pile of mud. I feel my knees buckle and my breathing stop. There is an arrow sticking out of his skinny back.

In shock, my eyes well up, and I rub them, forcing some air between my teeth. Then, with every breath I have, I struggle to move him, taking care to lift his braid out of the mud and pooling blood. Once he is lying on his side, I touch his face, his arms, his bony boy-man chest. His glassy eyes are staring at the sea, dead and blank.

"Abooksigun," I wail, struggling to push down grief. I would gladly give him my whole head of hair just to have him back, this fierce protector, this rescuer.

An eerie feeling comes over me. In that moment I realize that I am weaponless. My bow and arrows were left inside.

359

"Achak? Where are you?" It comes out as a whisper as I choke back a sob.

Standing quickly, I do an about-face, but I don't get far. Just as I am picking my way through the muddy yard, Logatha begins to scream. Looking up, I catch sight of her in the arms of one of Thorvard's thugs.

"Stop!" I scream as he strikes her violently from behind. As she falls, her hands jut forwards to protect her bairn. My legs freeze up. He strikes again, kicking at her, and she crumples in a heap.

Behind me, someone whistles a grey jay's song. It sounds like Nashushuk's call. He must be close. I spin around and come face to face with the man I hate. Thorvard's eyes are mere slivers in his hardened face. He has Achak by the throat, backed against the doorframe of the thrall's hut.

"Let him go," I shriek. Panic flares in Achak's eyes.

"This pond scum tells me you are his *oosuck*?" Thorvard over-pronounces the Beothuk word. I grit my teeth. "Have you become this Red Man's whore?"

In a *whoosh*, memories of Thorvard's mistreatment shove their way into my head. I scream again.

"Shut up, you two-faced bitch! Your *faðir* would disinherit you if he knew that you had a relationship with this worm. Your mother would collapse like she always does."

"By the gods, I beg of you, let him be!" I shout as Thorvard begins to squeeze Achak's throat. "He is nothing to you. Let him go!"

Thorvard growls before releasing Achak with a kick. My

baby's *faðir* doubles over with a heavy groan.

"Get up," Thorvard commands as Achak makes eye contact with Thorvard's knife. Thorvard lunges and Achak ducks.

Lurching forwards, I stop when Thorvard slices his knife across Achak's arm. He yells, and Thorvard reaches down and drags him up, twisting his arms behind his back, not caring whether he gets smeared by blood.

My legs are tree stumps growing roots. My palms are wet. Achak takes another ragged breath, squirming as he releases a war cry that snakes its way into the air. Thorvard snarls and jerks him back, lodging his knife against Achak's throat. Achak's shoulders sag and his face twists up. If I try anything, Achak is a dead man.

"You vicious animal! You violent brute!"

Thorvard drags his eyes across my face and his gaze comes to rest on my little bump. I blink at him owlishly. The muscles in my jaw tense up.

"Freydis, where were you for all these months?" The air slithers through his teeth. His eyes are cold. "I'll ask again. Where were you, Freydis of Gardar?"

Achak blinks. Thorvard digs the edge of his blade into Achak's throat, drawing a thin line of blood.

"Stop!" I screech. Achak's panicked eyes fix hard on mine. In silence he pleads with me to back away. Thorvard glances between the two of us.

"I see that you have been busy making *skraeling* friends," he snarls.

"I'll do anything to spare this Red Man's life," I beg softly, feeling chilled. My request is met with a crooked smile before Thorvard unexpectedly pushes Achak into a barrel where Achak bangs his head. Without flinching, Thorvard kicks him hard before leaning over him. Then, with a violent yank, Thorvard plucks him up. Achak looks too dazed to try to struggle free, and I stand there watching helplessly.

"This pond scum isn't worth it, but I'll be generous just this once," Thorvard smirks as he flips back his hair. He hocks a wad of spit into Achak's face. "How about we trade a life for a life?"

I will my pulse to settle down. "I beg for mercy," I manage, sucking back a building sob.

"Mercy?" Thorvard's eyebrows arch high. I know his tricks. I know his games. I know the timing of his posturing. My muscles twitch. Thorvard smirks again. I stare at him.

"Freydis Eiriksdóttir begs for mercy here on Vinland's shores where there is no Althing to adjudicate the fairness of her case."

My mind is racing. My breathing stops.

"Your lies cost me everything," Thorvard fumes.

"I have never lied," I manage as I gather courage and muster strength.

"You were never sick on your brother's farm," Thorvard scorns. "At Leif's house you duped me, you little wench! Then you destroyed my name when you chirped about the harshness of my fists. Thor give me strength, I should smite you down! Do you think I am a fool? I know your games, you little fox."

"Enough," I mumble pathetically.

"You are my wife and I'm in charge. When we return to

Greenland, you will restore my reputation. Then, for your impudence, I will take your lands and all your sheep. Afterwards, I will tell the good people of Gardar and Brattahlíð that you murdered our people here on Vinland's shores."

"You can't," I fume.

"I can," he yells. I glance at Achak. His face is blank.

"By Óðinn's beard, I'll make you take responsibility for all the hardships that we faced in this godsforsaken place. I'll blame you for the battle and the loss of lives. I'll blame you for the grief you caused and for the winter hardships that could have been prevented. The problem is that we left Greenland too late in the season. I swear to you, your name will be your ruin."

"It will not," I spit. "My family name will be revered throughout all time. It will never be destroyed by the likes of you! I am an Eiriksson!"

He cracks a grin before his eyes go cold. Then he rattles Achak's bones and I see my lover's blood-speckled ear. "Suit yourself, but if you want to save this Red Man's life, you will weave a story that clears my name."

My stomach falls. I hesitate. "What kind of story?"

He shrugs. "I'll tell our people that you entered the Icelanders' longhouses while they were still asleep and that you tied them up and murdered them."

"This is nonsense. It isn't true," I snarl.

"Listen here, you little wench..." Thorvard wrenches Achak and I go still. "I killed Finnbogi and all his men and Helgi, too. In fact, it was my good fortune to cleave that arrogant bastard's head right off his flimsy neck."

I gasp even as I feel my knees grow weak. Thorvard ignores me. "I killed Finnbogi to regain my honor, do you hear? You sailed west with Finnbogi without asking me. You killed our Greenlanders. It was you. Truly, Freydis, your men will back me. They say you murdered the innocent."

"I won't take the blame," I seethe.

"Then your Red Man dies."

My ears start ringing. My vision narrows. My chest constricts as I try to slow my breathing and draw my fists.

"As for all your fighting men – your loyal Greenlanders who sailed with you across the northern seas – many defected to my camp. I killed the remaining healthy ones here in Leifsbidur two weeks ago. The rest are marked for Helgafjell."

"I shall kill you," I say as I clench my jaw. If I had an axe, I'd smite him dead.

"*Oosuck,*" Achak gargles. His life depends on what I say, on what I do, on what falsehoods I claim as my own acts. Nervously I take a breath.

"If you release this Red Man in your grip," I say carefully, "I'll take responsibility for the evil deeds you committed here in Vinland. I'll tell the stories that you want told. With Loki's help, I'll do all this if you let us go."

"Well done," Thorvard laughs ruthlessly, "but we could weave an even better tale."

With a thudding heart, I glance around and almost miss spotting Askook hiding in the grass with his arrow nocked. I wonder why he doesn't take Thorvard out. Is he waiting for me to fall? I would expect his anger over Abooksigun to fuel his vengeance and make him do something rash. Instead he sits there until our eyes connect. An instant later, he is gone.

Thorvard grows cocky. "Your men are sick and mine are too," he spits. "To take the sick on board means death to all. We would be cursed. We could either leave them here to die on their own or you could kill them with my sword."

My mouth goes completely dry.

Thorvard smiles.

"We should kill them and tell our kinsmen that the sick chose to stay behind in Leifsbidur."

"You can't do that," I say, glancing anxiously at Achak's face. Suddenly it dawns on me that Thorvard has no intention of staying until the summer ends. Gathering up my strength, I shift my gaze. "Why this talk of sailing back to Greenland? I plan on staying here a long while yet."

"Freydis, you must know by now that I have had enough. I am going home." His face contorts in an angry scowl. "I am anxious to leave this Hel-hole behind. As for Finnbogi's longboat, it is filled with timber and many luscious furs and trading goods. My men were busy loading his ship while you were away."

"You thief," I spit. "How dare you steal Finnbogi's ship!"

"Finnbogi is dead. His men are too."

I am tempted to run at him and dig my fingernails into his chest and rip his heart out. Instead, I force myself to stand still. Thorvard has Achak by the throat.

"What about the women?" I manage in a quiet voice.

"I'll say that you attacked and killed them all."

"You'll be lying."

"*Neinn*." He looks smug. "You, Freydis Eiriksdöttir, will be the one who lies."

"Surely you don't expect me to travel back to Eiriksfjord and condemn myself?" I am so angry that I could gouge out his eyes and rip out his tongue. If Thorvard intends to leave the sick behind, Logatha and her bairn will die.

Achak shifts in place. This game must end. I will end it now.

"When we return to Brattahlíð, we will live apart," Thorvard whispers through his teeth, "but you will not breathe a word of our arrangement to anyone. If I hear you telling anyone that I spared a Red Man's life, I'll come for you, do you hear?"

"Why not divorce me now?" A sudden panic fills my chest.

"My *faðir* gave me trouble. Yours gave you land. We must stay married. It will serve me well. Your brother must pay me a portion of the profits he collects from the family lands, and I have the right to oversee your herds. If I leave you here and your brother thinks that you are dead, our clansmen will condemn me at the next Althing and accuse me of murdering you here on Vinland's shores. They will assume that I just want your land. I'll lose everything."

"Tell the good people of Greenland anything you want," I plead. "Just let me stay behind in Leifsbidur."

"You must come back to Eiriksfjord," Thorvard says unyieldingly.

I'm shaking. I cannot think.

Bracing myself against the surging fear, I bow my head.

"When will you leave?" I ask in a whisper.

"After I slice this *skraeling's* throat."

My head snaps up. The air wheezes through Thorvard's nose like dry reeds rustling in the wind.

"Come now, Freydis. What do you care? This Red Man isn't worth our time."

"I'll only leave if you promise to spare those who are gravely ill. You must also release the man you hold."

My voice is shaking. Achak squirms. He is helpless in Thorvard's grip. For a moment, we hold each other with our eyes. There is hallowed madness and gut-wrenching pain.

And love. There is that.

There is always that.

I will Achak to understand that I am stuck, to appreciate that there is no other way.

Achak, I give you up to keep you safe!

His eyes are glistening pools of light piercing me, holding me steady, keeping me from crying out.

"Freydis, have you lost your mind?" Thorvard scoffs. Once again, I glance at the *faðir* of my unborn child, the man whom I have come to love, the man who would do anything to rescue me, to save my life, to honor me.

It is my turn now to die for him.

Breathing a Beothuk prayer to the Great Creator, I brace myself and my stomach lurches. Our baby wakes and kicks me. Hard.

"I owe this Red Man nothing," Thorvard rages as he begins to squeeze Achak's throat. When Achak's hide shirt falls open, I see the raven tattoo on his chest.

"You gave your word…" I spit. My vision narrows and my thinking slows.

Thorvard glances at Achak's face. With a tight smile, Thorvard suddenly pushes Achak into the longhouse door. There is a wicked *thwap* and a heavy thunk before Achak bounces back and falls, hitting his head on the ground. Seeing his bloody face and death-like stare, I struggle to suppress a shrill, ear-piercing scream.

"Good riddance," Thorvard sniffs as he rights his clothing.

"*You troll*," I scream. "You killed him!"

Thorvard grabs me by the arm. "Shut up, woman! The ship is waiting. It's time to leave."

I bite my tongue and taste the metal tang of blood as Thorvard starts to drag me away from the settlement. Frantically, I begin to pummel Thorvard with my fists while desperately trying to twist my body to catch one last glimpse of the *faðir* of my unborn child.

"Achak!" I yell as I try to wiggle free but Thorvard's grip is strong. "Get *up*," I scream. My heart is cracking, bleeding out.

Thorvard pulls me forwards with his bear-like strength as I scan the empty yard in search of help.

Achak, my moccasins don't want to leave! They want to take a different path.

I send heartbreak soaring into the sky as the panic flutters down my back and a surge of sickness rips through my gut. In a flash, I see the kindness in Achak's eyes, his smooth brown skin, his tattooed cheeks. I love those cheeks. I give another tug, trying to rip myself away. I am suddenly aware that our unborn child will never see her *faðir's* eyes and never hear her *faðir's* voice. Achak will be dead to her. The Beothuk would want me to mutter prayers. I can't. Not now. Not yet. Not ever, if I am honest with myself. I have lost my faith in all the gods.

Thorvard half drags, half pushes me in the direction of the ships. When we finally reach the beach, I can't look back. I am too afraid of doing something rash that could get me killed. I must protect the only part of Achak that I have left. I must protect my unborn child.

Thorvard's men lift me, flailing, into the longboat. As soon as I am rid of them, I find a seat amidst the pelts, the kegs of water, and the salted fish. At my feet I find a tiny pinecone and I remember the lively Beothuk songs and the smell of smoke in Achak's tent. Through the mist I hear Achak's voice, the mispronunciation of his Norse words and the sound of his laughter as he nuzzles his nose into my neck.

My hands grip the gunwales. I feel the solidity of the wood. As the longboat lurches forwards in the rising wind, I realize that I am losing everything – the life I've built and the life I've found.

Memories of Achak break apart like fragile seed pods. From a far-off place, the coastal birds hovering over the pitching ship begin to shriek as they soar up high before plunging low in the drafts of wind.

A moment later I am shocked to see a familiar figure wading forwards in the foamy surf. Achak, my Achak, is still alive!

He stops when the water reaches his tattooed chest. Then he waves. He shouts. He waves again.

Leaning over the gunwales, I feel tears welling as the wind picks up with a whistling hiss. Achak calls. I can't find my voice. In the distance, his figure becomes a tiny dot that fades away, slinking into the blue. Suddenly, the wadmal sails flap open, the oarsmen cheer, and the longboat surges forwards like a sled on ice. Overhead, the seagulls cry as we head out across the sea.

That night, as I am pulling back my stringy hair, my fingers find Achak's raven earrings. I take them out. In my palms they are a treasured gift.

I trace the ravens with my fingertip and stare at the moonbeam etchings shining down. The memories come sliding in as slow as tree sap, too sticky to scrape away.

Oh gods, never again will I see the tattoo on Achak's chest. Never again will I breathe in his smell or feel his rough hands caressing me. Never again will he share my bed or hold me quietly in his arms. I yearn for him but he is gone.

The misery bubbles up and I feel the rawness of loss, the ache of sorrow entwined with a grief so bottomless I cannot breathe.

To calm myself, I look up at the nighttime sky, inky black and speckled with a spectacular array of dazzling lights in shades of green, gyrating wildly, swirling and blending as they come together. The bright patterns spiral upwards and loop down before hitting the horizon and bouncing back. Even higher, the stars – mere pinpricks of ethereal light – twinkle silently. And the moon, the moon is full. Tonight it weeps moonbeam tears that drop a string of sparkles across the dark white-capped sea.

Oh, Achak of the Beothuk tribe, with aching bones I promise to remember you.

When the moon shadows find me on Greenland's shores I will picture you, my love, my life.

I will recall your face, your red tattoos. I will remember you sitting cross-legged amongst your tribe, carving ravens into bone. In your absence I will honor you by teaching our *döttir* the Beothuk ways.

She will stand up to Thorvard. I will insist on it. Whatever happens, I will never let him rule her life. She will defy and dupe him if she must. Truly, I tell you, she will learn to defend herself. When she is grown, she will be just like you and grandmother. She will speak her mind from a place of wisdom. People will be drawn to her.

She will be skilled like you, Red Raven. I will teach her how to fight and how to hunt and how to honor the spirit of the animal. She will learn the art of sewing the hides the Beothuk way. I will show her. I have watched all of you long enough.

After the hides are smoked, I will even find some madder root to dye her clothing red to honor you.

Our *döttir* will be beautiful.

She will learn the lessons you have taught – that to place others above herself and care for them brings the greatest joy and happiness.

I will teach her.

She will follow in your footsteps and learn the importance of having an honorable family – a family who will protect, value, love, and defend her above all else. You will be proud of her when she spreads her wings.

She will learn your words, I promise you.

Together we will find the moon, that wondrous sky-pearl, that orb of light that links the three of us eternally. When we see it, we will think of you as you have asked.

As I have promised.

Always, my beloved.

Always.

Acknowledgments

To Jennifer Kaddoura for providing insightful and thoughtful editorial comments that left me musing and redrafting long after our meetings ended. Your passionate dedication to your craft, your keen eye, and your belief in me mean the world. Jen, you provided the loom that allowed me to weave Freydis's Viking tale. I am so grateful for our friendship and for the guidance that you provided allowing for travel into the unknown.

To my agents, Sam Hiyate and Emmy Nordstrom Higdon. Emmy, you believed in this project from the start, and I feel truly fortunate to have you representing my work. Your drive and determination to find the right home for this book speak to your willingness to help break the silence and bring attention to the plight of spousal abuse victims.

To the team at HarperCollins, including Charlotte Ledger, Lydia Mason, Andrew Davis, and especially Bethan Morgan, for her enthusiasm, encouragement, and editorial attention to detail as well as for her vision and guidance that helped make my writing soar. Also to Savannah Tenderfoot, the sensitivity reader for Salt & Sage Books, who provided insights and who raised awareness about some practical reasons why the Beothuk used red ochre.

To the field interpretive guides at L'Anse aux Meadows National Historic Site in Newfoundland, Canada, especially Paul Njolstad, Mark Pilgrim, and Kevin Young, who will be remembered for their storytelling in true *skald* fashion. To all the re-enactors at Norstead Viking Village, including Danecka Burden, Dillon Pilgrim, Annie Patey, and Sarah Colbourne. Thank you for allowing me to step back in time. Likewise, I am grateful to the staff at the Beothuk Interpretation Centre Provincial Historic Site in Boyd's Cove, Newfoundland, especially Karen Ledrew-Day. The beautiful people of Newfoundland, including Monty and Pansy Shears, who introduced me to cloudberry and partridge berry ice cream, were so generous with their time. Thank you for making my Newfoundland experience so memorable.

My passion for writing was fostered by many early influencers, including Janice Galleys, Genevieve Schulte, Guy Fuller and Veronica Wenterhalt. Thank you for encouraging me to write.

To members of the Victoria Writers' Society, especially Edeana Malcolm and Joy Huebert. Being part of a writing society presented me with opportunities that have made the publication of this novel possible.

To my early readers and cheerleaders, including Megan C., Lee B. and Michael G., Tiziana Hespe, Heather McEwen, Lise McLewin, Sheri Miller, Tammy B., Laura Gerlinsky,

Victor and Patricia Saavedra, Bev Rach, Bill and Barb Rogers, Seoyoung Ryu, Jonathan Penner, and especially Blane Morgan for our sisterhood and for holding my hand on this voyage.

To my family. My parents, with their background in teaching gifted education, the language arts, history, and creative drama, have been my champions throughout my life. I am so blessed to have both of them modelling a love of lifelong learning. I also feel grateful for the support of my brother, John Goranson, whose own writing, teaching, and grammatical expertise inspire me as a writer.

And lastly, thanks to Tavania, Taralyn, and Doug, who mean the world to me and who have gifted me with the time and space to immerse myself in Freydis's family life at the expense of our own. My gratitude to the three of you goes beyond what could ever be printed.

It takes a clan.

Author's Note

Freydis Eiriksdóttir is one of only a few women who are featured in the Vinland Sagas, a collection of medieval Icelandic writings penned in the 13th century about the voyages that the Vikings first took from Greenland to North America around 1000 AD. While there is much debate about where the Vikings first landed in North America, some believe that Freydis sailed to what is now L'Anse aux Meadows on the northern tip of Newfoundland, Canada. Viking longhouses were discovered in this area in the 1960s by Helge Instead and his archaeologist wife, Anne Stine Ingstad.

The location of Vinland remains as mysterious as the events that happened on Vinland shores. Freydis's tale would have been repeated orally by the Viking storytellers, called *skalds*, for centuries on end before it was actually recorded in writing. The skalds were like news reporters – the television talk-show hosts of their day – who retold stories of blood feuds and Viking expeditions, who kept track of the battles that were won and lost, and who shared the real-life dramas of the Norse. I am almost certain that their gender biases and clan loyalties would have influenced the way they described Freydis and the events that transpired. As such, the Vinland Sagas likely provide only partial truths.

What follows is the history. There are two versions of Freydis Eiriksdóttir's voyage in the Vinland Sagas. In the *Saga of the Greenlanders*, Freydis proposes to make the journey across the northern sea with two Icelanders, Helgi and Finnbogi. Before she departs from Greenland, she asks her brother, Leif, to use the longhouses that he had built during his first expedition to Vinland. He tells her that he would gladly lend the houses but not give them to her outright. She also asks the brothers to give her half of any trading profits made during the expedition. They agree, but Freydis doesn't trust the Icelanders. In fact, she breaks a pre-established agreement and instead of taking thirty fighting men with her on board their longboats, she takes thirty-five.

Once in Leifsbidur, Freydis has a disagreement with the Icelanders about who will stay in her brother's longhouse. A fight ensues and she is labelled as a woman of "ill-will" who is responsible for instigating conflict between the Icelanders and the Greenlanders. The group of settlers split in two, and Finnbogi and Helgi's men build themselves another longhouse farther from the sea on the bank of a lake.

In the spring, Freydis sneaks out of bed and wanders across the dew-covered grass in bare feet to go in search of

Finnbogi, who has announced an intention to stay in Vinland. She asks to exchange ships with him so that she can return to Greenland in a larger and safer longboat. When she rejoins her husband, Thorvard of Gardar, she accuses Helgi and Finnbogi of striking and dishonouring her. She is indignant when she threatens to divorce Thorvard if he will not avenge her.

Thorvard then takes his men and goes to the brothers' longhouse and enters while they are still asleep. He has Helgi and Finnbogi and their crews tied up and led outside, where Freydis kills them all. She even attacks and kills five women.

After performing her wicked deeds, Freydis swears her men to secrecy before she takes Finnbogi's longboat full of trading goods and returns to her farm in Greenland. According to the sagas, Freydis rewards her companions for concealing her misdeeds, but her brother, Leif, forces the truth out of three men under torture. The saga ends when Leif predicts that Freydis's descendants will not get along well in the world.

In *Eirik the Red's Saga*, Freydis is described as the illegitimate daughter of Eirik the Red who marries Thorvard of Gardar and sails to Vinland, where she encounters members of a Beothuk tribe who strike fear into the hearts of the Norsemen in her company. As her men are running away, Freydis chastises them for being cowards. After that, she is alienated.

In another passage, Freydis comes across a slain man whose sword lies beside him. Snatching up his weapon, she prepares to do battle against the Beothuk, but before she does, she exposes her breast and slaps it with her sword to announce her female status. This behavior on the part of a woman is considered to be so strange that the Beothuk retreat in fear and confusion.

In both versions of the Vinland Sagas, Freydis is depicted as a nefarious woman – a woman who is a liar, a murderess, and a thief. In the Greenland version, she is a rule-breaker, a troublemaker, and a sly and devious master manipulator. In the Eirik the Red version, Freydis shames her male kinsmen while acting in an aggressive and threatening manner, using her gender to instill fear. One can see why I was drawn to her and why I was motivated to shatter the wicked reputation that has ghosted her through the centuries.

While Freydis's character depiction provided the perfect threads for this revisionist retelling, the role of women in Old Norse culture also was a source of intrigue. In 1000 AD, Norsewomen could be tasked with managing the family finances, they oversaw the lands in their husband's absence, and they became landowners when they were widowed. Still, there were many gender inequalities.

By law, Norsewomen were under the authority and power of their husband or their father. They were neither allowed to participate in the local governmental assembly known as the 'Althing' nor were they allowed to seek divorce without obtaining endorsements from men who would be willing to speak up in their defence. Even then, divorce would only be granted under certain conditions such as when a man slapped his spouse on at least three occasions that were witnessed or when a husband inflicted large, life-threatening wounds which penetrated his wife's brain, body cavity, or marrow. In these situations, the woman could divorce and claim back her dowry and any inheritances she received, but the husband took back the bride-price and morning gift and two-thirds of the couple's common land holdings and possessions. The divorce declaration also had to list the reasons for divorce and be publicly announced in front of witnesses on three occasions: namely, in her bedroom, in front of the house, and before a public assembly.

I can't imagine being married to a narcissistic abuser and suffering secondary traumatization living in a society with these laws and stipulations. While Thorvard of Gardar's characterization is completely fictional, he represents the quintessential perpetrator of spousal abuse. He is a violator, a harasser, and a victimizer in a position of power who is physically, sexually, and emotionally abusive. Struggling to hide his own sexual identity, he tries to control Freydis using gaslighting strategies, false promises that foster hope, and intimidation tactics. He isolates her from family and friends and controls every aspect of her environment to make her dependent on him for everything. His violence is hidden behind closed doors, and he dupes his clansmen by presenting an image of himself as being a generous and protective provider.

It is hellish to live with someone who makes you walk on eggshells, who makes you fear almost everything, who leaves you feeling grief-stricken and devasted one minute and filled with rage and anger the next, and who makes you doubt yourself. In this novel, Freydis is the voice of all spousal abuse victims. She has been violated and belittled, hit and spit upon. Her world has been upended. Her life is not her own. When she tries to ask for help, she loses faith and trust in family members who silence her.

Spousal abuse is not time-bound. Family violence likely impacted the Norse in 1000 AD as much as it impacts couples and families today. While I hope that this work of historical fiction was able to normalize and validate the experience of people who are struggling to survive in abusive relationships, I also believe that the #MeToo movement inspires us all to speak out in an effort to protect vulnerable victims.

If you know of someone who is struggling to break ties with a narcissistic abuser, acknowledge and validate their experience and help them to escape.

If you are in an abusive relationship, try to find a safe way to leave. It takes so much courage, but it is possible just like it was for Freydis, who risked travelling into the unknown on a long voyage across the sea.

YOUR NUMBER ONE STOP

ONE MORE CHAPTER

FOR PAGETURNING BOOKS

One More Chapter is an
award-winning global
division of HarperCollins.

Sign up to our newsletter to get our
latest eBook deals and stay up to date
with our weekly Book Club!
<u>Subscribe here.</u>

Meet the team at
<u>www.onemorechapter.com</u>

Follow us!

 @OneMoreChapter_

 @OneMoreChapter

 @onemorechapterhc

Do you write unputdownable fiction?
We love to hear from new voices.
Find out how to submit your novel at
<u>www.onemorechapter.com/submissions</u>